THE TRIALS OF

RENEGADE X

CHELSEA M. CAMPBELL

1st edition published by Golden City Publishing, 2013

Cover art by Raul Allen.

ISBN: 0-9898807-1-0

ISBN-13: 978-0-9898807-1-8

Books by Chelsea M. Campbell

Renegade X
The Rise of Renegade X
The Trials of Renegade x

Harper Madigan: Junior High Private Eye

DEDICATION

FOR CHLOË, WHO PATIENTLY ANSWERED EACH OF MY QUESTIONS LIKE IT WAS THE FIRST INSTEAD OF THE MILLIONTH. THIS BOOK WOULD NOT EXIST WITHOUT YOU.

THE TRIALS OF RENEGADE X

CHAPTER 1

Kat pulls back a little as I kiss her. We're sitting on my bed in my room at Gordon's house. That's right. *My room.* It used to be my little brother Alex's room until Gordon remodeled the attic. Now Alex lives up there, and I live down here, on the ground, like any sane person. Any sane person making out with his really hot supervillain girlfriend, that is.

Kat's eyes dart toward the door, as if she expects it to spring open any second, even though no one's home. "Damien ... what about your mom?"

She means Helen, Gordon's wife, the mother of my three half siblings. I kiss Kat's neck, making her shiver— one of my favorite perks of being her boyfriend. "She's *not* my mom."

"She *really* hates me." Kat keeps her voice low, like she's afraid to say the words out loud. This should probably be the part where I deny it and reassure her that deep down my stepmom really does like her, but we'd

1

both know it was a lie. Kat's deceased grandfather was Helen's nemesis and the reason Helen lost her superspeed and why she walks with a limp. So how she feels about Kat isn't exactly a secret—one she doesn't mind telling me every chance she gets, as if I didn't hear her the first million times. She's also banned Kat from the house, and especially from my room—and, if she could, I'm pretty sure she'd ban her from my pants—but what she doesn't know won't hurt her.

Kat shakes her head. "What if they come home? You know I'm not supposed to be here."

"I also know what tomorrow is." Tomorrow's the day Kat moves into her dorm at Vilmore, the local villain university. Villains and heroes start college at sixteen, and not just because neither of them wants the enemy to get ahead, but because it turns out high school is boring and pretty much useless. And now Kat's starting up at Vilmore. *Without me.*

We were supposed to go together. We were supposed to sleep in each other's dorm rooms and partner up to ace all our classes and totally rule that place. Now she's going to do all that stuff—excluding the sleeping in other people's dorm rooms thing, I hope—on her own. Or, God forbid, with *other people*, even if they're not nearly as awesome as me.

I've had all summer to prepare for this, ever since Kat got her acceptance packet and I got my official rejection letter, but I honestly thought she'd tell me she'd changed her mind by now. I mean, if she has to go without me, what's the point? Just because her dad would kill her if she didn't go, and just because he'd *especially* kill her if she wasn't going on my account. Her parents aren't crazy about her making life choices based on "a boy," even if that boy is me, and even if I am not just "a boy," but "*the boy*" in her life. Plus, they've known me for about two years now, so they should understand why Kat would want her life to revolve around mine.

But anyway, tomorrow my girlfriend moves to Vilmore, *our school*, without me, and even though it's only a forty-minute train ride away, it feels like it might as well be the moon. I want to make the most of the time I have left with her, and that doesn't involve worrying about what Helen and Gordon will think of what we're about to do to each other. In my bed. Pants not required.

Plus, we've spent the summer doing it all over Golden City—we have a checklist of all the places we've graced with our love—and my room hasn't been covered. We even managed to do it in Kat's room last month, even though her mattress squeaks and her mom watches us like a hawk, but only because her parents were gone all day moving her grandparents—the ones who are still living, *not* Helen's nemesis—into a retirement home for supervillains. The home is really nice and has special walls, so when the residents lose control of their powers, they can keep it isolated and don't accidentally shoot anyone with laser beams or start any fires.

I wanted to put the retirement home on our checklist and volunteer to help them move, like the wonderful, upstanding citizens that we are, but Kat said it was probably our only chance to rip each other's clothes off under her parents' roof, so I gave in.

"You know, I saw your mom the other day." Something gets weird about Kat's voice, and she doesn't quite look at me, so I know that when she says she saw my mom, she means my *real* mom. "Damien, there's something you should—"

"I don't want to talk about her."

Kat hesitates, taking a deep breath. "Yeah, okay. But ..." She shakes her head, letting it go.

Good. Because my mom is the last person I want to think about right now, and not just because it's a total mood killer. It's been five months since she disowned me. Five months since we've spoken, and she probably hasn't thought about me once, so why should I think about her?

"I don't want to go tomorrow," Kat says.

I grin at her. "Liar." I wish she meant it, but I know she's excited about going. How can she not be? At least for now. A week or two in, when she's missing me like crazy, she might change her mind.

She smiles, but she still looks sad. "I wish you were coming with me, that's all. We were supposed to ..." She swallows and lets the rest of her sentence hang in the air.

We were supposed to go together. It was going to be the two of us, partners in crime. But that was before my sixteenth birthday. Before my thumbprint changed to form an *X* instead of a *V* like it was supposed to. Now she gets to go to Vilmore, and I'm starting at Heroesworth Academy on Monday.

Heroesworth. Ugh. Not exactly my dream school—the exact opposite, in fact, since it's a university for heroes, not villains—and not where I'd ever pictured myself. And yet I volunteered to go. It wasn't even Gordon's idea, though his whole face lit up like it was Christmas morning and he'd just opened a new pair of tights when I told him I wanted to enroll.

Want might be a strong word here. But I made my choice. I'm not a villain. I chose Gordon and his family— *my* family—over my mom. Over taking over Golden City and turning all the superheroes into zombie slaves. And I can fly. That's a superhero power if there ever was one, like even my genetics are trying to tell me this is who I am. A hero.

I've still got an *X*—thanks to my mixed parentage and the virus some scientists released years ago that marks heroes and villains with letters on their thumbs—and depending on my actions, it could still turn into an *H* or a *V*. But I live with heroes now. I have a sidekick. If I picked up a Magic 8 Ball and asked it if I'm going to get an *H*, it would say, *Signs point to yes!* Because they do. So I figure I might as well embrace it. I might as well try for an *H*, because then maybe it'll get here that much faster. Then I won't feel that hot rush of shame every time one of Gordon's or Helen's relatives comes over and asks if "that boy" is still staying here. Even though I *live* here and they know that. Or in the case of Helen's sister, glares at me like I'm some kind of demon spawn.

Which normally I'd take as a compliment. But not fitting in *anywhere* is getting old. And if I had my *H*, Gordon could tell people I'm his son without flinching. Without worrying about having to explain how he had a one-night stand with a supervillain. He wouldn't have to stand there, stammering, his whole face going red enough to match his cape.

"Let's not think about tomorrow," I tell Kat. "Or Monday."

"Or how we'll be going to rival schools and never see each other?" she asks.

"Exactly." I kiss a slow trail down her neck, making her melt against me and forget about what's going to happen after tonight.

She kisses me back, her tongue hot on my ear, and she might not be the only one who's melting. "I could change," she whispers. "Just in case someone comes home."

Kat's a shapeshifter. So even though normally she has shoulder-length black hair, blue eyes, and a thin nose, she could look like anybody in the world. But I don't want anybody else—only her. "Never," I tell her. "I'll risk it."

She sighs and relaxes into me, and I know that she liked my answer, despite her worries about getting caught. Her hands slide under my shirt, her fingers running up and down my spine. Resting just inside the band of my jeans.

There's a zap when I kiss her, a jolt of static electricity that sparks between us. She winces, but just for a split second, and then she's kissing me again. Ignoring anything else.

I forget about everything except the feeling of Kat pressed against me. Right now we're just two people making out, about to do way more and cross a significant location off our checklist, and it doesn't matter what letters are on our thumbs or what schools we're going to.

Her phone buzzes from inside her purse on the floor. That'll be her mom, checking up on her. Making sure she's not alone with me long enough to get into any "compromising" situations.

You know, like the one we're in now.

Kat ignores the phone. The buzzing stops for a few moments, then starts up again as her mom calls back.

"You know," Kat says, "it's not too late to, like, go out for ice cream or something."

Something our parents would approve of, she means. Though in Helen's case she's made it clear she doesn't approve of me spending *any* time with Kat, compromising or otherwise. Not that she gets a say in it.

"Oh, isn't it?" I ask, playfully pushing her down to the bed. It is *way* too late to go out for ice cream. In my humble, still unfortunately fully clothed opinion.

She grins. "We could go to that one place where they name the ice creams after zoo animals, the one where you kept pointing to the Bald Eagle flavor and saying you were going to report them to the endangered species people."

I smile at the memory. "The one we got banned from, you mean?"

"The one *you* got banned from." She pokes me in the chest. "I got a coupon for a free ice cream cone because they screwed up my order."

"You're going to be gone tomorrow. Do you really want to spend the rest of our time together messing with people? Because, I mean, if that's what you want, we can go—"

"Don't even think about it." She pulls me down to her. I

kiss her, my hand sliding under her shirt. My fingertips brush against her stomach, then up against the edge of her bra. "You're sure you want to do this?" she asks.

"Uh, when have I ever not been sure?" For the record, I am *extremely sure* I want to do this. Like, right now.

"Never, but that was before you decided you wanted to get your *H*. I'm the bad-girl villain. You're the hero now."

I swallow, not liking what that implies. As if choosing to go for my *H* means having Kat in my bed is off-limits. That makes it sound like what we're doing is wrong, and I so disagree. I love her, and so what if that means I want to take her clothes off?

Besides, I said I wanted to be a hero, not a saint.

"Are you telling me you want to be a bad influence?" I ask her.

"Definitely," Kat murmurs, kissing me again, her mouth hot against mine. She grips the edges of my T-shirt and starts to pull it over my head. So I don't see so much as hear when my bedroom door flings open and Helen, my stepmother, says, "Damien, are you—"

She cuts off there. Kat freezes. My heart pounds in my chest.

I pull my shirt back down—it's blue and says, SUPERHEROES DO IT WITH CAPES!—and run my hands through my hair. They weren't supposed to be back for at least another hour. Never mind the fact that no one was supposed to just *barge in*, like they, you know, own this place or something.

Helen's standing in the doorway, her eyes narrowed at Kat, who sits up and stares at the wall, not looking at anyone. She was already a bit flushed from our compromising activities—okay, more than a bit—but now her cheeks turn a bright, shameful red.

"You could have knocked," I say, shattering the tense silence that's filled the room. And even though I'm the one breaking the rules by having Kat here, I can't keep the annoyance out of my voice. There is such a thing as respecting other people's privacy, after all.

Amelia, my fifteen-year-old half sister, rushes up behind Helen, putting a hand over her mouth. She manages to both smirk and look genuinely horrified at the same time when she sees me and Kat in the bed together, even though we're both still fully clothed. "Oh. My. *God,*" she says, drawing each word out extra long. She makes the situation sound ten times more dramatic than it is, as if we'd been caught running a prostitution ring out of my room, which isn't exactly zoned for business. "You are *so* dead."

"Amelia," Helen growls.

But Amelia's already running off, shouting something about having a million phone calls to make.

"Tell them I charge one hundred dollars an hour," I call after her. "Kat's my reference if they have any questions about quality of service!"

Kat punches me in the shoulder. "*Damien,*" she says out the side of her mouth, her teeth clenched. She jerks her head ever-so-slightly toward Helen.

Helen, who is staring at us in shock, as if how I feel about Kat—or that I can't keep my hands off of her—is in any way news to her. "This isn't a free show," I snap. "You

9

can stop staring at us like we're animals in the zoo." *And to your left, everyone, you'll observe the mating ritual of the teenagers of the species. Notice how the male specimen becomes agitated when said ritual is so rudely, and prematurely, interrupted.*

"What's going on?" Gordon calls, his footsteps in the hallway.

"Your son and that—" She swallows back whatever she was about to say, but I can't help glaring anyway. Because I'm pretty sure "that wonderful supervillain girlfriend of his" isn't how she was going to end that sentence. I'm *pretty sure* Helen thinks Kat is a slut for giving it up to me, even though I'm the only guy she's been all the way with and we are in love and have plans for a pirate-themed wedding.

We don't find out what Helen was going to say, though, because apparently she can't even finish. She can't even look at me for one more second and instead holds up her hands in an "I'm done" gesture and turns away, leaving Gordon to deal with me.

He glances after her, then at me. He takes in the situation. Me. Kat. The slightly rumpled bed. Then he suddenly gets real interested in his shoes. This from the guy who did it with my mom in a dirty subway bathroom and made her lose her hairpin. He wasn't so shy *then.*

Kat's phone starts buzzing again. She reaches down and snatches it out of her purse, hitting a button to silence it.

"Damien," Gordon says, clearing his throat, "I think Kat had better—"

"I have to go," she says, not letting Gordon finish. "I'll

see you, um ..." She pauses, realizing that for the first time in months she doesn't know when we'll see each other again.

I lean in to kiss her good-bye, but her eyes dart toward Gordon, and she pulls away, too embarrassed.

She gets up from the bed, slinging her purse over her shoulder and stuffing her phone into it.

"Kat, wait—I'll walk you home."

I get up to follow, but she shakes her head, already hurrying for the door and pushing past Gordon. "I just ... My mom's going to be freaked." That's all the explanation I get before she makes her escape, though not without one last glance over her shoulder at me. Our eyes meet. She bites her lip. Then she rushes off, leaving me on my own to explain to Gordon where babies come from.

$$X \cdot X \cdot X$$

It's not that I dislike Helen. In fact, for a stepmom, she's pretty awesome. I mean, I'm her husband's illegitimate love child with a supervillain, and even if the little incident that spawned me happened before she and Gordon met, it's cutting it pretty close. She could have freaked when Gordon first brought me home six months ago, just out of the blue, no warning. She could have refused to let me stay here or had crazy ideas that I was evil or something. But no. She welcomed me into the family. And even if she misguidedly felt sorry for me for my supervillain upbringing, she never made me feel weird about it.

And considering that my real mom disowned me for disagreeing with her and showing even the teensiest signs of maybe leaning toward my hero side, Helen gets major points from me for treating me like one of her own kids. Even though we're not technically related. And even though we might disagree on who I should be allowed to associate with.

I sigh as I glance at the clock—it's almost six—and dial Sarah's number on my cell phone. Sarah's my sidekick. She's an ordinary citizen, not a hero or a villain, though she *is* pretty heroic. She's all for me getting my *H*, for obvious reasons. And, also for obvious reasons, she's on Helen's list of people that are actually allowed at the house.

Sarah answers after only two rings. "What's the emergency?" She must know it's me.

"No emergency. Can't a hero call his sidekick just to chat?"

I can practically hear her rolling her eyes. "What is it, Renegade?"

"It's a nice night for crime fighting."

"I thought you said you were busy?"

"I was." That was when I thought I was spending the evening with Kat, before Helen chased her off. "I had a change of plans."

My door opens. I half expect it to be Helen again, or Gordon, coming to tell me off for earlier. He was too flustered at the time to do much more than stammer. And then I told him that when a bird and a bee love each other very much, or when they meet randomly in a dirty subway

12

bathroom—which is *not* on our list, by the way—they want to rip each other's clothes off and do things to each other that birds and bees would never do in real life. And that sometimes when people meet randomly in a dirty subway bathroom, they don't use protection and end up with an illegitimate love child who then has to explain the facts of life to them sixteen years later. Because if they already knew, they wouldn't be gaping at him with their mouths hanging open like that.

Then he stormed out.

Which is why I expect him to be back for round two, but instead of Gordon, Amelia pokes her head in, her eyes darting right to the bed, as if she expected to catch a second showing. Which, considering that no boys will ever touch her—what with her sparkling personality and all—is probably the closest she'll ever get to the real thing.

Amelia's got dyed black hair, blond eyebrows, and is slightly pudgy. She also wears way too much mauve eye shadow, something that was popular for some reason with all her friends at our old school.

I glare at her. "You could have knocked." Just because she has no life of her own and has to live vicariously through mine doesn't mean she can barge in whenever she wants.

"Then you would have told me to go away."

"*Exactly.*"

"You had a change of plans?" Sarah repeats through the phone. "So I'm your second choice."

She makes that sound like it's a bad thing. As if it's not an honor to be chosen at all. "We could just hang out. You know, if you think all the evil-doers of the world are taking the night off or whatever."

"Your girlfriend bailed on you and you're lonely, you mean."

Okay, maybe there's some truth to that, but the way she talks, you'd think it was a crime to want to spend time with her. "We can watch a movie. Your pick."

She makes kind of a snorting sound. "You said you were busy, so I made plans. With *Riley*."

I make a shooing motion at Amelia, directing her toward the door. I mouth the words *Get out.*

Amelia acts like she didn't notice and plops down on the bed. I don't know if she's just misguidedly making herself at home, or if she's hoping to get a better look at the scene of the crime. The *almost* crime, anyway.

I ignore her and tell Sarah, "Cancel them. Wouldn't you rather spend time with me?"

"Spend time with you instead of my boyfriend? Yeah, right, Damien."

"I'll let you pick the movie. Something sci-fi, if you want. With a really technical plot I won't be able to follow." Sarah convinced me to go see some futuristic, super-convoluted sci-fi movie with her this summer while Riley was out of town, visiting his grandparents. My brain just about melted out of my skull, and I spent the whole time asking Sarah what was going on while she kept saying she'd explain it to me later, after it was over. I *considered* faking an illness and pretending I needed to go home, but the fact that I didn't and sat through the whole thing, melting brain and everything, just goes to show what a good friend I really am and how lucky Sarah is to have me.

"Riley and I are watching a rom-com. In my room. And I'm turning off my phone."

Erg. "Riley's a total douche. You know that, right?" He's also got an *H* on his thumb, marking him as an official hero—just Sarah's type.

"Uh-huh. Sounds like someone else I know. Funny how you only started wanting to hang out with me so badly after he entered the picture."

"Not true." Okay, totally true. I don't know why, but the guy just irks me. And I know I shouldn't care, but the fact that Sarah likes him better than me, and might actually believe he's a better *hero* than me, really pisses me off. I'm supposed to be the hero in her life. The only one. I don't need a do-gooder type like Riley showing me up. Especially since he's the type who will watch *The Crimson Flash and the Safety Kids*—my dad's kids show— with her while keeping a straight face. Something I could never do, though, thankfully, neither can Kat. It's one of our favorite shows, as long as we get to make fun of it the whole time. Sarah watches it intensely, like the Crimson Flash's words of wisdom about how to safely cross the street is the most important advice she'll ever hear. I'm surprised she doesn't take notes.

"And," I tell Sarah, "just to prove how not jealous I am, I'll come over and watch the movie with you guys. I'll even sit between you, to equally share my presence."

"The last time I let you hang out with us—"

"Let me? Don't you mean, 'was honored by me wanting

to spend time with you'?"

"The *last time* I let you watch a movie with us, you pretended Riley had gone invisible and that you couldn't see him."

Riley's superpower is turning himself invisible. *Lame.*

"I'm entertaining," I tell her. Which is true and she knows it.

"No, you're a jerk. You *sat* on him, Damien, and pushed him off the bed."

"I didn't push anyone. He fell in his frantic attempt to get away from me."

"He broke his finger! He had to go to the doctor."

How is this my problem? "It's not my fault he doesn't get enough calcium. I didn't *intend* for him to get injured." It was just an added bonus. "Plus, it healed, didn't it? I don't see why I can't hang out with you guys."

"Because you're not my boyfriend. And you're not the only guy in my life anymore."

I was her boyfriend, sort of, once upon a time. During a very brief period where I was mistakenly denying my love for Kat and thought fooling around with Sarah would be easier than dealing with my real feelings. Which it turned out wasn't true, and Sarah and I were better off keeping our relationship romance-free. Not that there was a lot of romance going on, just some making out, but whatever.

And yeah, maybe I enjoyed being the only guy in Sarah's life, before she met Riley at some sci-fi convention back in June. And it's not like I want to date Sarah now or anything. I just don't want Riley putting his mouth all over her. Or making her think that having an *H* makes him a better hero than me. "That doesn't mean you're not still my friend."

"But it does mean you don't have a right to be jealous."

I clench my fist. "I am *not*—"

"You only want to spend time with me because you can't have me. That's kind of the definition of *jealous*."

"You're my sidekick. How am I supposed to get my *H* if you're spending all your time making out with some guy?"

"You say that, but every time I have a mission for us, you're too busy with Kat. Slipping certain parts of your anatomy into certain parts of hers.'"

"*Language*, Sarah." The mouth on her. Seriously.

"Those were *your* own words, Damien. And besides, who says we're making out?"

"Great, then you won't mind if I—"

"We could be doing *much* more than that, but you know what? It's none of your business."

"Come on, Sarah, don't be like that."

"I have to go—Riley's here with the movie. Good-bye, Damien." She hesitates, then adds, "Don't call back," before hanging up.

"I'll watch a movie with you," Amelia says. She's sitting on the edge of my bed, idly kicking one leg against the mattress.

This is what it's come down to. Spending Friday nights watching movies with my half sister, who will always be free because she has no life. This is what I have to look forward to now that Kat's moving to Vilmore without me and Sarah's preoccupied with the Invisible Douche.

"Or I can go make sure Sarah's not doing anything I

wouldn't do."

Amelia snorts. "Is there anything you wouldn't do?"

I pause, thinking it over. "Homework."

She rolls her eyes, then brightens. "Have you started it? I bet you haven't. You're going to be *so* behind."

"On what? School hasn't even started yet."

"Um, hello? Didn't you get Miss Monk's email? We already have a project assigned in Intro to Heroism, and it's due *Wednesday*." She says *Wednesday* like it's the day the world's going to end.

Did I mention that it's not just me who's starting at Heroesworth next week, but also Amelia? Even though she's eight months younger than me and was a grade below me at our high school, she applied for early admission to Heroesworth this year, since she'll be sixteen in October. They let her in—a decision that probably had more to do with her dad being the Crimson Flash than it did the ten-page essay she wrote them—which she bragged about all summer. At least until I got accepted, too, and then she said they'd let *anybody* in.

"I don't even know what classes I'm in yet." What with us not being allowed to choose any of our classes our first semester, plus I was kind of a last minute addition, thanks to Gordon pulling some strings with a friend on the admissions board. But I'm going to take a shot in the dark and guess that my classes are all, how you say, really stupid?

Amelia gapes at me. "Didn't you read your intro packet? New students have to take Intro to Heroism. That means both of us." She narrows her eyes a little, as if waiting for me to argue. Then she clears her throat. "If you want, I could help you start the assignment."

Work on an assignment before I've even started school? For a class I may or may not even be in? "Yeah, that's exactly how I want to spend my Friday night. Don't you have flying lessons to get to? Oh, wait, that's right. You *don't*." Amelia spent months telling me how much better at flying she was going to be than me when she got her power. Then a few weeks ago she discovered she could teleport items to her, but only if she'd touched them before. It was apparently her great grandmother's power on Helen's side, meaning she didn't inherit "the family power" like I did. And after enduring months of her being a snobby bitch about it, I'm taking every chance I can get to gloat. "It's too bad, really. I wanted to see him push you off a building." Like he did to me, no thanks to her.

She flicks a piece of fuzz off her shirt. "You're such a jerk."

"Yeah, I am. But you, Amelia, you're *delightful*. A real pleasure to be around." Just thinking about falling from the tallest building in Golden City still makes me sick, especially as I remember the pavement rushing toward me, which I *still* have nightmares about. My fear of heights was bad enough, and then Gordon had to go and make it worse. This from the guy who supposedly teaches safety lessons to kids. Good thing my flying power kicked in at the last second, or else he'd have had a lot of explaining to do.

"I've changed my mind," Amelia pouts. "I'm *not* going to help you with your assignment. And you'll be sorry on

Wednesday."

Sure I will. And pigs will sprout wings and Gordon will sleep with a supervillain. Oh, wait, that last one already happened.

"You'll be the only one without a poster to present."

A poster. Yeah, I think I can make a poster in two days, *if* I'm even in that class. "I'll manage."

"Okaaaay," she says, drawing it out to convey just how skeptical she is. "But don't say I didn't warn you."

CHAPTER 2

My first class at Heroesworth on Monday morning is Intro to Heroism.

Fine. So Amelia was right for once.

All the new students have to take it, and there are enough of us that there's more than one session. And even though we have the same teacher, Amelia has it in the afternoon. Meaning that when I walk through the door, the one person I know in this school isn't here. It's just me, a half villain, alone in a room full of heroes. My least favorite people. And, judging by the looks they're giving me, I'm *their* least favorite person, too, though obviously only because they don't yet know how awesome I am.

Wait. Did I say I only know one person in this school? Because I counted wrong. I know *two* people, and even though his seat is empty, I recognize Riley's backpack slumped on the floor next to it. It's pretty hard to miss, what with having a big silver Theta—the symbol for the Cosine Kid, Sarah's sidekick alter ego—drawn on it. His notebook's also splayed open on his desk, and I catch a glimpse of some scribbling in Sarah's handwriting that says, *Sarah <3s Riley*.

Barf. Sarah only "<3s" Riley because she's too blinded by the *H* on his thumb to realize what an epic jerk he is. Or at least what an epic jerk he is to *me*. Which he was even before I broke his finger. I mean, before I innocently knocked him off Sarah's bed and he, all on his own, injured himself by not falling to the floor properly.

I glance around the classroom, hoping for better seating prospects. Two girls who were whispering to each other look away guiltily when I make eye contact. And not because they were discussing my amazing hotness levels, but like they already know who I am—or, more accurately, who I'm *not*. My face gets a little warm, and I can't help making a fist with my right hand, hiding the *X* on my thumb.

A couple of guys "accidentally" bump into me on their way into the room, not even pretending to apologize. They catch me off guard, and I stumble a couple steps into a desk, which makes a loud screeching sound as it scrapes across the floor. Then *everyone* turns to stare at me.

"Just rearranging the furniture," I tell them. *Nothing to see here.*

Hushed conversations carry on throughout the room. I make out words like *villain*, X, and *shouldn't be here*.

Great. Five seconds in, and I can already tell my list of people who need dealing with—that is, my list of people who tried to mess with me and are going to get what they deserve—is going to be a mile long this year. And by *this year,* I probably mean more like *this month*. Or maybe even *this week*.

It would be so easy—and probably safer for my classmates—for me to turn around, go home, and tell Gordon I want to go back to my old school with Sarah. Where the kids don't have superpowers or *V*s or *H*s. Or, you know, *X*s. I might have been one of a kind there, too, but at least if people whispered about me in the halls, it was because I switched all the ketchup in the lunchroom with hot sauce or because I rigged the school intercom so when the principal made the morning announcements, he sounded like a chipmunk.

But I picture how red Gordon's face was and how tongue-tied he got when he was trying to tell his parents why he suddenly had a sixteen-year-old half-villain kid and where I came from. He got *that* worked up just telling them about it over the phone. Big surprise, but they didn't want to meet me. Which is fine with me—I already have grandparents, and they rock—but Gordon moped around for days like someone had spilled chocolate ice cream on his favorite cape. Which, er, might have actually happened, but I can neither confirm nor deny my whereabouts that evening.

And I remember, in contrast, how happy he was when I said I wanted to go to Heroesworth. "My oldest son, following in my footsteps," he said, then ruffled my hair and went on and on about how great Heroesworth was and how much I was going to love it.

Love it. Right.

I take a deep breath and force myself not to leave.

Because as much as I really don't care about following in Gordon's footsteps, it was pretty cool seeing him beaming with pride at me. And, as an added bonus, witnessing Gordon's fatherly love for me made Amelia practically choke on her cereal.

Ignoring all the stares and whispers, I take the seat next to Riley's. Everyone else in this class might *think* they don't want to sit by me, but Riley *knows* he doesn't. If I have to sit by someone who hates me—a mutual feeling, of course —it might as well be the person who's going to be the most annoyed by it.

I drop my backpack to the floor and stretch out my legs like I own this place. Then I hear a dramatic sigh next to me and Riley appears in his seat. Which I guess means he was there the whole time, what with being able to turn invisible and all. Which, according to Sarah, is cooler than being able-but-not-willing to fly. Whatever. I told her invisibility was a lame power and that she just has bad taste in guys. Me excluded, I mean.

"I didn't pull my disappearing act because I *wanted* you to sit here," Riley says. He's got short light-brown hair that he styles to look casually messy all the time, which, according to Sarah, makes him "really cute," though, according to *me*, it just makes him really douchey. He's also wearing a T-shirt covered in quotes from the League Treaty, the superheroes' code of honor they all have to sign to be considered legit. And even though he's sitting down, I know from past encounters that he's taller than me. "It's called avoidance. Can't you take a hint?"

"I *can*. I just choose not to." I lean over and snatch the

24

notebook from his desk. He makes a grab for it, but I turn my shoulder to him and start writing in it before he can stop me.

"Like you choose not to take the hint about me and Sarah?" He gets a grip on the notebook and yanks it away from me, but not before I've written *Riley + Damien = BFFs* in a style that matches his handwriting. He makes a face when he sees it and slams the notebook down on his desk. "I heard about you trying to weasel your way into our movie night. Why can't you leave us alone?"

"Sarah's my best friend." Well, besides Kat.

"Right." Riley rolls his eyes at me. "If you were really her friend, you'd want her to be happy. And face it, X, *I* make her happy."

I try not to show how annoyed I am. I hate it when he calls me X. And I hate how there's an implied "not you" at the end of his sentence. "Good for you. She has a thing for heroes, and you're her latest phase. You might have the *H*, but she's *my* sidekick." Sidekicks are forever. Mr. Perfect is only a temporary problem.

He snorts. "Not exclusively."

"*What?*"

He grins and looks like he's about to open his stupid jerk mouth to say something else when our teacher walks in the room. Or at least I'm assuming that's who she is, since she goes and stands in front of the whiteboard, where it says *Mikayla Monk* in big letters. Other than that, though, she doesn't really look like a teacher. She's probably in her mid-twenties, blond, and has on this glittery, pink spandex superhero outfit. And she's painted on an eye mask with dark-blue makeup that looks like it's about 50 percent sparkles. Her thigh-high boots are bright pink and so glossy, they look like you could use them as a mirror. The only thing she's wearing that isn't pink is a blue cape that matches her face paint and only goes about halfway down her back.

The whole class shuts up and stares at her as she struts to the front of the room. She puts her hands on her hips and surveys the class, her gaze moving up and down each aisle. I might be imagining it, but I think there's a pause as she gets to me, and a slight tightening of her jaw.

She pulls a tube of lipstick out of a small pouch on her belt and twists the end, bringing it to her lips like she's going to redo her makeup right here in class. But at the last second, she gives it another twist, two red lights start blinking on the side, and she hurls the tube into the middle of the classroom.

Right next to me.

My muscles tense. I have no idea what's going on, and before I can figure it out, the lipstick tube beeps and flashes a blindingly bright light. I throw my arms over my face and turn away as fast as I can. I've spent enough time with Sarah to know not to stare directly into any flashing gadgets unless I want to go at least temporarily blind. The tube must have a speaker in it, too, because I hear a tinny *kaboom* sound.

I guess that's supposed to be it blowing up, but it sounds super fake and nothing like the real thing. Which I have experience with, also thanks to spending time with Sarah. But this was just a simulation.

Slowly, I open my eyes and pull my arms away from my face. Everyone else is blinking, a lot, but they're not blind. And they can see plenty well enough to know I'm the only one who thought it could be real. Most of them are laughing. At me.

Yeah, well, they should try being the only villain in a room full of heroes and see how trusting *they* are.

Riley smirks, like he's just one-upped me somehow but is too good to laugh in my face, which only makes me hate him even more. I don't get what Sarah sees in him.

Miss Monk isn't laughing, either. She's not even smirking. "You're all dead," she says, her voice so serious that the laughter dies and an uncomfortable silence settles in the room. "How many of you didn't take me seriously because of my costume?" She gestures to herself and her skintight glitter suit. "You assumed I was a superhero because we're at Heroesworth. And you assumed because I'm dressed like this you didn't have to take me seriously."

I lean toward Riley and whisper, "What did you mean about Sarah?"

"She hasn't told you?" He fakes surprise. "I guess you're not as close as you thought."

I feel like I'm falling off a building again, the world rushing by me, unreal and out of place. He's lying. He has to be.

Miss Monk paces the front of the room, continuing to stare us all down. "It doesn't matter what color someone's wearing or if they have a pretty face. I wanted you to let your guard down, and you did. If you're going to be that easily fooled, you're all dead."

"Sarah and I are a team. She wouldn't—"

"Let's take our resident half villain as an example," Miss Monk says, suddenly directing everyone's attention to me. "You'd never know what he is by looking at him. Rumpled T-shirt, worn-out jeans, muddy shoes. And it looks like he didn't even comb his hair this morning."

Wow. The way she says it, you'd think I was dressed in rags. "I didn't have time—I had to stand in line for my bowl of gruel." For the record, I *did* comb my hair this morning. It was just with my fingers.

A couple kids laugh, maybe with me this time instead of at me. Not that I'm keeping track.

Miss Monk's eyes narrow. "I want everyone to look to the person to your left. Now look to the person to your right. Statistically speaking, one of those people will be killed by villains because someone else slipped up. Because someone on your team underestimated the enemy. Because one of you didn't follow the moral code laid out in the League Treaty. Don't let that person be *you*. You all have your *H*s."

"Well," Riley whispers, "most of us."

"This isn't pretend anymore, this is life and death. How you act now, how you handle your studies here at Heroesworth Academy, will determine what kind of hero you're going to be. The decision of whether you're going to be a liability or an asset starts now."

She pauses to let that sink in, then turns to write something on the board. I'm pretty sure I fall into the "liability" category, since I could care less about their stupid League Treaty. I'm going to get through

Heroesworth and get my *H*, but I'm going to do things my way. I might want a place to fit in, but I don't need to fit in *that* badly.

"Sarah's my sidekick," I tell Riley. "She wouldn't betray me like that."

"Yeah, but come on, X, you're not really a hero. No *H*, essentially no superpower ..." He shrugs. "You can't blame her if she's tired of playing around and wants to get serious."

"You and her. You're fighting crime together now, is that what you're telling me?" My insides feel like they're too heavy and too light at the same time, and there's this awful ache creeping up my throat. Even though I know Sarah would never betray me like that. Even if she's right about me ditching a bunch of our hero missions this summer to spend more alone time with Kat.

Riley claps me on the shoulder in mock camaraderie. "Face it. You're only half a hero. A gadget goddess like Sarah needs the real thing. You might have been an okay starter, but, well ..." He shrugs. "Looks like you were just a phase."

CHAPTER 3

"**W**here have you been?" I ask Sarah that afternoon after school. I'm waiting for her on her front porch as she hurries up the sidewalk, her backpack slung over one shoulder. "I've been calling you all day!" You'd think my phone calls weren't important enough to, say, drop everything for. She was only at school—it's not like she was doing anything that mattered.

"What is it?" she says, trying to catch her breath and rushing past me, fumbling to get her key in the door. "I have my costume in my bag—I can be dressed and ready to go in two minutes." She pauses. "Five minutes. I haven't been to the bathroom since lunch."

"That's not why I'm here."

She looks me up and down. "Why aren't you in your costume? We've got to hurry, and ..." She blinks, my last sentence sinking in. "There's no emergency?"

"I needed to see you about something." Something involving the Invisible Douche and all the stupid jerk things he said to me today. Which Sarah will no doubt confirm as a bunch of big fat lies and then finally realize what an idiot he is. She'll dump his brittle-boned ass, and then I will be here to console her. And to find her a new boyfriend—I'm not heartless, after all—one who has no chance of ever upstaging me, probably of the ordinary-citizen variety.

Sarah pulls what amounts to a homemade cell phone out of her backpack. It looks more like an inside-out walkie-talkie with wires, buttons, and microchips sticking out all over.

"I didn't hear it ring. Or maybe it's malfunctioning. Plus, you *know* we're not allowed to use cell phones at school. It could have been confiscated!"

"Uh, Sarah? Trust me when I say you wouldn't have gotten in trouble for using a cell phone." For having a contraption that looks like it's some kind of explosive, on the other hand? Definitely.

Sarah scowls at her phone, her forehead wrinkling in deep thought. She shakes the phone a little. Something inside makes a rattling noise. She smacks the side of it pretty hard, and for something that looks so delicate, I'm surprised pieces of it don't go flying off. It stays intact, though, and the screen blips to life.

"There," she says, sighing in relief. "See? It works great." She stuffs it back in her bag and opens her front door, motioning for me to follow. "So, if there was no emergency"—she sounds really put out when she says that, like she's disappointed about the lack of disasters in the world—"what was so important? Because I have to walk Heraldo, and then Riley's coming over, so ..."

I clench my jaw, breathing in slowly through my nose. "So you don't have time for me. I get it. And I suppose whatever you two are meeting about is none of my business?"

"Do I ask you details about *your* love life? I know about your checklist, and that's already too much information." She makes a disgusted face at that, pausing with her hand on the back doorknob. Heraldo, her Great Dane, barks outside and jumps at the door, scraping his claws against it.

"I'm not talking about your love life."

"Then what are you—" She opens the door, and Heraldo comes bounding in. His tail wags back and forth, smacking into my shins as he greets Sarah with a huge slurp. Then he turns around and tries to jump on me. "Down!" Sarah commands.

Heraldo slams his front paws into my chest and knocks me to the floor. Probably *not* what Sarah meant. At least, I hope not. Unless she's training him to take down bad guys, and then it might be kind of cool. If it hadn't happened to me, and if my head hadn't thudded so hard against the floor, I mean. Whether he meant to knock me down or not, Heraldo slimes my face with his tongue, seeming pretty pleased with himself, then notices the stern look on Sarah's face.

"Time out," she says, pointing to his dog bed in the corner of the living room. Heraldo slinks off to do what he's told, but not before giving me another quick lick in the face, getting his dog saliva up my nose.

Yuck.

"Do you want to tell me what's going on?" Sarah asks, hovering over me with her hands on her hips.

I groan. Mostly, I just want to lie here in my defeat. I pat the spot next to me, indicating she should join me down here instead of looming like that, but she ignores me. "I know what you've been doing with Riley."

"*What?*" Her face goes red. "We haven't—I mean, I don't know how you—"

"Not like *that*. I'm not talking about what you and him ..." I wave my hand, dismissing it. "But I know you've been moonlighting as his sidekick."

"Damien, that's crazy." She squints at me and tilts her head in disbelief, like maybe she heard wrong. "And not very accurate. I don't know where you get your information, but it's not true."

"So, you're not replacing me?" I shut my eyes, letting the huge wave of relief I feel sink in. "Also, I think I should tell you I can see up your nose from here. Which I wouldn't be able to do if the lady would join me on the floor."

She sighs, giving in, and lies down next to me. "I'm not Kat. You can trust me."

I glance over at her, not sure how to take that. "What's *that* supposed to mean? I trust Kat just fine."

"*Right,*" she says, and her sarcasm isn't lost on me. "That's why you're freaking out because you think I might be doing something with another guy behind your back."

Okay, so, once upon a time, back when we hardly even knew each other, Kat did cheat on me. She mistakenly thought I was just stringing her along and made out with my former—and now deceased—best friend. We broke up, and I didn't think I'd ever be able to forgive her, but while I was busy not forgiving her, we kind of became best friends. And while we were becoming best friends, we kind of really got to know each other and fell in love. And when it came down to me being miserable for the rest of my life because I was holding a grudge about a stupid mistake that happened in the past, or letting it go and admitting I was totally in love with her, it turned out the choice wasn't that hard to make.

"Even if it's not on a romantic level," Sarah goes on. "I mean, Riley and I *are* doing things on a romantic level, it's just not behind your back. I mean—well, you know what I mean."

"Yeah, so maybe I was freaking out, just a little. But if you say it was for nothing, then I guess it was. It's just, when Riley said you weren't exclusively my sidekick, I—"

"Wait, he *said* that?" Sarah sits up, suddenly on edge.

"Yeah, crazy, right? I shouldn't have listened to him. I should have known he was just making things up to piss me off." Poor innocent me, the victim in all of this. That Riley should really stop antagonizing me, what with me being Sarah's best friend and all.

"Because we've talked about it, but it's not like I committed to anything."

I feel like someone just knocked all the air out of me. I push myself up into a sitting position. "Sarah, what do you mean you've been talking about it?!"

"He asked me if I'd ever consider doing some crime

fighting with him. As in, like, ever, hypothetically. And it's not like you and I have an exclusive contract—"

"We don't have *any* contract."

"Right, so I said I'd think about it. If the situation ever came up. I never said I'd do it."

"I thought our partnership meant something to you." As in, more than her relationship with Riley. Since I've known her longer and am obviously superior to him in every way.

"It *does*."

"But someday you might jump ship and leave me for him, is that it?"

Sarah grits her teeth. "Why do boys always have to be such babies about everything? You're jealous of Riley—"

"Uh, I think I've made it pretty clear that I'm not."

She makes a *psh* sound of disbelief. "Was this in an alternate universe or something? You're jealous of him, and he's jealous of you. That I'm your sidekick and we spend so much time together in dangerous situations. Both of you need to grow up. I told him if the right scenario came along, I'd consider it. But that's all."

"And what, exactly, is the right scenario?" I need to know so I can make sure it never happens.

"Well, you know."

"You mean if I suffer an untimely death?" And what if Mr. Perfect were to have an unfortunate "accident"? Well, besides the one he already had. But this time I'd make sure no one could prove it was me.

"That's one possibility."

"And another one is …?"

She swallows. "Well, you kn—"

"*Don't* say that I know, because clearly I don't."

"I'm sure this situation won't ever happen, okay?" Her voice is getting kind of high-pitched, like it does when she's really nervous. "But I have to think about my future. Or at least be willing to re-evaluate my future in the future, which will be the present. I mean, the future of the present, which will be in the future. Is it hot in here? I should turn on the air conditioning."

"Sarah. Please, just tell me." Not knowing is ten times worse than whatever she's about to say. Well, hopefully.

"Okay." She takes a deep breath. "But, just so you know, it's not like I *like* thinking about this or having to plan for it. But Riley asked, and I—"

"*Sarah.*"

"Right. Well, you see, there's a chance you won't get your *H*. Scientifically speaking, it could go either way. Do we really know how accurate this virus is? And it's not like there are a lot of people with *X*s to do tests on, and you won't let me draw your blood, even though I told you I practiced first on an orange. Plus, your future's not decided yet. As long as you have an *X*, it could still turn into a *V*."

"Based on the choices I make."

She peers over her glasses at me and raises an eyebrow, giving me an "and your point is?" kind of look.

"Yeah, okay, fine. So I'm not perfect." She's got me there. "But I'm going to get my *H*." Probably.

"And last year you were so sure you were going to get your *V*. Not that you thought to inform me about that. You just let me believe you were some kind of hero."

The way I remember it, she wanted to believe I was a hero. But I did also sort of not tell her I was raised by a villain instead of her idol, the Crimson Flash, as she mistakenly assumed, or that I was intending to shirk all of my hero genes as much as possible. So I can see how she might think I was somewhat at fault.

"I *could* end up getting a *V*," I admit. She's right—not that long ago, it was all I wanted. Now, I'm not so sure. Kat would be happy if I got a *V*, and her parents wouldn't exactly be too broken up about it, either. Mom might even start talking to me again. Not that I want her to. But it's not like I could go back to my old life, even if I did get a *V*. Plus, I'd lose my entire hero family. And now I find out Sarah would abandon me, too. So, it kind of has to be an *H*. It's just the only option that makes any sense.

"I can't be a sidekick for a villain," she says quietly, almost to herself.

I nod. I get it. Sort of.

"But even if that happens, we'll still always be friends."

I feel like I'm going to throw up. Why does that sound like a breakup line? Especially if we're not, you know, breaking up. She was supposed to realize she needs to ditch Riley in this scenario, not me. "Right. Just you, me, and good old Riley. Best friends forever." Until he mysteriously disappears and his body is never found, and *not* just because he can go invisible.

"It probably won't happen," she says. "It's only hypothetical."

Yeah, but I don't know how long it's going to take for

my thumbprint to change. It might stay an *X* for years, or it might turn into an *H* tomorrow. Except, if it really did change tomorrow, I have a feeling it wouldn't be into an *H*.

"So," I say, "hypothetically speaking, if I had a *V* but you still agreed with what I was doing—fighting crime and stopping bad guys and stuff—you'd have to leave. For Riley, just because his genetics have given him some seal of approval." Because I'm not going to change my ways just because I get an *H*, so I don't really see the difference here. I'll be the same person with either letter.

"Damien, it's not that—"

Heraldo barks, interrupting her. He leaps out of his dog bed and races to the front door, arriving just as there's a knock.

"—simple. That's Riley. I'm going to have a talk with him. About telling you things that aren't true."

But even as she's talking about scolding him, her face lights up when she says his name. And when she opens the door, Riley pulls her into an embrace and kisses her before she can say anything. It's a really intimate kind of kiss and pretty disgusting—not like when me and Kat make out in public—and I look away, feeling uncomfortable. And maybe a little guilty. Not because I shouldn't be seeing this, but because I'm pretty sure I never kissed her like that when we were together. We weren't exactly together very long, and the point *was* to be messing around ... But still. Maybe Sarah deserves to have someone kissing her like that, like they really mean it. I just wish it didn't have to be *him*.

My phone rings—probably Kat calling to tell me how awesome Vilmore is—and startles Riley, who was too busy kissing my sidekick to notice me. I let it keep ringing. I'll call her back when I get outside, plus as long as it's annoying Riley, I don't see any reason to stop it.

"Oh, hey, X," Riley says, finally breaking away from Sarah before they both asphyxiate to death, "I didn't see you there." He doesn't sound embarrassed, just surprised and annoyed. "Did you come over so we could help you with your homework? I know pretending to be a hero is hard for you, so here's a tip. Any of the questions that ask what you should do when confronted by a villain? The answer isn't to congratulate them on the crime they just committed. Or to make out with them. It's to put them in jail, *where they belong*."

Sarah jabs him in the ribs. "*Be nice.*"

And he's the only one in the room with an *H* on his thumb. Must be great for your genes to lie for you like that. I wonder if it would still be an *H* if the letter he got was based on his actions instead of his parents. I'm pretty sure stealing another hero's sidekick is a crime. Or at least it should be.

My phone chimes, indicating there's a voicemail. I ignore both it and Riley and pretend like he isn't even there. "Well, Cosine old pal, I know you're going to be devastated by this, but it's time for me to go. No, no, don't beg me to stay. I couldn't possibly."

"We're on for Saturday," Sarah says. "I have a new gadget for you to try out. We'll go out patrolling. There's got to be *some* bad guy out there we can test it on."

The way her eyes glint, I hope all the bad guys stay home on Saturday, at least if they want to keep all their fingers. But I don't tell Sarah that—I know from experience reminding her that crime-fighting tools don't have to be deadly is a waste of time. Instead, I say, "Wouldn't miss it," and then ever-so-casually bash my shoulder into Riley really hard as I make my way out the door.

My phone chimes again, not letting me forget I haven't listened to the voicemail Kat left me. I smile a little, thinking about calling her and telling her about my first day at Heroesworth. She's the only one who'll really get how stupid I felt in class today, being the only half villain in a school full of heroes. She's also the only person I'd admit that to. And she's going to laugh so hard when I tell her about how each wing of Heroesworth is named after a different heroic virtue, like Courage or Honesty. And how, despite one of the wings being Generosity, no one would lend me a pencil when mine broke during a pop quiz in Morality about who we would save if we had to make a choice—a runaway train full of gradeschoolers, or a loved one about to be hit by said train.

I grab my phone, ready to call Kat without even listening to her message first, when I notice the caller ID says the call wasn't from Kat at all—it was from Gordon. Great. He probably wants to know how my first day went and why I'm not home already for some quality bonding time about how great it is to go to Heroesworth. As if that's going to happen.

I almost don't even listen to it. He's going to say the

same things when I get home—why listen to them twice? It's going to be boring enough the first time around. But then I give in and call my inbox, just in case. Like maybe he was calling to tell me I got a letter from Vilmore saying this was all a big mistake and they want me there tomorrow.

Not that I'd go, but it would be nice to be *asked*. And then to throw the invitation in their face.

And okay, maybe I'd at least think about it first. I mean, being surrounded by superhero kids who won't give me the time of day because they think they're all better than me—even if it's actually the other way around—doesn't exactly compare to pretty much moving in with my girlfriend. Then there would only be two places on our checklist—my room and hers.

"Damien," Gordon's voice says in the message. He sounds out of breath. And kind of freaked. "There's been an accident."

My stomach clenches and my blood turns cold. It's the hiccup in his voice when he says "accident."

"Alex is hurt. We need you at the hospital."

CHAPTER 4

I call Gordon about a million times on my way to the hospital, but he doesn't pick up. I try calling Helen's phone, but it goes straight to voicemail. I would call Amelia—there's no way she would ever not answer a phone—but she doesn't have one, thanks to Gordon's and Helen's "it's a privilege, not a right" policy. Which translates to, "Really we think you'll run up our bill too much and get in trouble at school."

Obviously, Gordon doesn't know the first thing about phone usage. If it was up to me, I would revoke his "privilege" of having a cell phone, because *why would anyone leave a message like that*? There's been an "accident"? What the hell *kind* of accident?! My little brother is in the hospital, and Gordon calls me, freaks me out with his vague-but-terrifying message, and then doesn't even have the decency to answer his phone when I call back?

My thoughts race the whole bus ride there. I think

about how Alex is only eight and gave up his room for me without ever complaining. I think about our ongoing game of trucks vs. dinosaurs, and what if I never get to find out what happens? I play the T-Rex, and occasionally a very sneaky Velociraptor, and Alex plays everybody else. And you can't really play trucks vs. dinosaurs with only a Tyrannosaurus and his Velociraptor sidekick, who is usually away on spy missions and so is never around. You just can't.

The bus gets slowed in traffic, and it takes what feels like a million years to get to the hospital. I jump out the second the bus stops and race through the main entrance and up to the reception desk. I'm out of breath and sweaty, and I'm pretty sure my hair is all over the place, because I couldn't stop running my hands through it like some kind of hair-touching maniac.

"My dad called me," I pant, not waiting for the receptionist to look up at me or finish typing on her computer.

"One second," she says, frowning at the screen and clicking her mouse a few times.

"It's my brother."

She holds up a finger, signaling for me to wait, and it's about all I can do not to freak out any more than I already am. I want to shout that my dad's not picking up his phone, and this is an emergency, and if I don't find out what's going on *right this second*, I'm probably going to die of a heart attack. Except that I'm already in the hospital, so maybe I'll make it through. But still. That kind of anxiety can't be good for anyone, plus how's Gordon going to feel if both his sons end up in this place?

Then again, if he didn't want me to keel over from assuming the worst, maybe he should leave better messages or answer his phone once in a while.

I tap my fingers against the counter. I run my hands through my hair again. "Look, I really, *really* need to find out what's going on."

She ignores me for a few more seconds until she's done typing, then smiles and says, "Your name, please?"

"Damien Locke." I think I hear my phone beep, so I grab it to check. Nope. Just wishful thinking.

"Locke," she mutters, peering at the computer screen and clicking away on the keys again.

"Yeah, but that's not the name it's—"

"Here we are. Marianna Locke."

"That's my mom. But—"

"She's in room 214. I just need you to sign in right here"—she shoves a clipboard with a space for my name and sign-in time at me—"and then you can go see her."

"What?"

"Just make sure you knock first. There should be a sign on the door, but we don't want to startle her."

I'm pretty sure seeing me would be startling enough. "My mom's *here*?"

"Yes."

"In the hospital." Villains don't go to hospitals. At least, not if they can help it, and not if they don't want the police asking a lot of questions. There are plenty of villain doctors who make house calls, so what would she ever be doing here? Unless something bad happened. Something so bad that she had to be rushed here for immediate treatment.

I swallow, not sure who I'm worried about more, her or Alex. It *should* be Alex—he's the one I came to see. He's the one I've been freaking out about since I got that call, and he's never betrayed me or stopped talking to me. But ... I can't help thinking my mom would *never* go to a hospital.

I picture my mom and Alex getting into some kind of head-on collision and both being rushed here. Except Alex is only eight, and my mom doesn't even own a car. Or at least she didn't five months ago.

"Your mother and your brother are both resting comfortably. Everything went smoothly—no complications."

What the hell is she talking about? "So, Alex Tines, he's okay?"

She scrunches up her eyebrows at me. "Who?"

I feel like I've stepped into some kind of alternate universe where nothing makes any sense. "My *brother.*"

"I think there's been some kind of confusion. It says here your brother's name is Xavier Locke. He was born this morning at ten fifty-two a.m."

Oh. My. God, as Amelia would say. I don't know what I would say, because I'm too stunned to speak, but I think it would involve some choice expletives.

My mom had a baby and didn't tell me. She hates me that much that she wasn't even going to tell me I have a brother. An all-villain half brother. A perfect little replacement.

My phone rings. I'm still too stunned to register what the sound is, but my hand moves to answer it completely out of muscle memory. "Hello?" My voice doesn't sound like me. It sounds too numb, too dead to be me.

"Damien." It's Gordon. He sighs in relief. "I'm so sorry. I was so panicked, I left my phone in the car. I just realized I didn't have it and that you might have tried to call."

"Is Alex okay?"

"He fell down the attic stairs. He has a broken arm and a slight concussion, but he's going to be fine. He's getting his cast put on now, and Helen just took Amelia and Jess home."

"I *told* you they were a deathtrap." No one ever listens to me about the dangers of staircases, especially rickety ones that are about one stomp from Amelia's hoof away from disintegrating into a pile of rusty nails and splinters.

"Yes, well, we'll discuss that later." He pauses, and I hear muffled sounds in the background, like he's talking to someone else. Then he says, "Okay, I'll ask. Damien, Alex wants to know what color cast you think he should get. Green or purple?"

"Green if he wants me to draw a T-Rex on it, purple if he wants me to draw a Velociraptor." Ask me something I *don't* know.

Gordon laughs. "I'll pass that on. Where are you?"

"I'll be there soon," I tell him.

There's just one thing I have to do first.

X·X·X

I get to room 214 and knock on the door before I can chicken out. Because seeing my mom after all this time, when she didn't even call me to tell me she was having a baby—let alone that I have a new brother—doesn't exactly make me feel all warm and fuzzy inside. It's more like it makes my skin crawl and my stomach want to turn inside out.

There's a slight pause after I knock, so that I'm thinking maybe she's not here, maybe the hospital made a mistake and I should just go find Gordon and go home, but then my mom's voice says to come in.

She sounds tired but happy, and when I go in, she doesn't even look up at first, too busy gazing lovingly at the baby in her arms, all wrapped up in a light-blue blanket.

"Hey, Mom," I say, and *that* gets her attention. "Long time no see."

She stares at me, her mouth gaping open. "Damien."

"Hey, look at that. You remembered my name."

"What are you doing here?"

"No, Mom, what are *you* doing here? Can I still call you Mom, or would you prefer Marianna?"

"Damien, don't be ridiculous. Come here so I can look at you."

I stay where I am. "So. I have a new brother and you weren't going to tell me."

"I wanted to call you. I thought about it a thousand times."

"But you didn't." I shrug.

"I didn't know how you'd react. You were the one who

chose to leave, to go and live with *that man*."

"That's not how I remember it. You kicked me out."

"Based on the choices you made."

I swallow back a bitter taste in my mouth. "So you replaced me. What happened to making a name for yourself? I was some kind of burden to you, but I guess it wasn't having a kid that was the problem, it was just *me*."

Her eyes fill with tears, and I've officially made my mother cry. But I deserve some answers, and I'm not going to back down.

The baby—Xavier—makes fussing noises, and Mom holds him closer and tries to soothe him. "Damien," she says, keeping her tone falsely pleasant, "you're upsetting your brother."

"Yeah, well, he's upsetting me. I guess we have that in common. And it's been five months since you kicked me out, and he doesn't look like he was born early." I'm no expert, but he looks like a normal baby. Not like one who was born several months too soon. "So that means you were, what, four-months pregnant the last time you saw me? You had plenty of time to tell me then, and you didn't. So what does that say?"

The baby starts full-blown crying, despite Mom's efforts to calm him down. She glares at me, her lasers flashing in her eyes—did I mention her superpower is shooting lasers from her eyes?—and grits her teeth. "Damien, if you insist on making your brother cry, then *you* are going to hold him. So get over here. Now."

Fine. I do what she says—though only because I *do* want to see him up close, and this is probably the only chance I'll get—but I drag my feet about it.

"Here," Mom says, transferring a screaming Xavier into my arms. "Just make sure you support his head." She leans back against her pillows and watches me. Us. "Look at you. My two boys." Her eyes are watering again, but this time at least it's not because I'm pissed at her. She grabs her phone from her nightstand and snaps a picture of us.

"*Mom.*" I roll my eyes at her and sigh, so she knows how ridiculous she's being. For a moment, it's like nothing ever happened between us. Like I never got my *X* or went to live with Gordon.

Xavier's mostly calmed down now. He squirms a little in my arms, but he's stopped crying. I don't think I did anything to make him stop, other than not yelling at his mom. I look him over, trying to see if there's any family resemblance. He has a few little wisps of red hair on his head. So I guess he takes after Mom.

I have dark hair, like Gordon. And my eyes are green like his, too, and, according to Sarah at least, I look a lot like him. I disagree on that front, but I guess I can admit I look more like him than like Mom. I feel a little stab of jealousy, knowing Xavier's going to grow up actually *belonging.* He's going to grow up knowing who his father is and that both his parents are villains. He'll get his *V* when he turns sixteen, go to Vilmore, and have the life I was supposed to have. He'll probably have a girlfriend that goes there, too. And he'll have laser eyes, like Mom, or maybe be able to shoot electricity from his hands, like my grandpa. *Our* grandpa, I guess.

I shut my eyes, not wanting to think these things. He's just a baby—it's not his fault he's going to have everything I should have had, but couldn't.

"So," I say, "are you still with Taylor? I mean, is he—"

"He's Xavier's father, yes. And we're still together. We're getting married this Christmas. Taylor wanted to get married before the baby was born, but things happened so fast. And I wanted to be able to wear a dress that actually *fit*. Just because I'm almost thirty-five—"

"You're thirty-nine, you mean."

She clears her throat. "Just because I'm of a certain age doesn't mean I don't want to go all out for my wedding."

"So, I suppose you weren't going to invite me to that, either."

"I didn't think you'd want to come. You were never enthusiastic about Taylor's proposal, and after everything that happened ..."

"I get it." I do. Not that it doesn't still hurt. "You weren't going to tell me about any of this stuff before you kicked me out—"

"Before you *left*, dear."

"—so why would you tell me now? Did Taylor know? About the baby—is that why he proposed? And what was all that crap about you making a name for yourself and me being some kind of burden on you if you *knew*—"

The baby starts crying again, and I shove him at Mom and turn away from them, because I can't even look at her, knowing all the ways she's betrayed me. How much she obviously didn't want me. The last thing I want is for her to look at my face and see how much all this hurts.

"I never said you were a burden, sweetie—"

She tries to put her hand on my shoulder, but I pull away. *"Don't."*

"And Taylor proposed to me because he loves me. Not because of the baby—I wasn't even pregnant then, so, you see, I didn't lie to you."

"You mean you didn't know you were having a baby." I remember when Taylor proposed and how much champagne Mom was drinking that day. She wouldn't have if she'd known she was pregnant, right? Even she's not that irresponsible.

"No, that's not what I said. Damien, come here. If you're going to accuse me of something, at least have the decency to look at me while you do it."

I turn around to face her. She looks me over, studying me, as if she'd forgotten what I look like and is trying to memorize it for later. "You're taller, you know that? You probably need new shoes. I don't suppose *that man* keeps up with these things—"

"Mom. I'm fine. I got shoes last month. And my father's name is Gordon. If you can let him violate you in a subway bathroom, I think you can say his name."

She flinches and ignores what I said, changing the subject. "Anyway, Damien, I wasn't pregnant back when you were living with me. Xavier didn't come along until another month after that."

I raise an eyebrow. "I think your math skills are slipping. That would mean he was born after only four months. You don't really expect me to believe that, do you?"

"Well … Maybe you should sit down before I tell you."

"Before you tell me what?"

"Nothing. It's just, you remember that growth formula I was working on a few years ago?"

"That was for plants. But I thought you learned your lesson after those man-eating vines grew like crazy all over the house that one time and almost killed us. If we hadn't had that extra-strength herbicide to use on them—"

"Which I also invented, of course."

"—then we'd probably both be dead right now. So, yes, *I remember.* I also remember telling you to not to experiment with anything like that ever again." Not that she ever actually listens to me.

"Well, I modified it. So it would work on more than just plants. And don't look at me like that—I wasn't going to use it on myself. It was for cows. To make them grow faster. With faster gestation rates, they could get to the milking stage that much quicker. And of course the cows themselves would grow up at more than twice the normal speed, so you can see why dairy farmers would pay through the nose for this kind of thing."

"And did they?" I can't believe it. She wanted to make a name for herself as a villain and *this* is what she's been doing?

"They would have. I had an offer on the table, Damien —I'm not stupid. But I couldn't get it working quite right. The milk from these cows wasn't exactly something you'd want to drink. And the meat was inedible." She makes a face. "No one was going to pay for that. And then I found out I was pregnant with little Xavier here, and, well, I had to shut down my experiment. At least for the time being. But I guess I must have already had too much exposure to the formula, because here we are, four months and one healthy little baby later."

Healthy? I gape at her. Then at the baby in her arms. "You mean, he's some kind of experiment?"

"No! Of course not. He was exposed to one of my experimental formulas by accident, which is not the same thing. I was thinking maybe I could market it to busy women. Why take nine months to have a baby when you can do it in four? Or possibly three?"

"That's insane."

"That's exactly what Taylor said. *Men.* You just don't get it."

"But what's going to happen to him? To my brother? I mean, if he's going to age twice as fast as normal—"

"*At least* twice as fast, Damien. Give my formula the credit it deserves. Some of those cows grew at absolutely astounding rates, if I do say so myself."

"Then he's not going to live as long." Suddenly, I wish I hadn't held him at all, that I hadn't felt his weight in my arms or the way his tiny little legs wiggled inside his blanket. I was probably never going to get to see him again anyway, and now I find out he's only going to have half a life. Less than that, according to Mom. Less than half as many leg wigglings. Less than half as many times hanging out with his friends. Less than half as many kisses. Less than half as many *everythings.*

I gape at Mom, horrified, and back away. "How could you do this to him?"

She holds Xavier extra close and glares at me. "It wasn't something I did on purpose. Do you really think so little of me?"

"How could you let this happen? How could you want to let this happen to *other people*?!"

"Keep your voice down. Obviously my formula needs some more work before I put it on the market. And he's going to have a perfectly healthy and happy life, just like everyone else. The formula will wear off. I think."

"So he just doesn't get to be a kid for very long, is that it? Let me guess—he'll stop growing super fast once he turns sixteen, gets his *V*, and becomes my replacement?"

"Damien!"

Xavier starts full-out wailing, his little wrinkled face turning red and angry. I have to shout just to be heard over him. "So I guess that's why you weren't going to tell me about him! I wasn't good enough for you, and instead of making things right with me, you just have a new kid. One who won't waste any time growing up into a perfect teenage son, and then you can pretend I never even existed."

"I think you should leave."

"Yeah, I bet you do."

I turn to go just as there's a knock on the door and Taylor comes in, balancing a couple of bags of Chinese food in his arms. "They didn't have the pork that you wanted, but I got the— Damien?" He's so shocked to see me, he loses his grip on one of the bags and has to scramble to keep from dropping it. "What are you doing here?"

"*Leaving.*" I push past him, and the only reason I don't slam the door on my way out is for Xavier's sake. He's going to have a hard enough life as it is.

CHAPTER 5

I dial Kat's number for about the fiftieth time when Gordon, Alex, and me get home from the hospital. Today must be "nobody answers their phone" day, because she's not picking up. Even though it's after six and I know her classes must be over and she must be dying to tell me how it went.

After about ten rings, her phone sends me to voicemail. *Hey, this is Kat. I'm probably screening my calls right now, but if you leave an awesome enough message, I might call you back. Except you, Damien—you're always awesome and I'll always call you back.*

I don't leave a message. What am I supposed to say? *My mom had a new all-villain baby to replace me. How was Vilmore?* Right. Plus, it was bad enough Mom kicked me out—it's not exactly like I want to broadcast my latest demotion to the rest of the world. Or, in this case, Gordon.

I sigh and sink down on the couch, staring at my phone. Willing it to ring. Maybe I should call Sarah. She's probably still busy with Riley, though I'm sure she'd tell him to get lost once she knew I really needed her. As long as I exaggerated and made it sound like an emergency.

"Mom!" Alex shouts, rushing through the living room and looking for Helen.

"Settle down," Gordon warns. "The doctor said to take it easy."

The narrow, barely held-together attic stairs creak, and then Helen hurries down them like they're not some deathtrap that almost killed her only son today. And to make matters worse, she's holding Jessica, my three-year-old half sister, while she does it. Great. Why not endanger the lives of all my favorite siblings? Amelia tromps down after them. They're all on the stairs at the *same time*. I feel dizzy just watching and have to look away.

Alex points to the cast on his right arm, practically jumping up and down with excitement. Obviously, he's still too much in shock to realize how traumatized he should be. "Look, Mom! I got purple! It was the best one."

"I can see that," Helen says. She exchanges a slightly worried look with Gordon, then tilts her head toward me. Gordon quickly shakes his head.

As if I can't tell they must be talking about me. Helen's probably wondering if Gordon's had a chance to have some sort of heart-to-heart with me about the dangers of sleeping with supervillains. *You might* think *you want to sleep with her, son, but you'll be sorry sixteen years from now when you have to tell your parents where your illegitimate villain kid came from.*

Uh-huh.

"Damien's going to draw a Velociraptor on it later," Alex tells her. "But he can't right now, because ..." He glances over his shoulder to make sure I'm not listening, and then finishes in a whisper. " ...because he's depressed."

What? "I am not," I mutter. Then I sigh and pull the hood of my sweatshirt over my face and sink deeper into the couch. But, you know, not in a depressed way.

Amelia moves to stand in front of me with her arms folded and this smug smile on her face. "Looks like *someone* didn't have a very good first day."

She looks like she's going to sit next to me, but then thankfully Jess beats her to it, cozying up beside me and laying her head on my shoulder. "You know, Amelia, it's too bad your power only works on things you've touched before. Otherwise, you could, you know, summon up boys."

Her mouth goes sour, like she just ate something that tasted bad. Then she actually clucks her tongue at me. "I heard about what happened. *Everyone's* talking about how you thought that bomb was real."

"Oh, is *everyone* talking about it?" I'd like to see her last five minutes at Vilmore.

"They do that trick every year. I can't believe you fell for it!"

How the hell was I supposed to know? "I didn't hear you warning me about it." If she even knew. She's in the afternoon class, so she had plenty of time to find out during the day. Especially if *everyone* was talking about it.

Jess tugs my hood back so she can cup her hands to my

ear. "Hi," she whispers, then smiles real big at me.

Amelia's nostrils flare. "Jess. No secrets."

I cup my hands to Jess's ear and ask her to go get me a pen. She scurries off to do my bidding.

Amelia scowls at me. "Just try not to become the laughingstock of the school, okay? It's bad enough people already know we're related."

"Yes, it is." We can agree on that, at least.

"But, since I'm feeling generous, I'd still be willing to help you with your poster. Mine's almost done, so I have some spare time."

She has no life, she means. "Why don't you work up a first draft and I'll see if I can sign off on it." Like I don't have way better things to do than work on some poster, which is apparently supposed to be on "what heroism means to me." All I have to do is find a magazine picture of a kitten in a tree, glue it on my poster board, and I'm done. No problem.

Amelia scoffs. "I'm not doing your homework for you."

"Then mind your own business. I don't need your help."

"But it's due Wednesday, Damien. *Wednesday.*" She puts her hands on her hips, letting that sink in.

"And tomorrow's only Tuesday." Besides, I'm the idiot villain kid who thought a bomb was actually going off in class. Miss Monk's expectations of me can't be too high. She'll probably give me a gold star just for getting my name right.

Jess waddles back over and holds out the crayon she brought me. Not a pen, but close enough. I whisper to her again and ask her to get me a piece of paper. When she runs off, I say to Amelia, "Wow, look at that. I wanted something, and it just appeared. Almost like a superpower."

"Shut up."

I tap the end of the crayon, studying Amelia. "Can you put your arm out a little? And turn to the left."

"Why?"

Jess returns with a slightly used piece of paper that has one of her drawings on one side. I press it against my leg and ready the crayon. "Because I'm going to draw a Velociraptor on Alex's cast later and I need to practice first."

She clenches her fists and makes a frustrated noise of rage.

"What? I thought you *wanted* to be a model."

Before she can say anything to that, my phone chimes and a text from Kat pops up. *Sorry I missed your calls—hanging in the commons. It's so loud in here! What's up?*

I get up from the couch and head for the privacy of my room, already texting her back. *Call me.*

"Fine," Amelia says in a snotty voice. "Be a jerk like that and don't accept my help on anything. It's not like I care if you fail. But I think you might like to know that that's not your room anymore."

"What?" My phone rings, but I don't answer it yet, too busy raising a skeptical eyebrow at Amelia and putting my hand on the knob anyway. I mean, I think I know my own room.

"Dad didn't tell you?" She bites her lip in mock concern, though I can already see the smug "I know something you don't" smile creeping over her.

"Didn't tell me what?"

Gordon hurries over from the kitchen. "I'll take it from here, Amelia." He looks down his nose at her, indicating she should go somewhere else and mind her own damn business.

She gets this self-satisfied grin on her face and takes my spot on the couch next to Jess. She tries to whisper something in Jess's ear, but Jess pushes her away, having none of it.

"There's been a change of plans," Gordon says, right as my phone stops ringing and says I have a missed call from Kat. "Alex is moving back into his old room, and you're moving into the attic."

I laugh. Gordon thinks he's so hilarious. That or he's delusional. "Ha. Good one."

"I'm serious. Helen and I talked it over earlier, and after Alex's accident, we feel it's not safe for him to be living up there."

Because the stairs really are a deathtrap, he means.

I glance over my shoulder at Amelia, to see if she's eavesdropping, which of course she is. Her eyes go wide when I catch her watching us and she looks away super obviously. "I think there's been a misunderstanding," I tell Gordon, my hand on the knob to *my* room, "and if you'll just step into my office, I think we can clear it up."

"Grab a few things for tonight. We'll work on actually switching everything this weekend. All right?"

I swallow and look over at the steep, rickety attic stairs. The railing is practically falling off. And he seriously expects me to live up there? "Dad," I say through clenched teeth, "that's great that you're so concerned about Alex's safety. But let's not do anything crazy that we might *regret*. I'm more than happy to share my very safe ground-floor bedroom with Alex, especially since it was his room first and he was kind enough to share it with me." Even if that meant I had to sleep on the floor, curled into a cramped little ball. But it would still be better than living in the freaking *attic* and having to go up and down those stairs every day. I get why he doesn't want Alex up there, but wasn't pushing me off a building enough for him?

My phone starts ringing again, but I press the ignore button, sending it to voicemail.

"Damien." Gordon gets this gruff "I'm your father and I mistakenly think I know what's best for you" look.

"I would also be perfectly happy to sleep on the couch. But that's my final offer."

"Alex's room"—he means the ground floor bedroom, the one that up until two seconds ago was *mine*—"isn't big enough for you to share permanently. And you're not living on the couch. Not when we have a perfectly good extra bedroom upstairs." He puts a hand on my shoulder and leans in, keeping his voice low. "I know how you feel about heights."

"Obviously you don't." Even after pushing me off a building, he still doesn't understand, because if he did, he wouldn't be asking this. "I've been telling you those stairs are dangerous for months, and you didn't listen to me. And now that you know I'm right, because Alex nearly killed himself on them, you want *me* to move up there? Do you hear how ridiculous that sounds?"

"But you're older and more careful. Nothing's ever happened to Amelia," he points out, as if that should reassure me. *Well, we've only had fifty percent casualties. You* probably *won't die.* "And," he adds, giving me his gruff look again, "you can fly."

Says the man who's only ever seen me do it once. I have, in fact, flown two times, but both times only because I was in mortal danger. I'm not eager to do it again.

"If something does happen," he goes on, "and I'm not saying that it will, but if it does, at least I know you can handle it. I don't have to worry about you. Unless there *is* some reason I should be worried? You were awfully quiet in the car. How was your first day?"

I flash him an overly fake smile. "My first day was *great.* I made tons of new friends. I'm already at the top of my class. I might even run for class president because I'm so obviously a shoo-in."

Disappointment flashes in Gordon's eyes, though he tries to hide it by not looking at me and staring at his feet, which really only emphasizes it. "Well ... first days are hard."

"All the more reason why I should get to actually sleep tonight. In a room that isn't going to collapse. You do realize I've never even been to the attic, right? I've lived here for six months and I've never even been up there."

He sighs, as if my stubbornness about, you know, not wanting to die is really putting him out. "If you've never even been up there, then how do you know you won't like it? Think of this as a way to start getting over your fears. It'll be good for you."

Right. Until the whole floor collapses and I die a horrible, excruciating death, buried under all the rubble. That's like saying if you've never stuck your head inside a lion's mouth, then how do you know it's not a great idea? "You're kidding me, right?"

He claps me on the shoulder, acting like he didn't hear me, and says, "I know you can handle it, Damien. And that I can trust you to set a good example for your brother and sisters. So go get your stuff." Then he walks off to go help Helen in the kitchen with dinner. Or to go find someone else's life to ruin. It's really hard to say.

X·X·X

"I tried to tell you," Kat says on the phone later that night. I'm up in my new room in the deathtrap—I mean, attic—sitting on the bed. It took me about twenty minutes to get up the stairs, though it felt more like hours. Every time I even breathed, they shuddered beneath me like they were going to fall. Especially as I got closer to the top and they actually started to *wobble*. My vision blurred and my palms got sweaty, so I didn't even think I'd be able to grab onto the railing if I needed to. Not that I trust the railing, since it's falling off and obviously unstable.

I had to practically crawl up the last few steps. I also had to wait until everyone else had gone to bed, or at least to their rooms, since there was no way I wanted anyone seeing me like that. Even if showing Gordon firsthand what an awful choice he made might have been tempting.

And now that I'm up here, the wind howling outside sounds extra loud. And the way it presses against the house makes the whole attic feel like it's swaying. Like I'm in some precarious tree house, not a supposedly sturdy building suitable for living in.

My new room itself isn't too bad, if you can overlook the swaying, the rickety stairs, and the general life-threatening danger. It's technically bigger than my old room, but the way it's shaped makes it feel more cramped. The wall behind me is slanted, so that I can't sit up all the way or I'll hit my head. Something I've experienced three times already, and I've only been up here an hour.

The floor, the ceiling, and the walls are all a dingy gray, except for the new wall Gordon put in a few months ago, turning what was Amelia's giant room into two. That wall looks like it's made of planks fresh from the hardware store. And I discovered it's not just the stairs leading up here that creak, but all the floorboards. It sounds like the whole attic is about to give way every time Amelia stomps around her room. And either her TV's blaring or the walls in here are pretty thin, because I can hear every word of the documentary she's watching.

It's the one they made this summer about Gordon's superhero alter ego, the Crimson Flash, called *The Man Behind the Cape*. They interviewed the whole family, putting those blurry dots over everyone's faces and disguising their voices, so supervillains and overeager tourists wouldn't be able to track down his real identity. Well, I shouldn't say they interviewed the *whole* family, since they left me out of it. The lady making the documentary asked who I was, and Gordon got this look on his face like he was going to have an embolism or something. His eye twitched, and he started stammering about how families are made of all kinds of people and that we never know how they'll turn out. The lady looked like she thought he was crazy.

Then I stepped in and said I was a distant cousin from out of town and did she know when was the best time to visit the Heroes Walk? She bought it, and nobody corrected me. I mean, Gordon looked like he wanted to— he even opened his mouth to protest, but then ... he just didn't. And I get it. It was easier this way. Plus, it's not like I wanted to be on TV, broadcasting to the world that I'm some freak with an *X* on my thumb. Or to have some actor twice my age play me in the recreated dramatic scenes, like they did for Amelia. The actress who plays her isn't just older, but way skinnier and with much bigger boobs— a body type I know Amelia aspires to have, even if she's about a million calories and a boob job or two away from ever achieving it. Which is probably the real reason she's watched *The Man Behind the Cape* about fifty times since it first aired last month.

But once I get my *H*, things will be different. Well, for me, not Amelia. Then even if I'm not exactly part of their perfect nuclear family, at least Gordon will be able to tell people I'm his kid with a straight face. And then the only embarrassing questions he'll have to answer will be why me and Amelia are so close in age, not why he, Golden City's most beloved superhero, has a half-villain son.

"Are you watching that stupid documentary again?" Kat asks through the phone. "Is it on my part yet?"

Kat managed to sneak in as a random extra when they were interviewing people on the street. She used her shapeshifting powers to hide the fact that her thumb has a *V* on it, just in case they weren't open to interviewing supervillains. The only line of hers they kept was the part where her eyes get all wide and she says, "Gosh, is the Crimson Flash actually here, *right now*?!" Then she looks around, like he might be standing behind her and she just missed him or something.

It's definitely the best five seconds of the whole movie. That and the bit where the Crimson Flash's cape gets snagged on a sticker bush and it takes him a whole minute to get it loose again. They overlay it with him answering questions about his everyday life, I guess so the viewers at home can see what an ordinary guy he is. You know, getting his cape stuck on things.

"Of course not," I tell Kat. Unlike Amelia, seeing it a couple times—once with my family, and once with Kat, making fun of it—was more than enough for me, though I do have my favorite clips saved on my phone. "That's my wonderful new neighbor, Amelia, who is oh-so-respectful of my space." My phone beeps, reminding me to plug it in. It's been beeping every once in a while for about twenty minutes now, but I haven't bothered to charge it. I'm too busy jotting down a list of potential ways to get myself kicked out of my excellent new living quarters. Alex did it, and he's only eight—it couldn't be too hard. "And how could you not tell me my mom was having a *baby*?"

She groans, and I can practically hear her rolling her eyes. "You didn't want to talk about her, remember?"

"Yeah, but that's before I knew she was replacing me." The problem with Alex's method of escape is that it involved falling down the stairs and resulted in breaking his arm. I happen to like my arm the way it is—intact and pain-free—and falling down the stairs is *not* an option, for all the obvious reasons, like it being way too terrifying.

Kat's quiet a minute. "I know things aren't great between you and your mom, but do you really think she'd do that?"

"I don't know what she would or wouldn't do. And either way, that doesn't change the fact that I have a brother."

I tap my list with my pen, considering other possibilities. Like, what if Jess suddenly started having nightmares and I was the only one who could make her feel better and had to sleep downstairs in her room? I put that in the "maybe" column, since it would probably also involve me giving her the nightmares to begin with—I'd say with scary movies, but Jess is actually really terrified of this one puppet show that's on in the mornings—plus I'm not *that* horrible.

Or that desperate. At least, not yet.

"You already had a brother," Kat says.

"This is different." My voice goes quiet. The wind shakes the attic extra hard, making it feel like the floor's falling out from under me, and I forget about my notes and clutch Alex's bedspread instead. It's got blue squares with pictures of trucks on them. Someone—I suspect Alex

—has taken a Sharpie and drawn faces on all of them, giving them their own personalities. I like Alex. I'm even sort of glad he's my brother. But it's different with this side of the family. Gordon didn't raise me. And he took me in. My mom, on the other hand, kicked me out the first chance she got.

"She claimed she couldn't make a name for herself because of me," I tell Kat. "And all this time, I thought she'd eventually figure out she overreacted and that she still wants me in her life. I mean, there's no way I'd go back there, even if she did, but now I find out she hasn't been thinking of me at all. She's been too busy having another kid. One she's actually happy about. He might not have been planned, either, but at least he's all villain. He even looks like her." I pause, thinking about holding Xavier earlier. "I don't want to like him." I feel kind of ashamed to say it. Whatever Mom did, it's not his fault. But that doesn't change the fact that I wish he didn't exist.

"I used to wish my parents would have another kid," Kat says. She's an only child. We used to have that in common. "But that was when I was, like, two. If they had another one now? Ugh."

A girl's voice in the background shouts, "We're going to the student store, Katie, you want to come?"

"Can't," Kat says. "I'm on the phone." As if they were talking to her, even though they obviously used the wrong name. Crazy.

"Ooh," another girl's voice says, "talking to your *boyfriend*?" Whoever she is, she says the word *boyfriend* like it's the most scandalous thing in the world. Kat must have told her all about me.

Then both girls call out in a singsong voice, "Hi, Damien!" before giggling hysterically and leaving the room.

"Sorry about that," Kat says, sounding embarrassed. "Those are my suitemates, Tasha and Liv. I guess I kind of talked a lot about you today."

"Understandable. I mean, it is difficult to go a whole day without gushing about how awesome I am. I often have trouble myself."

There's a thumping noise. Then Kat says, "That was me, hitting you with a pillow. Hard."

"I guess there are *some* benefits to this long-distance thing."

"Seriously, I was one of those annoying people who wouldn't shut up about her boyfriend back home. I even showed them pictures of you on my phone."

"And they were so taken with me, they forgot to ask you why I don't go to your school."

"I kind of let them think you're a year younger than me."

Well, it's better than them knowing the truth—that I go to Heroesworth, their rival school—or thinking I wasn't good enough to get into Vilmore. Which is, er, sort of also the truth, since even before I got my *X*, I was apparently not an ideal candidate, or at least according to Taylor, my stepfather-to-be and the former dean of Vilmore. He resigned last year, after Pete, my ex-best friend and one of his star students, died during his and Mom's attempt to take over Golden City. But not before he'd made his final decisions on who would be joining Vilmore's freshman class this fall. Mom really should have waited to start sleeping with him until *after* the admissions process. But, as I said before, she never listens to me. "They're going to be disappointed next year when I don't show up."

"Well, I was kind of hoping … I mean, you know, Heroesworth might not be your thing." *That's* an understatement. "And you could reapply. Taylor's not the dean anymore. You just need to buff up your villainous extra-curriculars. I could help you. Between the two of us, we could pull off something really devious."

I'm silent a minute, taking that in. And even though I've decided I want to get my *H*, part of me is still tempted by what she's saying. "Who's Katie?"

"Oh." She swallows. "That's me."

"Yeah, I figured. You didn't tell them your name was Kat?"

"Well, at role call this morning in Thwarting Heroes, Mrs. Thorpe called me Katherine. I *said* I go by Kat, but then this kid, Tristan, he started teasing me and calling me Katie instead and it kind of stuck."

I can't picture her as a Katie. She's always been Kat to me. "So some guy starts flirting with you and now you have a new name?" Some guy who better hope I never do get into Vilmore, because I *will* murder him. And probably get extra credit for it.

"*Damien.* It wasn't like that."

But I can tell from the way her voice gets super high-pitched that it *was* like that. I switch my phone to my other ear. There's a sharp zap of static electricity when I touch it that sends my nerves racing. "So, what do you want me to call you now?"

"Kat, of course. Geez. Don't make a big deal out of it."

But it feels like a big deal. When we were making out in my bed on Friday, she was Kat. Now she moves away and talks to some other guy, and suddenly she has a new name, like she's a different person. Like that time I caught her making out with my best friend Pete and she'd shapeshifted to look like someone else.

Maybe Sarah was right. Maybe I do still have trust issues.

"Katie is still short for Katherine," she says, sounding defensive. "It's just another version of the same name."

Just another version of her. One that feels really far away all of a sudden.

"Damien, *you're* my boyfriend."

"I know that, but does Tristan?"

"Oh, my God, will you let it go?"

"I just don't get it."

"It's not my fault if guys flirt with me."

But that doesn't mean she has to change her name every time one of them does. I take a deep breath, letting it out slowly. I waited all day to talk to her, and now I don't know how our conversation got so derailed. "Imagine how you'd feel if it was me. If some girl started calling me by a new name and I just went with it."

"Uh, you mean like when Sarah named you Renegade X? I don't have to *imagine* it."

"That was totally different."

"You're right. It was worse. You weren't even supposed

to be a superhero. You were supposed to be a villain, with *me*. She shouldn't have been the one helping you pick out a name. Plus, I know you made out with her. And I know we weren't together then, but don't pretend it doesn't mean anything. And you still see her all the time."

"She's my friend." And just because I'd never want Sarah and Kat to be in the same room at the same time doesn't mean they can't both be important people in my life.

"She's your sidekick. Face it, Damien, if I was running around doing villain stuff with some guy I'd made out with, you'd be going nuts."

"No, I wouldn't. I would very calmly—*very* calmly; I really can't emphasize that enough—and methodically *destroy* him, piece by piece. Look, Kat, I know I didn't get into Vilmore and that our plans for the future got thrown out the window, but that doesn't mean I don't—"

My phone beeps again, reminding me for the millionth time to plug it in, except it's actually about to go dead this time. "Hold on," I tell her, grabbing my backpack off the floor and scrambling to find my charger.

"It's okay. Tasha and Liv are back. I really should—"

"Wait, hold on. Don't go yet. I'm sorry, I just—"

I plug in the phone, and the wall socket lights up. Sparks fly out of it and burn my fingers a little. The wall socket goes dark almost as quickly as it lit up, and then all the lights go out and Amelia's TV turns silent.

"I just miss you," I finish, even though she can't hear me because my phone has gone completely dead.

CHAPTER 6

The power's been out for less than five minutes before Amelia knocks on my door. I debate answering it, since that means getting up and risking my life by walking across the floorboards. There's one in particular between the bed and the door that I don't trust, since it sort of sagged under my foot earlier.

But then Amelia calls out, "Damien, I *know* you're in there. And I know you're awake—I heard you talking."

Wow, and here she thought she inherited the power to teleport stuff to her. But her power must actually be super hearing if she could pick up anything above her blaring TV.

"Damien?" she calls again, and this time she sounds kind of freaked out. Like maybe she's watched one too many horror movies and thinks everyone in the house might have disappeared along with the electricity, leaving her completely alone.

I groan and, wonderful half brother that I am, get off

the bed, take a deep breath, and try not to picture the floor crumbling beneath me, now that I can't actually see it. It's pitch black in here, and this is my first time in the attic, let alone in my new room, so I have a little trouble finding the door at first. But then my hand smacks into the knob, and I open it to find Amelia standing in the hallway with a flashlight.

"What?" I ask, trying not to wince as the wind rattles the whole attic and my legs kind of turn to liquid.

The beam from her flashlight falls directly on the crotch of my pajamas, which are green flannel and have pictures of holly sprigs, reindeer, and snowflakes all over them, except for the crotch, where it says, DO NOT OPEN UNTIL X-MAS! Believe it or not, my grandma got me these last Christmas. I'm sad because it hasn't even been a year and I'm already growing out of them. Mom's right—I have gotten taller.

Amelia's cheeks turn pink, and she hurries to point her flashlight somewhere else. She decides on my face. I squint in the brightness and hold my hand out to block the light.

"Oh, good," she says, sounding relieved that she's not in a horror movie after all and isn't the last person left alive. "You're up." She fidgets, shifting her weight from foot to foot and making the floor creak. She scratches her nose with her free hand and points her flashlight at my shins, where the legs of my pajamas come up a little high. "The power went out."

"I noticed." And my fingers still burn a little from the wall socket exploding on me. Not that the power going out was my fault or anything. All I did was plug in my cell phone—how was I supposed to know the attic had such crappy wiring?

"I thought you might want some company. Because it's kind of spooky up here when it storms, and now that the power's out ..." She swallows. "It's scary enough for me, and I'm not afraid of ... you know. Being up high."

I raise an eyebrow at her, pretending the idea of me being even the least bit terrified of heights is news to me. "It's almost midnight. Shouldn't you be in bed? I know you need an *awful lot* of beauty sleep."

She glares at me. "I can't sleep." She points her flashlight at my face again, then realizes what she's doing and focuses it on the wall. She twists the end of it, playing with the amount of light it gives out. "I thought maybe you wouldn't be able to sleep, either. So, do you want to play *Capes and Robbers* with me? It's a board game. We *always* play it when the power goes out. It's kind of a family tradition."

"Wow. That sounds *so fun*. Let me guess, you want me to be the robber?"

"Well, you can't play with just capes. But we could watch a movie instead. My laptop has enough battery power left." She gestures to it, tucked under her other arm.

It wasn't there a second ago, so she must have used her power to summon it to her. It's bright pink and kind of stands out, even in the dark, and was an early sixteenth-birthday present from Gordon and Helen. Her birthday isn't until late October, which is still almost two months away, but they wanted to give her something for starting Heroesworth. All I got for my birthday was this lousy *X*, and getting shoved off a building, though I don't think that counts. I didn't get anything for starting at Heroesworth, either, though Helen did leave some informational pamphlets on the dangers of teen sex lying around for me to find. Because she's thoughtful like that.

"Or we could, you know, hang out. Just until the lights come back on." Her flashlight flickers, like it might go out, and she sucks in her breath. "*Please?*"

"I don't know. I mean, here you are, the same person who claims she knew about that fake bomb trick in Intro to Heroism, yet didn't have the decency to warn me about it. That doesn't really sound like anybody I want to spend time with. At least, not at the reasonable discount I would have given you. I'll have to charge you the full hundred dollars an hour, even if we're just talking."

Her nostrils flare. "Okay. I'm sorry I didn't tell you." She thinks I'm joking about the money.

"Not good enough." I start to shut the door in her face.

"Wait! I … I didn't actually know about it." She says it really quietly while staring at her feet.

I cup a hand to my ear. "What was that?"

"I said I didn't actually *know*, all right?" She waves her arms, her flashlight sending shadows across the walls. "Are you happy now?"

"A little."

"*Good.*" She sounds exasperated, as if I'm the one in the wrong here. Then the wind picks up again, sounding like a thousand angry ghosts pounding on the walls. A roll of thunder shakes the house, rattling the windows, and Amelia cringes, letting out a tiny whimpering sound. She hugs her laptop, clutches her flashlight, and squeezes her eyes shut until it's over.

I'm pressed against the doorframe, holding onto it for dear life. My heart's pounding so hard, I can feel my pulse in my teeth. Cold dread slips through my veins. I picture going back into my room and facing this alone. In the pitch-black darkness with the storm outside and me feeling like the floor's going to give way any second. At least Amelia comes with a flashlight. "All right," I tell her. "You can come in. For a little while. But only because you pretty much begged me."

X·X·X

Amelia thunks down on my bed and sets up her laptop. She pats the spot next to her when she sees me still standing by the door, as if I need to be invited to sit on my own furniture, especially my bed. Well, Alex's bed. But whatever.

I take a deep breath and make my way across the room in the dark, cringing as the floorboards creak and sometimes give a little beneath me. At least when I lived with Mom it was on the ground floor. She would have never banished me to an attic. Kicked me out of the house, sure. But this?

The laptop turns on, the screen seeming extra bright in the darkness, and Amelia turns off her flashlight. I sit down next to her, tempted to keep one foot on the floor so

I can feel if it's falling out from under me. But then I think if it's going to fall, there's nothing I can do about it, and maybe it's better not to know.

Amelia's staring at me in the glow from her laptop, her hand poised above the touchpad but not doing anything, even though she's supposedly getting a movie ready.

"*What?*" I snap.

"Nothing. Geez."

"I know being in a boy's room is a totally new experience for you, but you don't have to gawk." Especially since I know she doesn't actually have the hundred bucks and I'm doing her a huge favor by letting her sit here with me.

"Uh, hello? I've been in here before. This was *my* room before it was Alex's and before it was yours." She says it in a "so there" voice. "Plus, I've been in your room dozens of times when you lived downstairs."

"Oh, really?" I narrow my eyes at her. "That's funny, because I can count the number of times you've been in there, *that I know of,* on two hands."

She realizes her mistake and tries to backtrack. "Well, er, maybe not *that* many."

"You've been going into my room, you mean. When I'm not there." I hope she didn't find the embarrassing baby pictures of her I stole from the family photo albums, just in case I ever need to blackmail her. Or in case she ever does bring a boy home, though by then I will probably be at least thirty and married to Kat and not living here.

Amelia sniffs and turns up her nose. "I'm allowed to go wherever I want—this is my house, too."

"You want to try that logic again? Because I know for a fact that you caught Alex going through your collection of celebrity body glitters and threw a fit."

"Those were expensive! And he was going to use them for some stupid art project. That's *not* what they're for. And anyway," she adds, glaring at me, "what I meant was, I live here, unlike some people who Mom says *aren't* allowed in the house—especially not in your room—who you had over anyway."

"You mean Kat?"

She smirks. The ghostly bluish light from the laptop goes dim, making her look really creepy, and she swipes her finger across the touchpad to make it bright again. "You're sleeping with her, right?"

"Wow." I guess sneaking into my room wasn't nosy enough for her. "Did Helen put you up to this?" Obviously the informational pamphlets weren't doing their job and she had to send Amelia on a recon mission.

"No. But she is pretty mad at you." I can hear the annoying smile in her voice as she says it, like she's enjoying the thought of me being in trouble. Not that any of that is news to me, since Helen hasn't really spoken to me since Friday. "So, are you?"

"Why? You trying to live vicariously through me because you know no boy will ever touch you?" A rhetorical question, since we both already know the answer is yes.

She glares at me. "Her grandfather tried to kill my mom, you know."

"Oh, no, I hadn't already heard that *a million times.*

Thank you *so much* for filling me in. Because, wow, if I'd known Kat was at all related to anyone who'd ever tried to hurt a superhero, even if it was before she was born, I would never have touched her."

Amelia's whole face lights up in an "aha!" expression, like she just tricked me into revealing all my secrets. "So, you guys *are* doing it." She thinks about that a little longer and then makes a disgusted face. "*Gross.*"

And she doesn't even know about our checklist. I shrug.

"Mom hates her, you know."

"And that's supposed to matter to me because ...?" It's not like Kat's parents are crazy about us being together, either. Not since I got an *X* on my thumb, got rejected from Vilmore, and then went to live with heroes. But they knew me before all that—plus I'm the only one who ever compliments Kat's mom when she gets a new haircut—so they haven't done anything crazy, like banish me from the house. Though her dad has mentioned that if I ever try anything "below the belt" with his daughter, no one will ever find my body. But I'm pretty sure he'd say that even if I wasn't half superhero, and what he doesn't know won't kill him. Or, in this case, me.

"I won't tell her. What you told me." Amelia sounds dead serious about that, even though she usually can't wait to spread even the teensiest bit of gossip.

"Technically, I haven't told you anything. But I don't care what you tell her. Tell her Kat and I are dropping out of school, eloping, and going to start our own circus act. Or a detective agency. Tell her we're going to be pirates and have lots of pirate children. Who will eventually rebel and not want to be part of the family business, but they won't have a choice, since we'll be at sea. Unless they mutiny against us, but—"

"What?"

"Nothing. My point is, I don't care what she thinks." Helen's already made up her mind about me. And about Kat. Nothing I say or do—or don't do—is going to change that.

Amelia raises her eyebrows. "So ... you don't want to know what she said about you, then?"

"No, because I can guess. I bet it was something really nice, about how she thinks I have great taste in women."

She snorts, either ignoring or not catching my sarcasm. "Uh, *wrong.*"

"Oh, wait. Did Helen say I'm her favorite? Even though I'm not really her kid? I bet that was it."

"You know that's not what she said."

"Wait." I gasp, faking surprise and putting a hand to my mouth. "It ... it wasn't something bad, was it?"

"Shut up," Amelia mutters, finally getting that I'm making fun of her.

"Because I don't think—"

"She said you were a bad influence. On *her* kids. Okay?!"

The words hit me hard. *Her* kids. As in, an exclusive group I'm not part of. And suddenly there's a tightness in my chest that wasn't there before. "I'm a supervillain—er, half villain. What did she expect?" I do my best to hide the hurt in my voice, but I know Amelia hears it.

She folds her arms, looking a little smug, but mostly

sorry. "I thought you didn't care?"

"Whatever. It's not like I didn't already know." Except that I didn't. I thought her problem was with Kat, not with me, her favorite illegitimate stepson. "She actually told you that?"

"No. I overheard her talking to Dad."

I draw my knees up to my chest and rest my chin against them. "I get why she doesn't like Kat, being Bart the Blacksmith's granddaughter and all, but it's not like you're going to go out with some supervillain now." Assuming Amelia could find anyone willing to go out with her at all, that is.

"Well, it wasn't just that. She said you—" Amelia glances over at me and clamps her mouth shut, possibly realizing she's done enough damage. "It was a bunch of stuff," she adds quietly. The laptop goes dim again, but this time she doesn't fix it.

"Like what?"

"Just ... stuff."

"I want to know."

Amelia sighs. "Fine. She said you're a bad influence because you're pretty much the same age as me and already sleeping around." As if Amelia and I aren't almost a year apart and at completely opposite ends of the maturity spectrum. "And you aren't even trying to hide it, like you have no shame."

"Great." I have monogamous, consensual sex with my steady girlfriend, and my stepmother acts like I'm some kind of man slut? That I should be ashamed? *That's* fair. And for the record, I am trying to hide it, just not from her. Kat's dad's the one who threatened to kill me, and I have to pick my battles.

"She said Kat's going to get *pregnant*"—she practically hisses the word, as if she might get in trouble just for saying it—"and that she won't have us related to *him* by blood. Because if you and Kat had a baby, that would make me an aunt to Bart the Blacksmith's great grandkid."

I hug my knees tighter. "That's not going to happen. We're not stupid." There is such a thing as birth control, after all, and just because my parents acted like they'd never heard of it doesn't mean I'm going to be irresponsible like that. Not that I don't like being alive and all, but it was still pretty careless of them. Plus, Helen's one to talk. Considering that Amelia's only eight months younger than me and that Gordon hadn't even met Helen yet when he and my mom randomly did it in a public bathroom, I'm pretty sure if I look up their marriage certificate, the date *won't* be nine months before Amelia was born.

But what if me and Kat want to have kids together in the future? Helen doesn't get to decide that, and especially not because it would mean *her* precious superhero children might appear in the same family tree as her worst enemy. I get why that might annoy her and all, but it's not like it actually means anything.

"She also said you were wild and undisciplined, because of your upbringing. And that Dad shouldn't get his hopes up about you ..." She purses her lips and doesn't finish.

"About me *what*, Amelia?" This is her chance to let me

have it—I shouldn't have to drag this out of her.

"Making it at Heroesworth. Being able to rise above your villain side. Even if you and Kat don't, you know, ruin your lives. And she said there's not that great a chance of you getting your *H*." She shrugs and looks away guiltily. "She said you're the oldest and the rest of us look up to you too much for you to get away with acting how you do. Though obviously *I* don't, so she must have meant Alex and Jess."

Right. "And what did Gordon say? When she told him what a bad influence I am?" I hate the way my throat feels too tight and the bitter taste that creeps into my mouth. As if I actually care that my stepmother thinks I'm ruining her kids. My own brother and sisters.

"I don't know. I couldn't hear that part."

Wonderful. So Gordon may or may not have stood up for me. For all I know, Mr. Subway Bathroom himself could actually agree with her.

Neither of us says anything for a while, the only sound the whir of the laptop and the wind howling outside. "Damien," Amelia says, her voice barely a whisper, "I'm sorry. I don't think you're a bad influence. And neither does Alex. Or Jess."

"Of course they don't. They're the ones being corrupted by me, so they just don't know any better." What does Helen even think is going to happen? That her kids are somehow not going to get their *H*s because of me? They have genetics going for them—it would be impossible for them to get any other letter. And why did she have to tell Gordon I'm going to disappoint him? She doesn't actually know that.

And, I don't know, I thought she actually liked me. I'm pretty sure she did, but I guess any warm feelings she had for me dried up when she realized me being half villain actually has consequences. Like, for instance, me being in love with the direct descendent of her arch nemesis, the guy who took her superspeed and ruined her career as a superhero, who she obviously still has a grudge against.

"Damien?" Amelia says.

"It's late and the storm's over. You should go. I won't even charge you. At least, not right now. You can owe me."

"Okay, but we haven't even started the movie yet."

"Seriously, Amelia. You've said enough. And you'd better get out of here. You wouldn't want any more of my bad influences to rub off on you."

CHAPTER 7

I sit at the kitchen table the next morning, listening to the rain slamming against the window and staring at my phone, which I was able to charge after Gordon reset the fuse earlier. I told him something needs to be done, since the attic isn't just a deathtrap for the obvious reasons, but that the wiring is clearly also about to short out and start a fire in the walls and kill me in my sleep. But he just laughed and ruffled my hair like he thought I was joking.

Apparently it was only the attic that didn't have power last night, because of the blown fuse, and I could have been charging my phone the whole time if I'd just gone downstairs. Not that an extra venture down the stairs was on my list of things to do, but I might have, if it meant calling Kat back. Of course, then I might have gotten this picture Mom sent me that much sooner and probably never fallen asleep at all. It's the picture she took yesterday of me holding Xavier, which she sent to me at one o'clock last night, according to the info on my phone. She actually sent that picture to me, like she has any right to even still have my number.

My thumb hovers over the delete button. I should just get rid of it. It's not like I want any reminders that he exists or that Mom didn't even tell me about him. Plus, I look awful in this picture. My hair's sticking out all over, and I look shocked and kind of terrified of the baby I'm holding. He's so wrapped up in blue blankets that it's not like you can even see him. So, it's basically just me looking crazy and holding a wad of blanket. Not really worth keeping.

Well, unless I want to make some informational pamphlets of my own to leave for Helen to find.

"What's that?" Helen asks, coming up behind me.

"Nothing." I quickly press the button on my phone to make it go dark and slip it into my pocket. After what she said to Gordon about me, I'm revoking her "getting to know anything about me" privileges.

"Okay." She sort of laughs, like she's not sure what to make of my reaction but also doesn't really care.

Jess waddles in and sits down in the chair next to me. Then she gets up, pushes the chair right up against mine, and sits back down. She leans in close and presses her forehead against my shoulder.

My eyes flick over to Helen, wondering what she thinks of this, now that I know how she really feels about me. She's too busy peering into the fridge and grabbing a container of orange juice to notice, though.

"Ow!" I feel a sharp pinch on my forearm and look

down to see Jess staring up at me. Pinching has quickly become one of her favorite forms of communication. I'm pretty sure Amelia's the one who introduced her to it, which I think makes her the bad influence, not me.

Despite having just pinched me, she very shyly points to the untouched blueberry muffin sitting in front of me. I take a bite of it, then tear off a piece for her. She smiles at me like I just handed her part of the moon, not an insignificant amount of my breakfast.

And, okay, if Xavier is anything like Jess, how could I not love him? But ... he probably won't be. And he'll probably be screwed up from Mom's stupid formula and growing up way faster than normal. Plus, it's not like I'm ever going to get to see him. This is the first time I've seen Mom in almost half a year, and that was by accident. And even if I did get to visit him or something, what would Mom have told him about me?

Look, Xavier, sweetie, it's your older brother who couldn't cut it as a villain and turned to the dark side. Be good and eat all your vegetables, or I'll have to send you away like I did him.

Just kidding. Mom would never care if anyone ate all their vegetables. If she even served any.

"Amelia!" Helen shouts off into the hallway. "You'd better get out here if you don't want to be late for school!"

I hope it's not lost on her that *I'm* the only one up on time and ready to go. Of course, that might have more to do with me getting up super early so no one would see just how long it takes me to get down the stairs than it does me being responsible, but I think it still counts.

89

"Hey," Helen says, smiling at me. "You want a ride, kid?"

"Nope." *Not from you.*

She frowns. "Uh … it's pouring down rain outside."

"Is it acid rain?"

"No."

"Then *I'll walk.*"

She stares at me, a tentative smile tugging on one side of her mouth, like what I'm saying is so ridiculous, I must be kidding. "It's over a mile. You'll get soaked. I'm already taking Amelia—it's no trouble."

Jess grabs a handful of my muffin and shoves it in my mouth, returning the favor, I guess. So helpful.

"Jess?" Helen says. "Why don't you focus on your own breakfast?"

"I'm full." Or so she claims, but then she immediately starts licking the muffin crumbs off her hand like there's about to be a food shortage we don't know about.

"Then why don't you go find your shoes so we can get ready to go?" Helen waits until Jess leaves, then steals her seat next to me. "I want to talk to you."

"Wonderful." I see how it is. When someone's watching, she offers me a ride to school. As soon as we're alone, she's going to tell me off. "And here I thought you were never going to speak to me again. Just like my mom. I do something you don't like, and you pretend I don't exist."

"*What?* Where's that coming from?"

"How about the fact that you haven't spoken to me in days? That's kind of the definition of not talking to someone." Plus, I know what she said about me.

"I'm sure I didn't ..." She pauses, trying to come up with a time she actually spoke to me since Friday. "I've been processing. Trying to figure out what to say to you."

I shrug. "I know what you're going to say to me."

"You do?"

"Yeah. You don't want Kat over here again. *Fine.* She's at school now, anyway. It's not like I'm going to get to see her. But when I do, I won't bring her here." At least, I won't get caught again. And my excellent compromising skills would be a great asset to anyone I might be an influence to. Just pointing that out.

Helen folds her arms and leans back a little. "Oh, I more than don't want her here."

"Okay. I wasn't going to say it. It's not like I don't know you don't want me going out with her. But you know what? It's not your call. I love her. And you can't tell me who to love. Even if she is related to your arch nemesis." Who Kat never even met because he died before we were born.

Her forehead wrinkles and she snorts in disbelief. "You might *think* you love her. And if it was the real thing, that might be different. But you're *sixteen*, Damien! And some girl letting you into her pants is not the same thing as love."

"Uh, yeah. I *know*. It's not about that." Besides, how does she know Kat's not trying to get into *my* pants? Why does she assume it's all me? I think there's an equal amount of pants-wanting on both sides. Or, okay, maybe more like a sixty/forty split. But that's close enough. "I know when I love somebody. I don't care if it doesn't make sense to you." And if she thinks that me loving Kat has anything to do with getting in her pants or not, then she really doesn't know me at all. That might be a perk—one we both enjoy—but it's not why we're together.

"Her grandfather was a murderer. He was a horrible, evil man, and I nearly died making sure he couldn't hurt the people I cared about, or anyone else, ever again. Losing my superspeed was the worst thing that ever happened to me, and I'm lucky I escaped with my life. But I'd do it all over again if I had to. I'd risk everything to protect the people I care about. *That's* love."

"Just as long as it doesn't involve anyone related to your arch nemesis, right? Look, I get why you hate her grandfather so much, but *she's* not a murderer. Her parents aren't, either." And her dad grew up estranged from his father—gee, kind of like someone else I know—so it's not like they were close or anything.

"But they're still supervillains." She tilts her head, giving me this pointed look, like she thinks she's got me cornered. As if them being supervillains automatically makes them evil. "So is she."

"So, I shouldn't be with her? You don't even know her."

"I don't need to know her."

"Wow. Letterist much? My mom's a supervillain. I guess that means you don't need to know me, either."

"I just meant if you want to be a hero, you have to start making hard choices about the people in your life. I'm telling you this for your own good."

"Sure you are."

Her jaw tightens. "I don't want you to get hurt.

Especially because of some girl."

"Whoa." I glare at her. "Kat isn't just 'some girl.' She's my best friend." Which she'd know if she'd been paying any attention instead of obsessing over who Kat's related to. "She's the most important person in the world to me. And you're telling me to ditch her because I'm going to hero school? Doesn't sound very heroic to me."

Helen glares back at me and doesn't say anything. An awkward silence hangs heavy in the air. Then Amelia clears her throat from the doorway. "I'm ready to go."

"Great," Helen says, jumping up from the table and sounding relieved to be done with our conversation. "Let me get my keys. Damien, are you coming?"

I glance over at the window. It's still pouring down rain, and she's right, I'll get completely soaked. But after she basically just told me all supervillains are evil and that I only care about Kat because I'm too stupid to know better, I'm not going to give her the satisfaction of accepting her help. "I told you. I'll walk."

Helen blinks and lets out a long sigh. "Fine," she says, not arguing. "Come on, Amelia. Let's go."

"I'm walking, too," Amelia says, glancing over at me. "I'll go with Damien."

Helen gapes at her, like she thought she was winning this game against me but just lost all her points. Then she holds up her hands, frustrated with both of us, and says, "If that's what you want," before storming off to find Alex.

X·X·X

"And that," Mr. Fitz, our fourth-period history teacher, says, "is how the Daring Do-gooder defeated the evil Professor Doomsworth. With a matchbook and a pair of safety scissors." He shoots the class a smug grin as he flips the book shut.

Everyone laughs. Ha ha ha. It's so hilarious that a superhero defeated a supervillain. Even if that's not how it happened. I don't know what it is about superheroes that makes them all idiots, but I hope my supervillain genes cancel it out.

Not for the first time today, I raise my hand.

"Oh, my God, stop," Amelia hisses next to me. She transferred into this class today after dropping some study hall for superpower practice that she said was a waste of time. Read: she didn't like being reminded that she can't fly. Especially since she told me last summer that she was basically going to become super fit once she could fly, since it's an athletic power or something—I haven't noticed, what with not using it—and that everyone would be jealous of her. And then she got a power that's not only *not* athletic, but encourages laziness. Something I have pointed out to her many times over the past few weeks.

Her dyed black hair is frizzed out from walking with me in the rain this morning, and she tries to straighten it with her hands while she glances around at everyone, worried they might be judging her for knowing me. Which they probably are. "*Let it go.*"

Mr. Fitz's nostrils flare. He's a short, balding man with bushy eyebrows and a mustache that looks like it's trying to eat his nose. I'm pretty sure throwing his authority around in this class is his only joy in life. "Oh, look, everyone. It seems Mr. Locke has something to say. *Again.*"

Damn right, I do. "Well, for one thing," I tell him, "Professor Doomsworth was one of the most brilliant supervillains of our time, but he wasn't evil." A stereotype I'm *so* sick of hearing. I swear, if one more superhero tries to tell me that supervillains are evil, I'm going to burn their house down.

A murmur runs through the class. A couple kids snicker.

Amelia covers her eyes with her hands. Like she might be regretting sitting next to me. Or siding with me this morning. Or ever having met me.

Yesterday, which Amelia wasn't here for, was mostly an intro day. Mr. Fitz only hinted at all the really biased, hero-centric history lessons he'd be programming us with. But today he's actually trying to tell us stuff that didn't happen. Or at least that didn't happen the way the book says.

"Well, Mr. Locke, supervillains are generally considered evil." He shares another little laugh with the class at my expense. Like the fact that they're dumb enough to put such a giant blanket statement on every supervillain who's ever lived is some kind of hilarious in-joke.

I ignore him. "And Professor Doomsworth was never defeated. Especially not by some idiot with a couple of matches and some safety scissors. That's just some story, probably made up by the Daring Do-gooder to impress people. Who I've never even heard of, by the way, so ..." I shrug. "He couldn't have done anything that important. And everyone knows Professor Doomsworth went crazy. He was just, you know, *too* brilliant."

"Too brilliant," Mr. Fitz repeats, stunned.

"Yeah. So if he was defeated at all, it was by his own mind. He had a lot of phobias. The guy spent the last month of his life in a recliner. He never got up—not once. He thought the recliner was the only germ-free place in the universe." Which probably wasn't true, considering he spent a whole month in it. But that's where the crazy comes in.

Mr. Fitz nods. "Driven to madness by his loss at the hands of the Daring Do-gooder."

"Uh, no." And what the hell kind of name is the "Daring Do-gooder"? How daring could he have been with a lame-ass name like that? "Maybe that's what you want to think happened, but it's not—"

The bell rings, interrupting me. Everyone breathes a collective sigh of relief.

"I think that's enough 'enlightenment' for today," Mr. Fitz says. "Read chapters two through four in your books tonight. I'll see you all tomorrow. Except you, Mr. Locke. I'd like to have a word with you."

I sigh and slide down in my seat, letting my legs stretch out past the edge of my desk.

"Don't sit with me at lunch tomorrow," Amelia says, almost tripping over my foot before hurrying out of the room with everyone else.

So much for solidarity. Not that I was planning to sit with her two days in a row. I have much better things to do than watch her inhale a turkey sandwich, like annoy Riley. I'm learning all sorts of fun things about him, like that he has a really hard time eating when someone is narrating everything he does. And that when he goes invisible, forcing me to start making things up in order to continue my narration, he gets *really* embarrassed when I get past a PG-13 rating.

Mr. Fitz puts his hands on my desk and leans forward, his beady little eyes meeting mine. "This is a classroom, Mr. Locke. Not a joke. I realize you've had a *different experience* than the rest of the students, but when you're in my class—"

"I wasn't joking. The book was wrong." *He* was wrong. "I was correcting it."

His eyebrows dart up. "Are you seriously trying to tell me you know more than the textbook?" He laughs.

"I know Professor Doomsworth was pretty crazy toward the end of his life. My girlfriend's mom's hairdresser used to date his cook. They almost got married, but then she found out he wanted her to quit her job and have, like, ten kids, so she said no way."

He blinks at me. "Fascinating. And you think this person is more reliable than the textbook, which was written by *experts*?" He says the word *experts* like no one could possibly rank any higher, especially not some hairdresser, even though she was there.

"The textbook was written exclusively by superheroes. You have to admit it's biased. Maybe they got some of it right, but I've been looking through it, and the stuff they said about villains was pretty much made up."

"Or perhaps you're the one who's biased. This is a superhero school, Mr. Locke. I don't know how you failed to notice that, considering you're enrolled here. But if you want to pass my class—and you have to pass my class if you ever hope to graduate and join the League—you will stop wasting everyone's time with your 'corrections.' There will be a test next week, and I can assure you it will be based on the textbook, not on your personal anecdotes. I suggest you study it. Understood?"

"You want me to lie. On the test. Doesn't the League Treaty frown upon that?"

He clenches his fists. "You are not in this class to fill everyone's heads with your colorful perversion of history. You're here to learn what I tell you. So either you will mark down the answers from the textbook, or you will fail."

"So, if I write down the truth, then I don't pass the class?" *That* makes sense.

He shuts his eyes, putting a hand to his forehead in exasperation. "Let me put it in terms hopefully even you can comprehend. There's a right way to get through this class and a wrong way. The textbook is the right way. *Do you understand?*"

"Yes," I tell him. "I understand perfectly."

"Good." He straightens the collar of his shirt, seeming pretty pleased with himself for supposedly putting me in my place.

"You want me to lie, and I'm not sure I can do that."

His back stiffens. His nose twitches, his mustache quivering and threatening to eat his whole face. "Then I'm not sure I can give you a passing grade." He says it in a "just you think about that" tone, like passing this class should be my most important goal in life.

"Well," I say, "at least we understand each other."

CHAPTER 8

"So," Sarah says Saturday night, while we're out patrolling, "I heard you failed your poster." She says it very matter-of-factly and pushes her glasses up to the bridge of her nose, or at least as far as they'll go with her blue eye mask on. Sarah's costume is blue and black spandex with a big silver Theta symbol on the front, marking her as the Cosine Kid. My costume is similar, except it's green and black and has a big silver X. They're her own designs, ones she came up with last spring when she decided she was going to be my sidekick or else. Back before Riley ever entered the picture.

And, okay, back before I mentioned I wanted to get a *V* instead of an *H*. But things have changed since then. Now I *want* to be a hero—sort of—and I don't know what I'd do without her as my sidekick.

I roll my eyes at the mention of the poster. And since I know I'm not the one who told her, and she's not exactly chummy with Amelia, that leaves only one other person.

"So, I heard Riley's been talking about me." Probably trying to convince Sarah that I'm not hero material and that she should ditch me and start being his sidekick instead. As if he knows anything about it. He can't even fall off a bed properly. Whereas I have fallen off a bed plenty of times without injury—just ask Kat.

We pass by a bunch of shops, making what are fairly usual rounds now in downtown Golden City. Sarah puts on a pair of homemade heat-vision goggles and peers into all the storefront windows, checking for any bad-guy activity.

"Don't blame Riley for your failure," she says, glancing over at me. Her goggles obscure her eyes, making her look kind of like a robot.

"It wasn't a failure. I got a *D*." *D* as in *didn't care*. Alex's class made posters last year, and he was in second grade. Plus, I'm pretty sure Kat and her classmates aren't sitting around at Vilmore obsessing over getting their magazine cutouts just right. They're too busy, like, actually learning how to defeat superheroes and stuff. It's as if the teachers at Heroesworth *want* us to get our asses kicked.

Sarah tilts her head, giving me a knowing look, or at least what I assume is a knowing look behind her goggles. "You're not going to get your *H* by getting *D*s."

I sigh. "Don't worry. I'm supposed to redo it. Since Miss Monk thinks I didn't understand the assignment." Which I *did*. She just didn't understand my vision.

"Riley said the poster was supposed to be about what heroism means to you."

"Right. I made a big collage with kittens in trees. And

it's not like there are just pictures of cats in trees in magazines. I had to splice them together, using the technological magic of scissors and glue. It took effort." Okay, about half an hour of effort, which I spent mostly watching an episode of a new detective show Kat and I got hooked on over the summer. It's about a superhero detective who solves all his cases by teaming up with a supervillain on the sly. It's really popular, even if all the reviews say it's unrealistic. Because a hero and a villain could never be in the same room, let alone work together for the greater good.

"That's what heroism means to you?" Sarah asks. "Kittens? In trees?"

"Don't sound so shocked. It's how I met my dad, remember? And it's not like it's the only thing I put on the poster. There were also old ladies crossing the street and a burning building." Though now that I think about it, the way I structured it, it might have looked like the old ladies were crossing the street *into* the burning building. Oops.

Sarah wrinkles her nose. "We never do any of that stuff."

Well, I did run into a burning building once, to save a supervillain kid, but Sarah wasn't there for that one. And I almost got myself killed and my dad had to rush in and save me, so I'm not sure it counts.

"Is that really what heroism means to you?"

"Of course not." I try to slip my hands into my pockets out of habit, but my Renegade X costume doesn't have any. "But it's what they want to hear."

"Obviously not if you got a *D*."

"I forgot to label the burning building as an orphanage."

"I don't think that's it. I saw Riley's poster, and—"

"It wasn't that great." Okay, it kind of was that great, but I don't like the way her face lights up when she mentions him. And I don't like how many times his name has come up already, even though this is supposed to be *our* time together.

Sarah gapes at me. "It was a breathtaking watercolor tribute to his dad, who sacrificed himself saving all those people during that bus bombing a couple years ago. There were kids on that bus."

I swallow and don't look at her. "See? That's practically a burning orphanage." And who told him to use watercolors, anyway? It was supposed to be a *collage*. But you don't see him getting docked any points. It's letterist, I tell you.

She puts her hands on her hips and stares at me through her goggles. And even though I can't actually see her eyes, I'm pretty sure she's glaring at me. "His was from the heart. Yours was just some cheap imitation of what you *think* people want to hear."

I feel my ears heating up, and I hope she can't see anything that detailed with her heat vision. "Fine. So I tried to fake my way through the assignment. But it's not like I would have done any better with the truth. I'm not exactly the typical hero, and you should see the way they all look at me, like I'm some kind of criminal. Riley included." Though, to be fair, he is the only person in the class who I've so far caused any bodily harm to, so I *suppose* he has legit reasons, even if he's still a douche. "They don't want to know what my actual opinions are."

She shakes her head. "You really think you're going to get your *H* by faking your way through Heroesworth? It's your body, you know. You're not going to be fooled by that crap. And," she adds, "neither is anyone else."

As if I can just wish my thumb to be whatever letter I want. If it was that easy, I'd have gotten rid of this stupid *X* months ago. Though I can't help noticing how disappointed she sounds in me, or the little ache that seeps into my chest because of it. "Good thing I'm going to redo it, then." Probably.

"Yeah? And what are you going to put on it instead?"

"A picture of you, of course." Done and done.

She sighs, tells me flattery will get me nowhere— which, if the past sixteen and a half years have taught me anything, isn't true—and pulls a new gadget out of one of the pouches in her utility belt. She hands me what looks like a cross between a raygun and a remote control with a flying saucer attached to it. "Here, you're going to need this. There's suspicious activity three stores down."

There's a red button on top of the remote control part and the word *caution* written next to it in several languages, even though I'm the only one who's going to be using this thing. "You want to give me the rundown first? And, not that I need to remind you, but you know how I feel about killing people. Or severing limbs." Like I said, we villains aren't evil. Er, not that I am one or anything.

She pushes her goggles up onto her head and rolls her eyes at me. "It's perfectly safe."

"So, when I push this button with all the warnings by it, nothing's going to explode?" I've heard *that* before.

"Well ..." She looks away. "That depends on how you define *explode*. But before you say anything, hear me out. It's mostly a homing device. See, you aim it at your target and press that red button. Then you pull the trigger."

"Uh-huh. And what happens then?"

"Then ninja stars shoot out of it and track down your target. That way, all you have to do is get close enough to set your sights on them. And if they run, you won't have to chase them. The ninja stars do all the work."

I raise my eyebrows at her. "And these ninja stars do what, exactly? Because, Cosine, these are jewel thieves we're talking about here, not ax murderers."

"You don't know what they'll do when cornered."

"Yeah, especially when cornered with exploding ninja stars."

"All they do is home in on the target, surround them, and then gently explode, throwing out interconnecting nets. So the bad guy gets tangled up and detained until you catch up with them."

"Oh, yeah, just a gentle explosion. No problem. Have you tested this thing?"

"Define *test*." She slips her goggles back on and grabs my arm. "Never mind all that. They look like they're about to run. We've got to go."

I nod, silently hoping this new gadget does what she says, and hurry toward the scene of the crime. The door to the jewelry store's been busted open. Flashlights sweep around inside, and though it's mostly dark, I can make out the shapes of two guys rummaging through the shop.

Sarah motions for me to point the new gadget at one of them. She mimes pressing the red button.

I take a deep breath and hold up the new ninja-star gun. I don't know how I'm supposed to tell if I'm aiming right, but being five feet away from the bad guys in the middle of a break-in is as good a time as any to find out. I press the red button, half expecting the whole device to explode in my hand.

It doesn't explode, but it does make a loud buzzing noise. I hear Sarah mutter, "Oops," just as the two guys inside immediately whip around to face us, their flashlights blinding me. One of them shouts, "Freeze! This is official League business!" He holds up a hand, palm out, like it's a weapon, and that's when I realize they're not bad guys.

But I'm too late. I don't know what happens then, only that I *don't* pull the trigger. But a wild tendril of fear flashes through me. Electricity sparks hot in my hand. It feels the same as it did the other night, when the light socket practically exploded. Except this time, I know it's not coming from some outside source—it's coming from *me.* I can feel the charge all the way down to my bones. But it all happens so fast, and before I really get what's happening, sparks shoot into the gadget I'm holding, and then there are ninja stars flying. Not just at their target— who is apparently a superhero and *not* a jewel thief, which, to be fair, you can't tell using heat vision—but in every direction. Sarah and I both hit the ground just as the ninja stars swoop toward us.

The superhero who told us to freeze really means it. He shoots out a blast of ice from his hand, and suddenly I'm so cold, my teeth are chattering and I can't move. His partner creates some kind of energy shield just in time for the ninja stars to bounce off of it and over toward us. There are some mild exploding sounds—kind of like popcorn popping—and then a couple of nets splay over top of us.

The two superheroes rush out of the building now that we've been thwarted. "Just a couple of kids," one of them mutters, sounding half disappointed, half exasperated. Like having to deal with a couple of teenagers is worse than if we'd been dangerous supervillains.

They make sure the new gadget is out of either of our reaches before pulling the nets off and helping us up.

The one with freeze powers takes out a walkie-talkie and mumbles something into it about having some villain kid in custody.

I'm still shivering so hard, I can barely talk. "I'm ... not ... a villain," I correct him. And why does he assume I'm a villain, but not Sarah? She's the one who made the thing.

He gives me a skeptical look. "Riiight, kid. You want to show me your *H*?"

I close my eyes, hiding my thumb in my fist. "We thought you were robbing the place."

"And we thought you were shooting at us. Oh, wait, you *were*. And it doesn't matter what is or isn't on your thumb, because we've got to bring you in either way. Unless," he adds, "you can give us a real good reason not to."

Sarah's eyes meet mine. We both know what I have to do and that I'm not going to like it. I groan and tell them to call the Crimson Flash.

"He a friend of yours?" the shield guy asks, stifling a laugh.

"Something like that." There's no way I'm telling them he's my dad. Then I'd have to watch his face get all red when he came down here and they started asking unwanted questions. Plus, think of the media backlash if this got out. I know I don't exactly fit into his world. I don't need any more reminders.

Freeze guy looks me up and down. "*You* know the Crimson Flash? Some villain kid like you?"

"I'm *not* a villain. And yeah, I do, so just call him already."

X·X·X

Gordon stays silent until after we drop Sarah off at her house. Then he sighs, adjusts his bright red cape, which is sort of caught up in his seat belt, and says, "You want to tell me what happened?"

Electricity shot out of my hand. Even though that's impossible. "It was a misunderstanding," I tell him. I turn my shoulder toward him and lean my head against the window, so I don't have to see if he's angry or not. I stare at my hand, flexing my fingers, half expecting to see sparks. But nothing happens. Probably because I only imagined that that burst of electricity came from me. It must have been the gadget backfiring somehow. Just like how it was the wall socket that shorted out or blew a fuse or whatever. It had nothing to do with me.

Except I know I didn't imagine that electric feeling in my hand. Or the sparks flying out of it.

"It feels like more than a misunderstanding," Gordon says. He stops at a red light and glances over at me. "I know you've been having a hard time at school."

"It's only been a week." Kind of early for him to be judging me. I mean, I'm still getting my bearings—clearly I don't know how to work the system yet, as evidenced by my poster grade.

"Yes, and I've already heard from all five of your teachers." Drops of rain splatter across the windshield, and he turns on the wipers.

"All good things, I'm sure."

I watch the wipers smear water back and forth across the glass. It's impossible to have more than one superpower, and I already have one, so whatever I think happened tonight *couldn't* have actually happened. Especially since electricity is a villain power. I should know because it's my grandpa's ability, which I guess means it runs in the family. Not that that matters, since, like I said, I already have my power. I've never heard of anyone having two. Though, then again, I'd never heard of anyone having an *X*, either.

"You know," Gordon says, his voice quiet compared to the rain pounding against the windows, "I'd understand if you wanted to try something else."

I lift my head and raise my eyebrows at him.

"Something else?" Like what, joining the circus?

"If you wanted to go back to your old school. It's early enough in the year—you could still catch up."

"You think I can't cut it at Heroesworth." I know that's what Helen thinks. I can just imagine what she'd say if she knew I had a villain power. Which, thankfully, I *don't*. Because even if controlling electricity is as much in my genes as flying, that doesn't mean I actually have it.

"That's not what I said. But, Damien, you've been acting strange all week. I can tell something's bothering you. And I want you to know that if you're going to Heroesworth for my sake, well … That's not something I expect of you."

"Yeah? But it's something you expect from Amelia, right? And Alex?" You know, his *real* kids.

He laughs. "I can't see Amelia quitting Heroesworth."

"But if she told you tomorrow she wanted to drop out, you'd be disappointed. And if Alex or Jess was old enough and told you they didn't want to go, you wouldn't just shrug it off like it was no big deal." Dropping out also sounds like something a bad influence would do. It sounds like someone who's not absolutely certain he knows where he belongs. Like someone who might have a villain power, despite not really being one, and who refuses to sever all ties with the girl he loves just because she's a supervillain. Not that I know anyone like that.

"I don't want any of you kids to feel like you have to do things that don't make you happy." He glances over at me, then back at the road. "Heroesworth might not be the right fit for you, son. I know you've been struggling. And I don't want you to feel obligated to be someone you're not.

That's all."

"By *someone you're not*, you mean a hero, right?" And I hope by *struggling,* he's not talking about the poster. Because, to be struggling, I would have actually had to try first. I fold my arms across my chest and sink down in my seat. "Tonight was a misunderstanding. Sarah and I go patrolling all the time. We catch tons of bad guys."

Gordon gives me a skeptical look.

"Okay, maybe not *tons.*" But we've scared off our fair share of low-lifes, mostly because of Sarah's gadgets, which are known for causing loud explosions and occasionally lasers that slice through anything that gets in their way. "And there was only that one casualty."

"There was *what?*" He slams on the brakes, and not to teach me a lesson in why it's a good thing I'm wearing my seat belt.

I wave away his concern. "It was nothing. An art thief tripped over my foot and chipped a tooth. And sort of dropped the really expensive painting he was stealing in an oil slick in the parking lot. But the owners were still happy to get it back. Mostly. And nobody pressed charges."

He actually pulls over, even though we're only a few blocks away from home. His face goes pale. "Damien, why is this the first I'm hearing about this?"

"Because it wasn't a big deal?" I shrug. "It happened over the summer. You were busy filming your documentary."

"Even if I'm busy, you know you can talk to me, right?"

"There was nothing to talk about. It didn't even make

the paper."

"That's not the point. I think you and Sarah should cool it for a while."

"Oh, so now I'm not supposed to see Sarah, either?" Who am I supposed to hang out with, Amelia?

"No, I mean you guys shouldn't be out on the streets on your own. No more … what do you call it?"

"Patrolling?"

He nods. "You need to be focusing on your school work anyway."

Yeah, right. "But how am I supposed to get my *H* if I'm not out superheroing?"

"Damien … there's more to getting your *H* than prowling for bad guys at all hours of the night. You don't have to catch criminals to be a hero. I thought you knew that."

I glance over at him, taking a deep breath. "I do. But if we stop going on patrols, Sarah's never going to hang out with me. She's too busy with *Riley*."

"Is that what's been bothering you?"

"It's a factor." I flex my hand again, remembering the feel of the electricity earlier. "Riley's a total douche and not worth her time. But he thinks he's better than me because he has his *H*. And he's trying to convince her to be his sidekick instead of mine." And there *may* have been a finger-breaking incident, though my involvement in that was minimal at best.

Gordon scratches the side of his head. "Well, I can't imagine Kat's too crazy about you going out patrolling with Sarah, either."

"Not exactly," I admit, not looking at him, in case he gets the idea that he's actually right about something. "But it's not like anything's going on between me and Sarah." Just the two of us trusting each other with our lives on a regular basis. Nothing special about *that*.

Gordon lets out a slow breath. "Maybe not. But it still sounds like you have some choices to make."

"Here it comes. You're going to tell me to ditch Kat."

He sounds shocked. "Damien, I can't tell you what to do with your life."

"Try telling Helen that."

"Helen?"

"Yeah, you know, Helen? Your wife? The mother of *most* of your children?"

He scowls at me. "I *know* who she is."

"Well, she made it pretty clear that she thinks Kat and I shouldn't be together." Or breed.

"She knew her grandfather. She doesn't know Kat."

I raise an eyebrow at him. "Neither do you." Though he might if she was ever actually allowed in the house.

"No, but I know *you*. I trust you to make the right choices about the people in your life. Just like I trust you to choose the school you want to go to. So, if you were having second thoughts about attending Heroesworth, you know I'd—"

"I *don't* want to quit." Where else would I go? Plus, they're not chasing me off after only a week. What kind of self-respecting supervillain would I be if I let that happen? Er, ex-supervillain. Whatever.

"Okay." He holds up both hands, surrendering. "But I'd

understand if you did."

But he'd also be disappointed. He doesn't say that part, but I know he would be. Going to Heroesworth might not be something he expects of me, but maybe it's something I *want* him to expect of me, like he would of his other kids. "I've made my decision. I'm going to Heroesworth. I'm getting my *H*. End of story."

"As long as that's what *you* want."

"Yeah. It is." It has to be. "So can we just go home now?"

CHAPTER 9

"Can I ask you something?" Kat says on the phone Sunday morning.

I sit up in my bed, trying to adjust my pillow so I can lean back without hitting my head on the slanting wall jutting over me. Nothing seems to work, and I can't get comfortable. It also doesn't help that I have to go to the bathroom, but everyone's back from church, and Helen's bitchy sister and her stupid, loud-mouth husband and her stupid, bratty kids are over, and there's no way I'm going down the stairs in front of them and humiliating myself. Which I guess is what I get for sleeping in. Of course, I didn't exactly fall right to sleep last night after everything that happened. Every time I closed my eyes, all I could think about was that electric feeling in my hand. Which was better than feeling like I was falling from a building, but still. Not exactly pleasant.

"Let me guess," I tell Kat. "You're dying to know how I managed to look so amazingly hot in that photo I sent you, right?" It was the one of me holding Xavier. I didn't end up deleting it after all and sent it to Kat, but only because she said if I didn't, she'd just get it from my mom. And I'm not exactly thrilled by the idea of her and my mom communicating, because Mom might ask her about me and think she's part of my life again, which she's not. Or, worse, she might not ask about me at all.

Kat laughs. "I'm printing it out and putting it on our bulletin board right now."

"What? Kat, I was joking. I look horrible in that one."

"It's adorable. You look so confused."

There's a loud burst of laughter downstairs. Helen's sister, Leah, squawk-laughs like some demented bird. And her husband lets out these really cliché guffaws, like he's auditioning for a laugh track. I hate them both, which I know for a fact is mutual, since Leah referred to me as "that tragic mistake" once while she knew I was in hearing distance. But at least their nasty children aren't allowed in the attic—probably the only good thing about living up here. Except last time they were here, I *know* their five-year-old daughter pulled Jess's hair, made her cry, and then lied about it. And if I'm up here, then who's going to watch out for her? And who's going to make sure little five-year-old Belinda "accidentally" sits in some chocolate in her Sunday best and has to go home in shame?

Even Amelia doesn't want to hang out with any of them, since I can hear her overly happy pop music blasting in her room. That's how awful they are.

"And anyway," Kat says, "that's not what I wanted to ask you."

I sigh. "Yes, Kat, I *will* pose for an all-nude calendar. And I'll even give you a discount."

She laughs. "It better be a *good* discount this time. Because, Damien, there are cheaper models out there. You don't own the market."

I tug on the bedspread, trying to pull it out from under me without actually getting up, so I can use it as more back support. I succeed in pulling it out, but not without a loud crackle of static. A wave of visible sparks races across the surface of the blanket. There's a biting feeling in my fingertips, and I jerk my hand away.

My heart races. A prickle of dread creeps down my spine.

"Damien, are you okay?" Kat asks. "You're breathing kind of hard."

"Just thinking of you."

"Ha. Sounds more like when you accidentally look down from the top of the stairs."

She knows me so well. "You were going to ask me something?"

"Okay. Well, Homecoming is coming up in a few weeks."

"At Vilmore?" I get up from the bed, not liking the way the floor creaks beneath me, but still a little freaked out from the crazy static and wanting to distance myself from the source. Except I think I know the source wasn't the blanket. I'm pretty sure it was *me*. Except, of course, for the fact that it couldn't have been. All of this stuff that's been happening lately, making it seem like I might have some kind of electricity power ... it's just coincidence. It doesn't mean anything.

Probably.

"Yeah," Kat says, "at Vilmore. And, I mean, if you don't want to go, I totally—"

"Of course I want to go." She just mentioned it, and already I'm forming plans to put our Homecoming pictures on the wall in the living room. Right in view of the front door, so Helen has to look at them every time she comes in the house.

"I just thought maybe you wouldn't, because of ... you know."

"Not getting in?" Which was a horrible mistake on their part that I don't forgive them for—or, well, that I don't forgive *Taylor* for, I guess—but who am I to hold a grudge? Especially when in this case holding a grudge means not going to this dance with Kat, and not having fancy pictures taken that will annoy the hell out of my stepmom, and, most importantly, not holing up in Kat's dorm room with her in a blissfully interruption-free zone. After we've at least made an appearance at the dance and had our photos taken, of course.

"There's another reason you might not want to go," Kat says.

"Because of my *X*? I can wear gloves." I switch my phone to my other ear and hold my right hand out in front of me. If this whole electricity thing is just a coincidence— well, a series of very suspicious coincidences—then I have nothing to worry about. And if it's real ...

If it's real, maybe I should just find out and get it over with.

I concentrate on my hand. I picture sparks of electricity shooting from my fingertips.

Nothing happens.

"Homecoming is about honoring alumni. Each year, they pick a famous supervillain who went to Vilmore and base the theme around them. My dad's sponsoring it this year."

"So, they're honoring him? What's the theme, computer parts?" Her dad's company makes computers that send out mind-control signals to their users, telling them to buy more Wilson Enterprises products. It's a pretty lucrative way to do business, though kind of weird for a dance theme. Still, I don't see why that's a problem, unless what she's getting at is that her dad is actually going to *be* at the dance, making sure I don't put my hands—or any other key parts of myself—on his daughter.

"Not exactly. Hold on a second. I'm getting another call. It's my mom."

I try to remember what the electricity felt like just a minute ago. What it felt like last night when there was that charge deep in my bones.

Maybe I feel a spark. A little twitch of power tingling along the back of my hand. *Maybe.*

There's more commotion downstairs. I hear Jess start crying, and I wonder what that Belinda—a.k.a. "Mommy's perfect angel"—has done to her this time. Talk about wild and undisciplined. Then I hear Helen's sister's voice say, "Well, I'm *not* surprised. Considering his mother."

And I know—I *know*—they're talking about me. I don't even know what they're really saying, but I can tell from her tone of voice that it's about me, and that it's not anything good.

Rage flares up inside me. I want to march downstairs and tell that woman to shut the hell up and to keep her supposed "angel" away from my sister. I want to get in her face and tell her she knows *nothing* about me, or my mom, or about supervillains.

Electricity crackles to life in my hand. And there's no mistaking it—it's definitely real this time. Real and possibly freaking me out, just a tiny bit. Or maybe, like, a lot. Because even if I had my suspicions—and even if I've seen my grandpa conjure up lightning before—I didn't expect this to actually *happen*. Not to *me*.

"I'm back," Kat says on the phone. "That was Mom, calling to tell me how adorable and confused you looked in that picture. See, it's not just me."

"If you think confusion is adorable, you should see me now." *Because I have no idea what's going on.* I gape at the sparks flying between my fingers and the waves of whitish-blue electricity flowing across my hand. It burns a little, like bathwater that's too hot, but otherwise it doesn't really hurt.

"What?"

"Nothing. And I can't believe you sent that picture to your mom. I told you it was just between us." Sweat beads on my forehead. I close my eyes and try to take calming breaths. Though with each supposedly calming breath, I just feel more freaked out. "So. Homecoming. You and me and … what? A party about your dad?" But not *with* her dad, right?

"Not my dad. That's what I was trying to tell you. Wilson Enterprises is sponsoring it, but it's not about him. It's about my grandfather, Bart the Blacksmith."

"Great, so, 60s theme, then?" I say, purposely ignoring the obvious reason why she thinks I can't go now. As if I care what Helen thinks. Though, since I'm not actually the horrible bad-influence stepson she thinks I am, I won't rub the fact that it was a dance themed around her worst enemy in her face or anything. I'll make sure the annoying pictures I put up don't reveal that part.

"It was the marketing department's idea. They thought it would make a good story. For publicity. Look, I understand if you can't go. Or if you don't want to now."

"Of course I still want to go."

"Okay, but then why do you sound weird?"

I don't know, maybe because my hand is covered in lightning?

I have a villain power. This wasn't supposed to happen. Not *now*.

And it sure was a great idea to try summoning up electricity when I don't actually know how to get rid of it. Because, really, now what?

I swallow. "Kat, I think maybe I should—"

There's a loud *ZAP* and a whoosh of light as the electricity suddenly shoots across the room, knocking me backward. The charge of energy blasts into the wall, the one Gordon built this summer, exploding a jagged, smoldering hole through it. Plank bits fly everywhere, and the air smells like a mixture of sulfur and woodsmoke.

But, hey, at least my hand is no longer covered in

electricity. At least there's that.

"Uh, Damien, what was that?" Kat asks.

I'm too dazed to speak for a moment, just staring at the wall. "I'm going to have to call you back," I say, and then hang up, dropping my phone to the floor.

Amelia's head appears on the other side of the hole in the wall, cautiously at first, then full-out gaping at me.

"Oh. My. God," she says, her expression a mixture of surprise and smugness. "You are *so dead*."

X·X·X

"Damien?" Gordon's concerned-but-muffled voice calls from downstairs.

Why does he assume it's me? Why couldn't Amelia have blown something up?

"Have you ever seen a picture of a deer in the headlights?" Amelia says, smirking at me. "Because that's what you look like right now."

"Shut up."

"What did you even do?"

I hear more voices downstairs, all talking at once. The awful relatives are still here. I can just picture the ugly, know-it-all look on Leah's face when she tells Helen, "I told you so."

I blink at Amelia, realizing she asked me a question, and tell her the first lie that comes to mind. "It was one of Sarah's gadgets."

She raises skeptical eyebrows at me, even though I think that sounded like a perfectly reasonable explanation.

Just because it doesn't happen to be the truth *this time* doesn't mean it's not believable. "If it was one of her gadgets, then ..." She trails off, glancing down at my hand.

Dread flickers in my chest as I follow her gaze, half expecting my hand to be covered in electricity again. Like there's nothing I can do to make it stop and *everyone* is going to know.

They're all going to think this means I'm a villain. Which I only sort of am. But they're going to think I don't belong at Heroesworth, or at this house. That me getting my flying ability was a fluke and that I'm never really going to get my *H*.

Which might all turn out to be true, but that doesn't mean I want them thinking it.

When I actually look at my hand, though, I see there's no electricity. I'm safe. Well, except for the hole I blasted through the wall.

Amelia wrinkles her nose. "If it was one of Sarah's gadgets, then where is it?"

"Why do you care?"

She sniffs. "Fine, don't tell me. It doesn't matter how it happened—Dad's going to be so mad at you."

"It was an accident." Just, you know, playing with lightning in the house. Totally not my fault.

She shrugs and doesn't even try to hide the gloating in her voice when she says, "He's still going to be mad."

"Damien?! Amelia?!" Gordon shouts. Then I hear the creak of his footsteps on the stairs.

He's coming up here. He's going to see this. He's going

to find out.

I glare at Amelia. "We're going to hide this, and you're not going to tell him. Got it?"

The corners of her mouth twist into an evil grin. "I suppose I *could* help you. If I *wanted* to. If I had a good reason."

"I don't have time for this. Don't you have any posters or something? If we cover this up and if you keep your mouth shut—"

"Oh, I have *plenty* of posters." She studies the back of her hand as if it's absolutely fascinating and she has all the time in the world.

"Amelia. Come on."

Someone says something to Gordon, and he pauses on the stairs, buying me a few more seconds.

"I don't know." Amelia sighs. "It would be awfully fun watching you squirm when Dad gets here."

But she says *would be*, not *will be*. I hate myself for what I'm about to do. But what choice do I have? "If you do this for me, I'll owe you."

"Mm hmm. You'll owe me a lot."

"Yeah, sure. Whatever you want. As long as nobody else finds out about this."

Her face lights up. "Whatever I want? You promise?"

I cringe inside, knowing I'll regret this. But I nod anyway, just as Gordon resumes his climb up the stairs. Maybe I'll get lucky. Maybe the really creaky step near the top will actually break and he'll get stuck or something. But it doesn't.

Amelia uses her power, teleporting a rolled-up poster

into her hands, which she shoves at me through the hole in the wall. "Here." She drops a couple of thumbtacks in my palm and then hurries to put her own poster up on her side.

I unroll my poster and make a face. It's from *The Crimson Flash and the Safety Kids* and has the Crimson Flash in the middle and a series of ethnically diverse kids around the edges, each demonstrating some important safety tip.

And I'm supposed to put this on my wall and hope Gordon buys it? But I don't have time to find something else. My hands shake as I hurry to shove the tacks through the corners before he gets here. The poster's slightly crooked—I'll have to adjust it later, or, you know, burn it —but at least it covers up the jagged hole I blew through the wall.

I finish tacking it up just as he knocks on my door. "Damien?"

I open it, maybe a little too quickly. There's a spark of static as I touch the doorknob.

"Are you kids all right?" he asks. "We all thought we heard something." He peers past me, into the room.

"Everything's fine." I try too hard to sound casual, so that it ends up coming out strained.

Amelia's door clicks open and she pokes her head out into the hall.

Gordon wrinkles his forehead. "But what happened? And what's that smell? Is something burning?"

"Um ..." I'd use the gadget excuse again, but then he might figure out that there was actually an explosion, which might lead him to discovering the hole in the wall. "I don't—"

"It's just an old candle I had," Amelia says, slipping out of her room and standing next to Gordon. "And Damien was practicing his flying. But he fell."

"You ... were?" A slow, proud smile slips over Gordon's face until he's practically beaming at me. I haven't seen him this happy since I told him I was going to Heroesworth.

I glare at Amelia. I know for a fact that she didn't find the embarrassing baby pictures of her I collected, so she'd better watch it.

"He's been practicing a lot," she adds, smirking at me. "He's thinking about joining the flying team at school."

Gordon's so shocked and elated by that, he whips around to look at her, to see if she really means it.

While his back is turned, I motion for her to tone it down. We want to keep this at least remotely believable. Even Gordon's not that gullible.

"I was captain when I went," Gordon says, grinning at me and apparently eating up every word of Amelia's lies after all. I guess he really is that naïve. Who knew? "Well, my senior year, anyway."

"I still have a long way to go," I tell him. "Before even trying out, I mean." Which isn't going to happen. *Ever.*

"But you're trying. That's what's important. You're getting over your fears and getting out there."

Getting out there? By trying out for some stupid flying team? He is so delusional, because even if we were living in some alternate universe where I was actually going to try out, and where I actually had control of my power—well, either of them—I wouldn't join some stupid team. Do I look like a team player to him? I don't even know what the flying team *does*. And even if I had a major head injury and somehow decided I wanted to join, they'd have to be pretty desperate to even consider me, what with me being an evil half villain and all.

"Dad, I'm not … I mean, don't get your—" I was about to tell him not to get his hopes up, but then I realized that sounded like something Helen would say. "Let's keep this a secret for now. Just between us."

"Of course," he says, but I don't think he actually heard me, because then he says, "I'm going to go tell the others," before hurrying off.

I wait until he's gone before swearing under my breath. Then I sigh and lean back against the wall, startling a little when my elbow presses against the poster with the hole behind it.

Amelia grins at me, looking pretty proud of herself for the stunt she just pulled.

"What does the flying team even do?" I ask her.

"It's like swimming," she says.

"Swimming?"

"Yeah, they do all these big synchronized numbers. It's really impressive."

"Synchronized flying." Nope. *Never going to happen.* "And Gordon was seriously involved in that? He was their *captain*?" He's an even bigger loser than I thought.

"It's excellent practice. It improves coordination, teamwork, and speed." She sounds like she's reciting a promotional flier.

"Great. You were supposed to be helping me, you know."

"I did. I pretty much just saved your life. So you should be a little nicer to me. After all, you *owe* me."

I shudder. The last time I made a deal with Amelia, I ended up getting pushed off the tallest building in Golden City. Maybe I shouldn't have been so quick to agree to anything, especially since she's smirking at me like she's already adding up all the ways she can exploit this. But it's not like I had a lot of time to think about it. Plus, it could be worse. At least she doesn't know what really happened.

"Uh, Damien ..." Amelia's not smirking at me anymore. Instead, her eyes are wide, and she's staring at my hand.

There's a little crackle of electricity, and I glance down to see a couple of sparks arcing between my fingers. I clench my fist, willing the sparks to stop. I glare at Amelia. "You didn't see anything."

She backs away from me, her face going pale. "What *is* that?"

"Nothing."

She turns toward the open door, starting to shout, "Dad!"

I grab her arm. There's a visible spark of uber-charged static, and she flinches and jerks away.

"*Ow!* Don't touch me!" She stares at me in horror. "I thought you could fly!"

"I can. This is something else." I shut the door, standing in front of it and blocking her from leaving. "And nobody needs to know about it, especially not Gordon."

"But you're a … a vill …" She can't quite make herself say the whole word.

"A villain? *Half* villain, and you knew that. What, do you think I'm going to murder you or something? I'm the same person I was five seconds ago." Except now I have a really dangerous superpower that can blow holes through walls, and I can't exactly control it. Nothing to be afraid of.

She makes a face, like saying I'm half villain is equivalent to saying I'm half evil. "You blew up the wall!"

"I told you, it was an accident."

"You also said it was one of Sarah's gadgets." She gives me a wary look, wrapping her arms around herself and keeping her distance, as if I've revealed myself to be some kind of criminal and she shouldn't get too close. "I thought you were trying to get your *H*. Was that a lie, too?"

"I *am*. I didn't ask for this. Promise me you won't say anything."

She glances behind me at the door, like she's still considering reporting me to Gordon. "Why should I?"

"Because. I owe you, remember? Now I owe you even more." Erg.

Her voice wavers. "Are you going to get kicked out of school?"

"Not if no one finds out. Look, this isn't a big deal."

"Liar." She doesn't say it with her usual gloating. No singsong voice or any hint of "I've got you right where I want you." Instead, she sounds sad and almost pitying.

My palms sweat and I wipe them on my jeans. This is so bad that Amelia's first instinct is to feel sorry for me.

She has the biggest dirt on me ever, and it's *so bad* that she's not even being smug about it.

"You can fly, and you can zap people." Her lip curls in disgust. "What are you?"

"I'm your brother."

"*Half* brother," she says, emphasizing the distance between us.

"Please, Amelia." My voice sounds too high, too desperate and panicked. "You can't tell anyone."

She bites her lip, studying my face for a while.

I hold my breath. I might be blocking the door, but I can't keep her in here forever. And if she decides to tell Gordon—or Helen, or anyone, really—I'm ruined, and there's nothing I can do to stop her.

She closes her eyes. "All right," she says, finally giving in. "I'll keep your secret. For now. But if you shock me again—"

"It was an accident."

"—or do anything evil, I *will* tell."

"Evil? That's what you think of me?" One tiny zap, and she's looking at me like she doesn't know me at all. Like me being half supervillain was only okay as long as there weren't any reminders of it. A perfect example of why no one can ever know. Or at least no superheroes.

"I don't want you endangering anyone." She looks down her nose as she says it, like she's the protector of the world now. "And remember," she adds, a hint of the old familiar smugness creeping over her, "you *owe* me."

CHAPTER 10

Sarah's dad lets me in after I practically run to her house later. He's on his way to the store, so, thankfully, he doesn't ask me how school's going, even though Sarah told me he's fascinated by the anthropological nuances of a half villain "outsider" trying to incorporate himself into a "tribe" of heroes. I think he's been watching too many documentaries. He tells me Sarah's home, but he doesn't mention she's with Riley, which I feel is false advertising. I find them sitting in her room with the door open, even though, unlike at Kat's house, Sarah's allowed to have the door closed when a boy is over. Like her dad actually, you know, trusts her or something.

Er, not that Kat's dad should exactly trust her. Or especially *me*. But that's not the point.

Sarah and Riley both look up as I lean against the doorway. Sarah's sitting in her computer chair, and Riley's perched on the edge of her bed, next to one of her gadgets. I've never seen it before, but it's a white plastic device that looks sort of like a hair dryer with a big green and red dial on the side.

"Hey, Sarah," I say, "I need to …" I trail off, noticing there's a tiny screwdriver on the bed next to Riley, as if he'd been using it. Were they working on one of her gadgets *together*? "I have to talk to you." I glare at Riley and jerk my thumb toward the door. "That means alone, Perkins."

Sarah and Riley exchange a knowing look, then Riley rolls his eyes. It reminds me of when Gordon and Helen think they're secretly talking about me, like I'm an idiot or something and won't notice.

"I'm not going anywhere, X," Riley says, though I see he slides his hands under his legs, like he's worried I might break his finger again. "And can't you tell you're interrupting something?"

Sarah adjusts her glasses. "Damien, I'm kind of busy."

"Yeah, but this is important." Like, *I can shoot lightning from my hands and blasted a hole in the freaking wall* important. And I certainly can't tell her that with Riley sitting there. He'd love to know I have a villain power— just another reason for him to think he's a better hero than me, even if he's not. I drum my fingers against the doorframe, then barge inside, since it doesn't seem like an invitation is coming anytime soon. "What, exactly, am I interrupting?" It couldn't be anything *too* important, right? I mean, they did still have the door open.

I don't like the way they have that gadget sitting there between them, with a couple of tools sprawled all over

Sarah's glow-in-the-dark night sky bedspread, as if they were both working on it. Even though I know for a fact that Sarah works on her gadgets *alone*. I'm not allowed to touch them until they're done, at least not since that time I accidentally broke the automatic nail trimmer she was working on, just because I misunderstood that it wasn't at the testing phase yet. And I was the one who almost lost a finger, so I don't see why she had to punish me further by banning me from touching anything. But Mr. Perfect strikes again, because apparently that rule doesn't apply to him like it does to me.

He and Sarah exchange another glance, only this time they look guilty. Or at least Sarah does. She swallows and looks away, pretending to be interested in her laptop, the one with the all the superhero stickers on it, including the one of the Crimson Flash. She flips the lid open, then closes it again.

"What's that?" I ask, crossing over to the bed and reaching for the gadget.

Riley grabs it, pulling it away before I can touch it. He puffs up his chest. "Get out of here, X. Sarah already told you, we're busy."

An electric tingle runs up my spine, making the hair on the back of my neck stand on end. God, I hate this guy. "Sarah, I *really* need to talk to you. I have to show you something." I glare at Riley and add, "In private."

"Can't it wait?" Sarah presses the lever on the side of her chair and lets it sink closer to the floor.

"No. And what were you two doing?" I eye the gadget Riley's trying to hide behind his back, but I can't get a good look. What with him not being invisible and everything. Why don't they want me to see it? Is Sarah making gadgets for *him* now? Like I can't guess that from the fact that they were working on it together. It doesn't explain why he's hiding it.

"Well ..." Sarah sighs. "I've been meaning to talk to you about something."

"Great. I want to talk to you, you want to talk to me. I don't see any need for a third person in that equation."

"That's exactly what she needs to talk to you about," Riley says. "About you. Being a complete and total douchebag."

"Who, me?" I pretend like I have no idea what he's talking about. "Sarah?"

Sarah smooths out the fabric of her jeans. She wraps a long, messy blond strand of her hair around her finger. "You *have* been acting like a jerk lately. To Riley, I mean."

Okay, but did she ever consider the fact that I wouldn't need to be a jerk if he didn't go around thinking he's better than me all the time and trying to steal my sidekick? He hasn't exactly been a bearer of olive branches or anything. More like a thrower of lighter fluid.

I sit down next to him on the bed, a little closer than he'd like. I can tell because he gets all nervous, probably remembering that time I sat on him. I sigh, like this is all a big misunderstanding. "I hope this isn't about what I wrote in your notebook the other day, about us being BFFs, because *obviously* that was a friendly gesture."

Obviously. Just like *this* is. I slip my arm around his shoulders, like we really are BFFs or something. Though that might just be something that happens on TV, since I don't think I've actually ever put my arm around any of my BFFs' shoulders, unless it was Kat and I was about to make out with her.

It does the trick, though, because Riley flips the hell out and jumps up from the bed. At least he doesn't break any bones this time, though you'd think he'd have learned his lesson by now. "Dude, what the hell is your problem?!"

My problem is that he's obviously trying to hide something from me. They both are. But now that he's not blocking the gadget anymore, I snatch it off the edge of the bed to inspect it.

Riley's eyes flash with understanding as he realizes he's been duped. He makes a grab for it. "Give it back!"

I quickly pull it away, out of his reach. My victory doesn't last long, because then he tackles me, shoving me down and trying to scrabble over me to get to it. I toss it to the far edge of the bed and bring my knee up, slamming it into the side of his stomach.

"*Boys!*" Sarah shrieks.

Riley falls on top of me and catches himself by jamming the heel of his palm into my ribs. He lunges for the device. I shove him away and scramble to beat him to it. There are a lot of flailing limbs, and then I twist around and get a leg under me and push myself across the bed. My fingers close around the handle of the device, and I jerk my arm back and pull it over to me.

And accidentally smash my elbow into Riley's face. Oops. He cries out in pain and climbs off of me, holding his nose.

Sarah glares at me like I'm some kind of monster as she rushes to Riley's aid. As if I would do something like that on purpose, while there were witnesses present.

A metallic, coppery smell fills the room as blood gushes from his nostrils, seeping under his hands and dripping on his shirt. His voice is muffled and nasally when he says, "I'm going to *kill* you."

He *says* that, but he's the one who's bleeding, and I'm the one with the device, and I don't see him coming over here for round two. "You're the one who attacked me," I remind him. "Plus, it was an accident." Plus, he and Sarah are keeping secrets from me and I want to know what's going on.

He holds back a scream of rage, sounding like an angry elephant.

"Are you happy now?" Sarah snaps at me. She tells Riley she's going to go get a towel, but not before glancing back and forth between us, like she's not sure she should leave us alone together, even for a few seconds.

I take this opportunity to inspect my prize. The dial on the side moves from green to red. The green side is marked *better*, the red side *worse*. So descriptive. I hold it up. "If this is some kind of homemade sex toy, you could have just told me." Instead of letting me touch it. Not that I really think that's what it is—I hope not, anyway—but I don't get what the big secret is. "A hint? You want to turn it to the side that says *better*."

Riley's face turns bright red, and not just because his nose is bleeding. "It's a personality enhancer."

"And you didn't want me to know that Sarah's going to

use it on you?" Wouldn't it be easier to just, like, get a better boyfriend?

Sarah storms back in the room with a clean towel and an ice pack.

I wave the device at her, even though she's still glaring at me. "You'll never really change him, you know." A common mistake girls make, at least according to all the sappy made-for-TV movies Amelia watches.

"She wasn't going to use it on *me*, you idiot," Riley says.

Not him? I turn to Sarah. "I don't know what he's been telling you, but you're great the way you are. You don't need this. I wouldn't change a thing about you."

She makes an exasperated noise. "Damien, I was going to use it on *you*."

"What?" I do *not* like the sound of that.

Riley smirks while holding the towel to his face. "You're the one who needs the attitude adjustment."

Sarah hands him the ice pack. "I want all three of us to get along. And I know you two could be friends"—we both make disgusted faces at that—"if you could just, you know. Go with it."

"So, what, you were going to change my personality in order to force me to be friends with him? And," I ask Riley, "you were okay with that?"

He takes the towel off his face and winces at the sight of all the blood. "I don't like you."

"Obviously, since you attacked me." Completely unprovoked, I might add.

"But I like Sarah, and if she says we could be friends …

I'll try it."

"Uh, right." Easy for him to say—he wasn't going to be on the receiving end of some "personality enhancement" treatment she concocted. Plus, I can tell from his tone that he doesn't really believe we could ever be anything but enemies. He must *really* like Sarah. "So, you two were conspiring against me."

An electric charge burns beneath my skin. Sarah's supposed to be *my* friend. I'm supposed to be able to trust her. And then Mr. Perfect comes along and ruins everything, like he can just waltz into Sarah's life and take her away from me. I get up from the bed, anger boiling inside me. I'm still clutching the personality enhancer, though I try not to squeeze it too hard in my rage, not wanting to give Sarah yet another reason why I shouldn't be allowed to touch her gadgets. Especially since I'm guessing Riley hasn't broken any.

"You're overreacting," Sarah says. "We were trying to help you. Like an intervention."

"An intervention? For my personality? I think that's called *not liking* someone." It's also called *betrayal.* "I thought we were friends, Sarah."

"We are. I just wanted you two to get along! You're both important to me, but all you do is squabble."

"Squabble" is putting it lightly. Riley must agree, because he goes kind of pale at that, though it might just be the blood loss.

"And it's not like it would have been permanent," she goes on. "We were going to put you back to normal, once you'd had a chance to get to know each other. It was just a time out."

That must be what the "worse" setting was about.

Electricity twitches in my palms. I clench my free hand and hold the device tighter so neither of them sees. And pray I don't go all electric again and, like, take out the wall. A little zap flickers from me to the device. A couple of lights flash, and then the dial twists by itself, over from "better" to "worse." Which I hope nobody noticed. "Face it, Sarah. The Invisible Douche and I don't get along. And we never will." If she doesn't want us fighting, she should just get rid of him. *That* would solve it.

"At least Riley's willing to try and work things out with you," she says.

"Sarah, there's nothing to 'work out.' Sometimes people just don't like each other." I look to Riley for some sort of agreement, but he's slumped down on the bed, pressing the ice pack to his face and not paying attention.

"If there's nothing to work out, then maybe you should leave." Sarah marches over to me. She holds out her hand for the personality enhancer.

I don't give it to her. "Come on, Sarah. You don't mean that."

"You can come back when you're ready to play nice."

"Sarah, that's basically banishing me *for life*. You can't do that. And you expect me to give this back to you, after what you planned to do with it?" Which, for all I know, she *still* plans to do with it.

"Drop it," she says, like she's talking to her dog.

And like Heraldo, I obey. I set the device in her hand, but only reluctantly.

There's a little jolt as the device makes contact with her skin. A visible spark. She blinks, staring at her hand and looking dizzy for a second. She wobbles a little on her feet.

I put a hand out to steady her. I am, after all, still her friend, and a way better one than Riley, since he's on the bed, nursing his injury, and not even noticing that anything's wrong. I mean, not that anything *is* wrong, since it was just a little static electricity, right?

And by a little, I might mean *a lot*, and that it wasn't static at all, but came from my hand. Which might make her wobbliness my fault, if you think about it, which I'm not going to.

"Are you okay, Sarah?"

Something flickers in her eyes. She blinks a few times, and then a wicked smile curves one side of her mouth, making her look really evil for a moment. She shakes her head and the smile disappears, leaving her perfectly normal again.

Weird. But, whatever. I'm sure it was nothing. And that it didn't have anything to do with my new power. Or her gadget.

Sarah seems to remember what she was doing before the shock, then points to the door and says, "*Out.*"

CHAPTER 11

R iley shifts uncomfortably in his seat across from me at the dining table on Tuesday afternoon. He has his book from Intro to Heroism out in front of him, along with his binder and the worksheet with our assignment printed on it.

I fold my hands on the table and smile at him. I haven't said a word since we sat down, which was, oh, almost ten minutes ago. I've just been watching him squirm, waiting to see how long it will take before he gives in and makes the first move.

Finally, he taps his pen against the paper and says, "We should probably get started. The sooner we get this over with, the sooner I can leave."

"Wouldn't want to miss an episode of *Train Wrecks*."

"*Train Models*," he corrects me, like I didn't already know that. *Train Models* is a stupid, boring show where some old guy repairs model trains. Really slowly. I'm pretty sure even Sarah thinks it's boring, though I know she watches it with him anyway.

And if he wanted to be home in time to watch it, he shouldn't have insisted we meet at my house. Like he didn't want me anywhere near his family or something, though I was already planning on flattering the hell out of his mom and making her wonder why her son was being so hostile to such an obviously nice young man.

He clears his throat and reads from the assignment sheet. *"In a team of two, list and discuss the five rules from the League Treaty you feel are most important."*

This is supposed to teach us teamwork. And I know Miss Monk partnered us up on purpose because she knows we hate each other—after all, I did spend fifteen minutes of class on Monday talking to an empty chair I pretended I thought Riley was sitting in, even though he was across the room and *not* invisible—and she wouldn't let Riley out of it when he whined to her after class that he couldn't work with me.

"So," Riley says, "what are your top five?"

There are more than five? "The first ones."

"Uh, the third rule says that heroes don't cause unnecessary bodily harm, even to their enemies. Are you sure that's your favorite?"

I grin at him. "It's my favorite one to *break*."

"You haven't even read them, have you?"

I shrug.

"Damien," Helen says, stepping out of the kitchen, a dishtowel in her hand, "does your friend want to stay for dinner?"

"My 'friend'?" Does he look like someone I would ever be friends with? "How do you know this isn't Kat in disguise?" I reach across the table and take his hand, rubbing my thumb lovingly against his palm. "Come on, 'Riley,' let's go up to my room and 'study.'"

Riley yanks his hand away—he really doesn't like me touching him for some reason—and looks like he's going to throw his textbook at me. Or storm out and leave, which I think is a perfectly acceptable option. But then, instead of either of those things, he flashes Helen a bright smile. "I would actually *love* to stay for dinner, Mrs. Tines."

What? No, he wouldn't. He's lying. And if he thinks him staying for dinner is going to annoy me more than it is him, he's dead wrong.

"All right," Helen says, not sounding like she believes him. She sets her dishtowel down, then goes upstairs to ask Amelia if she wants one serving of lard with her dinner or two.

"What was that about?" I ask him.

He grins, savoring his very minor victory. "What, you can't take a little payback? Besides, I want to meet your dad."

Of course he does. He and Sarah are practically in his fan club. I think they actually would be if the age limit didn't cut off at twelve.

"So," he says, tapping the assignment sheet with his pen again, "you don't even know five rules, do you?"

"Look, Perkins, why don't you just put down whatever *your* favorites are? I mean, we're such good friends that your favorites are my favorites, right?"

"That's not working as a team."

"Sure it is. I'm compromising by pretending I care, and you get to talk in class about your top five idiotic ideas to live by. Plus, I already know how to work as a team, because I have a sidekick, and we work great together."

"The point is that we can't always choose who we get to work with. We have to be ready for anything."

"Like working with a half villain whose sidekick you're trying to steal?" And who has a new villain power you don't know about, and who could accidentally fry you to a crisp if you piss him off too much?

I hear Amelia's tromping footsteps, followed by the stairs creaking, and then she comes bounding over to us. I'm surprised she didn't make an appearance sooner, though with her door closed, I guess she didn't catch the scent of fresh boy hormones until now.

Her eyes light up when she sees Riley. "Who's this?"

"He's taken. And even if he wasn't, I don't hate him *that* much."

She scowls at me. "I was just asking. You never have friends over. Not boys, anyway." She sits down next to me at the table, uninvited.

"Beat it, Amelia. We're working."

"Oh, this assignment," she says, idly kicking her leg against my chair. "Me and Kim already got ours done. We worked on it in class while Miss Monk wasn't looking so we didn't have to meet up."

"Sounds like a rush job to me. You should let me look over it for you in case you screwed something up."

She tries to share a look with Riley—as if he cares—and shakes her head. "Nice try, Damien. You're *not* copying my homework."

Not copying it. Just writing my name on it instead of hers. "If you're not going to make yourself useful, then you can't sit with us. Go back to your cave and finish filling out your quiz about which of your guy friends might secretly like you."

She gasps, like that's really what she was doing. Which she might have been, since I know that was this month's quiz in *Spandex*—the stupid magazine she subscribes to that caters to teen hero girls—because I saw it when it came in the mail last week.

"The answer, Amelia, is *none of them*." Of course, she'd have to actually have some first, but still.

Amelia kicks my chair really hard. "You'd better be nice to me," she threatens, narrowing her beady little eyes. "You owe me, remember? And if you don't behave, I might spill your secret. You wouldn't want your new friend to know that you're—" She cuts off there and flashes me an evil grin.

Riley's gaze flicks back and forth between us, like he's trying to figure out what she could possibly have on me.

"Amelia, I'm serious. Get out of here."

"But I've just figured out what I want," she says. "I know what you have to do for me, so that I don't tell anyone that when no one's watching, you like to—" She gasps as she glances over at Riley, as if just noticing him, and shuts her mouth.

I grip the edge of my chair and glare at her. Electricity

tingles along my arms. "Murder my least favorite sister, you mean?" I swear she gets more annoying every day. I don't know where she gets it from. "Because keep this up, and I won't care how many witnesses there are." She can't tell a secret if she's dead.

And even though Amelia's obviously a big fat liar and just making things up to annoy me, Riley's smirking anyway. Like he enjoys watching her try to one-up me or something.

"Tell me whatever stupid thing you think I owe you and then get out of here."

"Later," she says, still grinning at me as she gets up from the table and clomps back up the stairs.

Then my phone rings. I slip it out of my pocket and see that it's Sarah. Calling me, not Riley, even though I'm pretty sure she's still mad at me for what happened to his nose. "What's up, Cosine?" I ask her, using her sidekick name on purpose to annoy Riley.

"There's an emergency," she says. "I'm at the jewelry store downtown. Get dressed and get over here. *Now.*"

$$X \cdot X \cdot X$$

Sarah's camped out across the street from the jewelry store —the same one we didn't stop a burglary at last weekend —when we get there, wearing her Cosine Kid outfit, though without the eye mask. And yes, I said *we*. Because the Invisible Douche just had to tag along, even though Sarah's my sidekick, not his, and she called *me*.

Sarah motions for us to hide along the edge of the

coffee shop she's lurking by, in broad daylight, binoculars in hand. She scowls at me, still in my regular clothes. "I said to get dressed, Renegade."

"I'm in stealth mode. And there wasn't time." Plus, my Renegade X costume was in my room, and I wasn't about to let Riley see me go up the stairs. It's bad enough that he was at my house at all and that he knows Amelia has something on me. I don't need to go advertising my worst fear to him, too.

And Riley's in jeans and a T-shirt, just like I am, but you don't see her complaining to him.

"What's the emergency?" Riley asks.

Sarah hands him the binoculars.

Uh, *I'm* supposed to ask her that, and she's supposed to hand them to *me*. I grab them from him and peer at the jewelry store, even though it's only across the street. The store itself looks closed—the lights are off and no one's inside—but the front door hangs partway open.

"Someone broke in? In the middle of the afternoon?" Downtown Golden City isn't exactly deserted at four o'clock on a Tuesday. Or on any day, really. There are plenty of passersby on the street and in the surrounding shops, and as I'm watching, a couple of people stop and point to the open shop door, discussing it for a minute before moving on. "You're sure it's not those guys from the League again?"

Riley yanks the binoculars out of my hands. He succeeds, but only because I let him.

"No one's broken in," Sarah says. There's kind of a wicked gleam in her eye and she rubs her hands together.

"*Yet.*"

"So, why don't we just go close the door?" Since someone must have left it open by mistake. We can send Riley to do it, since he's not supposed to be here and Sarah might be wrong about there not being bad guys. Or superheroes. I don't need them calling my dad again.

Sarah shakes her head. "That would defeat the whole purpose. I didn't hack into their security system so you could close the door."

"You didn't … *what?*"

"You hacked them?" Riley asks, though he looks accusingly at *me* as he says it, as if it's my fault somehow. Like Sarah would only do something like that under my influence.

"It's a trap," Sarah says. "To figure out who the bad guys are. Whoever goes in that store is obviously a thief."

Riley gives me this look like I disgust him—more so than usual. "This is what you guys *do*?"

"Yeah, not what you expected, right? It's okay—you can just go home." Does he seriously think I go around luring bad guys into committing crimes? I mean, as far as I know, Sarah doesn't do that, either. Or at least she didn't. "Sarah, are you telling me you're the one who broke into that store? Because last I checked, that's illegal."

"I only did it to catch criminals."

"Criminals who wouldn't have committed a crime otherwise."

She whips around and gives me a condescending look over the top of her glasses. "But if they would commit a crime at all, that makes them bad guys. This way, we don't have to wait for someone else to act—we can figure out who all the potential criminals are and put them in jail right away."

Riley raises a seriously skeptical eyebrow at me, as if I had anything to do with this.

I take Sarah's elbow and lead her a little ways along the edge of the building, so she's not distracted by watching the jewelry store when I tell her how crazy she's being. She shoves her binoculars at Riley and tells him to man the helm. "Look, Sarah, I don't know what's gotten into you—"

"I don't, either," she says. "But after you left on Sunday, I couldn't stop thinking about how many criminals there are in the world and how unsafe they make it for everyone else. Don't good people deserve to feel safe?"

"After I left?" Because I accidentally bloodied up her boyfriend and she had ne'er-do-wells on the brain, or because I may have accidentally zapped her with her personality enhancer when it was on the "worse" setting? "Define 'good' people, Sarah."

"People who aren't criminals, obviously." She rolls her eyes at me and dismisses the concerned look I'm giving her with a wave of her hand. "And anyone who would be tempted to walk into that store because the door's open, and take something, is a threat to other people. But no one can see it yet."

"Unless they have a *V* on their thumb, right?" *I* don't believe that, but I remember what she said about not being able to work with me if I had one. "Then it's plain as day."

Sarah's face lights up, not catching my sarcasm. "I don't think I'll catch any supervillains with this particular trap— as you're always telling me, most of them have way better things to do than petty thievery—but I'm glad you understand. This is my way of branding ordinary people so everyone else knows they're bad guys and what they're capable of and can stay away."

"Can you hear yourself right now? Because you sound completely insane." Okay, maybe not *completely*. But close enough. Plus, who does she think she's talking to? "You remember I'm half villain, right?"

"Don't be offended. I'm not being letterist. I think all people have the potential to be criminals."

Great. That's much better. "Except heroes, right? Because I didn't hear you say anything about them falling into your trap."

She squints at me in confusion. "Why would they? Heroes stop robberies, not start them. Where have *you* been?" She laughs.

Riley wanders over to us and hands Sarah her binoculars back, slipping his arm around her shoulders. "Someone closed the door," he informs us. "So I guess they passed the test."

Sarah folds her arms, looking really put out by that. I can tell she wasn't expecting there to be any good citizens in this scenario of hers. "They ruined it, you mean. I hadn't caught any bad guys yet."

"So the criminal population isn't as rampant as you thought and the world is safe," I tell her. "That's *so* horrible."

She sighs. "You're right, Damien. The real criminals wouldn't have fallen for something like this. If I want to catch supervillains, I have to kick my efforts up a notch."

Riley glares at me.

I put my hands up. "Whoa, Sarah, that's *not* what I said. And I don't think you should be doing this, period."

"I mean," she goes on, as if she didn't hear me, "you're half villain and you weren't tempted by this trap at all, were you?"

"Sarah!" What the hell is wrong with her? "Being half villain doesn't automatically make me half criminal." Or half evil. Or half of any other stereotype.

"Yeah," Riley says, "I think it's obvious you're more than only *half* criminal."

He's smirking as he says it—like he thinks he's so hilarious—but Sarah still has this serious line on her forehead, and her mouth is drawn taut. "I'm going to have to do better next time," she says. "So, what traps *would* you have fallen for? I mean, I know you're not the best specimen, but you still have some insights."

"Wow. How about the trap where my best friend tells me there's an emergency and gets me to come down here so she can try and lure innocent people into going to jail?"

"They're not innocent. Not if they'd be tempted by robbing a jewelry store. Especially in broad daylight." She snaps her fingers. "Maybe that was my problem! It should have been at night, even if there would be less people out. And something bigger, like a bank vault, or maybe the genetics lab. Something that might lure in actual supervillains."

"Why bother even trying to catch them at all? Why not just shoot anyone with a *V* on their thumb and be done with it?"

Riley looks from me to Sarah, like he can't tell if this is actually a serious conversation or not.

"Damien," Sarah says, "don't be ridiculous. You know the League Treaty prohibits that kind of behavior. Or at least you *should* know that, since you're supposed to be studying it."

"I don't care what the League Treaty says. A piece of paper doesn't actually decide anybody's actions. And even if it did, it's not like you've signed it or anything." Plus, she's not a hero, or eighteen, the age you have to be to join the League. But those are minor details. "I'm pretty sure the League Treaty frowns upon breaking into stores and trying to lure in bad guys. You're the only criminal here, Sarah, did you notice that?" And I didn't hear her saying killing all villains was a bad idea—only that it was against the rules.

Riley shifts his weight from one foot to the other, looking uncomfortable. "Breaking into places is wrong. That's not really what you do, is it?"

"I didn't 'break' in. I hacked in. It's much different. You're being babies about this, even though you both have hero genes. I thought you guys would understand." She shrugs off Riley's arm, shaking her head dismissively at us, like we're the ones being crazy here, and goes to grab her backpack from where she left it against the side of the building.

While she's busy, Riley gives me this worried look. Not

accusing anymore, just concerned. As if his girlfriend just revealed that she's some sort of vigilante psychopath. Which I guess she pretty much did. "Did something happen?" he whispers.

Did something happen? Let me think, let me think. Oh, I don't know, I *might* have accidentally screwed up Sarah's personality enhancer device with my uncontrolled electricity power, and I *might* have accidentally shocked her with it and caused some sort of crazy to take over her brain.

But I don't tell Riley that. Plus, this isn't really my fault, is it? I don't know for sure that her gadget did this to her or that it was because of me. Sarah's not *that* different. She's always had a ruthless vigilante side. Maybe she's just finally decided to go with it.

"You spend all your time with her," I remind Riley. "Shouldn't *you* know?"

He shoves his hands in his pockets and gives me a sort of half shrug, looking a little guilty, like he's a bad boyfriend for not noticing before now that something was up with her. "I'm sure she's fine," he says, staring at the ground.

"Me, too." See? Miss Monk can take her stupid teamwork assignment and shove it, because us agreeing on something wasn't as hard as she thought.

We might hate each other, but we have one thing in common. Well, two things, because, besides caring about Sarah, we're both apparently big fat liars.

CHAPTER 12

I drop a flier for the Heroes in the Park festival on the coffee table after dinner, pretending to look it over. There's a picture on it from last year's event, with white Christmas lights strung all over the statues in the Heroes Walk. I look closely, but I can't tell whether or not any of the statues in the picture is Helen's, since killing Kat's grandfather earned her a space in the walk of fame. The flier also says there's going to be a bonfire and free barbecue with the ten-dollar entry fee, plus some local folk bands are playing that I've never heard of.

The tagline reads, *Honor your favorite heroes in Golden City Park—fun for all ages!*

I don't really care how much fun it is, as long as it takes place on Saturday and has a reasonable price tag. Out of all the fliers for weekend events posted at the downtown library—where I stopped on the way home earlier, *sans* Riley, who opted to go to Sarah's for dinner instead—this looked the most promising. After all, Kat's going to be home this weekend, and, after two weeks apart, I plan to show her a good time.

A *really* good time.

I'm also going to tell her about my new power, which I haven't mentioned to her yet. It'll be much cooler to show her in person and not have her freak out or think I'm some kind of criminal. Or at least, if she does, to not think it's a bad thing.

"What's that?" Amelia asks, coming out of the kitchen, where Helen's doing the dishes and Amelia was probably annoying her with an intricate play-by-play of everything she did at school.

"Nothing." I quickly turn the flier over, so she can't see what it's about.

"Was that Heroes in the Park?" She reaches down to take it, but I keep my hand on it, pretending I don't want her to see. It doesn't matter, though, because now that she's touched it, she just teleports it into her hands. "Yep," she says, looking it over. "We went to this a couple years ago. It was really fun."

"Well, you're not going this year." I snatch the flier away from her.

"Why?"

"Because *I'm* going. I don't need *you* hanging around."

She glares at me. "I can go if I want to. It's open to everyone. Last time, we all went, as a family. Well, except Jess, because she was too little then. But she's old enough now."

"Uh, you're not all coming. I just said I was going. Not

you and the whole family."

"It's not *your* festival. You can't stop us. Plus, Dad will buy our tickets." She says that as if saving ten dollars would be worth having to hang out with them the whole night. "And Mom's actually *in* the Heroes Walk, you know."

"Oh, wow, really?" I roll my eyes at her.

She smacks my leg as she slumps down next to me on the couch. "And Dad's been voted Most Beloved Superhero in Golden City a couple times. It's really fun when people recognize them and want autographs. That's what happened last time, and then we got to go backstage with one of the bands."

"This isn't going to be like last time, because *I'm* going and *you're* not."

"We'll see about that." She teleports the flier into her hands again and holds it away from me.

"Great. Just ruin my weekend, why don't you." I fold my arms and bring my knees up, pressing my feet into the edge of the coffee table, pretending to be sullen about it. As if she's pissing me off and not just falling perfectly into my trap.

Amelia makes a disgusted face. "Feet go on the floor," she says, like she's the manners police. "And the festival is going to be fun. You'll see."

I won't, because I will conveniently get sick or have too much homework—or possibly both—right as it's time to leave. But, selfless person that I am, I will insist everyone goes on without me. And brings me back the signatures of the last band that's playing. I don't know who they are yet, but they've just become my all-time favorite, and I will *die* if I miss out on at least getting their autographs.

I'll probably have to fake an illness to rack up those kinds of sympathy points. Something bad enough so that I couldn't possibly leave the house and everyone feels a little sorry for me—sorry enough to pick up the souvenir I want that will ensure they're gone the entire time—but not so bad that anyone gets any ideas about staying home to take care of me.

Amelia's still sitting on the couch, just kind of staring at me.

"What?" I ask her. "Haven't you done enough, or do you have more of my plans to ruin?"

She sighs, looking like she has something else she really wants to say, but then Gordon and Alex come home bearing ice cream, and I don't find out what it was.

X·X·X

I get a text from Kat at around eleven. It says, *Impromptu party in the commons! Wish you were here. All my friends say hi.*

I'm in the middle of putting my pajamas on, but I stop what I'm doing and type back, *I wish you were where I am, too.*

Where are you? she asks.

In bed. >:)

I finish getting dressed and then grab the phone to text her again right as there's a knock on the door. I stay to the edges of the room as I go to answer it, since I've discovered the floorboards creak less that way.

Amelia fidgets in the hallway. She almost looks too nervous to speak, but then she says, "I'm here to tell you what I want. Because you *owe* me," she adds, as if I'd already protested against it.

"Fine, but make it quick. Some of us have lives." I wave the phone at her.

For some reason, she takes that as an invitation to push past me and stomp over to my bed. I wince as the walls rattle. She sits down and grabs my pillow, hugging it to her chest and resting her head against it. Then she frowns at the wall where I replaced the stupid poster she gave me. "You actually *like* Superstar?"

Superstar is a pop band made up of about eight teens— sometimes they lose a member to a solo career, only to replace them later—who won a contest for a record deal. They look more like the type of stupid band I would expect Amelia to be into, not me. Their gimmick is dressing up like heroes and villains in their videos, even though they're not actually super themselves. Well, they weren't, but their newest member is an actual *H*-bearing hero, and I've read on the forums that it's causing major drama in the band and that they might break up soon. Which I hope is only a rumor, because their new, currently unfinished album is supposed to come out next year and I already pre-ordered it.

"They're so *lame*," Amelia says.

"It's Kat's poster," I lie. Kat also thinks they are, as Amelia so eloquently put it, *lame*. "Did you, like, actually want something?" Besides getting her makeup all over my pillow and insulting my décor.

"Close the door," she says, since I'm still standing there with it open, expecting this to not take long and for her to be on her way out in a few seconds.

She's being kind of weird. I close the door and lean against it. "I know you think I owe you, and that I'm evil or something, but I draw the line at killing people."

"That's not what I want to ask you." Her cheeks turn pink and she presses her face down into my pillow, leaving streaks from her mauve eye shadow.

One side of my face twitches. I may be having an aneurism. "Just tell me so we can both get this over with." And so she can stop touching my stuff.

"Well," she says, speaking directly into the pillow instead of to me, so her voice comes out really muffled, "Homecoming's in a few weeks."

"I know. I'm taking Kat."

"To *Heroesworth*? You can't do that."

"Um, no." Until she mentioned it just now, I hadn't realized Heroesworth was even having a Homecoming dance. Though as long as they're not at the same time, I don't see a reason why we couldn't go to both, especially since that means two sets of pictures to annoy Helen with. "I'm taking her to the one at Vilmore. Well, she's taking me, technically. Though I will also be 'taking her' later that night, if you know what I mean."

"*Eww!*" Amelia squeezes her eyes shut in disgust, then opens them again. "You can't go to Vilmore, either."

"Why not?"

"Because Mom and Dad will kill you."

"Yeah, but they can't exactly stop me." Good luck with that, parents.

Amelia shakes her head at me and my lack of respect for their authority. "Anyway," she says. "About Homecoming."

"Yes, now that we've established that you don't think I should go to either one. You know, with all your kind words and sunny disposition, Amelia, I'm surprised the boys don't *flock* to you."

She buries her face in my pillow again. I cringe inwardly. She takes a few deep breaths—inhaling my boy hormones for courage, no doubt—then looks up at me, determination flashing in her eyes. "I want a date to the dance."

"And I want a palace on the moon. Neither of those things is ever going to happen."

"You don't understand. I want *you* to find me a date." She manages to meet my eyes for a split second before her face turns bright red and she has to glance away in embarrassment.

I inspect my fingernails. "What makes you think I have that kind of money?"

Her face falls, and she sprawls out on my bed, lying down on her stomach and still clutching my pillow. "I know it's impossible," she says quietly. "You're right—you probably would have to pay someone to go with me, since nobody would ever want to on their own. And I know if you find somebody for me that they'll only be going because you made them somehow, that they won't *really* like me. But I've never been to a dance before. Or gone out with anybody."

She presses her cheek to my pillow and sniffs loudly. It takes all my willpower not to make a disgusted face at her in her time of need. Even though I suspect she might be tainting my bedding with her tears of desperation.

"I don't care if they like me," she says, as if she needs to emphasize how low her standards are in case I set my sights too high.

"So, you're saying to just get you a warm body. For your first dance."

"It's better than having no one to go with."

"No, it's not." She doesn't really think that, does she?

"You don't know. You always have someone to go with. Someone who actually *likes* you. And you're the one who's always saying how impossible it is for guys to like me."

"I'm your brother. It's called teasing." And, okay, it might be more than teasing—it might be sort of true, but only because she acts so desperate all the time. Not because there aren't, like, equally unpleasant boys out there who might actually go for her.

Amelia shakes her head, rubbing her nose into my pillow, which I think I might have to burn after this. "No. I already knew it was true before you came to live with us. No guys have ever liked me, not even Robert March. I know because Tiffany asked him for me at the end of last year, since I knew I wouldn't be going to that school anymore, and he said no way. That's what he said—*no freaking way.*"

"He's a loser." He really is. He played the tuba in the school band—badly, I might add—and spent all his free time playing trading-card games with his loser friends and possibly not showering. No one in his group had girlfriends, or even really talked to girls much. And I'm actually surprised he turned Amelia down so harshly. It's not like he had any other prospects.

"I know he's a loser, but so am I. That's why I thought he'd say yes."

Well, with that logic, how could she lose? "Maybe he likes boys."

"No. I heard he kissed Melanie Hargrove behind the bleachers this summer. She's *first chair flute* in the school band." She says that like it makes her a woman of loose morals.

Those first-chair sluts, always stealing all the guys. "So it didn't work out with him. That doesn't mean—"

"Don't try to patronize me. No boys have ever asked me out, or flirted with me, or shown any signs of being interested. I know I'm not pretty. I know I'm not funny or interesting. But I just want to go to one stupid dance. With a boy. He doesn't have to like me."

Yes, he does. She keeps saying that he doesn't, but she can't just whore herself out to the lowest bidder. And is she really going to be happy if I find her somebody and she knows it's only a setup? That she specifically told me she wants a warm body to play the part of "Homecoming Date Number One" and that she's expecting it to be fake?

If I do that, it's only going to confirm her suspicions that she's worthless. That having someone to go to a dance with is more important than having, say, any self-respect whatsoever. And if she'd stoop that low for *this*, what happens when some guy realizes how desperate she is and tries to take advantage of her? I mean, besides me killing him, of course.

Amelia notices me contemplating this and not, like, agreeing to it. She rubs her face with her hand and says, "You have to. I know it's impossible, but if you don't, I'll tell Dad. About your secret. The whole school, too. And you don't want that to happen, do you?"

No, I most certainly do not. I sigh, not liking this one bit, but not having much choice, either. "All right," I tell her. "If that's what you want."

"It is," she says, and then wipes her face on my pillow one last time for good measure.

CHAPTER 13

M r. Fitz singles me out at the end of class on Friday and asks me to stay behind. The way he holds my test we took at the beginning of the period, and the way his mustache twitches like it's signaling the mother ship to come beam it up, I know whatever he's about to say can't be anything good.

But I don't care. I *really* don't care. School will be over in another hour. And, like, eight hours after that it will be time to go to bed. And the sooner I go to bed, the sooner it becomes Saturday, the day that Kat comes home. Of course, I can't exactly see her until that evening, when everyone leaves for the Heroes in the Park festival. Not unless I want to blow my cover, that is. But at least when I call her tomorrow afternoon, I'll know she's only across town, not forty-five minutes away.

Mr. Fitz shows me my test, which he graded as soon as I turned it in, marking it with red pen all over. There's a big *F* at the top, though I apparently didn't fail *every* answer, just almost. After all, the book does get one or two things right.

"I don't know if you're aware of this, Mr. Locke, but this is not a passing grade."

I don't see how that's my problem. I told him I wasn't going to lie on the test, no matter what the book said, and he told me he was going to fail me. That's exactly what happened, on both accounts, so I don't understand what there is to talk about.

"I'm aware of it. I accept the consequences. Can I go now?"

He scowls at me, his bushy eyebrows coming together. "I'm not certain that you understand what those consequences are. You can't go around making up answers and expecting to get by in life. This is an *F*. For *failure.*"

"It's a piece of paper." Big deal. I take out a piece of paper from my binder and write *You don't know what you're talking about* on it and hand it to him.

He scans it, then crumples it up in a fit of rage.

"See?" I tell him. "That piece of paper said *you* were stupid, and you didn't take it seriously, either."

"Fortunately for me, that piece of paper doesn't decide my fate at this school. However, this one"—he holds up my test—"and others like it, *do* determine yours."

I wonder if Kat has to put up with this kind of crap at Vilmore. "I said I wasn't going to lie, and I didn't. You can't make me put down the wrong answers just because they're what you want to hear. You can write *F* on my paper all you want, but you can't actually change my mind or make me believe any of the nonsense in the textbook."

Mr. Fitz's hands clench, wrinkling the edges of my test. He grits his teeth. "Perhaps not, but I *can* call your parents." He pauses, waiting for that to mean something to me.

As if I can't handle them. I pull out my cell phone and bring up Gordon's number, then hold it out to him. "Go for it."

He doesn't take the phone, like the fact that I was so willing to call my dad makes him suspect this is a losing battle. He glares at me, his whole face red with anger, and then slams my test down on my desk. "Bring this back to me on Monday, *signed.*" He motions for me to leave.

I stuff the failed test in my backpack and get out of there. People are still hurrying through the halls on their way to fifth period. Only one more class, and then I can go home. And Kat comes home tomorrow.

Kat comes home tomorrow.

Kat comes home to—

"Damien!" I'm so obsessed with getting to see Kat again that I think I hear her voice. I know I must have imagined it, but then, right as I'm thinking that, someone comes running up to me in the hall.

She throws her arms around me, and I recognize the scent of her watermelon shampoo. "*Kat?*"

She hugs me tighter, then steps back, grinning at me. "I'm on a field mission," she says. "We had to pick a place to gather information, and I chose Heroesworth, because ..." She looks down, smiling stupidly at her shoes. "Because I hoped I might run into you. How silly is that?"

166

"Zero percent." I can't believe she's *here*. On some sort of hands-on assignment, and not, like, sitting around making stupid posters. Heroesworth should take note.

We're just kind of standing there, both of us grinning at each other, when some guy comes hurrying over, looking really put out. "Katie?" He has bleached-blond hair that doesn't match his eyebrows and a really pointy nose. "You just took off."

"Damien, this is Tristan. Tristan, this is Damien, my—"

I kiss Kat before she can finish, showing him *exactly* who I am to her. It's a deep kiss, a two-weeks-of-not-seeing-you kiss. The slow, intimate kind that makes other people uncomfortable to watch. Sparks race up my spine and the hair on my arms stands on end. There's a sharp zap between us when I break away. Then the bell rings, signaling I'm officially late to class.

"What was *that*?" Kat asks.

I'm not sure if she means the kiss or the zap at the end, but I pretend I didn't notice the zap and assume it's the first one. "I missed you." And I wanted to put Tristan in his place, of course. But *mostly* it was because I missed her.

Tristan makes a big show of clearing his throat to get our attention. I'm pretty sure he's the same Tristan who started the whole "Katie" thing, and now he's here, working with her on some field assignment. Almost like he was her partner in crime, or at least like he thinks he is. He's going to have a lot of trouble partnering up with her after I murder him.

Kat looks embarrassed, like she'd forgotten he was

there. "This is my boyfriend Damien."

"I gathered that," he says. "What's he doing here? You didn't invite him, did you? Because Mrs. Thorpe didn't say anything about—"

"I'm on a field mission, too," I tell him. I hold out my hand to shake with him, wondering how badly I can shock him before he notices it's not just static.

But he pretends like he doesn't see me and turns to Kat instead, leaning in to whisper to her and touching the inside of her wrist. He makes it look like a deeply personal gesture—like they *could* be just friends, or they could be something way more—as if he's trying to make a move on her right in front me.

And suddenly it's all I can do *not* to electrocute him. A charge burns beneath my skin. All my hair stands on end, and I have to take a deep breath and will the electricity to stay in check. I planned to tell Kat about my new power this weekend—she's not some superhero who'll freak out and act like I'm a criminal—but frying the other member of her team probably isn't the best way to break the news. Even if he hasn't spoken two words to me and I already hate him and really, really want to.

And maybe, since he's a supervillain, I wouldn't even get expelled for killing someone on school property.

"We're being timed," he says to Kat. "We've lost enough points already in this competition, and we're not supposed to get distracted. Or talk to outsiders."

Outsiders? Who's he calling an outsider? Just because I don't go to their school and am not part of their mission and have no idea what's going on.

Kat rolls her eyes at him. "It's fine," she says. "We'll still pass."

"I'm not coming in last so you can make out with your boyfriend."

"You might want to tone down the jealousy," I tell him. "Girls really hate that."

He glares at me.

Kat sighs, giving in. "Fine, I guess we should go finish our mission. Damien, do you know where the main office is? The records room is connected to it, and I had blueprints, but I sort of got turned around."

I point down the hall. "Take a left at the vending machines. If you get all the way to the cafeteria, you've gone too far."

"Thanks." She smiles and moves in to kiss me, then hesitates, like she can feel Tristan scowling at us. "I'll see you tomorrow," she says instead.

They turn to leave and haven't even gone ten feet before Tristan finds some excuse to touch her arm. I clench my fists, letting electricity crackle in my palms, now that no one's watching and they're far enough away that I don't think I'll lose control and actually, like, murder him. Plus, the way he's standing so freaking close to her, I'd probably hit Kat, too. And that's *definitely* not how I want her to find out about my new ability.

Then, out of nowhere, Riley's voice says behind me, "You're seriously going to let them walk away like that?"

I jump, startled, and turn just in time to see him go *un*invisible. He scares the hell out of me, and before I know what's going on, there's a loud crackle and a burst of

169

light as lightning arcs from my hands to the ceiling, hitting one of the emergency sprinklers. It's over just as quickly as it started, except now the fire alarm's blaring and water's raining down on us.

Kat's staring at me from the other end of the hall, her eyes wide, as if she's never seen me before. Her mouth drops open, and she blinks a few times, like that couldn't possibly have just happened and she must have been hallucinating, despite the water pouring down from the ceiling and the alarm going off.

I motion for her to call me. Then Tristan grabs her hand and the two of them make a run for it before anyone shows up to investigate.

X·X·X

I pull Riley into the nearest bathroom—which happens to be the girls', but is also empty—just as classroom doors fling open and everyone piles out into the halls to evacuate the building. He stands in front of the sinks, soaking wet, staring at me with his arms folded and an "I knew you were trouble" look on his face.

I wonder if I can use my electricity power to erase his brain. Or at least his memory of the last five minutes. But since I'm not about to try that, I pace in front of the door and run my hands through my hair, flinging drops of water all over, while I try to figure out what to do. Obviously, I can't murder him, even if that sounds like the most reasonable option right now, because Sarah would kill me. And because I'm not, you know, evil.

It's one thing for Amelia to have something on me, but I'm *not* going to owe Riley. I'm not going to be under his thumb. If he'd even go for that. I mean, what kind of bargaining power do I have when he just got everything he wants? He's got enough dirt to completely ruin his worst enemy, which I'm going to go ahead and assume is me, since I don't know of anyone else who's broken any of his bones lately. I don't have anything that can compete with the satisfaction of telling everyone he's been right all along and I'm a no-good villain who lets other villains just waltz around the school like they own the place and who has a villain power. And who obviously isn't hero material and that Sarah shouldn't be sidekicking with.

He's going to ruin me, and there's nothing I can do to stop him. And I'm sure as hell not going to give him the satisfaction of begging him not to. Especially since he has no reason to listen.

So, already regretting this and wondering if maybe I threw out the murder option too soon, I step away from the door so I'm not blocking him in. "Go ahead, Perkins. Just get it over with." So much for my weekend with Kat, since Gordon will be too busy yelling at me to ever let me out of his sight. I can already see the disappointment on his face when he finds out I'm expelled. And, of course, *why*.

Riley stands up straighter and looks down his nose at me. He sounds like a complete douche when he says, "You know I wouldn't do that."

"Wouldn't do what?"

"Stoop to *your* level."

"My level." Which is obviously so much lower than his, and not just because he's taller than me. "You don't want to go running and telling everybody what you just saw?" While he was spying on me. Don't forget that part.

He gives me this dramatic sigh, like he wouldn't expect someone of "my level" to understand. "Of course I do, X. But I'm better than that. I'm not *you*."

Okay, accidentally bashing his nose on Sunday obviously wasn't enough for him, since all I'm hearing is that he wants me to punch him in the face. "Watch it, Perkins. How do you know I won't just fry you right now?" I hold up my hands, as if I might actually do it, though I hold back on the electricity. We're both soaking wet, and even though I'm pretty sure I'm immune to my own lightning power, accidentally electrocuting myself to death in the girls' bathroom with Riley isn't exactly how I want to find out. "I'm a villain, right? Isn't this what we do?"

He rolls his eyes at me. "If I thought you'd really do something like that, then I *would* tell someone. But I'm not going to get you expelled just because I found out a secret about you and I happen to hate your guts. That might be what *you* would do, but it's not very heroic."

This is why everyone thinks villains are evil. Because when superheroes start spouting off crap about how much better they are than us, it makes it really hard not to kill them. "And it doesn't bother you that I can shoot lightning from my hands?"

He shrugs. "I never really believed you could fly. This explains it."

"Except that I *can* fly."

"Okay. Prove it." He gestures for me to get on that.

"What, like, now?"

"Yes, now. I'm not talking about some big demonstration. Just hover over the floor or something. If you can fly, that shouldn't be a problem."

I swallow. Flying, even just a little, means not being on solid ground. Which is probably my least favorite place to be. I've also never flown on command before, unless trying not to die counts, and I'm not sure it does. "I don't have to prove anything to you."

"Uh-huh." He smirks at me. "That's what I thought."

"No, it's not. I *can* fly. I just *don't.*"

"Well, I've seen you use lightning. And now you conveniently 'refuse' to fly when I call you on it. So I think I can draw my own conclusions. Plus, you don't really expect me to believe you have two superpowers, do you?"

"I don't care what you believe." Well, except for him mistakenly believing he's better than me.

"And I don't care what lies you tell. One thing I don't understand, though, is why you're even going to this school or how you expect to graduate. You catch supervillains wandering the halls, and you don't think anything of it? You not only let them go, but you *give them directions?*"

"Kat wouldn't hurt anybody." Not unless they messed with her secret collection of scrapbooking materials she thought I didn't know about and used them to put together a tribute to the world's scariest clowns and hid it under her pillow. Then I happen to know she's not afraid to fight dirty.

"Even if I believed that, she's still a supervillain," Riley says. "She's not supposed to be here. You're not supposed to help her do villainous stuff at our school." He puts his hands behind his back and shakes his head at me. "Are you really trying to get an *H*? Because you certainly don't act like it."

"If I wanted a lecture, I would have turned myself in. Stop acting like you're better than me, because you're not."

"Then stop making it so easy. Face it, X, you're never going to get an *H*. And you're never going to belong at this school." He sighs, giving me a really patronizing clap on the shoulder, which is pretty bold of him, considering the whole uncontrollable-electricity thing. "So you might as well do us both a huge favor and quit while you still can."

CHAPTER 14

I answer the door Saturday night wearing a white dress shirt with a black jacket over it, plus nice pants and a tie to match. Kat has on a faded T-shirt with an angry robot on it, jeans with a hole in the knee, and an old sweatshirt around her shoulders.

I gape at her. "Didn't you get my memo? We have a dress code. This is a *classy* hook up. I mean, really romantic evening. I'm not sure I can even let you in like that."

"I had to sneak out. And you might not know this, Damien, but it's kind of difficult to climb out the window in an evening dress."

"Shapeshifting, Kat. It's called shapeshifting." I cluck my tongue at her and shake my head. "I *suppose* I can still let you in." She did, after all, not freak out or suddenly decide I was evil when I explained my new electricity power to her on the phone last night. "But you're going to have to take those clothes off, what with not following my dress code and everything."

She rolls her eyes at me, then steps inside. "You're sure no one's home?"

"Would I be seducing you in the doorway if they were?"

"Trying to, you mean. And I wouldn't put it past you."

"They're gone until ten. We've got three hours." Three hours together to make up for two weeks apart. Two *very long* weeks. "And," I add, sighing at her outfit, "I hope you can get it together for Homecoming."

"I'll wear what I want and you'll like it, if you know what's good for you."

"I was thinking we could wear swimsuits. I mean, everyone's going to be in formal wear. It's *so* been done."

"Yeah, that's not going to happen. The publicity team from my dad's company is going to be there, and I'm supposed to take pictures with him. And I'm not doing that in a swimsuit."

Oh, great, so he *is* going to be there. "What? But you're supposed to be *my* date. Can't I just buy you from him already for, like, two cows or something?"

"The going rate is ten cows, at least. You'd better start saving up." She slips her hand into mine and leads me toward the attic stairs.

"You might want to tell your dad that he might not want to show up for Homecoming. Because I'm going to do some things to you that he's not going to approve of, and I think it'd be better for everyone involved if he just stayed out of it. And we can wear swimsuits to the one at

Heroesworth. I know your dad's not going to be at that one. That is, if you want to go with me next weekend." They're not at the same time—I checked. The one at Vilmore is the weekend after. "I mean, it's probably going to be stupid, since it's at Heroesworth, but think of all the people we can mess with." Assuming I've found a date for Amelia by then and am still alive.

"An evening with you, messing with superheroes who think they're better than us?" She grins. "How could I say no?"

"You couldn't. I don't even know why I bothered to ask."

"Are these *them*?" she says, gazing up at the stairs looming over us.

"Yes, but—"

"So, your dad's really making you live up there? You have to go up these every day? I thought he knew about the heights thing."

"He suffers from a rare condition called 'selective idiocy.' Unfortunately, it's spreading at an alarming rate. And these stairs are really dangerous, so I understand if you want to do it on the couch instead."

"Again, *not happening.* Plus, I want to see your room."

"Okay, but only take them one at a time, and don't touch the railing, because it's going to fall off. And the boards on the seventh, twelfth, and twenty-second steps are loose, so take those ones extra slowly, so you don't—"

She takes off, bounding up the stairs like she didn't hear a word I said, or like she has some sort of death wish. She stops on the seventh step, testing it with her foot and making it wobble on purpose.

"Hey!" I shout. "Weren't you listening?!" What am I supposed to do if she falls and kills herself in a tragic stair accident?

"It's not that bad." She comes back down, her hands pressing on either side of the railing, despite how flimsy it is. "Are you coming or what?"

"Before or after I die of a heart attack?"

"Okay. You stay down here, then. I'll just be upstairs, taking off all my clothes." She raises a seductive eyebrow at me before taking off again.

"That won't work on me!" I call after her. Even though it's totally working on me. I mean, the stairs are still terrifying as hell, and it's an effort to put one foot in front of the other, especially toward the top of the stairs, when everything starts wobbling, but I might be making progress a little faster than I normally would. Maybe a lot faster.

When I get to my room, Kat's still fully clothed—in fact, she zipped up her sweatshirt, which is the opposite of getting undressed, though that may have something to do with it being colder up here—and is smirking at my Superstar poster. "Is this the hole in the wall?" I told her about it last night on the phone, when I was explaining how I went all electric at school. She untacks one of the bottom corners and peers behind the poster, gaping at the damage. "Wow. You're right, your dad will *so* kill you if he ever finds out about this."

Just like her dad will *so* kill me if he ever finds out about *this*.

I come up behind her and kiss the back of her neck, trailing the tip of my tongue across her skin. She shivers and sinks against me. I put my arms around her, and she leans back and whispers, "You're sure they won't come home this time?"

"Kat," I whisper back, already leading her toward the bed, "it's been two weeks. I *made sure.*"

X·X·X

We're making out on my bed not even five minutes before my phone rings. I grab it off the nightstand, expecting it to be Gordon checking up on me or something, since he thinks I'm sick. Which is *almost* thoughtful of him, except for the fact that I told him I'd be in bed the whole time they were gone—not exactly a lie—and he's disturbing my supposedly much-needed sleep. I'm preparing to answer the phone in my most pitiful "everything hurts and I don't know why but am bravely soldiering on" voice when I see Riley's name on the screen.

I only have his number because I asked Sarah for it when all three of us went to the zoo early this summer— back before the finger-breaking incident, when I was still allowed to hang out with them—claiming I wanted it in case any of us got separated. I was, of course, going to use it to torment him later, but then I forgot. She must have given him my number, too, though I have no idea why he'd be calling me right now.

"Don't answer it," Kat says, lying half on top of me, resting her head on my chest while she undoes the buttons of my shirt.

"I just have to tell someone off. It won't take long."
Either Riley's calling to apologize for being such a douche
to me yesterday—unlikely, considering he's been a jerk the
whole three months I've known him and has never once
been sorry about it—or he's thought up more reasons why
he thinks he's better than me. Either one sounds like a
good excuse for me to put him in his place. Especially
since he has the nerve to actually call me.

"You've reached the hotline for Sex Addicts
Anonymous, how may I help you?"

"*Thank God.*" He sounds panicked and out of breath. "I
didn't think you were going to answer."

"It's what we do. Tell me the nature of your sexual
addiction."

"What? Look, I didn't have anyone else to call, and—"
There's a weird sound in the background, like lasers firing.
A sound that brings back memories of my childhood. "And
I really need you, so—"

"Oh, *that* kind."

"This is serious!" There are some scuffling sounds and
pounding footsteps and then a door slamming. When Riley
speaks again, his voice is hushed. "I'm trapped in some
building downtown. I need you to come get me out of
here."

I laugh. "Why would someone like you need someone
of *my level* to help you? Call Sarah."

"Sarah's the one who got me into this mess!"

"And you don't have any other friends? That's—" Kat
slides her tongue along the edge of my ear, catching me

off guard, and I gasp.

"What are you …?" Riley sounds like he's going to ask me what I'm doing, but then he must think better of it. "Look, X, you're the only supervillain I know."

"And that matters because?"

"Because I'm in a building owned by supervillains and there are killer security robots chasing me! And going invisible doesn't work because they're—" There's a loud crashing sound. Riley swears, and then there's a lot of commotion, and when he speaks again, he sounds like he's running. "They're tracking me by sound."

"Have you tried shutting up? What about not breathing?"

"Can't you do something?! Don't you, like, know some supervillain code or something?"

"Why, because all supervillains know each other and share their secret codes to deactivate their killer robots?" God, he's an idiot. "That's so offensive, I don't even know where to start. And this from someone who's *so* much better than me."

Kat finishes unbuttoning my dress shirt and pulls her T-shirt over her head. She presses up against me, her bare skin on mine, kissing my neck while her hands wander down my stomach to other, *lower* places. "Get off the phone," she whispers, unzipping my pants.

I swallow. "Look, Perkins, I *really* have to go." Otherwise this phone call is going to get indecent. "Good luck with those robots."

"No, wait! I'm sorry for what I said! I'm not—" There's a pause, and I can't tell if it's because the words are that hard for him to say, or if it's because he's having to evade a pack of killer robots. "I'm not better than you!"

For someone being tracked by sound, he sure does shout a lot. "Great. Can I call you back in three minutes?"

Kat punches me in the arm.

"Isn't there something you can do?" Riley cries. There are more crashing sounds and another door closing, and then, in between gasping breaths, he says, "I'm at Fourteenth and Cedar. In this really corporate office building. Please—"

"Wait, you're *where*?" I sit up suddenly, bonking my head against the slanting wall, and glance at Kat, wondering if she heard what he said.

"It's some company. They make computers. I don't know what it's called."

"Wilson Enterprises," I offer. Fine, so supervillains do all know each other. I take a couple deep breaths, trying to clear my head.

Kat raises an eyebrow. "What's going on?"

"This idiot I know is trapped at your dad's company," I tell her, not bothering to cover up the phone, so that Riley hears me calling him an idiot. "Do you know the codes to call off the security robots?"

She shakes her head. "You have to be in the building. And have a key card."

I sigh. To Riley, I say, "I don't suppose you have one of those?"

"I don't have *anything*. Sarah was doing something with the computers, and then she just left me here, and then the security system came on and there were all these robots and I thought I was going to die, and I probably still am, and—"

"Geez, Perkins. Did I *ask* you for your life story?" I roll my eyes and share a look with Kat.

"I have a card," she says, not sounding too happy about it.

I check the time. Still over two and a half hours left. "We can get down there and back and still have enough time to … you know. Finish up here."

"We'd better," Kat says. "And then no more phone calls." She puts her shirt back on and grabs her purse off the floor to double-check that she has the right card.

"All right, Perkins," I say. "We're coming to get you."

"You are?! That's—"

I hang up on him. He *so* owes me for this.

CHAPTER 15

I t takes us about twenty minutes to get down there, and then Kat uses her card to deactivate the security system. We find Riley on the third floor, where he's barricaded himself into the copy room. The door has big gashes on it and some scorch marks and a couple now-inactive robots crumpled on the floor around it. The robots are metal and vaguely human-shaped, except that they're on wheels and have saw blades and laser guns for arms. I tell Riley it's safe to come out—I tried to tell him over the phone when we got here, but he didn't believe me —and then there are some shifting sounds as he moves stuff out of the way and opens the door.

There are big circles of sweat under his armpits, and he looks like he's about to collapse. He tentatively pokes one of the deactivated robots with the toe of his shoe, cringing as he does it, like he expects it to come alive again and murder him. When he's satisfied that we have indeed rescued him, he steps past the robots and exhales. "Thanks," he says, rubbing the back of his neck. He takes us in, frowning a little at our disparaging outfits, but doesn't ask about it. Then he looks nervously at Kat, like he's afraid she might bite him.

"This is Kat," I tell him. "She's my girlfriend, and she's a supervillain, and she just saved your life."

"And you," Kat says, looking him up and down, "must be the idiot." She folds her arms and raises an eyebrow at him. "You want to tell us what you're doing here?"

Riley slumps down in an office chair at somebody's desk and puts his head in his hands. "It was Sarah. She said the computers they make here put out mind-control signals."

Kat looks over at me.

I scratch my ear and stare at a very interesting spot on the floor. "I *might* have mentioned it to her. At some point."

"Damien! That was confidential information!"

"Yeah, but it was just Sarah. She wouldn't ... I mean, I didn't *think* she would ever do anything." I sit down on the edge of one of the desks and glare at Riley. "What, exactly, did she do?"

"She hacked into the system. So she could change the hidden message the computers send out and tell all the bad guys to turn themselves in. She was being really weird, like she was the other day when she was watching the jewelry store."

"And you thought breaking in here and doing all that was okay?" Kat asks him, her hands on her hips. "Why?

Because we're supervillains?"

"No! Of course not." He glances up at her, then away again. "She told me it was a superhero mission."

"Which you went on without me," I remind him. Er, not that I wasn't exactly busy with my own plans tonight. And not that I would have gone along with it, for obvious reasons, which Sarah must have known, and which must be why she didn't call me. Not because she chose him over me or anything.

Riley shrugs. "She asked me to go with her, so I did. And then she brought me *here*, and I realized what she was doing was wrong, but it's not like I was going to abandon her."

"You mean like she did to you?"

"I tried to reason with her, but you know how she was the other day. It's like ... it's like she's a different person. Like her personality changed overnight."

Oops.

"Something's definitely wrong with her," he adds. "It was like she didn't care what happened to me."

"What, and it's impossible that she just finally realized what a loser you are?"

His eyes dart up to mine, a hurt look on his face, like he might have had that same thought. But then he shakes his head, dismissing it. "She finished what she was doing and *left*. And then the security system came back on, and I was trapped here, and the robots were destroying everything. You know," he says, addressing Kat, "it seems like a really expensive way to stop intruders."

"It's also the reason we never have them. Plus,

insurance pays for the clean up." She gives us both a confused look. "So, Sarah wants bad guys to turn themselves in? What bad guys?"

"All of them," Riley says. "She's got this idea that she can make the world a safer place by pre-emptively weeding out criminals. She was trying to lure potential bad guys into committing crimes the other day, but it didn't work, and she said that was too small scale, anyway. With her new plan, if somebody's done something they should feel guilty for—or if they're planning to commit a crime or something—then the mind-control messages from the computers will convince them to go to the proper authorities and confess. I thought it was messed up, but she wouldn't listen to me. I told her *she* was the one committing a crime, but she said using supervillains to catch other supervillains was fair play."

Kat gapes at me. "This is what you guys do? I thought you, like, helped people and stuff!"

"We do! I had nothing to do with this." I wave my hands, emphasizing that part.

"But she's *your* sidekick, Damien. It's bad enough you hang out with this guy"—she jerks her thumb at Riley —"who's obviously got a problem with supervillains, and now I find out Sarah's even worse?!"

Riley swallows, looking really nervous again.

"First of all," I tell Kat, "I don't hang out with this guy. And, second, Sarah's not normally like that."

"Riiiight."

"She's not! She's just a little messed up right now. Because I *might* have accidentally used her personality

187

enhancer on her." I say this last part out the side of my mouth, so my words are kind of unintelligible.

"What was that?" Riley asks.

"I said I might have accidentally used her personality enhancer device on her last weekend. On the 'worse' setting. And there may have been some stray electricity involved." I hold up my hand, letting a couple sparks flicker to life at my fingertips, in case he wasn't sure what electricity I was talking about.

Now he's gaping at me. And looking like he wants to kill me. "You *what*?!" He gets to his feet, his hands balled into fists at his sides. "And you weren't going to say anything?!"

"I'm saying something now, aren't I? And I didn't know for sure anything was wrong with her before. I mean, she's kind of just like that. Sometimes."

"I don't understand why Sarah's even friends with you. How could you do this?"

"It wasn't on purpose."

"It's *never* on purpose, is it? Not when you broke my finger—"

"Oh," Kat says, nodding and smirking a little. "*This* guy."

"—not when you bashed my nose the other day, and certainly not when you, like, damaged school property with your villain power! And now that you've screwed up Sarah and turned her into some crazed vigilante, I suppose *that's* not your fault, either?!"

"I didn't say it wasn't my fault—I said it wasn't on purpose. And I think you're making too big a deal out of this. All I have to do is get the device, turn it to the 'better' side, and use it on her again. Then everything goes back to normal." An excellent and foolproof plan, if I do say so myself.

"All *you* have to do? You're not going anywhere even near—"

A loud whirring sound interrupts him, followed by some beeping. Little lights start flashing on the dead robots.

"Oh, no," Kat says, squeezing her eyes shut.

I don't like the sound of that. Neither, apparently, does Riley, because his face goes pale and he starts shaking all over. "Not again," he says, watching as the robots pick themselves up.

"Kat?" I whisper.

"I thought I turned it off, but I must have put it on a timer. I've never done this before."

Riley starts muttering over and over that we're going to die.

"Shut it, Perkins," I hiss. "Just be quiet. They can't track us if we don't make noise, right?"

All three of us watch as the robots come to life again and start patrolling the room. One of them glides over to us. We hold perfectly still, hardly daring to breathe. Electricity flickers to life beneath my skin, but I will it to stay there, trying to remain calm. The robot comes right up to where I'm sitting on the desk, looking me in the face. I hold my breath, praying for it to go away. It can't know I'm alive, right? As long as I don't make a sound, it's going to wander off and not kill me.

And then Riley sneezes and I throw myself to the floor, narrowly avoiding a laser to the brain. The saw arm comes down and hacks through the desk I was just sitting on.

I grab Kat's hand and shout, "Run!"

"This way!" she says, leading the three of us down a hallway, the robots following.

"Can't you use the card again?" Riley asks.

A laser hits the ceiling above our heads, sending bits of tile and plaster raining down on us.

"Only if we can get downstairs." Kat turns a corner, taking us down another long hallway and then another after that, giving us a little lead time on the robots. The hallway's a dead end, but it's also where the elevators are.

She presses the button for the elevator to come, but it doesn't light up. She presses it again. Then a bunch of times. "It's not working. It must have turned off when the robots spotted us."

"I knew it," Riley says. "We're going to die!"

"For the last time, Perkins, shut the hell up! We're not going to die!" I shout this at him right as a laser narrowly misses my shoulder, blasting a chunk out of the wall behind me instead. The three robots chasing us are at the end of the hallway, and now there's nowhere for us to go.

"How?!" Riley says. "Because unless you have some brilliant plan you haven't told me about, that's exactly what's happening!"

The robots descend steadily down the hall, their saw blades whirring and their lasers charging.

Riley looks around frantically, as if he thinks there's another door or other escape route we were just too stupid to notice. There isn't.

"Kat," I say, nudging her with my elbow and ducking another laser beam, "do something."

"*Me?* I told you, I can't. There's nowhere to put the card! Not unless we get to the security office downstairs!"

Crap. I shut my eyes. Maybe Riley's right—maybe we are going to die. "Change into something else," I tell her. "Something quiet that runs fast, like a mouse or a rat. Get out of here!"

"Damien!" She squeezes my hand really hard, twisting to the side to avoid another laser.

"Do it, Kat! We don't all have to die!"

"No, you idiot!" She lets go of me and holds up her hands, splaying out her fingers and miming using magic powers or something. "Electrocute them!"

Whoa. Why didn't I think of that?

"Now!" she screams.

Right. I hold up my hands, sparks twitching to life in my palms. Waves of electricity flow over my skin. All my hair stands on end. The robots are only a few feet away. I gather up everything I've got and let them have it, shooting a beam of lightning at them.

The one in the middle takes the beam straight on and falters a little. It hesitates, fighting against the electricity, and then keeps moving. The other two, which are off to the sides and not getting the full force, don't even seem to notice.

"Oh, great!" Riley snaps. "I *knew* you couldn't do it! And now we're all going to—"

"If you say we're going to die *one more time*, Perkins, I

swear I'll electrocute you!" Rage boils up inside me. At Riley, for assuming I'm going to fail and for calling me down here in the first place. Kat and I could be safely holed up in my room right now, having lots of sex, but *oh no*, I had to drop all that to come down here and save his sorry ass. And this is the thanks I get.

A new surge of electricity bursts from my hands, fueled by my rage. The force of it pushes me back against the wall. Lightning crackles through the hallway, hitting the first robot and flowing into the others, stopping all three of them in their tracks. They twitch a little, their saw blades powering down, and then their lights go out and they stop moving altogether.

I'm breathing really hard and I feel kind of lightheaded. And even though this isn't the first time I've used my lightning power, I stare at my hands in disbelief.

"Well, X," Riley tells me, "I guess you're not completely useless."

"Gee, thanks."

"Wow," Kat says. "That was *amazing.*"

I sink back against the wall, wiping a bunch of sweat off my forehead with my sleeve. Being so amazing is apparently hard work. I pull my cell phone out of my pocket and check the time. "And we still have over an hour and a half left to get back home and—"

The elevator dings. The doors to my right open, and a familiar dark-haired man in a business suit steps out. "Hello, Damien," Kat's dad says, not exactly sounding happy to see me. He must have overridden the elevator, either using his CEO status or his superpower that lets him commune with machines.

I wonder why he addressed me and not Kat, but then I glance around and see she's turned herself into an office chair and Riley's gone invisible. Which is probably better for everyone, considering her dad's going to kill me enough as it is. He doesn't need to find me sneaking around with her, and I don't know how I'd explain Riley being here. There's no way I'm telling him my sidekick and her douche superhero boyfriend broke in and changed his mind-control message, which they only knew about because I apparently have a big mouth.

"Tom!" I say, stepping away from the wall to greet him and pretending like there's nothing weird about me lurking in his office after hours with some dead killer robots in front of me. "What are you doing here?"

"I was going to ask you the same thing." He folds his arms across his chest, looming over me.

While he's not looking, Kat shapeshifts back into herself and slips into the elevator, along with Riley, who turns visible again just in time for me to catch a glimpse of him before the doors close. Kat gives me an apologetic look and mouths something at me, but I can't make out what it is.

"You look awfully dressed up," Mr. Wilson says, eyeing my clothes. "Big plans this evening?"

I glance down at myself, hoping I don't look too disheveled from my activities with Kat earlier. "This is how I always dress."

"No, it is not. Did you know that my daughter's in town tonight?"

"Oh, is she?"

"You know that she is. And I was surprised that she didn't ask to go see you or have you over at the house. In fact, I found it somewhat suspicious. And then I got a call that the security system cut out. And that someone from the building next door saw two kids sneaking in here."

My mind is spinning. It could have been us, or it could have been Sarah and Riley. Either way, they're not here and I am. And I'm not going to have any trouble faking being sick later, since I feel like I'm going to throw up.

"Now," he says, "why would you and my daughter be sneaking around a deserted office building on a Saturday night?"

"We're not. I mean, we weren't. It's just me. I was, um, fighting robots. See, it turns out I can shoot lightning from my hands, and—"

"Don't lie to me, Damien. I'm not stupid, and neither are you. It was a rhetorical question. I know exactly what you two were doing."

Then why is he asking? Plus, that's *not* what we were doing, at least not here. "I think there's been a misunderstanding."

"I told you not to touch her," he says, staring down at me. "What part of that *didn't you understand*?"

X·X·X

Kat's dad is apparently not big on listening to explanations, because instead of giving me a chance to concoct some story about how I wasn't trying to sleep with his daughter, he grabs my shoulder in a death grip and hauls me into the elevator. And not to take me to the lobby and kick me out, either. No. He takes me to the *roof*.

This is how I die. He said he'd kill me, and now he's actually going to do it. And he knows I'm afraid of heights, so he's purposely choosing the worst way possible. Wilson Enterprises might not be the Golden City Banking and Finances building, but it's plenty high enough that the fall will kill me. Just glimpsing the drop surrounding it makes me dizzy and sick, especially knowing what's coming. I'm already reliving the last time it happened. My palms sweat and my vision blurs as he drags me through the garden—this is a *nice* roof, meant for people to, like, hang out on, which sounds crazy to me—and toward the ledge.

My lightning power has abandoned me, either because I need to recharge after killing those robots, or because I'm just that terrified. As is, my legs don't want to move and I can't get enough air. And even though my body is screaming at me to do whatever it takes to get out of here, it's like all my muscles are frozen and can't hear the signal to move. It's like I'm watching this happen to someone else and there's nothing I can do to stop it.

"Kat's going to be really mad if you kill me," I tell him, not liking how small my voice sounds. He's not really going to do this, is he? He's just trying to scare me. At least, that's what I tell myself. But when I look up into his face, and at the anger flashing in his eyes, I'm not so sure.

"The fall won't kill you," he says, sounding a little disappointed about that. "After all, you can fly. Because you're half *superhero*." He shoves me to the edge, his grip on me tightening. My shoulder burns and is going numb at the same time. "Do you think I want my daughter to end up with someone like you? Someone who's only *half* a villain?"

I'm staring down at all the empty space below me. My stomach drops and my mind reels and it's all I can do not to throw up. I shut my eyes, unable to keep looking at my surroundings, but then I open them again, because not being able to see the floor beneath me makes me feel like I'm already plummeting off the edge. "I think I should tell you that I haven't flown in months. I don't know if I can still do it. And this building's shorter than the last one— my power might not kick in before I hit the ground."

"Kat's going to Vilmore," he says, as if he didn't hear me. And while he seems pissed, he also seems way too calm for someone standing so close to a ledge. Someone who can't even fly. What if I freak out and fall and take him with me?

Not that I'm going to do that.

I hope.

"This is her chance to make something of herself. Her two short years there will decide her entire future, and she doesn't need some boy distracting her. Especially not one who couldn't even get in."

"I'm not—" I start to say I'm not just "some boy," but then he puts more pressure on my shoulder, shoving me that much closer to the edge, and I shut up.

"And she especially doesn't need someone who's trying to be a hero. I understand that you didn't make it as a villain, but you're *not* going to drag her down with you."

Nice word choice. I feel my legs start to wobble, and then my knees buckle, dropping me to the floor.

He yanks me back up again, forcing me to stand on unsteady legs. "What do you think you can do for her? What do you *possibly think* you can give her, except one problem after another?!"

My thoughts swirl together, trying to come up with a way out of this. "I love Kat," I tell him, since it's the truth and three words is about all I can muster right now.

"If you loved her, you would want her to be happy. How is she going to be happy when all her new friends find out she's dating a superhero? Who goes to *Heroesworth Academy*? How is she going to build a career as a villain? No one will trust her if she's with you. Tell me, Damien, are you going to sign the League Treaty? You want to get your *H*, don't you? How the *hell* do you think you're going to do all that and still be with her?"

"I'm not signing it," I say, shaking so hard I almost can't get the words out.

He snorts at that. "Doesn't matter. You'll have an *H* while she has a *V*. I know who your father is. Just wait until *that* gets out."

I'm pretty sure I'm delirious. I must be, because the next words out of my mouth are, "We're getting married." At least, I think that's what I say—I'm not coherent enough to know for sure.

But then he jerks my shoulder really hard, like he's getting ready to actually throw me off the edge, and I know I *did* say that. "That's never going to happen. You don't have a future with her. It won't work."

"We'll make it work."

"She deserves better. You and I both know you're not good enough."

"No, *we* don't."

"I should have told her she couldn't see you as soon as it happened, as soon as you got that *X*. But I thought it would blow over, and she would have only wanted to see you more if I told her she couldn't. So now I'm telling *you*, Damien. Do you want me to throw you off this ledge?"

I cringe, my legs giving way again, so that I sway a little and would probably fall if he didn't have such a tight grip on me. A cold gust of wind ruffles my hair. I lick my lips, my voice rough and strained. "*No.*" Please, God, no. What the hell is wrong with everyone in this town? When did it become acceptable to throw people off of buildings?

"Then tell me you'll leave my daughter alone. Tell her you're not going to see her again. She'll be upset, but she'll get over it, and she'll find someone at Vilmore. Someone with a *V* on his thumb who she doesn't have to be ashamed of."

"Kat's not ashamed of me." And she wouldn't just get over it. I know she wouldn't.

"Not yet. You're still young—you don't know how hard it will be. Say it, Damien. Promise me, or you go over the edge."

I feel hollow inside. The ground below looks impossibly far away, lit up by streetlights and the glow of nearby businesses. The back of my throat burns. He's right, I probably won't die. My flying power will probably kick in. But waking up every night in a cold sweat, endlessly reliving plummeting to the ground, is almost worse. Dread prickles in my stomach and down my back. And I would do anything to stop this from happening.

Anything except what he's asking, that is.

"No." I brace myself for the fall.

"No?" He grabs me with both hands, holding me as close to the edge as he can without actually dropping me, so that I'm leaning over it and my feet are precariously balanced. One more shove and I fall straight down. "The two of you can't last. One of these days, she's going to realize what she's missing out on. She's going to realize just how many things she's never going to have as long as she's with you, and she's going to regret it. It'll be easier on both of you if you break it off now. Promise me you won't see her again, or you—"

"I said *no*! I can't do that! I *won't.* So if you're going to push me off, then just do it already!" I twist out of his grasp as I say that, rage overcoming my fear at least long enough to make my muscles work. I shove myself away from him, my feet slipping on the ledge. A horrible, nightmarish feeling of not having solid ground under me —of not having *anything* under me but a dozen stories of air—washes over me. I remember with sickening clarity what the fall will feel like, already reliving it before it even happens.

And then Kat's dad reaches out and grabs my arm, hauling me back onto solid ground. His blue eyes are wide as he stares at me with a mixture of anger and disbelief. "What the hell were you thinking?!"

"Me? You were the one pushing me off a building!"

He throws his hands up. "I wasn't actually going to do it!"

Now he tells me. "Try being less convincing next time." Or, you know, not doing it at all.

He puts a palm to his forehead and leans his head back, looking pretty freaked out. "Don't ever do that again."

"You started it."

"I was trying to scare you." He tilts his head, giving me this stern look, like I'm the one in the wrong here for not knowing better. Right. "I didn't think you'd throw *yourself* off."

"I'm not breaking up with her."

"Yeah, I think you made that clear."

"You can't force me to. And I'm better than you think."

He sighs, not agreeing with me, but not denying it, either. "It'll never work." That's what he says, but he sounds way less sure about it this time.

"You don't know that." He doesn't. I gesture over my shoulder at the ledge, where I would have relived my worst nightmare rather than lie and say I'd do what he wanted. "I might not have a *V*, and I might not go to Vilmore, but none of that stuff matters, because I would do *anything* for her." I pause, letting that sink in. And then, even though all I really want to do right now is crumple to the floor and die, I look him in the eyes and say, "That's kind of more important, don't you think?"

CHAPTER 16

There's a knock on my door at a little after ten, and then Gordon's voice says, "Damien? Are you awake?"

I'm in bed in my pajamas, but my light is on and I am definitely still awake. I can't stop thinking about almost falling off a building. Or all that crap Kat's dad said about me not being good enough for her. I consider pretending to be asleep so Gordon will go away, but then I think maybe I could use the distraction. So I tell him to come in.

He opens the door and looks me over as he crosses the room, the floorboards creaking loudly under his weight and making me wince. "How are you feeling?" he says, sitting down on the edge of the bed.

"Terrible," I tell him, and it's not even a lie, though it's not for the reason he thinks. But it's still kind of comforting when I tell him that and he gives me this concerned look, like he wishes he could do something to make me feel better.

"I brought you this," he says, handing me a photo of the band whose signatures I asked for. They're called The Bottlers, whatever that means, and, sure enough, they all signed it.

I sit up to look it over and smile. My plan would have worked perfectly, had it not been for the Invisible Douche screwing it up. Not that I doubted it. Well, okay, maybe part of me wasn't sure if they'd *really* stay that long, even if I was sick. I kind of figured Jess would get cranky around nine or so and they'd decide I could just live with the disappointment and come home early. "Thanks."

"You know, they weren't too bad. I was surprised."

I raise an eyebrow at him. "You think I have bad taste in music?" I have no idea what this band sounds like.

"I didn't think I liked folk bands."

That's funny, because I would have pegged him for the type to like them a lot. "Neither did I."

He smiles a little at that, then says, "Can I get you anything?"

I try to think if there's anything I want, especially since I won't have to go down the stairs myself to get it. And while I'm still pretty shaken up after almost falling off a building, I'm also pretty hungry from taking out those robots.

"What about some cereal?" he offers. "Amelia always likes that when she's sick."

I make a face. I can't help it. "I don't know if you've noticed this, but I'm not Amelia."

"I know. And you're not Alex or Jess, either." He

pauses, and then his face suddenly lights up, like he just thought of something. "Hey, what about tomato soup? I know it sounds a little strange, but—"

"Did Mom tell you that?" I scowl, not liking the idea that she's told him things about me. Not that I really think she did, but I don't know who else would have.

"What? Damien, when would she have told me anything?"

"I don't know, but how else would you know I like tomato soup when I'm sick?"

He laughs. "I don't. I said that because it's what *I* like. None of the other kids do, though."

"Oh." Great. Now he knows we have something really stupid in common, and I'm never going to hear the end of it.

"Do you want me to make you some?" He looks so hopeful, so eager to share this with me.

I swallow and stare down at my bed. I don't know why, but I just can't give him the satisfaction. "I'd rather have a sandwich or something."

"All right," he says, sounding only a little disappointed, like he's still too happy that we have this weird thing in common to let my rejection get him down. "I'll see what we have." He pats my knee, still smiling about the stupid soup thing, then hesitates before getting up to leave. "You know, I've been thinking. One of these days, we ought to go down to the DMV and get you your learner's permit. When you're feeling better, of course."

"My learner's permit? What, like, to learn how to drive?" I thought I was supposed to be the sick one, so how come he's delirious?

"You're sixteen. Closer to seventeen. You're plenty old enough to have your license already."

"So?"

"So, Amelia's going to have hers soon. Don't your friends your age have theirs?"

Kat does. Sarah's still working on it. She would have gotten hers this summer if she hadn't accidentally run a stop sign because she thought she saw some guy stealing an old lady's purse. It turned out she was wrong, but the guy testing her was going to be lenient about it, at least until she said she'd been planning to run down the supposed purse thief with her car. "Are you trying to peer pressure me into this?"

"No, son."

"So ... it's some kind of punishment? Or a really weird reward?" I'm not sure what I've done either way to make him decide to do this.

"My father taught me, and I thought it was something we could do together."

"You would seriously get in a car with me behind the wheel?" I raise my eyebrows at him.

"I trust you."

Wow. "Is this because I'm going to Heroesworth?" Now that I'm supposedly following in his footsteps, he thinks I'm someone I'm not.

He sighs. "I just want to spend time with you. It has nothing to do with what school you're going to."

"Okay, but don't say you trust me when you don't."

"Damien, I *do* trust you."

"But I'm pretty sure I'm going to suck at driving. And I'll probably crash the car."

"That's ridiculous. You won't. Plus, we'll start out with the basics first."

"But if I did …" I let out a deep breath. "You'd be mad."

"I wouldn't. I might be upset at first, but I wouldn't be *mad*."

I give him a skeptical look. "You're always mad at me. I'm always doing things that piss you off. And I'm pretty sure crashing the car falls into that category. So … no."

"I'm not always mad at you."

"Yes, you are. Like when you had to pick me up from patrolling with Sarah." Well, maybe he wasn't that mad then, but he certainly wasn't happy with me.

"Damien, I was upset because you didn't tell me about it. You're always …" He hesitates, searching for the right words. "I get mad when you don't tell me the truth. When you keep things from me."

Keep things from him? Like, say, having a lightning power he doesn't know about?

"Or when you outright lie to me."

Like pretending to be sick so I can stay home and have my girlfriend over who's not allowed in the house? "I don't lie to you."

I think I say that with a pretty straight face, but he laughs anyway. "I know you have trouble trusting me with things, but I never know what's the truth and what isn't with you. I'd like to get to know you. Not who you think I want you to be, but the *real* you. And yes, I get mad when

I find out you've lied to me. But accidentally making a mistake is different. You're my son, and I want to teach you how to drive."

"So, if I crash the car, you *won't* hate me forever?" Because I'm still having trouble with that part. It's one thing for him to want to get to know me, but it's another if getting to know me means he's going to hate me. Because if that's the case, I'd rather just lie to him the rest of my life. After all, if I'd lied to Mom, she wouldn't have kicked me out. And I've learned from my mistakes—I might have ruined things with her, but I'm not going to ruin them with him, too.

"Of course I won't." He puts a hand on my shoulder. "I know we don't always see eye to eye on things, but, Damien, I could never hate you. You're my son."

I nod, because it feels really good to hear him say that, even though I'm not sure I believe it. *He* might, but I don't.

"And you're a smart kid. I know it's scary at first, but you'll do better than you think. I won't let anything happen to you."

I've heard *that* before. "This driving thing ... It doesn't secretly involve you pushing me off of any buildings, does it?"

"I promise you that it doesn't. So, what do you say?" He squeezes my shoulder and smiles at me, like he really does want to get to know me and spend time with me and stuff. And not because I'm going to Heroesworth or because I've made him think I'm better than I am, but just because I'm his kid.

"I ..." I take a deep breath. Me being his kid doesn't

mean he's going to automatically like spending time with me. And maybe he only gets upset when I lie to him, but it's not like I'm going to tell him the truth about me anytime soon. "I have to think about it."

"Okay." He nods, sounding relieved that I didn't just flat out tell him no. Like getting me to think about it at all is a victory. "It's your choice. Just let me know what you decide."

CHAPTER 17

Riley answers the door on Sunday afternoon, not even having the decency to look ashamed of himself. Or surprised to see me. In fact, if anything, I would say he looks smug.

"You're dead, Perkins." And not just because of what happened last night. "Where is it?"

"It's inside. And I was going to tell you about it."

"Sure you were. That's why you got up at the crack of dawn and went to Sarah's house to steal it out from under me." I push past him into the house, not waiting to be invited. I glance around the living room, but I don't see the personality enhancer anywhere.

"You're just mad that I beat you to it," he says, sounding pretty proud about that, even though he would be a chopped-up pile of robot-leavings right now if it wasn't for me. "As if I was going to let *you* get your hands on it. And anyway, I didn't steal it. I asked her for it, and she gave it to me."

Sarah doesn't know she owes her new-found vigilante status to her own device. Plus, according to what she told me, it's not exactly in working order. I went to her house earlier, intending to grab the device myself and use it on her before she knew what was happening. Riley must have had the same idea, because she said he'd already stopped by and that she'd given it to him. She didn't seem to think it was weird that he was still talking to her after what she did to him or anything. She also seemed pretty pleased with herself and kept checking the news, as if she expected to hear that all the bad guys of the world had turned themselves in already, her mission in life accomplished.

I didn't mention that I knew about her plan or that I had to go and rescue Mr. Perfect last night after she abandoned him.

"Sarah said it's not working," I tell him. A slight problem in my plans to have turned her back to normal already.

Riley glares at me. "Only because *you* touched it."

"Careful, Perkins. Don't make me regret saving your sorry ass any more than I already do."

Now at least he has the decency to look a little guilty, though then the next words out of his mouth are, "But if you hadn't broken Sarah's personality enhancer in the first place—or if you'd at least told me about it—none of us would have even been in that mess. Or in the one we're in now."

God, I hate him. "What I did was an accident.

Everything you did was on purpose. *You* were going to use the personality enhancer on me. *You* went with Sarah and broke into Kat's dad's company"—his eyes go wide at that and he glances around, like he's worried someone might hear, then motions for me to be quiet, which I most certainly will not—"and *you* interrupted my much-needed alone time with my girlfriend and begged me to help you and then almost got me killed!"

"Dude," he whispers, looking panicked. "Shut up. My *mom* is home. She'll kill me if she finds out where I was last night."

"What's that?" I cup a hand to my ear and speak extra loudly. "You're super grateful to me, a no-good supervillain, for saving your life when you went on that really dangerous supposed superhero mission? And you'd do *anything* to repay me?"

He folds his arms. "Okay, X. You made your point."

I gasp and talk even louder. "What?! You want to do *what* with me?! And, no, I don't think Sarah will understand, no matter how grateful you are! When you said *anything*, I didn't think you meant—"

He shoves me toward the hallway, his face going completely red. "Come *on*."

There are two doors at the end of the hall—an open one that must be his, and a closed one across from it with a sign that reads, ZACH'S ROOM—KEEP OUT!

Riley pushes me through the open door and shuts it behind him. Then he leans against it, looking really pissed off.

"This is how rumors start, you know," I point out. "I

mean, seriously, I say all that and *then* you drag me to your room? What's your mom *supposed* to think?"

He lets his head fall back and thud against the door, rubbing his face with his palms. "My life would be so much easier if you didn't exist."

"So much more boring, you mean." As evidenced by the … Well, okay, maybe his room's not as boring as I expected it to be. I thought it would be all stamp collections and pictures of grass growing or something. Instead, there are some drawings on the walls, mostly of farm animals in outrageous settings. Like a pig standing in a coffee shop, looking confused, or a cow waiting in line to buy movie tickets. His shelves are overflowing with fantasy novels and comic books and model spaceships from movies and TV. Really intricate ones that look like they would have been a pain in the ass to make and really, really tedious, but that are also sort of cool.

I gesture at one of them. "I thought you liked trains. Isn't that why you watch *Train Models* all the time?"

He shrugs. "I guess. Mostly I just like the show."

"And the drawings?" I point to one of a duck taking a shower. "Did you make them?"

"What do you care?"

"I don't know. I like them."

"They're kind of stupid."

I roll my eyes at him. "Geez, Perkins. Can't you take a compliment?"

"You really like my drawings?"

"I said that, didn't I? But if you're going to be such a jerk about it, we can forget the small talk. Do you have the personality enhancer or not?"

He crosses over to the bed, pulling his blue and green plaid comforter out of the way before leaning down and fishing the device out from under it. I grab it from him and turn it over in my hands, inspecting it, but it looks the same to me. Other than the dial being turned to the "better" setting, of course.

"It doesn't light up anymore or do anything," he says.

I test it out, pulling the trigger a few times, and see that he's right. "So, how soon can you fix it?"

"Uh … never? How am I supposed to fix this thing?"

"You were working on it with Sarah." You know, when he was conspiring with her behind my back.

"Not, like, the technical stuff. I was just helping her put the pieces together. She's the genius, not me."

"Obviously. So, we'll get her to do it." I'll just convince her Riley could use a few adjustments. It'll be easy, since it's true.

"She told me she already took a look at it. And that there was no reason why it shouldn't be working." He folds his arms and makes a point of looking down his nose at me. "Probably because *someone* zapped it and screwed it up."

"So, what you're saying is even Sarah can't fix it?" *That* sounds promising. I sit down on the edge of his bed and rest my chin in my hands, trying to think.

Riley clears his throat. "Isn't your mom a scientist?"

I glare at him. "No."

"But I thought Sarah said she—"

"Not *no* as in she's not a scientist. She is." A mad

scientist, anyway. "*No* as in that's not an option."

"But she could fix it, couldn't she? Because Sarah told me about the incident before. With her hypno device, and that—"

"Did she also tell you my mom stole it from her and kidnapped her dad? And tortured him?" Well, she had "honeybuns," a.k.a. Taylor, do that part. "Is that really the kind of person you want to bring into this?"

"Well, no, but you'd be the one asking. I mean, she'd be doing it for *you*, right? She wouldn't have to know she was helping Sarah."

"For me? Did Sarah forget to mention that me and my mom aren't exactly on speaking terms?"

"She might have said something, but—"

"Or that my mom kicked me out? That she never wants to see me again?"

"That can't really be true, can it? I mean, she's still your mom, right?"

I sigh. "She had a baby without telling me. A replacement. I only found out about him by accident. And she's getting married this Christmas, but she wasn't going to tell me about that, either. And she certainly wasn't—isn't—going to invite me." The last thing I need is to go crawling back to her because I screwed something up and need her help. I don't need her. Not for anything.

"Oh." Riley sits down next to me on the bed, taking a deep breath. "That's messed up."

"Tell me about it. I can't go back there, and there's no guarantee she could fix it, anyway. We'll figure something else out."

We're both quiet after that, trying to come up with some other way to fix it. Or at least I think we are, but then, out of nowhere, Riley says, "I'm sorry about last night."

"Why? Because now you know my mommy doesn't love me?" I say it in as mean a voice as I can, because I *don't* need his sympathy.

"*No*. Because I almost got you killed. And I interrupted your ..." He looks away, trying to think of the right words.

"Sex night with my girlfriend? Who I never get to see now that she's away at school?"

He swallows and looks like he kind of regrets opening his big mouth. "Yeah, that. You didn't have to come down there, but you did. And I was kind of a jerk to you on Friday."

"You think?" Wow, has hell frozen over? I double-check the drawing of the pig in the coffee shop to see if it's suddenly sprouted wings. "And I *did* have to, because you were at Kat's dad's company, and those robots are ruthless."

He shakes his head. "You hate me."

"So? Not enough to let you get dismembered by killer robots. And Kat had the card." I shrug.

"We grabbed the security tapes on the way out," he says. "I mean, she did. But I was the lookout."

I nod. Kat told me as much on the phone last night.

"She seems cool," Riley admits.

"What, for a supervillain?"

"No. Just ... She's not what I expected." He hesitates, glancing over at me, then says, "Her dad looked like he was going to murder you. But you're still here, so what happened?"

"He yelled at me for an hour for breaking and entering and destroying his robots. Or at least that's the version I told Kat."

"And the truth?"

I lean my head back, shuddering a little as I remember staring down from the ledge, waiting to feel that sickening drop. "It doesn't matter. I survived, no thanks to you."

There's a knock on the door. Riley shoves the personality enhancer back under the bed and then tells whoever it is to come in.

A scrawny-looking kid, probably only a year or so younger than us, with the same light-brown hair as Riley bursts into the room. "I got it!" he says, holding up a video game called *Aliens vs. Dinosaurs IV* that has a picture of space aliens shooting lasers at a bunch of cyborg T-Rexes on the cover. "This was the last copy and it's *mine*. And *you* said you would play it with me, and I'm going to blast your face off!" He grins at Riley, waving the game at him. Then he notices me on the bed and clams up, suddenly getting all quiet and taking a step back.

Either he's really shy or my reputation precedes me.

"Zach," Riley says, "this is Damien. He's, um, one of Sarah's friends. Damien, this is my brother Zach."

Zach glances over at me, then quickly away again. "Is … Is he the one you told me about?"

Riley ducks his head, looking kind of embarrassed, and nods.

Great. I wonder what kind of monster Riley's made me

out to be. He probably told his brother all about how I broke his finger and bashed his face in. Or how I'm an evil villain who attacked school property and let supervillains roam free in the halls. Not that I care what this kid thinks of me, but it would explain why he's staring at me like I'm some kind of freak show.

I get to my feet and look down at Zach—even though he's Riley's brother, he's a lot shorter than him—and clench my jaw. "*What?*"

He swallows and his eyes get real wide. "Is the Crimson Flash really your dad?" He sounds super nervous, like he can't believe he's actually talking to me. "Because that must be *so awesome.*"

I blink at him. That was so not what I expected. I raise my eyebrows at Riley. "*That's* what you told him about me?"

"Well, it's true, isn't it?" he mutters, not meeting my eyes.

Zach, however, is staring right at me. Gaping, actually. "I can't believe you're friends with my brother."

"Yeah, I can't believe it, either." Okay, so maybe I don't have the heart to tell him his brother and I don't exactly get along. At least, not when he's looking at me like that, like it's an honor just to be in my presence.

"And you're at my *house.*"

"*Zach,*" Riley warns. "Back off."

Zach's face gets a little red, like he just realized how much he was gawking at me. He holds up the video game again. "Do you want to play with us? It's really fun. I have the first three already, and—"

"Zach!" Riley glares at him. "Didn't I *just* tell you to leave him alone?"

"But ..." Zach's face falls, and he stares at his shoes, clutching the video game to his chest. "*Fine.*"

Sorry, Riley mouths at me behind his brother's back.

"Actually ..." I can't believe I'm saying this. But the game does look fun, plus with Kat back at Vilmore and Sarah turned crazy, it's not like I have anything better to do. And, okay, maybe the way this kid is looking at me, like I'm some kind of celebrity, is pretty flattering. "I could play with you guys. For a little while."

"You can?!" Zach says, his whole face lighting up.

"You can?" Riley says, sounding really skeptical and drastically less enthusiastic.

"Oh, my God!" Zach runs off into the living room, shouting something about setting it up.

"You don't really have to play," Riley whispers once he's gone. "I mean, if you don't want to."

"Nah, it's okay. Besides, I want to see him blast your face off."

"He'll blast yours off, too—he's really good at this game."

"How old is he?"

"Fifteen. He'll be at Heroesworth next year."

"And the ladies ... they're all over him?"

Riley snorts. "Are you kidding me? He'd probably throw up if one ever actually talked to him."

So I'm guessing it's a safe bet he doesn't have a date for Homecoming then. *Perfect.* Amelia's going to be so pleased when she asks him out and he vomits all over her. And she *is* going to ask him out, because, contrary to what she believes, I'm not doing it for her.

"Why do you ask?" Riley says.

"No reason," I tell him. "I just like to know who I'm going into battle with."

CHAPTER 18

"Ha! I told you you were dead, Perkins." I blast his alien with the cyborg T-Rex I'm playing, mashing the buttons on the controller.

Riley grits his teeth and leans forward, pressing a combination of buttons that make his alien do some weird spinning attack that blocks the lasers I'm shooting at him.

I mash some more buttons—after a little over two hours, I think I've mastered the art of button mashing, if not how to actually play—and resort to elbowing him in the ribs in real life, since he's sitting next to me on the couch. Zach's on the other side of me, waiting to play the winner, and has kicked both our asses in this game several times already.

"Ow!" Riley cries, trying to fend me off without letting go of his controller. "That's cheating! And it's not going to work!"

Sparks race up my spine as I struggle to beat him, not

for the first time since we started playing. I'm so worked up about this game, I can feel electricity burning beneath my skin, like my body thinks I'm in an actual fight. Possibly a sign that I should take a break, but there'll be plenty of time for that *after* I destroy him.

"Flip him!" Zach shouts, urging me on. "*Flip him!*"

"What? I don't know how to do that!"

"It's the most basic combo! Just do it!"

"That doesn't mean anything!"

"Like this," Riley says, making his alien throw my dinosaur across the screen.

I grip the controller really hard, frantically pressing buttons. I manage to make my T-Rex whomp him with its tail. While he's down, I shoot more lasers at him before he can block me. I've almost got him—just one more hit and I win—and then electricity flickers in my palms. It zaps the controller, which instantly goes dead. The game freezes as a message pops up on the screen, saying we need a second controller to play.

Oops.

"The battery needs charging," Zach says.

But Riley must have seen what happened, or at least suspect, because he looks at my controller, then at me, and says, "Nice going, X."

Zach scowls at him. "It's not his fault."

Well, that's what he thinks. "You should be grateful, Perkins. I was just about to kick your ass. Now you've been saved the humiliation."

"Yeah, right."

I lean back against the couch cushions and set the now-dead controller on the coffee table.

Zach gets up to turn the game off. I've learned several things about him in the past two hours. For one thing, he thinks I can do no wrong, which, I must say, is a great feature. He also likes Velociraptors—another plus—and is nice to his mom. Even when she made him stop playing for about ten minutes to help her put groceries away after she made a trip to the store. I think she would have made Riley help, too, if he hadn't had a guest over. Or, you know, if she'd known I'm not so much a guest as I am the guy who keeps injuring her son, but I wasn't about to volunteer that information.

All in all, Zach seems like a good candidate for taking my sister to Homecoming. I can't picture him turning her down, and he's more than just a warm body. After all, he's a warm body *I* approve of. More importantly, though, I'm pretty sure going on a date with Amelia would actually mean something to him. Possibly a lot. And that he wouldn't try anything.

But it won't mean anything to Amelia if I just tell him to go with her. Like I said, she's going to ask him— whether she knows it or not—and he's going to say yes. And they're going to do that all on their own, without knowing I'm pulling the strings. All I really have to do is get them in the same room together. Then their mutual desperation will take care of the rest.

"Well, Perkins," I say, "I guess I should be getting home for dinner."

Riley glances at the cuckoo clock on the wall that, to my disappointment, doesn't actually do anything on the hour, since the cuckoo part is broken. "It's not even four."

"But dinner's at five, and I wouldn't want to risk being late. I mean, I know *some* people don't take these things very seriously, but that's not how it is at *my* house."

"What? What's that supposed to mean?"

Zach comes back and sits down, watching us intently.

"Nothing. Just that it was really rude of you to skip out on dinner the other night."

"It was?" Riley wrinkles his forehead, scrunching up one eyebrow. "But *you* said it was okay. In fact, you specifically said that I *wouldn't be missed.*"

"Well, I have been known to be wrong on occasion. Because, see, my stepmom invited you, and she was real disappointed that you took her invitation so lightly. Especially after you promised you were staying."

"I ... I didn't really promise, did I?"

"You said you'd *love* to stay for dinner. *Love.* That's what *you* said, and she thought you meant it for some reason. And my dad was disappointed, too. You know how he hates letting down his fans."

Zach gapes at him. "You could have met the Crimson Flash?! *What* is wrong with you?"

Riley stares guiltily at the coffee table, but otherwise ignores him. "He didn't let me down—I'm the one who didn't show up."

"Right," I tell him, "but he feels bad, because you wanted to meet him. And my stepmom thinks you don't like her, and after you seemed like *such a nice boy.*" I shake my head.

His mouth falls open a little. He swallows. "I didn't

know they felt that way. Because *you* said—"

I hold up a hand. "I didn't know, either."

"Sure you didn't. Now the Crimson Flash hates me. And your stepmom, and she seemed really nice."

"Well ... They don't *hate* you. They're just disappointed in you."

"Good job," Zach says, scowling at Riley.

"And," I add, "they've been on my case all week to invite you over again. But I should probably just tell them you stood them up for a reason and that it's never going to happen. Because it's not like you *want* to come over or anything, right?"

"Well, that's not ... that's not true." He bites at his thumbnail, looking worried. "I mean, I *could* come over. If they want me to."

"They do. Really badly. And you'd be doing me a favor, since then they'd stop hounding me about it."

"Do it," Zach says. "I'll never forgive you if you don't."

"You should come, too," I tell him. "My dad would be upset if he knew you were a fan and I didn't invite you."

He looks like he's going to explode. "Riley, now I'm going to *kill you* if you don't say yes."

"Okay, okay." Riley holds up his hands. "We'll have dinner at your house."

"Yes!" Zach jumps up from the couch and punches the air, then looks like he doesn't know what to do with himself. "What day? Can we come over tomorrow? I've never met anyone from TV before. Do we have to dress up?"

Riley groans and rubs his face with his hands. "God,

Zach. Calm down. It's not a big deal."

"Uh, yeah, it kinda *is*."

"If you have to freak out, do it somewhere else." He shoos him away. "You're bothering us."

"But—"

"Go *away*."

"Fine." Zach rolls his eyes, as if Riley's the one exasperating *him*, and then takes off for his room.

"What?" Riley says when he catches me smirking at him.

"Nothing."

"He's never going to shut up about it, you know. I'm going to have to hear about the time he met the Crimson Flash for the rest of my life."

Especially if Zach and Amelia fall in love and get married and have tons of babies. But I'm getting ahead of myself. They just have to like each other long enough to go to Homecoming. After that, they're free to go their separate ways.

I pick up the dead controller from the coffee table, looking it over now that Zach's gone.

"There's no way the battery's just dead," Riley says. "I'm pretty sure I heard you zap it. Once you knew you were going to lose, of course."

"Yeah, right. I was *so* winning. One more hit and you were done."

He shrugs. "If only the controller still worked, we could have a rematch. But now we'll never know."

"Or ..." I make waves of electricity flow across my right hand, holding the controller in my left.

"Are you crazy?" Riley whispers. "What if Zach comes back and sees you? Do you *want* someone to find out?"

I ignore him and make a big show of bringing my right index finger and the controller together, zapping it again. Nothing happens. At least, not at first. I start to say, "Well, it works on TV," when the light on the controller flickers back on.

I blink at it, then press the power button. The whole system starts up. "Wow. I can't believe that actually worked. But I guess now we can have that rematch."

Riley's staring at me. Really seriously. Like he not only can't believe that just happened, but he also just figured out the secret to the universe. "Forget the rematch, X."

"Why? Because you know you'll—" And then it dawns on me why he's staring at me like that.

Our eyes meet as we exchange a look of understanding, and then I toss the controller on the couch and we both hurry down the hall to his room.

X·X·X

Sarah's in the living room, in front of the TV, when Riley and me get to her house. She has it on the news and is scowling and shaking her head as the anchors talk about how there's been a surge of innocent people turning themselves in to the police today.

"Those idiots," Sarah grumbles, folding her arms and sinking down in the poofy easy chair she's sitting in.

"Hey, Sarah," I say. I'm holding the personality enhancer, which now at least lights up after I zapped it again. I'm assuming that means it works, though neither of us was exactly eager to be a test subject.

Sarah glances up at me, then at Riley, from her position in the chair, which looks like it's trying to swallow her whole. She grips the armrests and pulls herself out of it. "Can you believe this?" she says, waving her hand at the TV. "I was trying to get guilty people, *criminals*, to turn themselves in. And instead there are all these cases of good people taking themselves to the police because they forgot to pick up their kid from daycare or get the oil changed in their car."

"I guess they still qualify as 'guilty people,'" Riley says.

"What are you talking about?" I ask Sarah, pretending like I have no idea, since she still thinks I'm blissfully ignorant of her crazy exploits last night.

She sighs. "I put out some mind-control signals." She conveniently doesn't mention that she had to break into Wilson Enterprises to do it. Or that she abandoned Riley there to a bunch of killer robots. Though, to be fair, she might not have known about the robots part. But still. If anyone should be turning themselves in from feeling guilty today, it should be her. "They were supposed to get criminals to take themselves to the police because they actually felt remorse. But mostly it hasn't been bad guys. It's been people who feel overly guilty about normal mistakes. Some of them were even superheroes. And there haven't been *any* supervillains." Sarah peers over her glasses at me as she says that, giving me an accusing look. As if I'm personally responsible for this. "They apparently don't feel guilty for their crimes."

That or they know better than to buy computers from Wilson Enterprises. "How do you know who's committed crimes or not?"

She ignores me, wrinkling her eyebrows at us. She takes in the fact that we're both here and that I'm the one holding the personality enhancer, even though she gave it to Riley earlier. "Wait. Did you guys come here together?"

"Well," Riley says, "we sort of, um ..."

I sigh and flop down on the couch. "I hate to break this to you, Sarah, but Riley and I are in love and will be going to Homecoming together. So I hope you didn't already buy a dress."

Riley looks like he's going to die. "That's not—"

"Is that your way of saying you guys aren't squabbling anymore?" Sarah asks, grinning at us.

"Not ex— Er, well," Riley says, stopping himself from blowing this, "something like that. I guess."

"And we didn't even need this thing." I hold up the personality enhancer. Which, as far as Sarah knows, doesn't work.

"Well, I *did* already get a dress," Sarah says, still grinning. "So even though I know you don't have a date, Damien, you can't have mine."

"What? Yes, I do. I'm taking Kat." Assuming her parents don't figure out why she wants to come home so badly that weekend. Though I'm pretty sure they don't keep up with events at Heroesworth, so even if they'll know she's going somewhere with me that night—since apparently her *not* begging them to get to spend time with me is, understandably, highly suspicious—they probably won't suspect anything. Which is good, because I don't think they'd approve of her going to a dance at Heroesworth with me, even if her own school sent her there on that field mission last week. Which is also how I'm going to spin this if we get caught, telling them it was all in the name of homework.

Sarah narrows her eyes at me. "You can't bring her to the dance. She's a supervillain. She's not allowed at Heroesworth."

A supervillain who saved her boyfriend's ass last night, after she abandoned him. "No one will know."

"You'd jeopardize the safety of the entire school? A whole generation of heroes? For a *dance*?"

"Who said anything about jeopardizing anyone?"

"She goes to Vilmore. You can't knowingly sneak her into Heroesworth! It's—"

Riley clears his throat, interrupting her. "Hey, you said you got your dress?"

"Yeah," she says, taking a deep breath and seeming relieved to not have to deal with me, since I am apparently being impossible. "I showed it to you last week, remember?"

"I forgot what it looks like. Can you show it to me again?"

"Yeah, sure," she says, getting up from her chair. "And, Damien, you don't have to have a date to come to the dance. You can hang out with us. It'll be fun."

Um, right. Because going alone and having to watch them make out all night sounds so appealing. But I don't mention I'll still be going with Kat, because I have more

228

important things to worry about right now. Like shooting Sarah with the personality enhancer as soon as her back is turned.

"I'll think about it," I say, pretending to sound dejected, like she's actually convinced me I can't bring my girlfriend to Heroesworth. Kat being a supervillain is a minor detail, one no one has to know about, especially since she can shapeshift and make her thumb not have a *V*. She can even have an *H* if she wants. And what my fellow classmates don't know about her won't hurt them.

Sarah smiles at me and then turns to go to her room and get her dress. I hold up the personality enhancer, aiming it at her back.

Riley mouths, *Now*, not daring to actually say anything, in case she turns around.

I take a deep breath and pull the trigger.

The lights on the device flicker on. There's a flash as a bright beam shoots out from the end of the personality enhancer and hits Sarah in the shoulder. It makes contact just for a split second, and then the beam sputters and dies. The lights on the device go dim again. A little curl of smoke comes out the end.

Sarah turns around, rubbing her shoulder and frowning, like she's not sure what just happened.

I hide the personality enhancer behind my back, hoping I don't look too conspicuous.

For a moment, I think Sarah's going to put two and two together and call me on it, even though the device is supposedly broken. But then she seems to decide nothing happened after all and continues on to her room.

"*Voila,*" I say, holding up the device again and blowing the smoke from the end, like gunslingers do in old Western movies. "One Sarah, back to normal. Our work here is done."

But Riley's got this concerned look on his face, like he's not so sure about that. "It didn't look like it worked properly."

"Oh, yeah? And what is it supposed to look like?"

"I don't know, but probably not all flickery like that. And should it be smoking?" He takes the device from me and pulls the trigger again, aiming it at the wall. The lights don't come on and nothing happens. "See, it's broken again."

"Yeah, but only *after* I used it on her. The beam hit her."

"Just barely."

"But she obviously felt it. And," I add, pointing to the dial on the side of the device, "it was definitely on the 'better' setting this time."

"That's true," he admits, scratching the side of his head, "but *something* went wrong. What if you zapping it just powered it up again? What if it didn't actually *fix* it? Maybe it didn't make her better at all."

"I'm sure it's fine."

"But how do you know that it worked?"

Well, if he wants to get technical about it, I guess I don't. But now the device is definitely broken, and I don't think a jolt of electricity is going to bring it back to life this time. So it kind of has to have worked. "It did," I assure him. "We both saw it."

He opens his mouth, looking like he wants to argue with that, but then Sarah returns with a sparkly silver dress draped over one arm, and he doesn't say anything.

CHAPTER 19

Dinner Tuesday night is a disaster. A complete and total disaster.

For one thing, Zach, who was energetic and outgoing when we played video games last weekend, just sits there and says nothing. He occasionally looks up from his food to gape a little at Gordon, then quickly stares down at his plate. I even set it up so he's sitting next to Amelia, and he hardly looks at her.

And Amelia's not much better. She asks him some basic questions, like what school he goes to and if he's going to Heroesworth next year, and then gives up on him. Though that might have something to do with the fact that he mumbles the simplest answers possible and doesn't invite much conversation. But she doesn't have to glare at him when he accidentally bumps her elbow and makes her drop her forkful of mashed potatoes. Especially since she's the one who then spatters gravy on his sleeve and tries to wipe it off with her finger, succeeding only in rubbing it in. And she doesn't have to then completely ignore him and try to talk to Riley instead.

"So," she says to Riley, giving him a smug grin, "Damien said he redid his poster for Miss Monk's class, but he won't tell me how he did."

Riley looks kind of smug himself. "Well, actually—"

I punch him in the shoulder. Hard. "*Shut up*, Perkins."

"You redid your poster?" Gordon says, looking from me to Amelia, catching on that there's something he doesn't know. "How did it go?"

"We had to make posters in class," Amelia informs Zach in a really patronizing voice. "About what heroism means to us."

"I *know*," he tells his plate of roast beef.

I take a drink of water, glaring at Amelia. "We don't really want to talk about school at the dinner table, do we?"

Helen wipes a smear of mashed potatoes off of Jess's nose. "I'd like to hear it."

"Tell them," Riley says. "Since you put *so* much work into it."

Is it too late to uninvite him? Or to point and say, "Look over there!" and then electrocute him to death while everyone's head is turned?

"What did you do?" Alex asks. He's sitting on my other side, staring up at me with wide eyes and sort of kicking my chair with his foot. He's built a volcano with his mashed potatoes and smashes it with his fork—a little awkwardly, since his right arm is still in a cast and he has to use his left—releasing gravy-lava all over his plate.

"Well?" Gordon says.

Fine. But he asked for it. "It was blank. Because heroism is all around us and undefinable." I spread my hands out, indicating all the places heroism might be, and look up at the ceiling.

Riley snorts. "That's *not* what you said in class."

I grit my teeth, feeling sparks race up my spine. "It's pretty close."

"No, it's not."

"Damien?" Helen raises her eyebrows at me.

I fold my arms and lean back in my chair, ignoring the way Amelia's smirking and eating all this up. "I *might* have said that heroism is just a word. And that it doesn't mean anything. But," I add, when Gordon's jaw drops and his fork clatters against his plate, "I only said that because everyone at that school thinks they're better than me." Well, mostly because of that. Partly because I meant it. "You should have seen how pissed they looked after my presentation."

Helen groans. "Was that really worth it?" She makes it sound like my presentation wasn't a rousing success, as if everyone getting angry over it was a bad thing and not completely the point. "What grade did you get?"

"Grades aren't important." I didn't have grades for sixteen years while Mom was homeschooling me, and I'm still here, aren't I?

Alex whispers, "Whoa," very quietly, like he'd never thought of that before. Or like he can't believe I'd say something so outrageous, even though he's known me for over six months now.

Helen's jaw tightens as she looks from me to Gordon, like she wants to know what he's going to do about this.

"Is that why you failed your history test, too?" Amelia asks. "Because grades *aren't* important?"

Damn it.

"You what?" Gordon says. "Damien, if you need help with—"

I wave away his concern. "The teacher's the one who needs help. I was just making a point." And forging Gordon's signature on the test I had to get signed.

Amelia shakes her head. "He failed *on purpose*, he means."

An angry crease forms across Gordon's forehead. "You did *what*?"

I hold up a hand, signaling I'm not listening, and address Zach instead. After all, getting him and Amelia together is what we're here for—even if no one else knows it—not interrogating innocent half villains. "So, Zach, what's your favorite episode of *The Crimson Flash and the Safety Kids*?" Amelia won't be able to resist a guy who likes her favorite show. Especially since bragging about being related to the Crimson Flash is a hobby of hers, one she's very passionate about.

"*Damien*," Gordon growls. As if we don't have guests over.

"Hopeless," Amelia says, shaking her head. She glances at Riley to see if he agrees with her, then, as an afterthought, at Zach, who isn't paying attention.

Zach looks up at me, then at Gordon, his mouth falling

open. He looks like a lost fish. "I, uh ... The one with the cows. No, the one at the film studio!"

Gordon smiles, despite still being mad at me. "That was the same studio we film the show in. It's kind of fun to see it from the other side."

"No, wait! I think my favorite is the one where you go to the, um ..." He sucks in a deep breath, clutching his forehead like his brain is about to explode. Like this is some sudden death question and he'll have to leave if he gets it wrong. "The, um ... space museum! Wait, no, I meant ... I think I meant a different one."

"Well," Amelia says, as if anyone asked her, "I don't have a favorite. I like them *all*."

I lean toward Riley and whisper, "What the hell is wrong with your brother?"

"What?" He glances over at Zach, who's rubbing his forehead and looking like he's going to have a heart attack if he doesn't think of the perfect answer in the next five seconds. "Oh. That's how he gets when he's nervous."

Nervous. Great. Nervous isn't going to get Amelia to Homecoming.

"You know," Gordon says, "I think my favorite is the one about the studio. But I also really enjoyed filming the one where we visited the space museum."

Zach swallows and nods, his whole face turning red.

Amelia scowls at him, like it's his fault Gordon didn't tell her how awesome she is for liking every single episode of his show equally.

"You know, Amelia," I say, "if you hadn't applied for early admittance to Heroesworth, and if you'd gone to a high school for heroes instead of a regular one, you and Zach would have been in the same grade and gone to the same school. You guys would have, like, known each other. How weird is that?"

Amelia scoffs, giving Zach a withering look, like she really doubts she'd have had anything to do with him. For someone so desperate to have a boy actually like her, you'd think she'd be less of a bitch. "My birthday's in five weeks," she tells him. "When's yours?"

"May," he croaks, hardly getting the word out.

"Do you even have your power yet?"

He doesn't answer, too busy trying to clear his throat. He reaches for his glass of water, but his hand's shaking so bad that he just ends up knocking it over, dumping ice water into Amelia's lap.

She jumps up, screaming and holding her hands above her head, as if that will help anything. Her nostrils flare as she takes deep breaths and generally acts way more dramatic than necessary.

"Sorry," Zach manages to mumble.

"It's *fine*," she snaps.

Helen starts to get up from the table. "Let me get you something to clean that up with."

"No. I'll get it. I *do* have my power." She says that last part very obviously for Zach's benefit, in case he wasn't clear on the fact that she thinks he's beneath her. She holds her hand palm up, closing her eyes and making a big deal about using her ability.

Then Zach's shirt appears in her hand.

At first I think she did it on purpose, because she's

actually *that* mean, but when she opens her eyes, shock and horror spread across her face as she realizes what she's holding. She looks down at Zach, her face going completely red as she openly gapes at his naked torso.

Zach looks just as mortified, closes his eyes, and says in a squeaky voice, "Can I have my shirt back?" It's the most he's spoken to her all night.

Amelia tosses his shirt at him and runs from the table.

Zach turns invisible. Kind of too little too late, I think, though I guess it means he has his power after all.

X·X·X

"I don't suppose you know any available guys?" I ask Kat on the phone later. I'm up in my room, sitting on my bed, long after the brothers Perkins have fled the house in shame. Well, Zach may have fled in shame. Riley seemed somewhat amused and said we'd have to do it again sometime. Though I'm pretty sure he was joking, especially since he said it in front of Zach, who, I'm fairly certain, will never step foot inside our house again. "Preferably someone under sixteen with no *V* on their thumb, since my stepmother would freak out. Though, at this point, I'll admit I'm not too picky."

"I know how you like them young," Kat says.

"I like being *alive*. So, do you know anyone or not? What about Julie's brother?" Not that Helen wouldn't flip the hell out if I set Amelia up with Kat's cousin, but it would only be for one night. Plus, they're from her mom's side of the family, so they're not even related to Helen's nemesis. I mean, they're still supervillains and everything, but setting Amelia up with him wouldn't make me *completely* a bad influence.

"Will? He has a girlfriend now. Plus, I wouldn't subject him to your sister. He's kind of shy, and she's kind of ..."

"A total bitch?" I sigh. Maybe Sarah knows someone. Well, someone other than Zach, that is. "I hope you didn't have your heart set on me being around for very much longer or anything. Because if I don't find someone for Amelia before Homecoming this weekend, she's going to spill my secret and Gordon is going to kill me. Also," I add, reading from the quiz in *Spandex* that I stole from Amelia, "when you go to the movies with your guy friend, does he *a*, offer to buy your ticket, *b*, share his popcorn, or *c*, flirt with other girls the whole time?"

"Your dad won't actually kill you, will he? I mean, it's not your fault you got that lightning power. And definitely *b*."

"You're right—if you think about it, it's actually *his* fault. If he didn't want a kid with lightning power, he shouldn't have slept with my mom. And what do you mean, *b*? Who have you been sharing popcorn with?" I tap my pen against the shiny magazine pages, not marking that one down.

"It was the midnight premiere showing of *Pirate Zombies from Hell*. You *know* how much I wanted to see that one, and everyone was going. And what kind of quiz is this?"

"Uh, not everyone, Kat," I say, ignoring her last question, "because I don't remember being there. We were supposed to see that one together. I can't believe you went without me."

"I didn't know when we'd get a chance to, and I didn't want to miss it. Plus, it was fun."

Fun? Without me? I find that very hard to believe. "And the popcorn?"

"Jordan got too much, so he offered to share it with me."

So he'd have an excuse to sit next to her, she means.

"*And*," she goes on, "before you say anything about how he just said that so he'd have a reason to sit by me or something, you should know that he's gay."

"Why, Kat, I would *never* say something like that. You make it sound as if I think every guy out there is trying to get somewhere with you." Which they are. Well, except for Jordan, apparently. "Though, while we're on the subject, are you sure you don't know anyone desperate enough for your attention that they would, say, take your boyfriend's superhero half sister to a dance at Heroesworth? As a personal favor for you?"

"Why don't you just tell your dad about your lightning power? Then she won't have anything on you. And don't you think he'll take it better, coming from you?"

"You know I can't do that. He's actually sort of proud of me right now, going to Heroesworth and trying to get my *H* and everything." And supposedly trying out for the flying team, though that's one area where he will just have to be disappointed. "And if he knew I had a villain power, especially such a destructive one, he'd think I'm dangerous."

"You *are* dangerous. I saw what you did to the wall. And to those robots."

"Yeah, okay, but I don't want *him* to think that. Plus ... if he finds out, he might think that even if I do get my *H*, I'm never really going to be a hero." Just like how villains would never see me as the real thing because I can fly. Though I guess now that I can shoot lightning from my hands, I could probably fake it, except for the whole *X* on my thumb thing. "And he's the Crimson Flash. He's been voted Most Beloved Superhero or whatever. They made a documentary about him. A stupid one, but still. There's a reason I wasn't in it. He *can't* have a son with lightning powers."

"But, Damien, he already does."

"But he doesn't know it, and neither does anyone else, and I'd like to keep it that way." He's ashamed enough of me as it is. I don't need to give him one more reason. Plus, I know how he'd look at me if he knew. Like I was some sort of criminal. Like I didn't belong in this family or at Heroesworth. And, okay, maybe saying I "belong" at Heroesworth is pushing it, but I don't want him to think I shouldn't be there.

"And when someone finds out?" Kat says.

"No one's going to find out. At least, not as long as I find someone to go to Homecoming with Amelia. Which, I admit, is going to be difficult, especially after tonight. I mean, I brought her a perfectly good candidate, and do you know what she did?"

"Didn't have the same taste in guys as you?"

"She stole his shirt. With her power. Like, right off his

back. And that was after being a bitch to him the whole night."

Kat laughs.

"Laugh all you want, but you're the one who's going to have to find some way to go on living without me once I'm dead. It's not going to be easy."

"Are you sure it went that badly? Because I'm not hearing anything that means she didn't like him."

"Just because the night ended with her half undressing him does *not* make it a success. As I've heard her say very loudly through the walls several times while on the phone with her friends, tonight was the most embarrassing night of her life."

"So, what you're saying is she cares what he thinks. And that she stole some of his clothes and told all her friends about it." Kat waits for that to sink in.

"I don't know. You weren't there. It was a—"

A knock on the door interrupts me, followed by Amelia's voice saying, "Damien?"

"Hold on," I tell Kat, sighing and getting up to answer it.

"Do you have my magazine?" Amelia says when I open the door.

"*No.*"

"Isn't that it, on your bed?" She holds out her hand and calls it to her. She looks it over, seeing that I've partially filled out the quiz, and raises her eyebrows. "You want to know if your guy friends *like* you?"

"No, I already know they do. The quiz just confirms it. And you could have just taken that back without coming over here."

"But then I wouldn't know that you *stole* it. And also, I need to talk to you." She stands there, biting her lip, not saying anything.

"Well?"

"It's private."

I gesture to the fact that there's no one else here.

She glances over at the stairs, like she's afraid someone might be listening below. Which I highly doubt. "Can't I just come in? It's about what you *owe* me."

I'm pretty sure what I "owe" her at this point is a pair of cement shoes and a drop off the Golden City Bridge. But I move aside and let her in anyway. "Fine, let's get this over with. And don't touch my pillow." I close the door and grab my phone, telling Kat I'll have to call her back.

Amelia sits on the edge of my bed. She rolls up her magazine and then unrolls it again. She plays with the corner of the cover, bending it back and forth.

I fold my arms and glare at her. "It's funny you should want to talk to me, because I want to talk to you, too. Just because I 'owe' you doesn't mean you can be a bitch to my guests."

Her mouth drops open. "I—" Her face goes red and she makes a grab for my pillow, either forgetting or not caring that I told her not to.

I snatch it off the bed before she can get her hands on it.

She uses her power and makes it appear in her arms anyway, clutching it to her chest.

"Seriously? You couldn't, like, call up your own

bedding to ruin?"

She ignores me. "I didn't mean to be a—" She swallows, not finishing that thought. "Zach didn't even talk to me. He's the one who was rude."

Uh, right. Blame the kid who was too terrified to look up from his dinner all night. "Being quiet isn't a criminal offense." A lesson she could stand to learn. "You're the one who kept putting him down."

"I was nervous," she says.

"*Mean* I think is the word you're looking for."

"I just wanted him to … you know."

"What? To know you think you're better than him? I think you established that."

"I just wanted him to notice me." She stares at the floor.

"Is that why you stole his shirt?"

She lets out a squeak and then flops backward onto my bed, holding my pillow over her eyes. "That was an *accident*. I didn't mean to do it. And now he probably hates me."

I grab my pillow again, not letting her hide under it, and make her look at me. "He probably thinks that *you* hate *him*."

"But I don't." She sighs and sits back up. "That's what I wanted to talk to you about. I changed my mind. About what you owe me."

"Oh, no. That's not how it works. You made it perfectly clear what you want. So, unless you're telling me I'm off the hook"—which I wouldn't trust anyway—"then we have nothing to talk about."

"I want Zach." As soon as she says it, she must realize what it sounds like, because then her cheeks go red. "I mean, I want to go to Homecoming with him."

I raise an eyebrow at her. "Why? So you can drop a bunch of pig's blood on him?"

"I like him. He's cute, like his—"

"Don't say it."

"—brother. Do you think he's already going with someone?"

"Well, I don't know." I study the back of my hand, like I have better things to think about than whether or not the guy I was trying to set her up with is available. "I don't think so, but I don't see what it would matter to you." Unless of course Kat was right and my mission tonight wasn't as big of a disaster as I thought. Which is what it's starting to sound like.

"Because. I just told you. I *like* him. And you have to get me a date to Homecoming, and I want to go with Zach. So you have to make that happen."

"No. You said a warm body. You said *anyone*." Not that there is anyone else, but I'm not telling her that. And even if she's decided she likes Zach, she still has to be the one to ask him. I haven't come this far just to be thwarted. Plus, does she really think it will work out between them if she makes me ask him for her? Especially after how she treated him tonight.

"I changed my mind."

"That wasn't the deal. And anyway, Zach is my friend." Sort of. "And you can't date my friends." What was that Kat's dad said about how forbidding her to see me would only make her want me more?

"He's not your friend. He's your friend's *brother*. You're not even in the same grade. And you can't tell me who I can go out with. It's not like you've asked anybody else, right?"

"I'll find someone. There's got to be somebody else out there who isn't busy Saturday night."

"But—"

"Anyone but Zach. After the way you acted tonight? He'd probably think I was joking or setting him up for something. I'm not doing that to him."

"Well, maybe if you brought him over again, I could apologize, and—"

"And what? I told you, I'm not asking him out for you. You can't take Zach to Homecoming, Amelia, and that's final."

CHAPTER 20

I throw a stick for Heraldo in the park on Wednesday afternoon. He watches it sail off and land a ways away, but doesn't chase it. Not until he looks up at Sarah and she says, "Go get it, boy!" Only then does he go bounding after it.

Slighted by a dog. Go figure. "So," I say to Sarah, "you're, um, feeling better now, right?"

She wrinkles her eyebrows. "Better than what?"

"Than before. I mean, since Sunday." Since I secretly shot her with her personality enhancer.

"What happened on Sunday? You mean since you and Riley are friends now?" She smiles at that. It's an "I told you so" smile.

I cringe inwardly and roll my eyes at her. "Let's not put a label on it." The Invisible Douche and I are *not* friends, but if it makes Sarah happy to think that, I won't correct her.

Heraldo comes running back. He shoves the stick—which is now covered in drool—at Sarah, even though I'm the one who threw it for him. She takes it and throws it again, wiping dog slobber off her hand on the side of her jeans.

"And," I add, "that's not what I meant."

She frowns, considering that. "I don't know what else you would mean."

I shrug. "Just ... Do you feel different? Since Sunday?"

"Well, now that you mention it, I— Heraldo!" She claps her hands with a loud *smack* to get his attention.

Heraldo stops chasing the unfortunate jogger he decided should now throw the stick for him and comes slinking back. Not that he does a very good job of slinking, being a Great Dane and all, but he is definitely cowed after Sarah's scolding.

"Sit," she says, and he sits. Right on my foot. "And I guess I have felt kind of ... I don't know. Better than I have in a while."

See? Riley can shove it, because I was right. The personality enhancer worked, thanks to the little jolt I gave it. And no one ever got to use it on me. Which they might have if I hadn't accidentally broken it in the first place. So, all in all, a successful blundering. "That's great, Sarah," I say, extricating my foot out from under Heraldo. Who is not the world's lightest dog, that's for sure. "And you're not still, um, mad about your mind-control signals not working?" Which have since been fixed, thanks to an anonymous tip Kat called in.

She laughs. "No. I don't know what I was thinking."

I breathe a sigh of relief and feel my shoulders relax. *Not* that I didn't think she was better. But it's kind of reassuring to hear her sounding like her old self again. "Let's just forget it ever happened." Especially since it was sort of my fault.

"Right." She hooks the leash onto Heraldo's collar and starts walking. "So, are you coming with us on Saturday?"

"*With you?* No. But I will be there." And, if everything goes according to plan, Amelia and Zach will be there, too. Though I guess if things don't go according to plan, I won't be anywhere, but whatever. "In my best swimming trunks."

Sarah makes a face and gapes at me, as if I was already wearing them. "You're going to *what*? Damien, don't you know Homecoming is supposed to be formal?"

"Of course I know. I'm not an idiot." It's also almost October. Do I really think even Heroesworth would be stupid enough to hold a beach-themed dance when it's practically freezing out? Besides, if it was a beach theme, I'd show up in a parka. She should know that.

"You'll look ridiculous if you arrive in just your underwear."

"Underwear? Who said anything about underwear?" An orangey-red leaf flutters down from one of the trees as we walk by, and I snatch it out of the air. I spin the stem back and forth between my fingers, watching the leaf twirl. "Swimming trunks are an acceptable form of being dressed."

"Right, and wearing a bikini *isn't* like wearing lingerie." She rolls her eyes. "Swimming clothes might as well be

249

underwear. Everyone's going to be staring at you all night."

I grin. "You think—" I stop myself from saying, "You think Mr. Perfect will be jealous?" since that's probably not something I would say if I was friends with him. Well, actually, it probably *is* something I would say, but I suspect Sarah might not see it that way and take it as a sign of us not getting along. So instead I tell her, "That's kind of the point."

"Don't you want to look nice?"

"Oh, Sarah. I am going to look *very* nice." I decide I'm done with the leaf, but I don't want to just abandon it, so I tuck it behind her ear. "That's a present," I tell her. "You can't ever get rid of it or my feelings will be hurt."

She half snorts, half laughs as she reaches up to touch it. "You're going to look stupid, is what you mean. You're supposed to get dressed up. Even if you don't have a date."

Heraldo sees a squirrel and suddenly tugs on the leash, jerking Sarah's arm as he lunges toward it. Sarah scolds him, and he reluctantly lets it go.

"First of all," I tell her, once Heraldo is behaving again, "I will not look stupid." Or, if I do, it will be a carefully calculated amount of stupid, which will quickly be overshadowed by how bad-ass I'll be for being the only guy there brave enough to show up in little more than his underwear. "Second, I will be getting plenty dressed up next weekend for the Homecoming dance at Vilmore." Since Kat's dad will be there and Kat has to dress appropriately. And because her dad already thinks I'm not good enough for her, and also because this is her first chance to show off her amazing boyfriend from out of town to all her new friends and delusional would-be suitors. "And, third, I *will* have a date, because I'm bringing Kat. Who will also be in a swimsuit, so I won't be the only one."

Sarah stops walking, startling Heraldo when he gets to the end of his leash. She scowls at me. "You really think that's a good idea?"

"No, I'm pretty sure I won't like the kind of stares she gets"—and will spend the whole night trying not to fry everyone with my electricity—"but it will be worth it, since we'll definitely be the most interesting couple there. No offense."

"That's *not* what I meant. I already told you, you can't bring a supervillain to Heroesworth."

"Yeah, but that's when you were—" I don't finish that sentence, since Sarah doesn't need to know she was messed up, due to me accidentally changing her personality. "It won't hurt anybody." Well, except for anyone who gets mad because their date is staring at either of us a little too hard. But that's not exactly my problem.

Sarah bites her lip. She looks up into my eyes, studying me, searching for something. "You don't see anything wrong with that? You don't feel ... guilty?"

"She's my girlfriend. I can bring her to a school dance if I want to." I stick my hands in the pockets of my sweatshirt and look down at my feet, not liking the way Sarah's staring at me.

"And you're not worried about going to Vilmore?

251

You're half superhero. What if everyone finds out?" She puts a hand on my arm, she's so concerned about this, like any of it is actually a big deal.

"Geez, Sarah, What do you think's going to happen? You think I can't cut it at Vilmore for even one night?"

"They're supervillains. If they find out, who knows what they'll do."

"What, you think they're going to beat me up or something?"

"Or worse."

I laugh. And she thinks *I'm* the ridiculous one? "You think I can't handle them?"

"Not all of them, not all at once. And they won't feel bad about hurting you. That's what my mind-control experiment taught me. I was a fool to think I could catch any of them with it, because supervillains don't feel guilty for their crimes. They're *sociopaths*."

"*What?*" I jerk my arm away from her, taking a step back. "You don't mean that, Sarah."

"Yes, I do. You just can't see it because you're ..." She trails off and suddenly gets real interested in watching the leaves fall.

"Whoa. You did *not* just say that." Well, technically she didn't, but we both know what she was going to say. That I can't see that all supervillains are sociopaths because I *am* one.

She swallows, still not looking at me. "You're half villain. You were raised as one. It's only natural that your judgment would be clouded on this."

I scowl at her. "My judgment's not the one being

clouded here. You're the one who's talking like you were when you ..."

"When I what?"

When she was under the influence of the personality enhancer, on the "worse" setting. An uneasy feeling settles in my stomach. "Being a supervillain doesn't make someone a sociopath. You know that."

She shakes her head. "Supervillains were the only ones not affected by my mind-control signals. Superheroes turned themselves in for stupid, everyday stuff, but supervillains who'd committed real crimes didn't do *anything*."

"You don't know who heard those messages or not. Plus, you've committed crimes, and you don't feel guilty for them."

"I only committed crimes because I *had* to. To catch bad guys. It was for a good cause. And I know your mom almost took over the city last year, and she didn't feel bad about it, did she? She killed your best friend—"

"*Ex*-best friend. And only to save my life."

"—and didn't care. She was going to enslave all the superheroes, and that seemed like a good idea to her." Sarah tilts her head and puts a hand on her hip.

"She had her reasons." Selfish reasons, but not insane ones. "And you don't know she didn't care about what she did to Pete. What she *had* to do."

"You mean she had to kill him because he was a villain and a sociopath? One who would have killed you and me and Kat without even a second thought? And you don't know how she felt about it, either, because you haven't

253

talked to her. Because her crimes were so terrible, you never wanted to speak to her again. I can't believe you're attempting to defend her."

"She might have made mistakes, but she's not a psychopath."

"*Sociopath*. All villains have at least some sociopathic tendencies. I made a chart. I can show you later. And even without the chart, you have to admit that it's true. After all, you've done plenty of things you should feel guilty for, and yet you don't. And you're only half villain. I'm kind of worried about you."

I glare at her. "Same goes for you."

"I was hoping your superhero side would be enough to counteract it. But the fact that you don't think there's anything wrong with bringing a supervillain to Heroesworth and endangering hundreds of lives is just proof that it isn't."

"God, Sarah. You *know* Kat's not dangerous!" Electricity races up my spine and crackles in my palms, reminding me that *I'm* the dangerous one, and I clench my fists. The last thing I need is for Sarah to find out I have a villain power, now that she thinks all villains are criminally insane. And, okay, maybe Riley was right. Maybe shooting her with the personality enhancer last weekend didn't work. Or at least I hope it didn't, because even if I have no idea how to fix her now that the device is broken again, I don't want to believe this is really *her*. The real Sarah might have a tendency to judge bad guys too harshly, but she doesn't think all supervillains are evil. Or insane. Or whatever it is she's saying they are.

And she certainly doesn't think *I* am.

Sarah gives me a pitying look. Like it's so sad I can't see the truth. "She's going to Vilmore. Where they learn how to kill superheroes."

"Now, wait, that's not—"

"You can't trust her anymore. How do you know her going to Homecoming with you isn't just some recon mission? How do you know she's not going to go back to school on Monday and report everything she saw? And knowing you, you'd probably *give her* information."

"No, I wouldn't." Just directions to the records office. That's all. And Sarah doesn't even know about that.

"You would. Because she's got you wrapped around her finger. And because, at the end of the day, you identify more with supervillains than with superheroes." She shrugs.

"That's not—" Okay, maybe that's a little true. "So what if I do? You can't expect sixteen years of being a supervillain to just go away overnight."

She sighs. "No, I can't. Which is why you probably shouldn't even be going to Heroesworth. It's obvious you can't be trusted."

"Come on, Sarah. You trust me with your life." And I trust her with mine. Or at least I did, before I screwed her up. "You're not serious."

"If you think you belong at Heroesworth, then prove it. Come to the dance Saturday night and hang out with us. *Without* Kat."

"Yeah, sure, and why don't you leave Mr. Perfect at home, too."

She narrows her eyes at me. "I'm warning you, Damien. *Don't* bring her."

"You can't tell me what to do."

"You're half hero and half villain. You have to make a choice." She takes the leaf I gave her out of her hair and holds it in her palm, like she's considering crushing it. "And if you bring her to the dance, then I'll *know* what side you're on."

X·X·X

I open the front door Thursday afternoon to see Zach, who I invited, and Riley, who I did not.

"Hello, Zach," I say, purposely ignoring Riley. "Why don't you come in?"

He glances around warily, probably making sure Amelia isn't lurking anywhere, waiting to strike. She's up in her room, but he doesn't know that, and otherwise we're the only ones home. When he sees that it's safe, he takes a deep breath and steps inside. Riley tries to follow him, but I put up a hand to block him.

"What are you doing here, Perkins? I distinctly remember messaging Zach, not you."

"Ah, but we're *such good friends*, X, that I assumed the invitation was for both of us. Besides, he didn't want to come here alone after what happened last time. And I don't blame him." He goes invisible and sidesteps me, then reappears again.

"Fine, I suppose you can come in." But only because I need Zach here. And to not freak out or run away

256

screaming when he finds out Amelia's home.

"So, what am I beating you at today?" Zach says. "I mean," he adds, grinning, "what are we playing?"

I turn on the TV and grab the controllers, tossing one to Zach. I turn on the system and put in the best game I have, which is a fighting game simply but appropriately titled *Villains vs. Heroes*. Alex is the only one who will play it with me—well, besides Kat, who isn't allowed in the house—and Gordon and Helen don't exactly look favorably on it. Even though it's just a game and you can pick any characters you want—you don't have to have heroes and villains fighting each other. But they don't really have anything to worry about, anyway, because Alex always gets distracted with making his character fly all over and do crazy jumps—he *always* picks the superhero who can fly—and doesn't actually care about the fighting part. Which means, realistically, that I don't have *anyone* to play it with.

Riley shakes his head at me as the game starts up. "*Heroes vs. Villains*? Let me guess—you're playing a villain?"

"It doesn't matter which character I play—I'll still kick your ass." I grab the remote and turn up the volume on the TV until it's annoyingly loud. Just loud enough that it will attract the attention of the noise police upstairs.

"Does it have to be so loud?" Riley says, slumping down on the couch next to me.

"Yes, to drown out your whining."

Zach smirks at that and starts flipping through the characters, trying to decide who he's going to be.

I automatically select the villain with lightning power —the one I always play, or at least that I *used* to—and then think better of it and hit cancel.

"Great choice," Riley mutters, though it's hard to hear him over the blaring TV.

Zach picks a bad-ass-looking superhero girl with freeze breath. He notices I'm having a hard time choosing and says, "You can fly, right? You should pick the guy who can do that."

"He can't actually fly," Riley says.

"Shut up, Perkins. You don't know what you're talking about."

"I thought Sarah said you could fly," Zach says to me. "What other power would you have?"

Riley folds his arms and sinks back into the couch, looking real smug. "Yeah, what other power would you have?"

"Flying power is lame," I say. Even if it maybe comes in handy sometimes, like when people throw me off of buildings. I end up picking the supervillain guy with laser eyes, because I know all his moves, and try to ignore the fact that it reminds me of my mom.

"Freeze breath vs. laser eyes," Zach says. "I like it."

"Flying isn't lame," Riley corrects me. Like he's the superpower police. He's as bad as Amelia. "You're just saying that because you don't actually have it."

"Like I said before, I don't have to prove anything to you." The fight starts up and our characters appear in the middle of a tall building under construction. A place where flying power might actually be useful, though I regret nothing.

Zach immediately shoots me with freeze breath and then spin kicks me and jumps away. I recover from being frozen and laser him. Besides the game music, which is kind of blaring, there are a lot of sound effects from us kicking and punching and shooting our superpowers at each other. So I'm not surprised that the fight isn't even halfway over before I hear Amelia's door open and then her angry, tromping footsteps on the stairs.

"You'd *better* turn that down," Amelia shouts, coming into the living room, "or I'll—" She stops short, noticing I have guests over. Well, noticing I have one guest over in particular.

Zach glances nervously at her, looking away from the screen and giving me a chance to push him off the edge of the building. Something I would *never* do in real life.

"Go away, Amelia," I tell her. "Can't you see we're busy?"

She makes a *hmph* noise and picks up the remote from the coffee table and turns the TV down. "I can be here if I want. You don't own the living room."

"Yeah, well, it's not up to me. *Zach* doesn't want you here."

Zach gasps, looking over at me like he can't believe I just spoke for him, then sort of ducks his head and hunches his shoulders.

Amelia's mouth hangs open, mortified that it might be true.

"Right, Zach?" I say, kicking his character as he climbs back up the building. "You want her to leave, don't you?"

"Well, um ..." He glances over at her guiltily, then at the screen.

"See, Amelia? He doesn't want you here. He's just too polite to say it."

"That's not ... I mean, I don't ..." He swallows and clears his throat. "She can stay."

Amelia gets this really pleased look on her face. She sits down in an easy chair and watches the game, her chin in her hands. Then she scoffs at me. "Laser eyes, Damien? Isn't that your *mom's* power?"

"Shut up, Amelia. He said you could stay. He didn't say you could talk." I use my laser eyes at the same time as Zach uses his freeze breath, and our two powers collide and we end up in a button-mashing duel to see whose power actually overtakes the other. I win, but my victory is short-lived, since Zach manages to duck and roll away, avoiding my lasers.

"I told him he should pick flying," Zach says, his eyes darting over to Amelia, then back to the fight.

"Yeah, right," she says, actually trying to sound friendly for once. Something I wasn't sure she was even capable of. "He *hates* flying. He's probably too scared to do it, even in a game."

I grit my teeth, trying really hard not to zap the controller. Or Amelia. Even if she kind of deserves it for not keeping her stupid mouth shut.

Riley sits up, suddenly interested. "Wait, you mean he actually *can* fly?"

"Yes," Amelia says, basking in the fact that somebody actually cares what she's saying for once. "But not very well. It's wasted on him, really."

Geez. I set her up with the guy she likes to help her self-esteem, without her knowing it, and *this* is the thanks I get? "You want to talk about superpowers? Stolen anyone's shirt today, Amelia?"

Her face goes completely red. So does Zach's.

That's what I thought.

"That was an accident," she says quietly. "I didn't mean to do it."

Zach nods, not looking at her.

I lean forward and get a couple more hits on him before he finally takes me out and the fight is over.

"That's right!" he says, forgetting about being shy in light of his victory. He drops his controller and throws his hands up. "First time playing, and I totally beat you!"

"I'm out of practice." Which is true.

"He was still better than you," Amelia says.

Zach looks over at her, his eyes a little wide, probably not expecting her to compliment him. Then he gets over his shock and grins. "What can I say? I'm a natural."

"You're a natural *ham*," Riley says. He rolls his eyes at Zach and holds out his hand for my controller.

But before I can give it to him, Amelia asks, "Can I play?"

"Uh, no," I tell her. "You hate this game. You refused to play it before, remember?"

"Well, maybe I just didn't want to play it with *you*."

"Besides, it's Riley's turn and he's not going to just let you have it."

"Well," Riley says, "I can go next. It's not a big deal."

"Cutting in line isn't a big deal? Right. I'll remember that at lunch tomorrow." He always gets there way earlier than me, though that may have something to do with my third-period class being on the second floor and the cafeteria being at ground level. "And anyway, Amelia, you don't know how to play. Someone would have to teach you, and I'm not doing it."

"It's not that hard," Zach says.

"For you, maybe. I mean, maybe it wouldn't take *you* that long to show her how to play, but you're my guest, and she shouldn't be bothering you with things like that."

"Well, it's not ..." He looks up at Amelia, meeting her eyes, then stares down at his knees. "It wouldn't be bothering me. And you're right, it probably wouldn't take me very long to teach her, and then we could all play."

"Seriously?" I give him a skeptical look, then shrug. "*I* wouldn't have the patience for it, but if you really don't mind—"

"He doesn't," Amelia snaps, grabbing the controller out of Riley's hand. "You just don't want him to teach me because then you know I'll beat you."

"Unlikely," I say, sighing and pretending to sound annoyed. Which I will be if he actually does teach her how to beat me, though I doubt that will happen within the next million years. I get up, giving Amelia my seat so Zach can show her what all the buttons do, and then tell Riley I need to talk to him.

He's kind of smirking as he follows me into the kitchen. "What?"

He leans against the counter. "Nothing. Just picturing

you flying."

"Well, don't, or I might picture you with another broken finger."

"Can you *really* fly? You have two powers? Because I want to see it, if it's true."

"You're not going to see it, so I guess that means it isn't. And we have more important things to discuss, like the fact that Sarah's still screwed up."

He scrunches his eyebrows. "What do you mean? And you're not getting out of it that easily. You think you can just bring up Sarah and I'll forget about the flying thing?"

"There is no flying thing. Amelia's a liar. You shouldn't believe a word she says. And yes, I do think that, because I'm trying to tell you that you were right. When you said the device didn't work. She's definitely not better." If anything, she might be *worse*.

"Why? What happened?" Now he looks worried. "Did she go on another crazy mission?"

"Well, no. Not that I know of."

"Okay. So, what did she do?"

"It's not so much what she did as what she said. We were talking about the dance on Saturday, and I was telling her how I'm going to wear swimming trunks, and she—"

"You're going to wear *what*?" His mouth twitches, like he can't decide if he should laugh or frown.

"That part's not important."

"Yeah, but swimming trunks? That's it?"

"Yes."

"I'm going to be wearing a tux, and you're just wearing

shorts?"

I glare at him. "You're missing the point. Which is that *after* I said that, I mentioned I was still bringing Kat, and she said it wasn't a good idea."

Riley scratches his ear. "Well ... I kind of have to agree with her. *Not* that I'm not grateful for you and Kat saving me or anything, and not that I think she'd do anything bad. But you're not supposed to bring supervillains into Heroesworth. What if people find out?"

"They're not going to. She can shapeshift and have an *H* on her thumb." And show me up. Whatever. "So, problem solved. Nobody will know the difference."

"Okay ..." he says, not sounding at all convinced. "But if they did, you'd be in serious trouble. You know that, right?"

"They *won't*. And Sarah is the one in trouble here, not me. She said I couldn't bring Kat, like she has any say in it, and then she said all supervillains are sociopaths."

Riley sighs, taking that in. "That is kind of extreme."

"And offensive. She even said *I* had sociopathic tendencies and that I didn't feel guilty enough for all the bad things I've done."

"Well, do you?"

"Will you stay on track here, Perkins?! We're talking about Sarah, not me. And you know how much I hate admitting you're right, or at least you can imagine it, since it's never happened before, so you know I wouldn't be saying this if it wasn't true. The device didn't work, and Sarah's not back to normal."

"Based on the fact that she doesn't think you should

wear your bathing suit to Homecoming? Or bring your supervillain girlfriend to Heroesworth?"

"No, just the second one. And that she thinks all villains are sociopaths, which they're not."

"I don't know. Is that really proof that she's not okay?"

"You're the one who thought she wasn't. You're the one who said it didn't work, and now you're arguing that she's fine?"

"I didn't say that. I *am* still worried that the device didn't work. I'm just not sure that what you're saying confirms it."

"So, what, you agree that all supervillains are sociopaths? Because *you know* that's not true."

He holds up his hands. "I'm not saying that. But let's not jump to conclusions. Let's just wait and see."

"Yeah, that sounds like a brilliant plan."

He glares at me. "You don't know that anything's really wrong. So she has an opinion about supervillains—so does *everybody else*. And we're not messing with her personality until we know for sure we need to. Not that I know what we'll do, since the device is broken, but we'll figure it out. But *not* until we know for sure. That cool with you, X? Or do you want to screw her up even more than you already have?"

Electricity sparks at my fingertips, but I take a deep breath and hold it back. "Fine," I tell him. "We won't jump to any conclusions. But I'm telling you, Perkins, something's not right."

"Yeah, well," he says, not looking at all happy about this, "let's just hope you're wrong."

CHAPTER 21

I wear dark-blue swimming trunks with white stripes down the sides on Saturday night. Kat wears a shimmery light-green one-piece with big pink and yellow polka dots all over it. Both of us are wearing flip flops. I have to give her my phone to put in her purse, because any weight in my pockets starts dragging down my entire ensemble. And while I might want people looking at me tonight, I have my limits. Kat is the only one who gets to see *that*, at least without paying the appropriate fees first.

Everyone stares. And whispers about us. And they might know who I am—that weird half-villain kid nobody likes—but they don't know that Kat isn't the real thing. She shapeshifts her thumb to look like it has an *H*, just in case anybody looks up close. Something her parents would kill her for if they knew. But they don't know, and neither does anybody else, because everybody gives me *those* looks. The "how the hell is he with *her*?" kind. Which I take as a compliment.

Everyone looks at me like that, that is, except for Amelia, who spots me after we get our pictures taken and then looks like she's going to die. She's here with Zach, exactly as I planned. They spent the whole afternoon on Thursday playing video games and not giving anyone else a turn, though he got pretty nervous when Gordon came home and asked if he'd like to stay for dinner again. Then Zach and Riley were out of there. But not before Amelia asked Zach if he was busy Saturday and if he'd like to go to Homecoming at Heroesworth with her, even though it was such short notice. Luckily for me—and for her, I guess —he said yes. And *even though* I supposedly didn't fulfill my part of the bargain, Amelia said I didn't owe her anymore, since she wouldn't have met Zach if it wasn't for me. She thought she was being really generous and kept lording it over me, which meant it took real effort on my part to keep my mouth shut.

Now, Amelia's wearing a pink dress she already had in her closet, and Zach, like all the other guys here, is wearing a tux. I have never been so underdressed in my life. It's perfect.

"Oh, no," Amelia says when she sees me. She puts her hand over her eyes, though I can't tell if it's to show how embarrassed she is for me, or if it's to block the view. Then she lets her hand fall and shakes her head.

"Hi, Amelia," Kat says. She nods at Zach—who's gaping at us and can't decide where to look, since everywhere seems to be inappropriate—and adds, "You must be the idiot's brother."

"This is Zach," Amelia tells her, grabbing his arm. "He's my ..." Her cheeks turn red and she doesn't actually finish that sentence, even though I'm pretty sure the word she was looking for was *date*, preferring instead to flare her nostrils at me. "Do Mom and Dad know you're wearing that? Because that's *not* how you left the house."

"Why do they care what I'm wearing?" Besides, they'll find out soon enough when we get our pictures back and I put them up on the wall. Then Helen—and anyone else who walks through the front door—will have to see me and Kat, practically in our underwear, having a good time together. Every single day.

"Because," Amelia says. "You're supposed to get dressed up. Not show up like that and embarrass me." She glances apologetically at Zach, who's still trying to decide where to look.

"Zach," I say, ignoring Amelia, "this is my girlfriend Kat."

"Hi," he tells her. "Do you go here, too?"

"*No.*" Amelia gives me a sharp look. "She doesn't."

Kat inspects her thumb, letting Amelia get a good view of the *H* there. "I don't know. I was thinking about transferring."

Amelia's mouth turns down and her face goes pale before she realizes Kat's joking. Then she grabs my arm and pulls me off to the side, far enough away where Kat and Zach won't hear. "What do you think you're doing? Mom and Dad are going to kill you when they find out you brought her here. To Heroesworth." She says that last part like I might not have realized where I was.

"Yeah? And what are they going to do, ban her from the house?"

A group of girls walks by, pausing to look me over. I smile and wave at them, and they burst into embarrassed laughter before continuing on their way to the buffet table.

Amelia's eyes go wide, and now she *really* looks like she's going to die. She smacks me in the arm, hard. "I have classes with some of them! And now all I'm going to hear about on Monday is how my idiot brother dressed like a freak!"

I sigh and put my hand on her shoulder. "Amelia, Amelia, Amelia. I think you're missing the big picture here. If everyone is looking at me, then no one is looking at the crud hanging out of your left nostril."

"The what?" She clamps her hands over her nose, then not-so-subtly tries to wipe away the imaginary crud. "Why didn't you say anything?"

"And if everyone's distracted by my near nudity, then they're not noticing that big green fleck between your two front teeth, or the underwear lines showing through your dress, or the awkward way you're walking in high heels. And they're not even that high."

She slides her tongue across her teeth and glances down at her hips, trying to smooth away the pretty much invisible lines with her hands. "Oh, my God."

"And I wasn't going to say anything, but ... Well, never mind."

"No, tell me."

I shrug. "It'll just upset you."

269

"*Damien.*"

"Fine. I'm sure no one else has noticed, but you did remember to put on deodorant tonight, right?"

"*Yes.* Why?"

"Oh." I look away and scratch the back of my head. "No reason. Pretend I didn't say anything."

"It's hot in here! I can't help it if I ..." She lifts one arm up and tries to sniff without being obvious about it, which she fails at. "You don't think Zach will notice, do you?"

"No, he's probably too busy noticing that your boobs are bigger than the last time he saw you."

Her mouth drops open. "It's the bra I'm wearing! It has extra *support.*" She glances over her shoulder, back toward Zach, who's telling Kat about something that involves waving his hands around a lot. "You don't think he actually noticed, do you?"

I raise an eyebrow at her. "What do you think?"

She puts a hand to her forehead. "I thought tonight was going really well."

"Hey, I didn't say he'd *mind.* Tonight *is* going really well. And because everyone you know is busy staring at me, no one's going to be scrutinizing you or noticing that this is obviously your first dance. So, you know, you can thank me later."

She sucks in a deep breath, taking all that in.

The group of girls comes back to get another look at me, only this time Kat comes over and hooks her arm through mine, resting her head on my shoulder and glaring at them. "Get your own," she mutters.

I smile and kiss the top of her head. "Aw, don't be

jealous," I say, even though I kind of love that she is. "You know they could never afford me."

Zach comes over, too. "Hey," he says to Amelia. "Do you, um, want to go get some punch or something?"

"*Yes.*" She says that like she can't wait to get away from me . She also crosses her arms over her chest and keeps licking her teeth. Before leaving with Zach, she looks over at me and says, "*Don't* embarrass me."

I give her an angelic look, like the idea never even crossed my mind. I wait until they're gone before telling Kat, "You're lucky you don't have siblings."

She pokes me in the chest, her fingernail digging into my bare skin. "You're lucky I don't have brothers, because I'm pretty sure they'd kill you."

"True." And her dad is bad enough. "Hey, look, there's Riley," I say, spotting him partway across the room. "Let's go make him uncomfortable. I mean, let's go say hello."

Riley is standing against the wall by himself, though since he's holding a sparkly silver shoulder wrap that matches the dress Sarah showed us, I'm pretty sure that means she's here. He takes a deep breath when we come up to him, letting it out slowly and shaking his head while he looks us over. "Wow. You were serious."

"You knew I was."

"Shorts. Just shorts."

"Yep. *Just* shorts."

He sighs and gives Kat an acknowledging nod. "It's, um, good seeing you again."

"I'll *bet*," I say. "Eyes up here, Perkins."

His face goes completely red as he glares at me. "I

wasn't—" He doesn't finish that thought, too embarrassed to say that he wasn't looking, even though I'm pretty sure he really wasn't. "Sarah went to the bathroom," he says, like he hopes she shows up soon so he doesn't have to talk to me. "She should be back any moment."

Good. I want to show her she can't tell me what to do. She can't stop me from bringing Kat here. And not that I want to sour our evening or anything, but maybe if she starts in on her "all supervillains are sociopaths" spiel, Riley will see that we need to take action.

"Your brother's cool," Kat tells him.

"Um, thanks? It's his first dance. He's really excited."

"He told me." Then she grins at me and says, "He and Amelia are really cute together. You did good."

Riley looks from her to me, frowning as he tries to make sense of that.

"*Kat.* I don't know what you're talking about. I have never done a good thing in my life. Present company excluded, of course."

She laughs.

Then Riley sees something behind me and his eyes go wide. He starts to say, "Sarah, what—"

But before he gets a chance, there's a loud blast. One moment, Kat is smiling at me and laughing. And the next, she's hurtling toward the wall. There's a sickening crunch as she smashes into it and then crumples to the floor.

"*Kat?!*" All my blood runs cold. It's suddenly freezing in here, and not because I'm hardly wearing anything. I start shaking and I can't make sense of what just happened.

And then Sarah's voice behind me says, "I told you not

to bring her here, Damien. I *warned* you."

X·X·X

I sink to my knees, crouching on the floor with Kat, trying to see if she's okay.

She has to be okay.

She has *to.*

My heart's pounding and I can't think. My thoughts jumble together, too fast and too slow at the same time.

"Sarah!" Riley shouts, a shrill edge of panic in his voice. "What the hell are you doing?!" He gets down on the floor with me, trying to help. "I didn't know," he mutters. "Oh, God, I didn't know."

Blood covers one side of Kat's face. Her left wrist is swollen and bent funny. Her eyes are closed, but she's still breathing.

I'm not sure if I am. I look up at Sarah, who's holding one of her homemade gadgets. It's shaped like a gun and is pointed right at me. She takes another one out of her purse. This one's smaller, more compact, but when she fires it at the wall, a laser blasts a chunk out of it and bits of debris rain down on us.

"Nobody help her!" Sarah shouts. "She's a supervillain! We can't let her leave!"

People scream. Some of them run. A room full of superheroes, and nobody does anything.

Instead, there are shocked gasps and snide whispers of agreement. Because they know who I am. They can believe that the half-villain guy bold enough to wear a pair of swimming trunks to Homecoming would also be bold enough—or maybe crazy enough—to bring a supervillain as his date.

Sarah points both guns at me. "Riley, get back. Didn't you hear me?"

"Sarah," Riley says, holding up a hand, trying to reason with her, "I know you're not yourself right now, but this isn't—"

"Get away from her." She points the shockwave gun at him, keeping the raygun aimed at my chest. "You, too, Damien. You won't get another warning shot."

Riley goes invisible while her attention is focused on me. She doesn't even hesitate. She pulls the trigger and he slams against the wall, turning visible again and crying out in pain as he clutches his shoulder.

"I'm sorry," she says to him, "but you don't understand. You don't know what's at stake here."

I get to my feet, staying in front of Kat, blocking her from Sarah. Electricity burns beneath my skin. All my hair stands on end, and there's a loud crackle as lightning arcs between my hands. I don't think about it—it's just there— and I couldn't stop it even if I wanted to.

Sarah's eyes widen in surprise, but then she shakes her head sadly, as if she should have known.

And if there was any doubt about who the bad guy is in this situation, it's gone now as everyone stares at me. Kids and even some adult chaperones gape as sparks flicker across my bare skin and electricity crawls over my arms in waves. Phones come out. Pictures get snapped. More people run while they can.

Someone comes tearing through the crowd, pushing people out of the way to find out what's going on, and I see Amelia staring, horror-stricken, at the scene before her. At Sarah, one of my closest friends, pointing a raygun at me. And me, trying really hard not to fry everyone in the room. "Damien?!"

"Amelia, get back!"

"No wonder," Sarah says, her voice choked with emotion. "No wonder you brought a supervillain into Heroesworth! Even though you knew all it would take is one wrong word from her back at Vilmore and a whole generation of superheroes would be wiped out!"

More gasps from the crowd as the idea spreads like wildfire. They don't have any trouble believing it. They don't know that Kat wouldn't do that. They're probably pretty sure that *I* would.

"You're one of *them*." There are tears in Sarah's eyes now, as if she can't believe how I've betrayed her.

Riley's face is pale. He's still clutching his shoulder and his voice is strained when he says, "Sarah, stop. You're overreacting."

Something about the way he says that—or maybe the way he *doesn't* freak out about me going all electric—makes her gasp and gape at him in horror. "You knew?!"

A couple of chaperones arrive on the scene. One of them swears when he sees two injured kids and then me, covered in electricity. He says something about a supervillain infiltration and needing backup before taking off again. The other one waves her hands and shouts at the crowd not to come any closer.

"Sarah." My voice sounds weird. Shaky and thin and not like me at all. Waves of electricity wash over me, and I can't tell how much of it is beneath my skin, or there on the surface for everyone to see. But I feel myself losing it, losing control, because I want so badly for this to be over. For Sarah not to be pointing a gun at me. For Kat to not be lying helpless on the floor. "You're my *sidekick*. You know I wouldn't—"

"I can't be a sidekick for a villain. And that's what you are, isn't it?" Again, the hitch in her voice, the hurt because she thinks I've betrayed her. That both me and Riley have. "You have a *villain power*."

One that's going to get out of hand really soon. I wish the crowd would move farther back. I wish the people next to me weren't people I cared about. "Sarah, please, this isn't you. Just—"

"You endangered all these people, Damien! You're doing it again, *right now*!"

"Put the guns down, Sarah."

"You first," she says. "Stop using your villain power and move away from her, or else I'll have to hurt you, too."

I don't trust her, and even if I did, I don't know how to stop. And this *isn't* Sarah. And it's my fault she's like this, because I screwed her up in the first place with my stupid electricity power, and I insisted she was fine last weekend, because I wanted her to be. And if I'm all that stands in the way of her pointing that gun at Kat, then there's no chance in hell I'm going anywhere. "You know I can't do that."

"And you know I can't let her go back to Vilmore."

"Sarah," Riley says, "just stop. We can talk about this."

Giant waves of electricity arc between my hands. Somebody's going to get hurt soon if I can't stop it. Maybe lots of people. Amelia's still there, on the edge of the crowd, only now Zach's there with her. Both of them are watching this play out, their eyes wide. Riley's leaning against the wall, thinking he can still talk Sarah out of this. Or maybe he's just too stunned to know that he should get the hell out of here.

I'm pretty sure I could take Sarah out. I'm pretty sure I could take *a lot* of people out. But I'm not a killer, and this isn't really her. Somewhere in there is the real Sarah, who would never do this. Who I would trust with my life.

More adults arrive. Screaming at me to stop. One of them uses her power to make a protective shield, but it's not enough to cover more than a few people. Another points his hands at me. I don't know what his power is, but he shouts something about not being afraid to shoot.

I hear Amelia's voice shrieking, begging them not to hurt me.

Sarah takes aim, her raygun pointed right at my heart. Her finger moves against the trigger.

This is it. She's going to kill me. And I can't hold it back anymore. Adrenaline spikes through my veins. Electricity surges over my entire body, forcing all my energy into my palms. I raise my hands up toward the ceiling, right as I completely lose control.

Lightning blasts a huge hole through the roof. People scream and run for their lives as plaster and tiling and other crap rain down on them. All the lights go out and the music stops. The sprinklers come on and the fire alarm blares.

The blast from my electricity knocks Sarah back, and her shot misses its target and hits the wall above my shoulder. The superhero who kept shouting that he wasn't afraid to shoot finally does. A beam of white light clips my arm, leaving an angry burn across my skin. I have just enough time to realize how much it hurts before the doors burst open and the cavalry arrives.

Some guy says, "Oh, it's you again," and then blasts me with his freeze rays.

CHAPTER 22

I get arrested. Sarah does not. They lock me up in a special containment room at the police station that's meant to hold the most dangerous supervillains. Which, in what feels like another lifetime, I would have taken as a pretty big compliment. They fingerprint me—making sure to get the *X* on my thumb—and take my picture. A picture I will *not* be putting on the wall. They ignore the burn on my arm, and I don't say anything about it, even though it hurts like hell.

I use my one phone call to call Gordon. I consider using it to call Kat, because I'm desperate to find out if she's okay and I know Amelia will have already told Gordon what happened to me. But I figure Kat's probably not in any condition to answer her phone. Or mine, since it's still in her purse. In fact, all my stuff I had with me tonight is either with her or in my locker at school, and I have absolutely nothing on me. No phone, no ID. Nothing. Just shorts and a pair of flip flops.

I keep telling the police and the guys from the League who brought me in that I'm not a supervillain. But after what happened, I don't exactly blame them for not believing me. And it doesn't help that the only other villain in the containment room recognizes me and asks me how my mom is doing. I tell him she's fine, and he notices I'm shaking all over and tells me not to worry, that getting hauled in occasionally is just part of the trade, and that it's going to be all right. I don't believe him, but I nod anyway and try not to feel like I'm going to throw up.

It's well after midnight by the time Gordon comes to get me. He takes one look at me after they let me out of the containment room, his face an angry mask, and says, "Where are your clothes?"

In my backpack, in my locker. But somehow I don't think he meant it so literally. "I was trying to be different."

He makes a disgusted noise, like he's not surprised. Not by me screwing up and not by me getting arrested with almost nothing on. He stands there, glaring down at me, looking me over and obviously not liking what he sees.

I'm still shaking, and my arm hurts really bad, and I would give almost anything for him to hug me right now and tell me he knows it was all a big misunderstanding and that he's just glad I'm safe. But instead he looks at me like I'm a criminal, like he's never seen me before. There's a moment where I'm actually afraid he's going to tell them he doesn't know me after all and that they should lock me back up again.

"I saw the videos," he says. "Online."

Videos that I'm betting *don't* include the part where Sarah attacked Kat out of nowhere. Probably nobody started taking pictures or filming until after I went all electric. I wonder if he somehow didn't notice I was only wearing shorts in the videos, or if that comment about my clothes was just him taking a jab at me, pointing out what a disappointment I am.

"What were you *thinking*?" He keeps his voice low, and I get the impression it's taking a lot of effort on his part not to yell at me. At least not until we get home.

I swallow and wrap my arms around myself, being careful not to touch the burn on my arm. "Is Kat okay?"

He shakes his head dismissively, like he can't believe I had the nerve to ask that, like maybe I have no right to after what I let happen to her. And now he does yell. "I don't know, Damien! Maybe you should have thought of that *before* you endangered her life!"

I feel hollow and absolutely worthless. My throat goes tight, and hot tendrils of guilt and self-loathing slither through my chest, ugly and painful.

Nobody was supposed to know she was a supervillain. Sarah wasn't supposed to go psychotic and start *shooting* at us. But all my reasons for taking Kat to Heroesworth sound really stupid in retrospect. I wanted to defy the rules. I wanted to prove that I could bring her there and that nobody could stop me. I wanted to flaunt the fact that we were together.

Or maybe I just wanted to have a good time. I wanted to be able to take my girlfriend to a stupid school dance and not have to think about what letters are on our thumbs. But even that sounds lame. I risked her life, I almost got her killed, because I wanted to spend a few hours wearing nothing but swimsuits so people I don't even like would stare at us? Not that I knew I was risking her life. I wouldn't have been, if not for Sarah, and that's kind of my fault, too. Okay, no, not *kind of*. It's completely my fault. Sarah going crazy, Kat and Riley getting injured, and me blowing up part of the school and getting arrested is all completely and totally 100 percent my fault.

"Do you know how humiliating this is?" Gordon says as he leads me toward the lobby. "To find out that my son has a *villain power* because he got arrested for blowing up part of Heroesworth? And that he got *expelled*? Do you know what I had to do to get them not to press charges?! Never mind," he snaps when I open my mouth to speak. "Whatever smart-ass comment you have to say to that, I don't want to hear it!"

For the record, I was simply going to say, "They're not?" because I can't actually think of anything he could have done to get them to let me go, sexual favors or otherwise.

Amelia's waiting for us in the lobby. She's changed out of her dress and into jeans and a sweatshirt. She jumps up out of her chair when she sees us, her eyes darting back and forth between me and him, looking relieved to see that he hasn't murdered me. At least, not yet. "It wasn't his fault," she tells him. And with a surprising amount of conviction, considering she didn't see how it started.

"*Amelia*," he growls, like this isn't the first time she's

said that and he didn't believe her the first million times.

She looks me in the eyes and says, "Riley told me what happened. He said it wasn't your fault."

Well, if Mr. Perfect said it, then it must be true.

I think that, and then I feel this overwhelming wave of guilt. For what happened to him tonight, because of me. And because, even after all that, he still said I was innocent, even though he must know that I wasn't. I might not have pulled the trigger on Sarah's gun, but I was the one responsible for it, and he knows that as much as I do. I don't deserve for him to defend me. Just like I don't deserve the concerned looks Amelia keeps giving me, like she's worried about how I'm doing. *Me.* Her stupid, idiotic brother who ruined her big night and is, no doubt, going to be the talk of the school on Monday, but not for the reasons she thought. And she's not going to be Amelia anymore, she's going to be "the sister of that villain kid who blew up part of the gym." Good luck living that down.

And Sarah thinks I'm a sociopath, that I don't feel bad for anything. She should see me now.

Gordon walks ahead of us, like he can't stand to look at me. He leads us outside, toward the car. An icy wind blasts me as soon as I step outside, giving me flashbacks to when that freeze guy used his power on me at the school. And at the jewelry store. But mostly at the school. I can see my breath in the air, and I start shivering after only a few steps, what with it being so cold out here and me wearing pretty much nothing. I guess nobody thought to bring me a coat.

I catch Gordon's arm as he's about to get in the car. Because I need him to look at me. I need him to turn around and acknowledge that I exist and that I'm still his son and not the evil supervillain the internet has probably already made me out to be. My teeth are chattering as I start to say, "Dad, I didn't—" But he jerks his arm away from me, and then, yes, he looks at me. But it's not the look I wanted. It's a mixture of anger and fear and even revulsion. It's a look that stops me in mid-sentence and makes me want to go crawl under a rock and never come out again.

And then, in a tone that doesn't leave any room for arguing, he says, "*Not now*, Damien."

I get in the back of the car, because there's no way I'm sitting next to him in the front. Amelia gets in the back, too. She should be as mad at me as Gordon is, but instead she doesn't know better. Because Riley mistakenly told her it wasn't my fault. Because she saw all those superheroes yelling at me, and Sarah pointing guns at us. And she saw how freaked out I was. And maybe I didn't mean for anyone to get hurt, or to lose control of my lightning power, but she should still be mad. She must realize that her life is pretty much over, all because of me.

But instead she reaches out and touches my arm. Like I'm still a real person. Like I'm still her brother. "Kat's okay," she whispers. "Riley was there at the hospital, and I made Zach find out, and he told me. She has a concussion and some broken ribs, and her wrist is broken, but she's going to be okay."

I swallow and nod, not trusting myself to speak. And

then I turn away, pretending to see something really interesting out the window, so she doesn't see the tears in my eyes.

X·X·X

Gordon calls a press conference Sunday afternoon. No, not Gordon—the *Crimson Flash*. Because that's what he had to promise in order to keep me out of trouble. He has to go on live TV and confess to the entire world that the half-villain kid who destroyed part of Heroesworth is his *son*. That he slept with a supervillain seventeen years ago and that, all this time, he hasn't been the pinnacle of morality his fans thought he was. And that he's kept me a secret from them, even if it was only for the past seven months.

A secret that obviously had serious consequences.

He also has to claim that it's his fault I was attending Heroesworth in the first place, that he deceived the administration into thinking I wasn't dangerous, despite being half villain. He's taking the blame so the school can pretend they had no idea I was a liability or that I might have been a danger to the other students. Instead, everybody gets to think it was the Crimson Flash, of *The Crimson Flash and the Safety Kids*, who knowingly risked the lives of everyone at Heroesworth, so that his secret delinquent son could go to his alma mater.

As if any of that is even remotely what happened.

He explained all that to me last night, before he let me go to bed. He made sure I knew just how badly I'd screwed up, as if I didn't already. Now I'm hiding in my room. I know the press conference is on because I can hear the TV downstairs. And because Amelia knocked on my door and told me it was starting, though I pretended to be asleep and didn't answer. Everyone else is down there, watching him ruin his life for me, but I can't.

So instead I'm sitting on my bed, pretending it isn't happening. I have my phone back, thanks to Amelia using her power to get it for me last night, and I dial Kat's number for the millionth time today. And, like all the other times, it goes straight to voicemail.

Hey, this is Kat. I'm probably screening my calls right now, but if you leave an awesome enough message, I might call you back. Except you, Damien—you're always awesome and I'll always call you back.

Hot guilt wells up in my chest. Always awesome. Yep. That's me.

I don't know why she's not answering. Maybe she's that hurt, that she can't. Or maybe she's mad at me for, you know, almost getting her killed.

Or her battery could be dead, but somehow I doubt that's it.

Gordon says something very solemn sounding on the TV downstairs, though I can't make out what it is, and then there are a lot of angry noises from the crowd.

I pull my blanket over my head to try and muffle the sound more. Then I suck it up and call Kat's house. I hope Kat answers. I hope her mom answers. Anyone but—

"How dare you call here," her dad says. He sounds pissed. I don't blame him.

"Can I talk to her?"

"Can you *talk* to her? No. No, you cannot. *You* are never talking to her again."

In the background, I hear Kat's mom say, "Is that Damien? Is he all right?"

Her dad sighs. He says to me, gruffly, "You're all right, aren't you?"

My arm still hurts, though not as badly as it did last night, since I put medicine on it and a couple of giant band-aids. The most popular video of me blowing up part of Heroesworth has over 1,000,000 views. My little brother looked at me this morning like I wasn't the same guy who drew a Velociraptor on his cast, but instead like he thought I might be planning to burn the house down, and was too scared to talk to me.

"I'm fine," I lie.

"He's *fine*," he repeats, talking to her mom. Then, to me, "You listen here. After what you did, you don't speak to Kat ever again. You don't call her. You don't message her. And you sure as hell don't see her in person."

"*Tom*," Kat's mom scolds.

But he ignores her. "I told you you were trouble. And then you and her lied to us, and you took her to *Heroesworth* and almost got her—" Too much emotion clouds his voice, and he doesn't finish that thought. "You stay away from her, Damien."

I'm not going to do that, but I keep my mouth shut. I might be trouble, but I'm not stupid. "Is she okay?"

"She will be. The doctor said she'll be able to shapeshift herself back to normal, once she gets her strength back. She should be better by tomorrow."

I exhale in relief.

"Until then, she's in a lot of pain. Because of you."

I wince. "Will you tell her I'm sorry?"

"No. I won't." And then he hangs up.

I just sit there, under my blanket. It's too hot and I can hardly breathe. And I can still hear the TV downstairs. I think they might have turned it up. I catch part of a sentence where Gordon's saying how ashamed he is, and my blood runs cold and my heart beats too loud.

I call Riley. I don't think real hard about it, I just do it.

He answers after three rings. "Hey, X." He sounds relieved to hear from me. And worried. "Are you watching this?" The press conference is on in the background.

"*No.*" I pause. "Can you turn it off?"

He moves away from the TV, the sound getting fainter, and then I hear his door close. "So," he says, "some party last night."

"Are you okay?" The words just come out, before I even realize I'm going to say them.

"Me? Am *I* okay? What about you?"

"Just answer the question, Perkins."

He sighs. "I've been better. But I'm all right."

"And your shoulder?"

"Dislocated. It hurt like hell when they put it back, but it's fine now. Kind of sore. That's all. And what about—"

"How's Zach?"

"He's fine. *You're* the one that got hauled off last night."

I don't say anything to that, and we're both silent for a minute. Then my attention wanders to the sound coming from the TV downstairs. I hear a reporter ask Gordon how he could put all those kids in danger, and I feel sick.

"So," I say, desperate to distract myself, "when do you think we'll get pictures back?"

"Listen, X, about last night."

"We'll figure something out. About Sarah." Actually, *we* won't, because I already have a plan, one that doesn't involve him. Because I don't need to risk anybody else getting hurt again in all this. But I have a feeling he'd argue with me if I told him that, so I keep it to myself. And when Sarah's back to normal and she and him are happily reunited, he'll forgive me for not including him.

Well, probably.

"No," Riley says, "that's ... I mean, we will, but that's not what I—" He swallows. "I'm sorry. God, I'm *so* sorry. I should have listened to you. You said Sarah wasn't better, and I said we should wait. Look how that turned out! I was there with her all night, and I didn't know she was *armed*. How did I not know that?!"

"You couldn't have known."

"I should have stopped her. I saw her coming, holding a freaking gun. If I'd warned you guys, if I'd ... You *told* me she thought supervillains were sociopaths, and I brushed it off, like it wasn't important. And maybe there wasn't any way we could have fixed her between now and then, but if I'd been paying attention, maybe I would have noticed sooner, what she was going to do. I could have stopped it." His voice shakes. "And if I'd realized she was going to actually *shoot* me, I could have ... I don't know. I just should have been able to stop her."

"Perkins, if you think Sarah doesn't come armed to

pretty much any situation, then you really haven't been paying attention."

He *almost* laughs at that. "I thought she was actually going to kill you."

She was. If the blast from me losing control of my lightning hadn't thrown her off, she wouldn't have missed, and I'd have taken a laser to the chest. "It wasn't her. And it's over now. And we're going to find a way to fix her."

"Right."

"It was my fault. Not yours. You know that."

"No, X, I don't. Maybe you started all this, but you never meant for any of that to happen. You didn't do anything wrong last night."

"I brought a supervillain to Heroesworth. Sarah warned me, and I did it anyway."

"Yeah, and you also showed up in what pretty much amounts to your underwear. Both were unconventional. Neither one was a crime. And you didn't mean to blow up the roof. If you hadn't, you would have blown up *people*. You did what you could."

I'm quiet, thinking that over.

I hear an outraged eruption from the crowd on the TV. Reporters snapping at Gordon. Snippets of questions make it past my blanket shield. *Who's his mother? Did you cheat on your wife? What does it feel like to be a fraud?*

"Well," Riley says, "I guess ... I guess I should go."

"Oh." So much for my distraction.

"I mean, you probably have things to do."

"Yeah. Lots of things. Very important ones." Like cowering in my room.

"Okay. Right. I mean, unless ... You never answered me. About how you're doing."

"You were watching the press conference. What do you think?"

"That bad?"

I wince. "I don't want to keep you. I'm probably the last person you want to talk to, and ... You probably have things to do, too."

"Yeah," he says, "really important ones. Like talk to this half-villain guy I know. He's kind of famous right now, and I bet the tabloids would pay a lot for behind-the-scenes information."

I smile. Just a little. "Not as much as you'd think. I already called them. It wasn't worth it."

He laughs. "Do you actually have anything to do?"

"Only if hiding in my bed counts."

"Do you ... do you want to come over?"

Yes. I want to be anywhere but here. Except ... "I don't think I'm supposed to leave. But maybe ... maybe don't hang up. At least, not until the press conference is over."

"Yeah. Okay. I won't." There's a pause, and then he says, "So, what do you want to talk about?"

"Anything. Tell me about all the stupid TV shows you watch."

"They're not stupid."

"Sure they're not. But, you know, now's your chance to convince me. Pick one. And it better have a good story. And it better not be *Train Models*."

He scoffs, and I can picture him rolling his eyes at me. "*Train Models* doesn't have a story. It's not that kind of show. You know that."

"It's just that boring, you mean."

"You said anything."

"Seriously, Perkins? You're really going to tell me about an old guy fixing model trains?"

"*No*. But there's this one I started watching this summer, about this hero and this villain who have to work together to solve crimes, and—"

"I already watch that one."

"Oh. So then what did you think of last week's episode?"

"I missed it. But ... spoil it for me. I want to know what happened. And I ..." I need the distraction.

He seems to get that part without me saying it, because then he says, "Right. Well, Zach hated it, but I thought it was awesome."

"Great, that means it sucked." As if there's ever a bad episode.

"You don't know that. You don't even know what it was about yet."

"Yeah, well, start from the beginning," I tell him. "And don't leave anything out."

CHAPTER 23

"Jess, take a letter." Jess is sitting on my bed early Monday afternoon with a notebook I gave her and some crayons. I clasp my hands behind my back and pace a little, keeping to the floorboards that creak the least and skipping any that sag. Which means I can really only go a few steps before I have to turn around again. "Rumors of my demise have been greatly exaggerated. Yes, I have been expelled from school, and yes, several gossip sites have speculated that I never cared much about going there. Which, as you know, isn't true. Don't write that part down."

She scribbles furiously in the notebook with a green crayon.

"Blue or black only," I tell her. "No one's going to take green seriously."

"Whatever," she says.

She may have picked that one up from me. Whatever.

"All right. Back to the letter. My grades at Heroesworth were not excellent. In fact, they kind of sucked. No, wait, don't say 'sucked.' Nobody's going to take that seriously, either. What I should say is that my grades were less than spectacular. I'll just assume you know how to spell that. So, yeah, not great. It could be said that I didn't try very hard. Actually, it has been said, by several of the previously mentioned gossip sites. But they've also said that me blowing up part of the gym was a publicity stunt to get into Vilmore. Which it wasn't."

"Done," she says, and pushes the notebook toward me.

There's a rough drawing of what might be a mouse, or maybe a cat, with a smiley face on it. I nod my approval and turn the page for her. "And it was my choice not to be in that documentary this summer. Not Gor— Not the Crimson Flash's. So, the fact that they're already talking about releasing a new version, called *The Man Behind the Lie*, is just mean. And unnecessary. Maybe the first one left out a few things, but nothing important." I turn to face her and sigh. "And I know what you're going to say, Jess, that leaving me out of it was kind of a big thing. And maybe even somewhat important. But it didn't hurt anything. I never meant to hurt anybody. That's what all the websites and news articles don't realize."

She leans in really close to the page, scribbling in red now.

"It's not like I *wanted* to be able to shoot lightning from my hands. I never meant to become bad-ass enough to blow up the roof of the school. Part of the roof, anyway. Plus some robots. And my bedroom wall. Whatever."

"Whatever," she repeats.

"Right. So. I *may* have made some less-than-spectacular choices. But I never meant to be dangerous. Or to let Kat get hurt. Or Mr. Perfect. I mean, Riley. Do *not* write down that I called him Mr. Perfect. Just white it out or something. And I didn't mean for Sarah to get messed up. Most of all, I didn't mean for Gordon—for my dad—to throw away his life for me. Which is why I'm going to run away and join the circus. If they'll have me. I mean, I don't actually know how to do any circus stuff, and I don't do heights, so the trapeze is out. So is riding elephants. And clowns are terrifying, so I won't be able to be in the same room with them. And I'm not actually sure how you go about joining the circus. But I'll figure it out. I'll fix Sarah first, and then I'll leave. Gordon will be better off without me, and once I'm gone, all of this will blow over. He'll rescue some orphans or something and everyone will forget that he ever had a half-villain son."

"Clowns," Jess mutters, frowning very seriously at her drawing.

"No, *not* clowns. I can't emphasize that enough." I sit down on the edge of the bed and let my hands fall between my knees. "Some people might see me running away and joining the circus as a sign of defeat. But it's not. I know when to graciously bow out. And it's not like I have a lot of other career options at this point. Vilmore didn't want me, I got expelled from Heroesworth, and apparently the regular school I used to go to won't take me back, because your mom already called them. No one will have me. So, I might as well not waste any more time here, ruining things for everyone. I'll miss you, though," I tell her. "You'll probably forget about me, after a while, but maybe when you're older, we can be friends on the internet."

The stairs creak. That'll be Helen, probably coming to snatch up Jess and drag her away before I accidentally electrocute her or something.

"Okay, write this down quickly. This last part is important. Because Kat's not going to understand why I left. I mean, she will, because I'm sure she's noticed the media exploding with stories about me. And her. And our scandalous relationship, what with my stepmother killing her grandfather and everything. But—"

There's a knock on the door.

I ignore it. "But Kat's going to think I wasn't thinking about her when I made this decision. That I was maybe being selfish and possibly even a little cowardly. But I *am* thinking about her. A lot. And I'll send her postcards from the circus. She'll be the only one I send them to, and once everything's blown over ... Maybe she'll come visit me."

The door opens. Which I guess is Jess's cue to leave.

But then it's not Helen who steps inside my room, but *Kat.*

"What is Kat going to think is selfish and cowardly?" she says, closing the door behind her and raising her eyebrows at me.

I kind of freeze up and just stare at her. The last time I saw her, she was lying broken on the floor of the gym. Bloody and unconscious. Because of me. "What are you doing here?"

"Hi," Jess says. She waves at her.

Kat waves back, then looks guiltily at the floor. "I kind of broke into your house." She can use her shapeshifting power to turn her fingers into lockpicks. It's kind of creepy, but it works.

"My stepmom's home. She—"

"She didn't see me. And I know you're probably in enough trouble as it is, and it'll be even worse for you if I get caught here, but I figured you couldn't leave the house, and I had to see you." She crosses over to the bed and stands in front of me. "So, what decision did you make that I'm going to think is selfish and cowardly?"

I swallow. "It's all in the letter Jess took down. You can read it later."

She glances over at Jess and her scribbles, which are very obviously not any kind of writing. "Or you could tell me now."

I stare at her. At her wrist, which isn't swollen anymore. And her ribs, which I guess were broken. And her face. Not covered in blood.

She glares at me. "You'd better be picturing me naked."

I am picturing her lying in a hospital bed. In horrible pain. I'm picturing her lying helpless on the floor while Sarah pointed a gun at her. I flinch and look away. "I'm joining the circus."

"Great. I'll come with you. I think I'd do pretty well there."

"Yeah, probably, but you can't come with me."

"Why? Because I'd show you up?" She sits down on the bed and nudges me playfully with her elbow.

I turn away, angling myself so she can't see my face. "You have Vilmore. You have options. You don't need the circus."

"But I want to be with you."

"You don't know what you'd be getting yourself into. There's no money in it. At least, I don't think. And there are probably going to be clowns, though we won't talk to them. I mean, *I* won't talk to them. You won't be there."

"Are you doing this because of what happened to me? Because you think I'll be better off without you or something? Because that's not—"

"No. We both know you won't be better off without me —you'll be devastated. You'll hardly be able to go on living."

"Wow. You're right. You running off *is* selfish and cowardly."

"*You* won't be better off, but Gordon and everybody else will. It's actually pretty selfless of me, if you think about it."

"Except for the part where you leave me devastated and unable to go on."

"Yeah, but you'll forgive me." She actually, like, still loves me and stuff. "He won't."

Jess tugs on my sleeve and shoves another picture at me. This one is ... I can't actually tell what this one is supposed to be, but it might involve an alligator and a zebra. Which probably makes it a crocodile, except it might also be a picture of a snake and an oddly striped cow. Who knows?

"Good work," I tell her. "Now draw something for Kat.

It'll be my going away present to her."

"You don't get to have someone else draw me a going away present from you. And I should be the one giving you something, since you're the one leaving, right?"

"Yeah, but I'm thoughtful like that."

"Uh-huh. And your dad's not going to forgive you if you run away."

"He's not going to forgive me if I stay, either. Not for this. The best I can do is minimize the damage."

"That's the best you can do?"

I shrug. "It's not the worst."

She takes a deep breath, watching me. Her eyes search my face, and I stare at her, and in my mind I hear Sarah accusing me of being a villain and telling me to stop using my lightning power all over again.

"Don't do that, Damien," Kat whispers.

"I'm not doing anything." Just remembering what it felt like when I thought I might lose her. When I had a gun pointed at my chest and was worried I might accidentally fry a bunch of people, Kat included.

There are footsteps on the stairs. Kat's eyes go wide and she shimmers and turns into a pillow right before there's a knock on the door. And it's a good thing she does, because Helen doesn't wait for me to answer—or to hide any girls who aren't supposed to be in my room—before opening it and saying, "It's time for Jess's nap."

Jess stares at the pillow at the foot of my bed. "Kat," she says.

"Does she have to go? She's kind of my secretary."

"She's going to get really cranky in about five minutes,"

Helen says, coming over and picking her up from the bed. "And, Damien, I've been meaning to talk to you. About that video—"

"I don't want to talk about it." I can't help glancing over at Kat. Or at least at the pillow that's secretly her. She must have seen it by now. She must have seen what happened after Sarah shot her.

"Well, we're *going* to talk about it. I saw what you did. When you were covered in electricity. When Kat was hurt and you used your power to sa—"

"No, you didn't see!" I don't mean to yell at her—it just bursts out of me. Because it's not just her that doesn't understand, but *everyone*. And Kat is *right there*, even if Helen doesn't know that, and I don't want her dredging up everything that happened or talking about how she thinks all supervillains are evil, including me. "You saw what you wanted to, like everybody else!"

"*Damien*. Don't raise your voice to—" Her eyes go wide. And kind of scared.

Sparks of electricity fly between my fingertips. And along my arms. Because it feels like everybody in the world thinks they know what happened, that they know *who I am*, and who I'm *not*, and I'm sick of it. And maybe I could make the sparks stop, but I don't. "I know what you said about me! You told Gordon I was a bad influence on *your* kids. You said I was going to fail at Heroesworth and disappoint him. And now you're right, and you don't get to gloat about it. And you don't get to talk about that video of us—of me—because you weren't there!"

She winces and gets this mixed look of hurt and guilt

on her face. Hurt because of all the awful things I just said, and guilt because of all the awful things I know *she* said. Her eyes don't leave the electricity on my hands as she takes a step back, wrapping her arms tight around Jess. "You need to calm down."

"Then you need to leave me alone."

"Damien, I just wanted to—" She takes a deep breath and holds up a hand. "Fine. We'll talk about this later, when you can control yourself."

"No, we won't!"

She backs out of the room, and I get up and slam the door behind her. I wait until I hear her angry footsteps creaking on the stairs before flopping back down on my bed. I bring my knees up and take deep breaths, trying to make the sparks die down.

Kat shapeshifts back into herself and crawls over beside me. "Wow," she says.

"Yeah."

"I didn't know you had that in you."

"Me, neither."

"So ... what's our circus act going to be? Because there's no way I'm letting you go without me."

I smile. "I thought I would be part of the freak show. People could pay twenty bucks to look at my *X*. It's going to be called *X-Rated*."

"Twenty bucks? For twenty bucks, it better actually *be* x-rated."

"Fine. Ten bucks."

"There's only one problem with that. Well, two, because I said what's *our* act going to be, not yours. But your *X* is going to change someday, right? And then you'll have an *H* or a *V* and you'll be out of a job."

"Right. Well, I hadn't thought that far ahead."

"You *so* need me."

"Plus, maybe it won't change, because I don't know what I am. I mean, I have two powers, right? And I've kind of screwed up as both a villain and a hero." I used my villain power to save Kat. But also to blow up part of the school and kind of ruin everybody's lives. So what does that make me?

Kat shapeshifts her thumb to have an *X*, just like mine, and holds it up. "Or I could take over your act."

"Don't cheapen it." But I smile at her and we press our thumbs together. "I bet our act would do a lot better with you in it. What with being called *X-Rated* and all."

She punches my arm. Right on my burn.

"Ow!" I wince and hold my hand there.

"Oops. Sorry."

"No, it's fine. It only hurts when you hit me."

She rolls her eyes at me. Then she lies back with one arm under her head. "You know you can't really join the circus."

"I'm sure I can think of a better act."

"That's not what I meant."

"I know." I slide my hand over hers. "But I don't know how to fix this."

"Maybe you can't. Sometimes bad things happen. Like when Mr. Wiggles died and we couldn't put him back together and he came back as a zombie."

Mr. Wiggles was her old dancing flower toy she gave

me for my birthday. He got broken—no thanks to Amelia snipping him in half—and no amount of duct tape could fix him or make him dance again. And he didn't really come back as a zombie, though he kind of looked like one after all the duct tape. "It was *Dr.* Wiggles, Kat. I didn't put him through grad school for nothing."

She laughs. Then she whispers, "You can't fix everything, Damien."

"No, maybe not," I admit, squeezing her hand. "But I can sure as hell try."

CHAPTER 24

I t's not particularly hard to break into Sarah's house on Tuesday. In the middle of the day. Which might not be the best time for covert operations, but it *is* the best time for no one being home, since Sarah has school and her dad has work. And Heraldo has ... running around in the backyard and barking before I even step foot on the front porch.

It helps that I have a key. I had to dig it out of the back of the drawer I shoved it in when she gave it to me a couple months ago. She said it was in case there was ever a superhero emergency and I needed to either grab some of her gadgets or save her from bad guys who'd taken over the house. I told her that second one was pretty unlikely, since I didn't exactly think I could win a fight with someone who could take her on and live to tell about it. *Ha.* I also told her there's no way I'd be randomly taking some of her gadgets, either, unless I already knew what they did. You never know when one of them's going to explode or try to chop off your finger. And then she said I should still take the key, because she needed me to walk Heraldo while she and her dad went out of town that weekend.

And since I have a key, I'm not even sure if this is breaking and entering. Entering, sure, but there's no breaking involved. I simply unlock the door and step inside. And I'm still Sarah's friend—the real Sarah, before I screwed her up—and this is all for her own good, so there's no real reason why I shouldn't be here. Though I'm not sure that would hold up in court if I get caught.

The house is quiet, except for Heraldo barking his head off in the backyard. I can't tell if he knows I'm not supposed to be here, or if he's expecting me to let him in, so he can slurp me and knock me to the floor again. Either way, I leave him where he is and hope the neighbors aren't home, or at least that they don't get suspicious. This will only take a minute. I just need to grab the personality enhancer, which we left here last time because it was broken and we didn't need it anymore, and then I can get out of here.

I creep down the hall to Sarah's room. Her door is closed, and there's a moment where I worry maybe she's not in school. What if she stayed home today? Not that Sarah ever stays home from school, but she could be sick or something. Even Sarah is susceptible to germs. And if she's in there and I come waltzing in ... I'm going to have some serious problems. Like a laser to the chest or a gentle explosion to the head.

My palms are sweating. I wipe them on my jeans and try not to think about how convenient it would be to be able to go invisible right now, because that might be like admitting invisibility isn't a lame power. Which it is. Even if it might come in handy sometimes.

I put my hand on the knob and turn it slowly, listening for any sounds of movement on the other side. Nothing. I turn it all the way and fling open the door, and—

Still nothing.

I breathe a sigh of relief and look around, spotting the personality enhancer in a pile of other non-working gadgets that Sarah keeps for spare parts. Luckily, she hasn't dismantled it yet. I grab it off the pile. Mission pretty much accomplished. I'll be home before Helen gets back from the store and even has a chance to realize I'm gone, since I'm grounded and not supposed to leave the house, like, ever again. And I didn't even need Riley's help. Nobody had to get hurt, not even me, and ...

A piece of paper on Sarah's desk catches my attention. I walk over to it and get a closer look. It's a drawing of what looks like a tall rectangular cage. Which seems kind of weird, since what would Sarah need a cage for? And there's a list of parts off to the side, like she's actually building this thing. Whatever it is, it must be more complicated than just a bunch of metal bars stuck together, because she's got little diagrams of wiring drawn in one corner.

I have no idea what it could be for, but I'm pretty sure it can't be anything good.

I'm still trying to figure out what it might be when I

hear footsteps in the hall. And then Sarah's voice, saying, "I'm going to need part number 5A31 and also three of R34. Industrial strength."

I feel a jolt of panic and my heart pounds in my chest. She's home after all, and she's heading for her room. I didn't even close the door, not all the way, and she's going to see me if I don't do something. I consider hiding under her bed, but I happen to know that she keeps a bunch of shoe boxes full of nuts and bolts under there, plus some spare tools and other parts for her gadgets. All that junk doesn't exactly leave a lot of room for someone to hide. So instead I choose the closet and manage to close the doors behind me just as Sarah comes in.

Her closet doors are the kind with the tilted slats in them, so I can still kind of see out. Though I hope for my sake that she can't see in. I also hope she doesn't notice that her personality enhancer is missing and not still in the to-be-dismantled pile.

She has her homemade cell phone up against her ear and listens to the person on the other end for a few moments before saying, "I need them as soon as possible. I've got to get this done by Friday."

She pauses, listening again. Then she glances over at the closet and frowns.

Uh-oh.

She comes over, and I shrink back as far as I can, which isn't nearly far enough, since there isn't a whole lot of empty space in here. I'm pressed up against the wall, clutching the personality enhancer to my chest and praying she hasn't actually spotted me.

"Why is this open?" she mutters, tugging on one of the closet doors, which I guess I didn't close all the way. It's not the one directly in front of me, but she'll still see me when she opens it.

If she opens it. I can hope, right?

I squeeze my eyes shut for a moment, like not watching will make her not see me.

The closet door creaks a little. She starts to pull it open, and I am *so* dead. I hold up my hand, letting a few sparks come to life, even though I don't really intend to use my power on her. I don't think I could make myself hurt Sarah, though I know she's plenty willing to pull the trigger on me. But maybe it will be enough to scare her. I mean, she saw what happened to the roof at Heroesworth.

But then she stops. She only opens the closet door a few inches, just enough to kick a shoe that was wedged there back inside, and then she closes it.

She didn't kill me. I blink, hardly daring to breathe, and marvel at the fact that this didn't just go horribly wrong.

"Okay," she says to the person on the phone. "That'll work great. I'll come down right now." Then she thanks them and hangs up.

She grabs her backpack off the floor, stuffing the phone inside it, and leaves.

I wait until I hear the front door close before letting myself exhale. I open the closet, ready to get the hell out of here with the personality enhancer, but before I can step outside, I notice a red laser beam in the air in front of me. Lots of them, actually, criss-crossing the room like a security system in a spy movie.

Which Sarah has obviously seen too many of.

I pick up one of her shoes from the bottom of the closet and toss it into the room, disturbing some of the beams. As soon as it touches them, *real* lasers—like, the lethal kind that blow stuff up—fire and blast the shoe to pieces.

Great. When did she put this in? I'm going to assume it was after I screwed her up. Because if it was before that, then I think I should have had some warning. What with having a key to her house and all. Not that it really matters right now, because either way, I'm still trapped. By a lethal security system.

And there's only one person I know of who might be able to get me out of this.

And he's never going to let me live it down.

X·X·X

Riley waits until we're safely outside of Sarah's house to say anything, though it's obvious he's pissed. He just used his invisibility power to sneak in through the window and get past the lasers to disarm the system, after I used my cell phone to call him from the closet and tell him I needed his help. He should be smirking at me and gloating about how the tables have turned, especially since this may be his only opportunity for it—what with me not planning on needing him to save my life again or anything —but instead he's mad.

Which actually kind of sucks, because I really don't need one more person mad at me.

"What the *hell*, X?!" he says when we're out on the

sidewalk, moving away from Sarah's house. He shoves me in the shoulder really hard. Luckily it's my left arm, the one without the burn.

"I believe the words you're looking for are 'you had it coming' or maybe even 'I told you so.' I mean, you didn't tell me so, but you were probably thinking it."

"No. I wasn't. What were you doing?"

I hold up the personality enhancer. "You know what I was doing. Stealing this. Obviously."

"Yeah, so why didn't you call me? It's not like I can turn *invisible* or anything!"

I wince. "I had a plan. To fix things. You didn't need to get involved."

His shoulders sag and his arms flop down at his sides. "You weren't going to include me. After everything that's happened, you were seriously going to leave me out of it? I thought we were friends."

I glance over at him, at the hurt look on his face, and then I stare very hard at the sidewalk. I step over a crack with a plant growing through it. "Why would you think that?" My voice sounds very small. Very small and very guilty.

"I don't know, X, I thought— You know what? It doesn't matter! I just left school in the middle of the day— and missed a test, no less—to help you out after you decided to break into Sarah's house to get the device without even telling me, but apparently I did that for no good reason! Just, you know, didn't have anything better to do, so why not?" He shakes his head. "God, I'm an idiot."

"No, you're … you're not."

"I'm not? Then what do you call it?"

I let out a deep breath, rubbing my face with the palm of my hand. "You're not an idiot, because we *are* friends." I might mumble that last part.

"What was that?"

"We *are* friends, okay, Perkins?! Do you want me to tattoo it on my forehead? Geez."

He looks kind of startled by that. He raises his eyebrows, then lowers them. "Okay. If we're friends, then why did you do this without me? Try to, I mean."

"Because. I got us into this mess. I was going to get us back out."

"Yeah, but I thought *we* were working on this? That's what you told me on Sunday. You said we'd figure something out. Is this because I screwed up? Because I couldn't stop Sarah?"

"No. Look, it wasn't anything you did. I just … I've caused everyone enough problems as it is, including you. No, especially you, because I not only got you hurt, but I messed up Sarah."

"I'm not hurt. I'm fine. And—"

"Your girlfriend *shot you* because of me."

"It wasn't her. The real Sarah would never do that. I know that and so do you."

"Well, it doesn't need to happen again. That's why I left you out of this. I was going to fix everything on my own, and when everything was back to normal, *then* you could be mad at me."

"I'm not mad."

I give him a really skeptical look.

"Okay. Fine. Maybe I'm a little mad, but I get why you did it. It was stupid, but I get it."

"I'm going to get this fixed"—I indicate the personality enhancer again—"and then I'm going to— I mean, then *we're* going to use it on her."

"Yeah, sure, you're just going to pop down to the local evil genius store and have them fix it right up."

I lean my head back and sigh. "Something like that."

"You— *Oh*." He swallows. "Can you do that? I thought you said that wasn't an option? That your mom never wanted to ..." He trails off and glances away.

"Never wanted to see me again?"

"Yeah, that. And I thought you weren't exactly talking to her."

"I'm making an exception."

"Do you think she'll do it? Do you think she even can?"

I shrug. "I'll find out. But ... probably." As in probably she *can* fix it. I have no idea if she will.

He considers that for a minute. "And then you call me. Whichever way it turns out."

"Yeah. Then I call you. And then we take down Sarah."

"Right," he says. "And then we take down Sarah."

CHAPTER 25

I t's about ten o'clock at night when I finally sneak downstairs to grab some food from the kitchen. Dinner was at six, but I didn't eat. Like yesterday, I stayed up in my room, because I couldn't face Gordon. Or anyone. I couldn't handle sitting there at the table while Alex made sure not to sit next to me and Gordon refused to speak to me. Or, worse, to even look at me. And I couldn't take Amelia recounting everything everyone said to her at school—since everyone wants to know how she's handling living with a dangerous supervillain in the house, especially one who's destroying her famous dad's reputation—or Helen talking about her day and acting like keeping the shop closed on a Tuesday is normal and isn't because she had to stay home and keep an eye on her evil half-villain stepson who got expelled and who nobody trusts to be on his own.

As if the second their backs are turned, I'm going to run

off and blow up another school or something. I mean, I did run off the second her back was turned, but only to break into Sarah's house and steal her personality enhancer. Which, er, maybe sounds kind of bad, now that I think about it, but it's not like I didn't have a good reason.

So, anyway, I'm pretty hungry by the time I sneak downstairs. I'd meant to wait until ten thirty, just to be on the safe side, but I couldn't hold out. But maybe I should have made more of an effort—or stocked up more snacks in my room when I had the chance—because Gordon is still up. He isn't getting ready for bed like he's supposed to be. He's sitting at the dining table, which is right in my path to the kitchen. I don't know why he's here—doesn't he know some of us have to eat?—but I turn around, intending to slink back upstairs and not come down again until at least midnight.

Or to send Amelia down here instead. I'd have her use her power, but I'm pretty sure she's eaten all the food she's ever touched.

"Damien."

I stop in mid-step. He sounds tired when he says my name. Exhausted and fed up and like he doesn't want to talk to me. Which is fine. I think more people should do what they want. Like, say, *not* talk to their son that they hate. Because it's not like I can't tell he hates me. It's not like I don't see it in his face or hear it in his voice. I'm avoiding him for a reason. And he should be happy about it. He should be glad that I'm staying out of his way and letting him pretend I don't exist.

"Come here."

Seriously? He could just let me walk away, and we could both act like he didn't speak to me, like he only said my name as a reflex, like the way Jess says "cat" or "dog" whenever she sees a picture of one. But no, he has to make this messy and more complicated than it needs to be.

I turn around and approach the table.

He looks me over, like he hasn't seen me in a long time, even though it's only been a couple days.

"Sit down. I want to talk to you."

"No, you don't." My stomach growls and I stare longingly into the kitchen. All that food, so close and yet so far. "We don't have to do this."

"Yes, *we do*." He gets to his feet, anger blazing in his eyes. "Do you have any idea the kind of sacrifices I've made for you?!"

I swallow, suddenly not all that hungry after all. "Yes, and I—"

"No, I don't think you do! And if I say you're going to sit here and talk to me, then you are going to sit here and talk to me, damn it!"

I sit. I spread my hands out against the table and examine my fingers.

"Why didn't you tell me?"

I know he means my electricity power. I shrug. "I was hoping I wouldn't have to. That it would just go away."

"Just go away." He laughs. It's not, like, a happy laugh or anything. It's more angry and mocking, like he can't believe I said that. "Superpowers don't just go away!"

I wince and hunch my shoulders. Him yelling at me

sounds especially loud when the rest of the house is so quiet. And I'm sure everyone else can hear him—they all know he's chewing me out right now. "I didn't want you to look at me like you didn't know me. Like I wasn't who you thought I was. I was hoping I could keep it a secret until it wasn't a problem anymore. You should understand that better than anyone."

"*I* should understand? You endangered hundreds of people and made me the most hated superhero in Golden City, but I should *understand*?!"

"I didn't tell you about my lightning power for the same reason you didn't tell people about me. Because you were hoping you wouldn't have to, that I would just ... maybe not go away, but that I'd stop being someone you were ashamed to admit was your son. You couldn't tell your fans you had a half-villain kid any more than I could go up to you and say, 'Hey, Dad, I can shoot lightning from my hands—that cool with you?'" I shake my head. "Maybe after I got through Heroesworth, and maybe if I got an *H* on my thumb, then telling people about your mistake wouldn't have been so bad."

"My mistake." He lets out a deep breath, some of his anger draining away and leaving a pained expression on his face.

"You sleeping with my mom. With a supervillain. And yeah, okay, I guess I mean me. I'm not exactly someone your fans would approve of. I probably never will be, if we're being honest here, but I thought I could at least look good on paper. So that you could tell people about me with a straight face and not have to answer awkward questions." Or, you know, ruin his career.

"So, you lied to me and pretended you wanted to go to Heroesworth." His voice burns, angry again.

"It wasn't a lie. I—"

"Did you know already? Did you knowingly get me to pull strings to get them to enroll someone with a *villain power*?"

My stomach growls again, despite how sick I feel from him yelling at me. "It didn't start until after that. And the way you said 'villain power' just now, like it's disgusting ... That's why I couldn't tell you." My hands start to shake. Probably from hunger. Definitely not from the way he's looking at me like everything I say just reminds him how much he hates me.

"You should have told me the second you knew."

"Why? You couldn't have done anything about it."

"I could have pulled you out of Heroesworth!"

"I didn't want that."

He slumps down in the seat next to me, staring at his hands. "Damien, I told you you didn't have to go there for me. Now it's obvious you really didn't want to be there. And you didn't take your classes seriously."

"They didn't give me a reason to. The history book was wrong, and everything was stupid, and—"

"You made a poster on what heroism means to you, and it was *blank*." He shakes his head. "I should have known this wasn't going to work. You never wanted to go, and ... there was no flying team, was there?"

"No. I mean, I think there is one, but ... Look, you're wrong, because I *did* want to go."

"Because you thought I wanted you to."

"That's not it. It's part of it, but mostly I just wanted to belong." I don't look at him while I say it. It's hard enough to admit, and I don't need to look over and see the disgust and disappointment on his face. "I was supposed to get a *V* and go to Vilmore, but I didn't. Nobody else has an *X*. Not very many people, and not anyone I know, anyway. I didn't want to be the only one of your kids who didn't go to Heroesworth. I didn't want you to think I wasn't good enough. And I wanted to prove that I could. And, okay, maybe I don't agree with everything they teach there, and maybe I don't want to join the League or anything, but that doesn't mean I wanted to be left out."

"You went to Heroesworth because you wanted to belong?" He sounds extremely skeptical. "You expect me to believe that?"

"It doesn't matter what you believe. It's the truth. And if I'd told you I got a villain power, you would have made me quit. You would have pulled me out of school and stuck me in the attic and never let me leave the house, just like you're doing now. You would have had even more reason to not want people to find out about me."

"So you were just never going to tell me. You trust me so little that ..." He holds up his hands, exasperated. "I don't know what I'm supposed to do with you!"

"I'm sorry."

"Sorry isn't good enough, Damien! Do you have any idea how much damage you've caused? Not just to the school, or to your friends, but to *me*? To this *family*?!"

"I didn't mean for any of this to happen! I—"

"I know you didn't." He gets to his feet. "But it doesn't change the fact that it *did* happen. Because of *you*."

I nod. I cross my arms on the table and press my forehead to my wrists, so he can't see my face. So I can't see his. "I'm going to fix it."

"Fix it?! You can't fix this! You— You've done *enough*. I'm going to figure out what to do with you, and then whatever I say, you're going to do it. Do you hear me? And in the meantime, you had the right idea. Just stay away from everyone and don't cause any more trouble."

"Just stay in the attic and don't talk to anyone or use my villain power, you mean?"

"Yes. That's exactly what I mean. Do you think you can handle that? Do you think you can do *one thing* I ask you without arguing or screwing up? *Do you?!*"

I swallow down the bitter taste in the back of my mouth. My eyes water, but I keep my face pressed to my arms. "Yes."

"Look at me when I'm talking to you, Damien!"

I lift my head. A tear slides down my cheek, and I kind of hate him for it.

"Do you think you can do what I asked you?"

"I said yes, didn't I?"

For a second he looks like he's going to chew me out some more for that, but then suddenly he just looks sad. "There are leftovers in the fridge," he mutters.

"I'm not hungry," I say, right as my stomach growls again.

He makes a scoffing noise, like he can't believe I lied to him about even one more thing, and then says, "Fine. Suit yourself," before storming off into the other room.

X·X·X

"So," Kat says on the phone later, "my dad kind of forbid me to bring you to Homecoming on Friday."

"What, he doesn't want me blasting a hole through the roof? Because I happen to know it will make it onto the evening news. How's that for a publicity opportunity?" I brush crumbs off the edge of my bed and consider eating another granola bar. After scarfing down a turkey sandwich in the kitchen after my run-in with Gordon, I grabbed two boxes of granola bars—the unfortunately healthy kind with giant chunks of nuts in them and no chocolate—plus three apples and a bag of chips, and hauled them back to my room. I decide to wait on the second granola bar and stuff it back in the box.

Kat laughs. "What time will you be there?"

Gordon wants me to stay locked up in my room and not cause trouble. I'm pretty sure going to Vilmore—especially a dance honoring Bart the Blacksmith—would count as trouble. At least it would as soon as someone snapped a picture of me and posted it online. Then the whole city would know the Crimson Flash can't actually keep control over his delinquent villain son. It would look like I was openly defying him. "I don't think I'm going."

"Why? Because of my dad? You're not scared of him, are you?"

"Of course not." The man's insane, that's all. "But I don't think I should. And it's just a dance, right?" Just one

320

I actually wanted to go to. Whatever.

I catch a snippet of the eleven o'clock news coming from Amelia's room. It's something about the Crimson Flash, and I'm glad the sound is too muffled for me to make out any more of it.

"Right," Kat says. "It's just a dance. But my dad still wants me to go with someone. For the photos and stuff."

"Oh." Since when does she do what her dad says?

"So, if you're not going, then I'm taking someone else. You're okay with that?"

No, I'm not okay with that. "You're going with Jordan, right?"

"Jordan has a boyfriend."

"So do you." My fingers tighten around the edge of my blanket.

She hesitates, then says, "Tristan asked me."

I grit my teeth and have to prop my phone between my ear and my shoulder because electricity flares to life in my palms. Of course he asked her. He knows she's with me—the whole world knows that, thanks to all the media coverage—and he still asked. Just like he kept finding excuses to touch her arm right in front of me.

"Damien, did you hear me? I said *Tristan* asked me."

"I heard you." He's going to call her "Katie" all night. Stupid douchebag can't even get her name right. And he's going to stand too close to her and ever-so-casually touch the inside of her wrist. And convince her to dance all the slow songs with him, so he can put his arms around her and maybe press up against her a little.

And definitely get electrocuted if he's ever stupid

enough to cross my path again.

"Well, I'm going with him. I mean, if *you're* not coming."

This is the part where I'm supposed to say of course I'm coming, if it means keeping her away from some guy I hate who wants to put his hands all over her. But I can't.

Amelia turns up the volume on her TV until it's blaring. A news anchor talks in her stupid news anchor voice about how there was a band of protestors today outside the studio where they film *The Crimson Flash and the Safety Kids*, saying that they should cancel the show, since obviously the Crimson Flash isn't fit to teach safety to anyone, especially children.

I shout at Amelia to turn it down.

She does, but only a notch or two. It's still blaring, and I can still hear them talking about how the Crimson Flash isn't who he led everyone to believe and that you can't trust *anyone* these days.

"Damien?" Kat says.

"Maybe you should go with him."

"That's what I— Wait, what? Seriously?"

"You're just going as friends, right?" Well, she is. He's not.

"Of course. But—"

"Then it doesn't matter who you go with." Just saying that makes my mouth taste bad. Of course it matters. She's supposed to go with me. We're supposed to go together, even though she's going to Vilmore and I'm not, and even though I'm half superhero. Those things weren't supposed to get in the way, but now I can't go because of who my dad is. Because he's a superhero and me being half villain has hurt him enough already.

"Tristan's the one who started calling me Katie. He's the one I was partnered with for our field assignment, when we went to Heroesworth."

"I know who he is." And how he's going to die.

I hear more choice audio blasting from Amelia's TV. Something about how the superhero-themed diner downtown is taking "The Crimson Flash Special" off the menu.

"And you're seriously okay with me and him going to Homecoming together?"

Absolutely not. "Is there a reason why I shouldn't be okay with it?"

"Well, no, but—"

"Then it's settled." She'll take that douchebag to the dance, and he'll spend the whole night trying to feel her up, while I stay locked in the attic where I belong. Where I can't cause any trouble or get in Gordon's way. Wonderful. Just how I always pictured it.

"But, Damien, if you don't go, my dad's going to think it's because of him. He's going to think he's getting what he wanted. And he wants me to be seen with someone else. So the media thinks we broke up and stops associating me with you."

I take another deep breath. "It doesn't matter what people think. We're still together."

"I know, but it doesn't feel right. For them to think that."

"No, it doesn't." In fact, it makes me sick. "But this

way, maybe some of the scandal will die down." That's a good thing, right? At least on some level?

"You want us to pretend like we're not together anymore because of some scandal? You sound like my *dad*."

"Maybe he has a point this time." And maybe the world's going to end because I said that.

"No, he doesn't! He just doesn't want us together! He's trying to keep us apart."

"But he can't." He's not the reason I'm not going, even if I can't say I was exactly looking forward to facing him or anything. "It's just one night."

"Sure it is. Just one night where it matters if I'm seen with you. And he's going to think you didn't show up because he forbid it. Like he has any control at all over whether or not we get to be together."

"It will look bad if I go. Because of my dad. And because of everything that's happened."

"It might look bad if you go, but it feels like it will actually *be* bad if you don't. Like everything that's happening really is keeping us apart."

"You mean because I'm half superhero? Because I've completely ruined my dad's life by being half villain, and now I can't be seen with a supervillain, especially at a place like Vilmore? The school *we* were supposed to go to together?"

"Yes."

"I thought you would understand."

"I do, but I don't want to lose you, Damien."

"You're not losing me." *She's* the one going with

someone else.

"No, you just think we shouldn't ever be seen together."

"That's not what I—" Fine, maybe that's what I said. Sort of. "You know why I can't go."

"Because of your dad. Because it might look bad for people to see you with me. To know that you're still my boyfriend."

"Just until this blows over."

"And when is that? When I'm not a supervillain and you're not half hero? When people forget you're his son? Because now that people know who you are, it's *always* going to look bad!"

I swallow. "Kat. It's not like that."

The TV in Amelia's room seems even louder. I don't know when she turned it up, but it's obvious she did. Is it really asking too much for her to not blast horrible news stories at me? I shout at her to turn it down again, but this time she either doesn't hear me or doesn't bother.

"If you can't see me because it looks bad," Kat says, "and it's *always* going to look bad, then when can you see me? When will it be okay for us to actually be together?"

When she's home from school on a weekday and breaks into my house. Obviously. "It's one night." My voice comes out a whisper, as if saying that more quietly will make it sound like less of a lie.

"Oh, so how about you come over on Saturday, then?"

"You know I can't."

"Then next weekend. I'll come home and we can go to the zoo and pretend we think the zebras are weird-looking horses."

"I can't do that, either."

"Superstar is playing a month from now. I'll go see them with you."

"*Kat.*"

"Don't say it's just one night, Damien."

"Fine. But it won't be forever. This doesn't change things between us."

She lets out a deep breath. "It better not."

"I know I said I wasn't really going to run away and join the circus, but let's not rule it out. In case we need a backup plan."

"It's not fair. Because you saved my life, now we can't see each other?"

"I can't cause any more trouble for him."

"Like dating a supervillain? One related to your stepmom's arch nemesis?"

"Our wedding may have to have a circus theme. Clown-free, of course."

"And we can't invite anyone we know."

Well, that goes without saying. "It's going to be all right, Kat." Somehow. I hope.

"Okay." She doesn't sound convinced.

"I mean it," I tell her. "I—"

"Damien, I'd better go. It's getting late."

"Right. But—"

"I'll talk to you later, okay?"

"Yeah, okay. But, listen, I—"

She hangs up.

And I have no idea when I'm going to see her again.

Maybe it's just the fact that I'm not on the phone

anymore, or maybe it's because I'm pissed that some douchebag is going to Homecoming with my girlfriend, who I can't be seen with ever again, but Amelia's TV sounds even louder than it did before. The news is playing interviews from kids at Heroesworth, talking about how they knew all along I was more villain than hero, and that the Crimson Flash must have pulled some serious strings to get me in there.

And this time I don't waste my energy shouting for her to turn it down. I reach out my hand and zap the wall socket, and then a second later the room goes dark and her TV goes silent.

So much for staying in my room and not using my villain power.

CHAPTER 26

Taylor answers the door when I go over to Mom's house on Wednesday with the personality enhancer. It feels weird to knock at my own house. Except it isn't my house anymore, which feels even weirder.

"Damien?" Taylor blinks at me and scratches his scraggly beard, like he never thought he'd see me again, and especially not here. That makes two of us.

I fidget and shift my weight from one foot to the other, just wanting to get this over with. "Is Mom home? I need to see her."

He glances over his shoulder, which I guess means she *is* home, and then back at me, looking worried. Like he's thinking I'm the last person she ever wants to see again and maybe he shouldn't let me in.

"It won't take long," I tell him, "and then she can get back to pretending I don't exist."

He sighs. "That's not ..." He clears his throat and leans

in closer to me. "We're getting married this Christmas. Your mother and I are."

As if I didn't know who he meant. I roll my eyes at him. "I *know*. She told me. At the hospital, when ..." When Xavier was born. "It's not like I didn't know you guys were engaged. I'm not going to, like, flip out or anything. I know you must have seen the videos, but I'm not here to blow up the house."

He flinches a little at that. "What I'm trying to say is that I think—I know—she wants you there, but I'm afraid she doesn't know how to ask you."

"She doesn't know how to ask me to her own wedding?" The one she wasn't even going to tell me about? I shake my head, not buying that. "That's because she *doesn't* want me to come." Not, like, in a million years.

"But I'm certain that she does. And I want our wedding day to be perfect for her, and that's not going to happen unless you're there."

I laugh. I can't help it. The idea that she needs me at all, but especially at her wedding, is ridiculous.

"I know this is difficult for you," he says, "but it's true. She's not really going to be happy unless you attend, and you've made it very clear you don't want to have anything to do with her."

"That goes both ways. Don't pretend like she wanted to talk to me all this time, like she didn't just go out and get herself a new son to replace me with."

He holds up a hand. "This means a lot to her, and I know she doesn't know how to ask you. Not after everything that's happened between you. And I also know she'll regret it if she doesn't. So, *I'm* asking you."

I raise my eyebrows at him. "You're seriously inviting me to your wedding right now?"

"Yes."

"And you think that's a good idea?"

"I think it's—"

Mom's voice interrupts him, shouting from within the house, "Honeybuns, who was at the door?"

"It's ..." He seems to think better of telling her I'm here. "Just a minute, sugar lemon!"

Barf. I do *not* miss hearing their stupid pet names for each other.

Taylor gestures for me to come inside. I step into the hallway, and for a moment, it feels like I never left. Like nothing's changed at all. And then we get to the living room, and I see that *everything's* changed.

For one thing, it's not messy. I mean, not that there's no mess at all—there's a bunch of baby stuff on the coffee table and a big pile of laundry on the couch, though it's folded—but there are also new shelves lining the walls and some big plastic drawers. Everything is organized, and all the drawers are color-coded and labeled alphabetically. It's like stepping into opposite-world or something.

"We've made some changes," Taylor says. "We had to baby-proof the house, and it just made sense."

"Wow, really? Cleaning up and putting everything away 'just made sense'?" I smack my palm against my forehead. "Why didn't *I* ever think of that?" My mom's been messy and unorganized my whole life, and now stupid Xavier comes along and she turns over a new leaf?

Taylor glares at me. "Stay here." He runs off into Mom's bedroom—er, their bedroom, I guess, which is gross—and returns holding a fancy white envelope. He hands it to me. "For the wedding," he says quietly. "And if you decide not to come ... I'd appreciate it if you didn't mention this to her."

As if I'm going to mention it to her either way or speak to her any more than I have to.

The envelope has silver writing on it that says, *You're invited.* I open it, and inside is a cream-colored card claiming that Marianna Locke and Taylor Lewis, along with their son, Xavier Locke, are inviting me—well, not me specifically, but the recipient of the card—to attend their very special day. As if Xavier has any say in it or any feelings about it whatsoever. Though I guess if he did, he'd probably be happy, since they're his parents. It's not going to be gross or make him feel weird to see them together, like it does me.

"You don't have to bring anything," Taylor says, noticing me still staring at the card with all the wedding info on it.

"Right, because I won't be there." Not that I want to go, but even if I did, if I can't go to Homecoming with Kat because she's a supervillain, then I sure as hell can't go to my mom's wedding. Then people would figure out *exactly* which supervillain the Crimson Flash slept with, which would be yet another scandal. Plus, I know Mom would throw a fit if I showed up and ruined her wedding day, no matter what Taylor says.

"Please, at least think about it." He gives me this sad

look, like he already knows that I'm not going to, then says, "She's in the nursery."

The nursery? This is only a two-bedroom house, so I don't know where there'd be room for a— Oh. He means she's in my room. Or what was my room, I guess.

I slip the wedding invitation in my pocket and go down the hall. My door—er, the nursery door—is open.

"Who was at the—" Mom cuts off, gasping in surprise when she sees me in the doorway. She's sitting on the floor with … Well, with what must be Xavier. He has the same red hair as her, but he's a *lot* bigger than the last time I saw him. I don't know how fast newborns are supposed to grow, but I know that at not even one month old, he definitely shouldn't be crawling around on the floor. Or holding Mom's hand and trying to stand.

She gapes at me, her jaw trembling.

"Hi, Mom. I do *not* like what you've done with the place." The walls of my room used to be blue, but now she's painted them yellow. Like blue wasn't good enough. Like she's over it. And instead of my bed, there's a crib and a changing table. And of course there's the toddler on the floor, which I could really do without.

Mom gets up, leaving Xavier in the lurch with no one to steady him as he tries to stand. "Damien, what are you doing here?" She sounds surprised. And maybe worried.

I hold up the personality enhancer and get right to the point. "I need your help."

She glares at me. "*That's* why you're here? I watched you get shot at on the evening news and had to hear from someone else that you were all right, because you didn't even have the decency to *call your mother* and tell her you were okay, and now you're here because you want something from me?!"

Xavier starts crying—probably because she's yelling—and sinks down to the floor, giving up on standing. His crying is sort of a high-pitched wail-scream that makes my ears feel like they're going to bleed.

I swallow and take a step away from them. "Need, not want. And who told you I was all right?"

"Mary. Wilson," she adds, as if I didn't know she meant Kat's mom. "I was worried sick, no thanks to you."

"It couldn't have bothered you that much. I mean, it's not like you don't have a backup son." One who's growing freakishly fast and should be fully replacing me in no time.

"*Damien Locke*, I am still your mother, and don't you come into my house and talk to me like that! Do you think it was easy for me to see you on TV and not know what happened to you? You could have been hurt—you could have been *dead*—and you didn't even think to tell me."

"I was kind of busy." What with my whole life falling apart and everything. Making sure my estranged mother's feelings weren't hurt wasn't exactly my top priority. "And it's not like you called me, either. If you were so desperate to know what was going on with me, you could have picked up the phone."

She shakes her head. "I couldn't. I wanted to, but what if you didn't answer? I wouldn't have known if it was because you were hurt—or worse—or if you just didn't want to talk to me."

"I would have answered," I mutter, not looking at her and not knowing if it's true.

"I called Mary, but she didn't know anything about you either, only that Kat was hurt and in the hospital. And then she called me Sunday afternoon and said Tom had talked to you and that you were all right. But I didn't hear a word from you. You talked to Kat's parents, but obviously you couldn't be bothered to let your own mother know you were still alive."

Uh, yeah, maybe because they don't hate me. Except for her dad, I mean. "Well, I *am* alive, and I'm here, and— Hey!" I spot something familiar in Xavier's crib and march over to it. It's my old teddy bear, Damien II, my favorite toy when I was growing up. He's gotten pretty shabby and kind of awful-looking over the years, and one ear is worn through, making him really stand out among all the new baby things. I snatch him out of the crib. "This is *mine.* When I came to get my stuff before, you told me you didn't know where he was!"

"Oh, sweetie, you're sixteen. You're too old to have stuffed animals."

"So you lied to me? And now you're giving my stuff to *him*?" I can't believe her.

"It reminded me of you, and you didn't need it," she says calmly. "And now Xavier likes it."

Apparently. It looks like one of the ears has been slobbered on recently.

I wish I hadn't come here. I wish I wasn't standing in my old room, now turned into my replacement's nursery, clutching a broken gadget and an old stuffed bear. And I really, *really* want to turn around and walk away, but I can't leave without getting her help first. "I'm taking him," I say, holding the teddy bear to my chest and gesturing with the personality enhancer, as if he's my hostage.

"Fine," Mom says. "If you want to be selfish and deprive your brother of his favorite toy."

"*His* favorite toy?! He's not even one month old! He'll get over it. And you shouldn't have given it to him."

Xavier, still crying and making these annoying little wail-gasps, watches me holding the bear and stretches his arms out for it. Fat chance, kid. The little usurper has everything I ever wanted—he doesn't get to have this, too.

Mom sucks in a deep breath, like she's trying to stay calm about me actually wanting to keep something from my childhood. "You said you came here because you need my help."

"I need you to fix something." I hold up Sarah's gadget again. "It's important. I wouldn't ask if it wasn't. So, just do this one thing for me, and then I'll get out of here and you never have to see me again."

X·X·X

"Damien, what did you *do* to this thing?" Mom asks, frowning in horror at the personality enhancer, which she's got opened up on her lab table in front of her.

"I didn't say I did anything. I just said it was broken." I set Damien II on the table, inspecting him for more signs of Xavier abusing him. I think he chewed on his nubby bear tail, and there's a dried up, slimy-looking smear on his foot.

Mom tilts her head, giving me a look that says she knows better than that.

"Fine. I zapped it." I hold up a hand, letting a couple of sparks flare at my fingertips. "Twice."

She breathes out slowly through her teeth.

I drum my fingers on the edge of the table, not liking that reaction. "You can fix it, though, right?"

"Sarah made this?"

"Obviously."

"Wasn't she the one shooting at you?"

"Yeah, but it wasn't really her, and … it's a long story. Just tell me you can fix it."

She bites her lip. "Are you really in that much of a hurry to never see me again?"

Kind of. Maybe. But I don't like the sad way she's looking at me, like I just kicked her favorite puppy or something. I swallow and look away. "I just need it. To fix Sarah, before …" Before she does something else crazy. "I just need it, all right? As soon as possible."

She turns away from the personality enhancer, looking me over and studying my face. "I saw the press conference."

I nod and squish Damien II's nose up into his snout, then let it pop back out again. "What does that have to do with you fixing the device or not?"

"If I'm going to fix it and never see you again, the least you can do is talk to me. Are you all right?"

"You can see that I'm fine." Except for the bandage on my arm, which I guess she can't see, since it's hidden by

336

my sleeve. But it's not a big deal, and she doesn't need to know about it.

"I was referring to everything that's going on. With that —with your *father*—and your lightning power. Your grandfather wants you to call him, by the way."

"What, and he can't call me, either?" I haven't spoken to either of my grandparents since before my birthday, when I got my *X*.

"He thinks someone else might answer, and he said if he gets one of those superheroes on the line, he's going to give them a piece of his mind, whether you want him to or not, for putting you in that school in the first place. I tried to tell him he'd be calling your cell phone, not the house, but he wasn't satisfied."

I shake my head. "Going to Heroesworth was my idea."

She raises an eyebrow. "It was? You're sure *someone* didn't pressure you into it?"

"*Someone* meaning Gordon? Yeah, I'm sure. I mean, he was happy about it, but he also tried to talk me out of it, and I didn't listen."

"Well, call your grandfather and tell him that."

"Why? So he can hate me, too?" Yeah, right. Not that I want him unjustly thinking about electrocuting Gordon every time he comes on TV or anything, but is it so bad if I have *one* relative who doesn't think I'm the scum of the earth?

"You think I hate you?" Mom says, her voice going funny and her forehead wrinkling and her mouth dropping open a little.

"I meant Gordon, but now that you mention it, I know

I'm not exactly your favorite person or anything." Certainly not her favorite son. I mean, I used to be her *only* son, so I guess I was the best and worst by default, but not anymore. "And what the hell's up with Xavier? He's way older than I thought he would be."

"Never you mind about Xavier. He's fine."

"He's *walking*." I rest my elbows on the lab table and put my chin in my hands.

"And someday, when you're older and have children of your own, you'll understand how wonderful that is."

"Uh, no, I don't think I will."

"Well, you'll at least understand why I wanted to get through certain phases of his development more quickly than others. I'd forgotten just how much work newborns are. I wasn't getting any sleep."

I sit up. "Wait, what are you saying? Mom, did you give him *more* of that formula?!"

She holds up a hand. "Calm down. Like I said, you'll understand when you're older."

"You're saying if I have kids someday, I'll understand why you didn't want him to have a childhood?" Yeah, *that* sounds right. "How's he supposed to learn stuff?"

"Ah." She gets this proud smile on her face. "I've already thought of that. Everything he needs to know, that he'd normally take months to learn, I feed into his brain at night through music with subliminal messaging. I wish I could take credit for it, but these supervillains in Switzerland created the system. It's all very well done. Information isn't just pumped in, but it's delivered through memories fabricated to have the right results. I'm thinking of making him think he crashed his bicycle and was nearly thrown into traffic—those things can be dangerous, and I don't want him getting run over."

I stare at her. Like she's crazy. Which she obviously is.

"Now, Damien, don't look at me like that. I'm not going to do it until he's older. He's too young to ride a bicycle right now."

"I had a bike and I'm not dead."

"But I *worried*. You were always so daring, and every time you went out with your friends, I worried about you getting hurt. But with Xavier, I don't have to go through that again."

"You're just going to make him afraid of everything?"

"Not everything. I enjoy ice skating. I thought we could do that together."

Wow. "That's messed up."

She grits her teeth. "I did not bring you into my lab to be criticized. I love little Xavier, just like I ..." She trails off, unable to say it.

I make it easier for her. "Just like you *used* to love me?"

She shuts her eyes for a moment, then opens them again. "I'm your mother, Damien. I still love you."

I go back to inspecting Damien II again, noticing how there's hardly any fur left across his stomach. "Yeah, sure you do. That's why you kicked me out of the house. That's why you replaced me and never want to see me again."

"I never said I didn't want to see you again."

"You didn't have to. I was your son for sixteen years, and I thought I mattered to you. But then I did one thing you didn't like—"

"You became a *superhero*. I was always afraid that you ... with *his* genes, and ... You made it clear which of us you take after."

"I blew up part of Heroesworth. I have a villain power. I got expelled and arrested and millions of people have watched it all online. I did all that, and Gordon took the fall for me. He took me in when you decided you were done with me, and now he's ruined his life, trying to protect me. It's more than I deserve, and I kind of wish he hadn't done it, because he hates me now, but ... Look, don't try and tell me you're better than him."

"You never went against my plans before you met him. That day at the Banking and Finances building, when you pulled that raygun on me, and after I saved your life, I just ... I didn't know who I was seeing anymore. You'd changed so much. And you could *fly*." She sounds disgusted, and I can't help feeling a twinge of self-loathing. "But, despite your mistakes, I never stopped loving you, Damien. And I'm sure your father hasn't, either."

I shake my head. "Five minutes in a subway bathroom with him doesn't mean you know him." She hasn't seen the way he looks at me. Or, more accurately, the way he *doesn't* look at me. "Millions of people hate him now. He's never going to forgive me."

"You were protecting Kat."

"And endangering lots of other people. Everything that happened that night was my fault. And it doesn't matter why I did it, because he's still the most hated superhero in Golden City because of me. Because everyone thinks it was his fault instead of mine. They're even talking about canceling his show."

"So," she says, speaking slowly, "a lot of people think things that aren't true because of something you did."

I roll my eyes at her. "I know what you're going to say."

"That it wouldn't be the first time?"

"Yeah, but this is different. It wasn't something I did on purpose, and it's *a lot* of people. The whole city. Maybe even the whole country."

"Damien, I don't know if you've noticed this, but you're very good at getting people to believe what you want them to. Like that time last year when you convinced that family down the street to move because you didn't like their kids."

"*Nobody* liked them. They were so obnoxious." Always shrieking and playing right outside our house. "And I know one of them peed in our yard that one time, even if I couldn't prove it. Plus, they kept trampling Mrs. Murdy's flower beds." Mrs. Murdy is an old lady who lives across the street. She's really cranky and mean, but she likes me because I'm the only person she knows who's not afraid to argue with her. And I happen to know it's not easy for her to work in her garden these days—not with her arthritis—but those stupid kids were messing up her plants like it didn't matter.

"You made them think their house was haunted."

I grin. "They're lucky that's all I did. I was considering making them think there was a sewage leak." I had several backup plans, actually. I went with haunting because they couldn't prove it was true or not.

"My point is that you can be very persuasive, when you put your mind to it."

"You think I can convince Gordon not to hate me?" That seems unlikely. I mean, if it was that easy, I would have done it already.

"I think you can make people believe what you want them to, whether that's a family down the street or the entire city."

"Nothing I say can change what happened. The Crimson Flash still has a half-villain son who blew up part of Heroesworth with his scary lightning power. I don't think I can spin that."

"Well, I think you underestimate yourself." She smiles a little. Then she sighs and looks at the personality enhancer again. "This is going to be a lot of work, you know that?"

"But you can fix it?"

"Most likely. It's going to take me a while, though."

"How long?"

She takes a deep breath, looking it over. "Your friend Sarah has a very *interesting* method of construction. It's too bad she wasn't born a villain—she'd do well at Vilmore."

I laugh. "I'm *not* telling her you said that." Not until I fix her, anyway.

"Give me a couple of days on this. You can come get it Friday morning. I'm afraid we're going to have to see each one more time, after all."

"Yeah, well, maybe it doesn't have to be the *absolute* last time. I mean, I'm not forgiving you for what happened or anything, but maybe ..."

"Maybe you could come over for dinner once in a

while?"

"I've had your cooking, so ... no. But something like that." Not that I'm allowed to leave the house or anything, or go hang out with supervillains, so I probably won't actually ever come over. But the idea of it doesn't sound like the worst thing in the world anymore, at least.

"I'd like that," she says. "And maybe it wouldn't kill you to call me once in a while? Especially if you end up on the evening news again."

"Deal. And same goes for you. If you, like, have another kid or something, you should probably call me. Not that you should have another kid or ever have sex again or anything, but if something life-changing happens, then I guess I want to know about it."

"All right," she says. "Then we're agreed."

"Yeah," I tell her. "I guess we are."

CHAPTER 27

I know Kat's classes are over at three today, and I kind of expect her to call me and tell me she's crazy for even thinking of going to Homecoming with anyone else but me, and that if I won't go, she's going to lock herself in her dorm room all night and listen to really emo music and not go to the dance at all, not even to take pictures with her dad, no matter how much he begs her. And probably cry. A lot.

Okay, so I don't really expect her to do any of that. But I do expect her to call and try to get me to change my mind again. So after I get home from Mom's house, I sit on my bed, staring at my phone, waiting for it to ring. Like someone who has no life. Though I do text Riley to tell him about Mom fixing the personality enhancer, but that doesn't really count. And when it gets around three thirty and Kat still hasn't called or texted or anything, I figure she's either mad at me, or that she realized how serious I was about not going. Probably both, I guess. I think about calling her, but I don't really want to hear in her voice that she's still hurt over the fact that I can pretty much never see her in person again. Which, I admit, really sucks and kind of puts a damper on our plans to spend the rest of our lives together.

But since I can't do anything to change that at the moment, I decide to take a more pro-active approach and get online to stalk Tristan. If the douchebag is going to take my girlfriend to Homecoming, he's going to have to face the consequences. And murdering a supervillain doesn't count as trouble, does it? Maybe if I kill him, the public will think that I'm more hero than villain after all and stop hating the Crimson Flash, since his son is obviously so much better than they thought. I mean, Riley said the League Treaty prohibits causing unnecessary bodily harm to your enemies, but clearly killing Tristan is necessary. I would be following the rules *and* enjoying what I'm doing. It's a win-win situation for everyone. Well, everyone except Tristan.

He's not hard to find, since he's friends with Kat on Facebook. He even posted on her wall earlier today, saying, *Can't wait for Friday!* It has three likes. One of them is him. He liked his *own* stupid message to her. Douchebag. I almost add my own comment that says, *Can't wait to electrocute you!* but I stop myself. That might alert him to the fact that I intend to murder him, which might make it more difficult. I mean, he should know already that I'm going to kill him, since he's taking Kat to the dance, but obviously he's underestimating me.

I go to his profile and see that he has two brothers and a sister. He also likes field hockey, whatever the hell that is, and listens to a strange mixture of stupid pop bands and metal. Thankfully, he doesn't like Superstar, and I don't have to kill myself for having something in common with him. Most of the shows he watches are reality shows. I notice the most recent movie he added to his favorites is *Pirate Zombies from Hell*, like that's going to impress Kat or something and make up for all his bad taste, especially since most of the other movies he likes are weird indie films I've never heard of.

I have several options here. One, I could convince Kat that she should go with all her friends to the movies again, since I won't be able to make it. Like, ever. Except I'll make it to that one, secretly, and then zap Tristan when he goes to the bathroom or something. That option might take a while, since it involves a movie coming out that everyone wants to see, plus there's no guarantee I'll be able to get him alone, and I don't want to murder any more of Kat's friends than I have to.

Option two, I create a fake profile and make him fall in love with me. Which has the added bonus of him getting distracted from Kat and leaving her alone. Then I ask him to finally meet me somewhere—somewhere very private, where there will be no witnesses—and kill him. I like this plan even less, though, because it involves actually interacting with him and leaving a trail online that could be traced back to me. You know, if anyone ever actually missed him enough to try and figure out what happened.

And, unfortunately, neither of those options involves

killing him before Friday evening.

I sigh, going back to the drawing board, when there's a knock on my door.

"Go away, Amelia! I'm busy!"

"Oh, okay," Zach's voice says. "I'll come back later!"

"Wait!" I get up from the bed and open the door.

Zach's standing in the hallway. "Me and Amelia are going to play *Villains vs. Heroes*," he says. "I thought you might want me to kick your ass again, but if you're too busy ..."

I wave my hand in front of his face. I don't understand why he's here, or why he's still talking to me. "Did I accidentally zap your brain and erase your memories? You saw me blow up part of Heroesworth last week. With my villain power."

"*Yes.*" His eyes light up. "That was the coolest thing I've ever seen in real life! I— Er, I mean," he adds, trying to tone down his enthusiasm and look appropriately somber, "that was really awful. What happened at the dance. Riley told me your girlfriend's going to be okay, though, right?"

"Yeah, she's fine."

"And he said Sarah's not really insane."

"Right."

"So ... can I see it?" He holds up his hands and wriggles his fingers.

"*No.* Shouldn't you hate me for pretty much ruining the Crimson Flash's life?"

"I already knew you were half villain." He shrugs. "And all that stuff he said, about knowingly endangering everyone at Heroesworth by having you go there, obviously isn't true. He's the *Crimson Flash*. He wouldn't do that. Plus, it's not like you're dangerous or anything."

I raise an eyebrow at him.

"Okay, okay," he says. "So maybe you're *a little* dangerous. Not dangerous enough to beat me at *Villains vs. Heroes*, obviously. But I trust you. I'll even prove it to you. You show me your lightning power right now, and I promise I won't freak out."

"Nice try, Zach. I'm not showing it to you."

"Aw, man! Why not?"

"Because. You already saw it. And I almost killed people with it."

"What about your flying power? Can you show me that? Or have you, like, killed too many people with it or something?"

"Yeah, hundreds. It's terrible."

"So, can I see it or what?"

"You've seen me use my lightning power, I've seen you go invisible. I think we're even."

"Your math is wrong. You've seen all of my powers, and I've only seen half of yours."

"Why do you want to see it so badly?"

"Uh, because you're awesome, obviously. And because we're friends. I mean," he adds, suddenly looking nervous, "I know you're my brother's friend and older than me and stuff, but I thought maybe you liked hanging out with me, too." His face goes kind of red, like he's worried I might tell him he's just Riley's annoying little brother and that he should get lost.

"You saw what I did at Homecoming, and you still

think I'm awesome?"

"Are you kidding me? I think you're awesome *because* of what you did at Homecoming."

"Because I blew up the roof?"

"No, no. Well, yeah. But mostly because you didn't back down. Sarah was going to *kill* you. Your girlfriend was hurt, and so was Riley, and nobody else was even trying to stop Sarah. Everybody thought you were the bad guy, but you still stood up to them. If everybody thought I was doing something wrong, and they were all yelling and pointing guns at me and threatening to use their powers on me and stuff ... I don't know if I could do it. Stand up to them, I mean. And now everybody's saying that you're a criminal and that the Crimson Flash isn't who they thought he was, but he *must* be, if you're his son, because what you did was really heroic. And not that being a hero is easy or anything, but it must be especially hard to be one when everybody thinks you're a villain."

Wow. That wasn't what I expected, and I just kind of stare at him for a minute. Then I take a deep breath and run my hand through my hair. "You really want to see my flying power?"

"Yeah."

"Come in. And close the door. And don't tell anyone about this."

"Don't tell anyone about what you showed me in your room with the door closed? Got it."

I smirk at that, though only for a second, because even though it's just Zach here and he thinks I'm awesome and I kind of trust him, I'm still really nervous about this.

He closes the door, and I go and stand in the middle of the room. "Okay, so, I haven't exactly done this in a long time. And I kind of hate it. And I'm just going to lift off the ground a little bit, okay? Nothing, like, amazing or anything."

If I can do this at all. I'm not even sure I know how.

I think about what I do when I use my lightning power —how I just sort of think about it and then it's there. And then, as I'm thinking that, I feel a tingle of electricity along my arm. Oops. I make it go away and switch gears, thinking instead about lifting off the ground. My least favorite thing.

I imagine my feet not being on the floor and how sick I'm going to feel when I'm hovering in the air, with nothing solid beneath me. I mean, not that the attic floor is exactly my idea of a safe place to stand, but at least it's something. I picture it crumbling out from under me, in an attempt to trick myself into feeling like this is another life or death situation. But all that does it make my hands start to shake.

I close my eyes and try a different tactic. Because thinking about possibly dying, and about how horrible I'll feel when I finally do use my power, isn't exactly working. So instead I imagine something even worse—I imagine actually *liking* it. Which takes a lot more imagination than, say, reliving falling from the tallest building in Golden City. But I think about wanting to rise up off the ground. About how being able to fly means, in a way, never *not* being safe, because I can't ever fall. I imagine floating, and I have such a good imagination that it feels like I really am, which makes my stomach twist up and my insides squirm. But I ignore that and try to pretend it's as cool as Zach probably thinks it is.

Then I bump my head on something, and Zach says, "*Whoa*," and I open my eyes and see him below me. Because I'm touching the ceiling. Because I wasn't imagining floating—I was really doing it.

A jolt of panic lights up my nerves. My flying power cuts out and I *drop*. One second, I didn't even realize I'd left the ground, and the next, my blood runs cold with overwhelming terror, and the floor is rising up to meet me.

So much for not being able to fall.

I don't land gracefully, but I do manage to land on my feet, in sort of a squatting position with one arm out behind me. Sweat prickles up and down my back, and I feel like I can't breathe, but I grin at Zach anyway, hoping he doesn't notice how freaked out I am, and say, "Happy now?"

"Yes."

"Good."

Because I'm *never* doing that again.

X·X·X

I get dressed up Friday evening—dress shirt, jacket, pants, bow tie, everything—as if I was going to Homecoming with Kat.

Not that I am. I mean, only someone who was awful and didn't care that they ruined their famous superhero father's life would even think about going to Homecoming at Vilmore. Which can't be me, because I'm not awful. Or, at least, I'm trying really hard not to be.

But I talked to Kat on the phone yesterday, and it was weird. Not because she said anything about the dance or about me not going—or about her going with someone else—but because she *didn't*. And I didn't, either, because I didn't want her to think about how I can't really see her right now. Or possibly ever. Not that I really believe that, because *ever* is a long time, and something's bound to change eventually, right? I'm going to fix this. Somehow. And then ... Well, then I'll still be the Crimson Flash's son.

But anyway, it was obvious there was something wrong, even though neither of us said anything about it. I wanted to tell her I was sorry, but it wouldn't really have helped anything. Me being sorry doesn't mean I can see her. It doesn't mean me not going to the dance isn't the first in a long line of missed events.

I think about all the days stretching out before us, of me not seeing her. Of our conversations getting weirder and weirder as we slip away from each other, and as we never say anything about it, because calling attention to it might make it too real.

I think about Gordon and all the things I've done to hurt him, and about how much worse it will be if I go to the dance. At Vilmore. Honoring Helen's arch nemesis, my girlfriend's grandfather. And how it will look to the entire city like I'm defying him, and that I'm just as villainous as everyone thinks I am. But it's not like he's ever going to forgive me as it is.

So maybe I've already lost him. I can't lose Kat, too.

Or maybe this will be the last straw and he'll decide to send me away. Maybe there's some boarding school for delinquent superhero kids. Because it's not like having superhero genes makes you perfect. There's bound to be plenty of other screwups, and they've got to put them somewhere. For all I know, he's already got something like that in mind for me. But maybe he's hoping I can stay, just like I am, and maybe me going to the dance at Vilmore will push him over the edge.

But I can't lose Kat. I *can't*. And yeah, she'll still love me, even if I don't go. But it'll hurt. She might not spend the night listening to emo music and crying in her room, but she'll miss me, and me not being there—me not being able to be *seen* with her—will hurt. A lot. And she'll know I let this get between us. That I fought to save her life, but that I didn't fight to be with her. And I'll hate myself for it. I kind of already do.

So I get dressed, as if I was going.

The personality enhancer—now fixed, thanks to Mom— sits on my bed. I glance over guiltily at it, because *if* I was going to sneak out tonight, it should be to use it on Sarah. Not to go to the dance.

But Sarah can wait one more day. This can't.

I finish getting dressed and creep downstairs. As if I'm going to leave.

Which I'm not. Because, like I said, only someone who was awful would do that. Only a really terrible person would add one more offense to the long list of terrible things they've done to hurt their father. And their family.

And pretty much anyone ever associated with them.

Gordon's not home yet, even though it's a little after five. Amelia's in her room, talking on the phone. I don't know where Helen and Jess are, though I can smell dinner cooking, so Helen must be home. But they're not in the living room, and my only witness is Alex, who's sitting on the floor, watching TV. He looks up at me when I come in, his eyes wide, then hurries to face the TV again, like *he's* the one worried I might see him. I wonder if he has any idea that I'm not supposed to leave the house, that I'm even doing something wrong.

I put my hand on the doorknob. Because I love Kat and I don't want her going to the dance with that douchebag, but more than that, I can't just not fight for her. I can't just stay home and never see her again.

But if I go ...

I hesitate, letting go of the knob. I step away from the door. Gordon doesn't deserve me doing this to him. He thinks I'm enough of a lost cause already, and if I go, then he'll *know* I am.

My phone rings. I hurry to silence it and see that it's Riley. He knows I was picking up the personality enhancer today—he probably wants to figure out when we're going to use it on Sarah. I can't exactly talk right now, so I ignore the call and set my phone to silent mode.

I walk away from the door. Then I change my mind and march back over to it. Then away again, then back. And I know I have to do this, I *have* to go, or else—

"*Damien*," Helen's voice says behind me, "what the hell do you think you're doing?"

Damn it.

I pause in mid-reach, pulling my hand away from the doorknob and turning to face her. I should have just left. If I hadn't waffled, if I'd stopped kidding myself about maybe staying home and being good, I'd be out the door already.

"I wasn't going anywhere," I lie. Or maybe it's not a lie. Maybe I really wasn't.

She glares at me. "You know you're not allowed to leave the house."

"I just said I wasn't!"

Alex turns his head, risking a glance at us, looking nervous.

"And you expect me to believe that?" She takes in how I'm dressed and shakes her head. "After everything your father has done for you, you couldn't even ... Were you going to see Kat?"

I look away.

"Of course you were. Did you even think about the fact that someone would see you? That pictures of the two of you would wind up online? Do you know what that would look like?! He doesn't need this! He—"

"So don't tell him!" I squeeze my eyes shut, my face heating up with guilt. Does she really think I don't care? "*Please*. Just ... Look, I didn't go anywhere! I was thinking about it, but I didn't, so—"

"Unbelievable!"

She's going to tell him. I didn't even go, and now he's going to know just how much he should hate me. My heart pounds, and I wish I hadn't gotten dressed up, that I'd stayed in my room. I don't know what's wrong with me.

I don't know why, after everything I've done, I can't stop ruining his life.

"You think because I caught you *before* you could leave means you didn't do anything wrong? That he doesn't need to know his son was carelessly running off to go on a date with a supervillain? Like you don't even care what you've done or what happens to him?!"

"Of course I care!" Electricity zaps along my spine and makes my hair stand on end. But I keep the sparks down this time. I don't want to fight with her—I just want this to be over with so I can go hide in my room again. "And it wasn't just a date. I know what it would look like, if people saw me with her, and— You think I'd be doing this if it wasn't important?!"

Alex gets up and runs off to his room.

I hear Amelia's door open upstairs. She doesn't come down, but she doesn't close her door again, either, so I know she's listening in. Because, you know, what I really need for this is an audience.

Helen sighs. "Honestly? I don't know what you'd do right now. And what could possibly be so important?"

Me going to Homecoming. At Vilmore. Which is going to sound even worse than whatever she thinks is going on. "Never mind. It wasn't anything." Just my life. No big deal. "Forget it."

I go to move past her, but she blocks me. "Damien. You don't get to walk away when I'm talking to you."

"Tell him whatever you want. It doesn't matter."

"If I have to tell him you were sneaking out to see her, that you were going to hurt him again, then I at least get to know *why.*"

"Fine." I'm dead at this point, anyway. She's going to tell him, and he's going to hate me more than he already does. He's going to keep me locked up in the attic forever, or ship me off to a place bad superhero kids go and forget about me. I'm really never going to see Kat again, or any of my friends. I'll give Riley the personality enhancer, and he can fix Sarah, and I'll just disappear. "I was going to Homecoming."

"Homecoming was last weekend." She raises an eyebrow, like she thinks I've lost it. Like maybe I fried my brain with all that electricity, or like all the bad stuff that's happened has made me snap.

"Yeah, at Heroesworth. This one's at Vilmore."

She folds her arms, her mouth an angry, thin line. "You were seriously going to a dance with Kat *at Vilmore*? Are you kidding me?" She puts a hand to her forehead, like she kind of wishes she hadn't asked, because now she's going to have to tell Gordon just how bad this is.

"I know how it sounds. But her dad's sponsoring the dance, and his publicity team's going to be there, taking pictures all night."

"And you wanted to make sure people saw you there?" She gapes at me in horror.

"No! I mean, her dad forbid me to go, because he thinks I'm not good enough for her, and because it's my fault she got hurt last weekend. He doesn't want her to be seen with me. He thinks if she goes to the dance with someone else, and people see her with someone less scandalous, then the media will back off and leave her alone. They'll think we're not together anymore." I make a face, still not liking that, even if it might be for the best.

"And you don't want people to think that."

"Of course I don't. But that's not what this is about."

"So, this is about you being jealous of someone else?"

I shake my head. "I told her to go with him. With another guy, I mean. And I told her her dad's right, and that we can't be seen together. Not just at the dance, but, like, *ever.*"

Helen takes a sharp breath in through her nose, understanding dawning on her. "You really said that to her?" She gives me a worried look, like I should know better than to say something that stupid and hurtful to my own girlfriend, even if she's not on Helen's list of favorite people.

"I pretty much told her I can never see her again. And I know what you're thinking. I know you're probably happy about this, because you didn't want us together in the first place. But it's not about what other people think, or about her going with some other guy." Who's going to die horribly from electric shock. "It's about her thinking we can never be together. But, I mean ..." I swallow. "I don't want to hurt Gordon any more than I already have. And I know what me being with her looks like. And I'm *always* going to be his son, even if he hates me, and she's *always* going to be a supervillain. And related to your arch nemesis." So maybe we really can't be together, after all.

"That's why you were sneaking out of here?"

"It's stupid."

"Damien. It's not stupid."

"It's not like it matters. Not after everything I've done."
I mean, it *does* matter, to me. But what I want doesn't
factor into this.

She shakes her head. "I *saw* the video. You saved her
life. You stood there with a raygun pointed to your chest,
willing to sacrifice yourself for another person, and that's
not something you do when it doesn't matter. When you
could live without somebody. I saw you use your villain
power to blow up part of the school, but I also saw you
use it to *save* her. That means something. And even if I
don't like who you ..." She swallows, stopping herself
from telling me for the millionth time that she hates my
girlfriend. "That's what I was trying to tell you the other
day, when you freaked out on me. And now ... what? You
did all that, but you're going to just walk away?"

I blink at her. "First you're mad at me for trying to
leave to go see her, and now you're pissed that I *wasn't*?
Besides, what do you care? You told me to my face I'm just
some stupid kid who couldn't possibly feel that way about
her. That I couldn't love anyone." I know she said that
because she doesn't like Kat, because she doesn't like that
I'm with a supervillain related to her arch nemesis, but she
can't pretend it didn't happen.

"That's not exactly what I said, but ..." A pained look
creases her forehead, like it physically hurts her to admit
this. "I was wrong."

"I didn't mean to blow anything up. I was trying not to
hurt anyone."

"I know. And I'm sorry for what I said. About you not
really caring about her. Obviously you do, and if she's that

important to you, then ..." She grits her teeth. "I might not like where she comes from, but if she means that much to you, then she couldn't be all bad. So, I'm sorry for that, and for what you overheard me tell Gordon."

She doesn't know it was Amelia who overheard her, not me. "You mean when you told my dad I was going to disappoint him and not make it at Heroesworth?"

She looks at the floor guiltily. Then she meets my eyes and nods. "I was mad. Because you had Kat over, when you knew you weren't supposed to. You *knew* how I felt about it, and you knew the rules, but you threw them in our face and had her over here anyway, so you could—" She stops herself from saying "so you could sleep with her." Or however she was going to put it.

"So, you knew all along I was going to fail. Good for you."

"I *didn't* mean it. And I certainly didn't want to be right. You're not a bad influence. You weren't supposed to hear that, but I never should have said it in the first place, no matter how mad I was. I'm sorry that I did, and that you had to hear it. I was wrong."

"I wasn't trying to hurt Gordon or anything. When all that stuff happened at Homecoming. But if it happened again, I'd still do the same thing. Because I couldn't let anyone hurt Kat. And maybe I shouldn't have brought her there, but Kat wasn't going to do anything bad. She *wouldn't*—she's not like that."

Helen nods, taking that in, though she cringes a little, like she can't quite believe it. "I get it, and I understand why you were trying to leave."

"So, are we done here? Can I go to my room now?" Where I'll apparently be waiting for Gordon to come home so she can tell him how horrible I am. I wonder if he'll come yell at me, or if he'll decide I'm not worth it.

"No, you can't." She looks at me like I'm an idiot. "You have to go."

"Go?" Dread prickles in my chest, because, for a moment, I think she means permanently.

She takes a deep breath, and I get the impression she doesn't like what she's about to say. "To the dance."

"I can't do that."

"You have to. You'll regret it if you don't."

"It's at Vilmore. People are going to see us. And Gordon will never forgive me."

"You'll never forgive yourself if you stay home tonight."

"You said he doesn't need this."

"No, he doesn't, but let me talk to him. He'll be mad, but he loves you, and he'll understand. Eventually. You won't get over losing her."

"I didn't say I was losing her."

She tilts her head. "Damien, you told her you can't see her anymore."

"Just because I can't see her doesn't mean I'm not *with* her. I'm going to talk to her on the phone every day." Until I die or decide to run away and join the circus.

"You have to go. I think you know that."

"Yeah, but the dance is honoring Bart the Blacksmith. It was the publicity department's idea, not her dad's, but—"

"It's okay." She puts her fingers to her temples, like just the thought of anyone honoring him gives her a headache.

"Are you sure?"

"No. But you'd better get going anyway. Before your father gets home."

CHAPTER 28

It must be about seven thirty by the time I get to Homecoming, since I missed the first train and had to wait a while for the next one, and the dance is already well under way when I arrive. The main door to the event hall is open, so I don't need a *V* on my thumb to get in, and Kat already gave me my ticket a couple weeks ago, anyway. I pretty much walk right into the dance, no questions asked.

It's kind of loud in here and really crowded. There are pictures of Bart the Blacksmith up on the walls, and of some of the power-binding jewelry he made, plus a couple of Wilson Enterprises banners strewn across the ceiling. I ignore all that and make my way through the crowd. I think I might recognize a few people from back when I still lived with my mom, before I got my *X*, but it's hard to tell, and I don't exactly stop to make sure. People seem to recognize *me*, though, or at least think they do, because some heads turn as I walk by.

And I'm not even in my swimming trunks.

Then I spot Kat. With Tristan.

She has on this light-purple dress that I've never seen her wear before, and she's shapeshifted her hair to have streaks in it to match. He's wearing a tux, and they look like any other couple here. Both of them have *V*s on their thumbs. Both of them go to this school. And everyone's going to see the photos of them from tonight and think they belong together. Like him having a *V* on his thumb and *not* being the son of the Crimson Flash makes him better for her than me.

I thought I could handle it. I thought I could just walk up to them and tell him to get lost. But seeing them together makes my blood boil and electricity run up my spine. And it's not even that he's touching her or anything, because he isn't. They're just standing there together, hanging out, but then he grins and says something to her, and she *laughs*. A lot. Like whatever he said was really, really funny.

I'm supposed to make her laugh. Not this jerk who has bad taste in movies and nothing in common with her, other than going to the school *we* were supposed to go to together. He thinks he can take my place as her partner in crime, but he can't replace me as her boyfriend, or as her *best* friend, or as the guy who makes her laugh like that.

And that's when I lose it. Something inside me snaps.

I'm going to punch him.

I'm going to punch that douchebag right in the face.

Kat notices me first. She blinks, not believing I'm here,

and then her whole face lights up. "Damien? What are you doing—"

I shove Tristan in the chest with both hands, startling him and knocking him back a couple steps. "Get the hell away from her!"

"Dude, I don't know what your problem is, but—"

"*You're* my problem!" Can't he take a hint? I mean, seriously.

I lunge at him. I've never actually punched anyone before—though I have been on the receiving end once—but this seems like a good time to start.

"Damien, stop!" Kat shrieks. "I didn't come here with him!"

I pull my arm back. "You what?"

"He's not my date! I came alone!"

She did? Does that mean I can't hit him? "But he asked you, right?"

"Well, yeah."

Good enough for me.

Except before I can hit him, Tristan gets his bearings and shoves me away. Fire flares to life in his hands, and he says, "Dude. *Back off.*"

It's like he *wants* me to kill him. Electricity arcs between my palms. There's no way he didn't watch the videos, so he's seen me blow up part of a school, and he still wants to do this?

It's right about now that I notice people are staring at us. Nobody gets too close, but everybody takes pictures.

Kat moves between us and holds her hands up. "Both of you, just stop!"

"He started it," Tristan whines.

"You asked my girlfriend to Homecoming!"

"And she turned me down! She said she only wanted to go with *you*. You don't have to rub it in!"

The lightning in my hands subsides a little. I look at Kat. "You turned him down? But I thought—"

"I couldn't do it." Kat stares at her feet, looking embarrassed and kind of guilty. "I was going to, and *you* even said you were fine with it, but ..." She sighs. "*I* wasn't fine with it. I didn't want to be here with anybody else, not even just as friends, and I almost didn't even come."

"Then why did he post *Can't wait for Friday!* on your wall?"

"Uh," Tristan says, "because it's *Friday*. Also, I post that every week. It's kind of an in-joke." He says that like there's than unspoken "you wouldn't understand" at the end.

Great. He has in-jokes with her. But at least he's not her date.

Then a familiar and very angry-sounding voice says, "What the hell is going on?!" Kat's dad marches up to us and takes in the situation. He looks really annoyed when he sees I'm involved. Not surprised or anything, but annoyed.

I make the rest of the electricity disappear and put my hands down.

Tristan hesitates, like he doesn't trust me, then does the same with his fire.

The crowd stops staring at us, though I know they've

probably already posted pictures of this online. I can see the headline now: *Son of the Crimson Flash Picks Fight in Supervillain Love Triangle*. I wonder if anybody got video of it and how many views there will be by tomorrow.

"It's nothing," I tell Kat's dad. "We weren't doing anything."

"He attacked me first," Tristan says, pointing at me.

I'm going to attack him again if he doesn't shut up. What the hell is wrong with this guy?

Kat's dad sounds annoyed and unimpressed. "You look fine to me."

"But—"

"Unless you *want* to get kicked out of here for fighting? Because I can certainly arrange that."

Tristan hesitates, like he's considering whether trying to get me in trouble would be worth it. He seems to decide that it isn't and retreats into the crowd, though not without telling Kat he'll see her in class on Monday, and not without glaring at me one last time.

"And *you*," Kat's dad says to me once he's gone. "I told you to stay away from her!"

Kat scowls at him. "*Dad*. He's my boyfriend! You can't tell me—"

"*You're* in trouble, too, because I told you not to bring him. In fact, I forbid it." He pulls out his phone and hands it to her, using his power to commune with machines to make it go online and find pictures of what just happened. He doesn't have to wake it up or push any buttons or type anything—or even touch it—he just talks to it with his mind or something and it does what he wants. And, yeah, there are pictures of me fighting with Tristan posted all over Twitter and Facebook. One of the gossip sites has even picked up on it already. They have a particularly good pic of me with lightning in my hands, and Tristan with fire in his, and Kat trying to get between us.

It does look pretty scandalous, actually.

"This is exactly why I didn't want you here," her dad says to me, taking his phone back. "And I can't imagine your family's very happy with you right now, either."

Nope. Probably not. But it doesn't change anything. "I'm not going to stop seeing her."

He raises his eyebrows and takes a step toward me, getting right in my face. "You think after everything you've done that you have a *choice*?!"

"Dad!" Kat cries. "It's *my* choice! And I love him!"

"Kat. Stay out of this. It's for your own good." He keeps his eyes on me. "She got seriously injured last weekend because of you. It's *your* fault she ended up in the emergency room. This isn't a game, and now you're here, causing even more trouble for her! I told you you didn't have anything to offer her, and I was right! And now that everyone knows who your father is, they're never going to leave you two alone. If you really loved her, you'd turn around right now, go home, and *never* see her again!"

He is *really* scary. And I kind of want to be anywhere but here right now. Well, anywhere but here or at my house, obviously. But even though it's really hard to meet his gaze and not look away, I don't back down. In my peripheral vision, I see Kat wipe tears from her eyes. Like she thinks this is it, like she thinks he's *right*, or at least that I'm going to listen to him. And maybe he has a point. But even if us being together is going to cause problems for everybody, I can't just give her up. "You told me to stay away from her, and I told you I can't do that! I said I'd do *anything* for her, and I meant it!"

"Anything? Like ruin her life?!"

"Stop it!" Kat says, swallowing back tears.

"You said I wasn't good enough," I tell her dad. "You said I didn't have anything to offer her but trouble. But I'm here, and I'm not going away. No matter what happens. No matter who says we shouldn't be together or how much you yell at me. And that's something. No, that's a whole hell of a lot, actually, because it's *all I have*. And if you want me to stop seeing Kat ..." I swallow. "You're going to have to kill me."

His nostrils flare. He looks like he *wants* to kill me. Then he straightens and adjusts his jacket. "You're serious."

It's not a question, but I answer it anyway. "I've never been more serious about anything in my life."

We stare at each other. I will him to smile and say, "Well, you two kids go have fun, then!" But of course that doesn't happen.

"You're still half superhero," her dad says. "You're still *his* son."

"We'll work around that." That and the fact that I'll probably be shipped off to a boarding school for delinquent superheroes as soon as I get home. It's probably somewhere far away, like France or Siberia, and my cell phone won't work there, and Kat and I will have to continue our romance through postcards.

Her dad looks me over, like he just hasn't stared at me scarily enough yet and I might still back down. But when I don't, he sighs. "I'm not going to kill you," he says. "But that doesn't mean I like it."

Which I guess is as much of his permission to be together as we're going to get.

Not that we need it or anything. Though I could do without him threatening to throw me off of buildings.

His phone rings. It's something work-related, and he walks off to answer it.

Kat throws her arms around me. "Did you seriously just win an argument with my *dad*?"

"Looks that way," I say, hugging her back. "Do you think he'll knock down the bride-price to something more affordable? Say, like, only five cows?"

"I didn't think you were going to show up. I didn't think ..." She chokes up a little, then says, "I didn't know if I was ever going to see you again. Not after what you said. You're really stupid sometimes, you know that?"

"Yeah, I do. And I have to warn you that our reunion might be short-lived, since I'm pretty sure *my* dad *is* going to kill me. So, I hope you have something in black, since you're going to need it to wear to my funeral."

She starts kissing me. Like she might never get to again. I kiss her back, and when we finally stop to breathe, she says, "You want to go to my room? Since it's your last night on earth and everything."

"I thought you'd never ask." And if her dad notices we're gone and decides he wants to kill me after all, well, he can get in line.

She grabs my hand, but before we can sneak off, a familiar voice behind us shouts, "Wait!"

I turn just in time to see Riley go uninvisible in the middle of a crowd of supervillains, somewhere I *never* thought he'd be. It's so unexpected, I blink a few times to make sure I'm not hallucinating. Which seems more likely than Riley Perkins showing up to a social event at Vilmore. Uninvited, I might add. But Kat's eyes go wide, too, so I know we both see him. I also notice he's holding the personality enhancer, which, last I checked, was still in my room.

"Wait," he says again. "We've got a serious problem, and you guys are going to want to hear this."

X·X·X

I glare at Riley. "How long have you been standing there, Perkins?"

"Not ... not that long." His face goes red. He looks from me to Kat, then swallows. "But I couldn't appear with her dad there, and then ..." He looks away.

"So, you mean you were there the whole time?! And then, what? You thought you'd just watch us make out for a while?!"

"No!" He winces, making a disgusted face. "But I didn't want to just interrupt! It looked important."

"What's going on?" Kat asks.

Riley glances guiltily at the floor. "Sarah's here."

Kat goes pale. "She's *here*?!" She looks behind her, like

she expects Sarah to be standing right there with another raygun pointed at us.

"Not *here,* as in this room." Riley glances around, looking kind of nervous, probably because he's in a giant event hall full of supervillains. "Look, can we go outside or something? It's kind of loud in here!"

"Yeah, *and* you're seriously underdressed." I shake my head at the jeans and faded striped T-shirt he's wearing. "Don't you know Homecoming is supposed to be *formal?* I'm embarrassed to be seen with you."

He rolls his eyes at me as we make our way to the entrance.

Once we're outside, I say, "You want to tell me what you're doing here?"

"Sarah's here," he says again. "At the school. I mean, I think she is."

"You *think* she is, so you went to my house, got the personality enhancer, and then came all the way down here? What happened to your phone?"

"*My* phone? What happened to *your* phone?! I called you, like, a hundred times!"

I pull out my phone, remembering that I put it on silent before I left the house, right after he called me. Oops. I have thirteen missed calls. I check and see that eleven of them are from him. One is from Gordon, and the other one is from Sarah. A cold prickle of dread creeps up my spine and settles in my stomach.

Riley's still seething. "Do you think I *wanted* to sneak into your house and steal this thing? Do you think I *wanted* to drive all the way over here and crash some villain dance?!"

"Why do you think she's here?" Kat asks.

"Because I ran into her dad at the store today, after school. And he actually stopped to talk to me, which I thought was weird, because there's no way he doesn't know Sarah attacked me last weekend, right? So then I thought maybe he was going to apologize, or maybe tell me he's on Sarah's side and I deserved it or something. And I kind of wanted to pretend I didn't see him, but he was already coming over to me, so—"

I tap my foot. "Get to the point."

"Yeah, okay. So, he came up to me and said he was glad that Sarah and I had made up. I didn't know what to say, because why would he think that? And then he said he'd just assumed that we had, since we were going to Homecoming tonight. He thought it must have been at Sarah's school. But I know that one was last weekend, too, the same as the one at Heroesworth. And when I just kind of stared at him, her dad said maybe he'd made a mistake. But I knew you'd said you were going to Homecoming at *Vilmore* tonight, and I know how Sarah feels about villains. Right now, I mean," he adds, glancing nervously at Kat. "While she's crazy."

"Is that it?" I ask him. "You're basing this on something clueless her dad said? Because if you were that desperate for an excuse to come to the dance tonight, you should have just asked. I mean, I would have shot you down— Kat's a hotter date and *much* lower maintenance—but you still could have saved yourself the trouble of coming all the way out here." I notice my phone says I have one new voicemail. "Did you leave me a message?"

"No, I didn't. And no, that's not it."

That means the message is either from Gordon or from Sarah. I'm not sure which one of them I hope it's from, and I'm kind of too terrified to listen either way. What if it's from Gordon, saying don't bother coming home ever again? What if it's from Sarah, saying ... I don't know, that she's going to kill me or something? Actually, on second thought, I hope the message *is* from Sarah. Because I already know she wants to kill me. I don't know for sure that Gordon never wants to see me again.

"After I talked to her dad," Riley goes on, "I went over to her house. In invisible mode, of course. She wasn't there. It looked like she'd already left, because her backpack was gone. Anyway, there was a map of Vilmore on her desk. She'd marked up some of the buildings, and one of them was the one next to this one. And, look, I know it's not a lot to go on, but she's up to something. I *know* she is."

Enough to come all the way over here, to *Vilmore,* which has got to be pretty low on his list of favorite places. "I believe you," I tell him—words I *really* never thought I'd say—"but what are we going to do about it?"

He holds up the personality enhancer. "You got this thing fixed, right? So, we just get to Sarah and blast her with it." He takes a deep breath and stares at his shoes, like he knows it's not going to be that easy.

It's not, and we're going to need as much information as we can get, so I clench my jaw and call my voicemail. It might be from Sarah. And if it's from Gordon, I'll just hang up before I can hear him say anything too horrible, like that he doesn't like the choices I've made and is kicking me out.

"Damien?" Kat says.

"Hold on. This might be her."

Please be Sarah. Please be Sarah. Please be—

"Hello, *Renegade*," Sarah says in the message. And even though she says my superhero name like it's the worst word on the planet, I'm still really relieved that it's her and not my dad. "You know how I said you were endangering a whole generation of superheroes last weekend? Well, that gave me an idea. A really *good* idea. Why not do the same thing to a whole generation of supervillains? Why not stop them all before they have a chance to commit horrendous crimes that we both know they won't feel guilty for?"

Kat and Riley are staring at me, waiting for some sign. I nod, indicating it's her.

"So," Sarah's voice goes on, "I'm here at Vilmore, and I've got everything set up to wipe out a whole bunch of criminals. And you know some of them are very, *very* dangerous. Maybe of Bart the Blacksmith's level. That's who the dance is honoring, right? But we don't know who that's going to be yet, so they'll all have to die. Except, you know what, Damien? I think I know who the *really* dangerous one is. It's *you*. So here's the deal. Turn yourself in, and nobody else gets hurt. Come to me tonight before eight o'clock and I *don't* destroy an entire generation of villains, including Kat. Call me when you get this message, and I'll tell you where to go. And you *will* call me, because

I know you. Your worst trait—the one that makes you so dangerous—is that you actually think you're a hero instead of a villain."

The message ends. A computer voice asks me if I want to save the message or delete it. I tell it to delete it.

"Well?" Kat says.

"What did she say?" Riley asks.

"She's here," I tell them, a cold, sick feeling twisting in my stomach. I check the time on my phone and see that it's seven fifty. "She's going to kill everyone at Vilmore, in about ten minutes, unless ..."

Riley screws up his eyebrows. "Unless what?"

"Unless I go talk to her."

Kat's shaking her head. "That doesn't sound right, Damien. And I don't trust her."

"I'm supposed to call her, to find out where she is."

"I know where she is." Riley points to the tall building next door. "She's on the roof."

"She wouldn't be on the roof. She wants me to meet her, and she knows that I'm—" She knows that I'm afraid of heights, but I don't need him to know that. "It doesn't make sense."

"It overlooks the dance, doesn't it? And I'm the one who saw the map. That's where she is."

"We don't have time for you to be wrong."

"I'm not. Just *trust* me for once. Because if she wants you to call her, then I don't think you should. I agree with Kat—this doesn't sound right. Nothing about it does. And if you call her, she'll know we're coming. This way, we can surprise her. I mean, how do you know she's not just going to shoot you with a raygun as soon as she sees you?"

He looks really worried, like that could actually happen. It probably *is* going to happen, since that's what Sarah wants, isn't it? She didn't *say* she was going to kill me, but she wants me to trade myself for the lives of everyone else, and she thinks I'm the most dangerous supervillain here. She thinks stopping me is worth letting a whole generation of supervillains go free. And as far as her not killing me goes, that doesn't sound too promising.

I hope Mom did a good job on that personality enhancer. Because if I go up there and I *don't* shoot Sarah with it before she shoots me, or if it doesn't work, then ... I'm not coming back down.

"You guys stay here."

"*No.*" Kat grabs my arm and glares at me. "We're all going, and we don't have time to argue about it."

"But—"

"I'm not waiting around here, not sure if I'm ever going to see you again. I already did that, and I didn't like it the first time. Besides, I'm a shapeshifter, and he can turn invisible. She doesn't have to know you didn't come alone."

"Yeah," Riley says. "We've been through this already. Don't be an idiot."

"Okay," I tell them. After all, it's not like I *want* to die tonight. If there are three of us, then maybe we stand a chance. Plus, Sarah said if I turned myself in, she wouldn't hurt anyone. I hope that includes the two of them.

I also hope that, if things go really badly tonight, they won't have to watch me die.

CHAPTER 29

"You take the personality enhancer," I tell Riley as we race over to the building next door. "We go up there, and then I'll distract her while you go invisible and sneak up behind her."

"I think you mean while *we* distract her," Kat says. She stops at the door to the building and grabs the handle. It doesn't budge. She tries it again, but of course it still doesn't move. She starts to turn her fingers into lockpicks, then notices the door doesn't have that kind of lock. It's electronic, with a number pad you have to type the right sequence into in order to open it. Kat swears under her breath, then says, "There must be another door or something. Or a window we could—"

"You think Sarah's going to make it that easy?" I ask. "She had to get up there somehow, right? So she's probably also the one who locked it behind her. She would have locked all the other doors to the building, too, and made sure there's no way in. She wouldn't have taken the chance that someone might get in the way of her plans."

"Damien, you don't know that."

"But I know *her*, and I know she's going to kill everyone in only ..."

"Five minutes," Riley says, glancing at his phone.

I cringe, because with only five minutes left, then I definitely know what I have to do. "Five minutes." I swallow. "Even if we did find a window or something, there might be more doors on the way up. She probably locked them, too, and there's no way we'd get through all of them in time."

Kat puts a hand on her hip. "Then what are we going to do? Turn around and go home?"

"I think you mean 'run for our lives before Sarah murders us.' But you know what has to happen." I glance up at the roof. I feel dizzy even thinking about it.

"*No.*" She grits her teeth and shakes her head.

"Can't you just fly up there or something?" Riley asks.

Just fly up there. He makes it sound so easy.

Kat glares at him for bringing it up, as if I hadn't already thought of it on my own. As if we weren't just talking about it. "Damien, you *can't*. You can't go up there alone! She'll ... She didn't really say she just wants to talk to you, did she?"

I don't answer her. My arms and legs tremble. And I really, *really* don't want to do this, and not just because I'll probably end up with another raygun pointed at my chest. But I have to. "I'm the only one of us who can get there in time." And it's my fault she's up there in the first place.

"So, *call* her!" Kat clenches her fists. She searches my face, her eyes pleading with me. "She *wants* you to go up there. She'll unlock the doors, and we'll all go. If she knows you're coming, she'll wait a couple minutes before doing whatever it is she's going to do to hurt people. You said yourself, Riley can go invisible and sneak up on her."

But maybe not before she kills me. Or Kat. Plus, like Kat said before, this doesn't feel right, and I'm pretty sure it's a trap. I just don't know what kind yet.

I exchange a look with Riley, who's shaking his head. "Don't call her," he says. Then he looks at his phone again and goes sort of pale. "Four minutes."

Kat's voice is frantic. "Damien, you can't do this! You can't go up to the roof—you can barely get up the stairs! She *knows* that. She knows how afraid of heights you are!"

"Wait, what?" Riley says. "You're afraid of heights?"

Damn it. He really didn't need to know that, though I guess he would have figured it out in a minute anyway.

"Is *that* why you said flying is lame?"

For the record, me being afraid of heights and flying being lame aren't mutually exclusive, but I don't bother saying that, and instead I ignore him and tell Kat, "She won't be expecting me to fly. This is our best chance at stopping her. And we *have* to stop her, because if we don't, she'll kill everyone here. Everyone at the dance. Your dad's there, and your friends, and a whole bunch of other people who don't deserve to die." Let alone get massacred. "And I don't know what she's planning or how big it is. She might kill you guys, too."

"You think I'm letting you go up there alone?" Kat says. "You think I'm going to let her kill you?!"

I hold up my hands and make a few sparks fly at my fingertips. "She's not going to kill me."

Kat looks anything but convinced. But it doesn't matter. We're out of time, and it's now or never.

I take the personality enhancer from Riley. "I'll fly up there and blast her with it," I say, looking up at the building, which suddenly seems a lot taller than it did a minute ago. And a lot blurrier. My chest gets tight and I already feel like I can't breathe, but I try to keep the strain out of my voice when I lie and tell them, "I'll be fine."

"We're going to find a way in," Kat says, as if she didn't hear anything I said. As if she didn't believe a word of it. "You don't get to die."

"Three minutes," Riley says.

And it really is now or never.

I shut my eyes and picture floating up, like I did in my room the other day. When I—

When I panicked and fell.

I tell myself that's not going to happen this time. It *can't*, because if I fail, if I can't do this, a lot of people are going to die. In only three minutes.

I try pretending I actually like flying, because it worked the other day. But I can't shake the nervous feeling clawing at my stomach. I couldn't pretend it was a life-or-death situation then, and I can't pretend this isn't as serious as it is. So instead I think about just how badly I need to get to that roof. I think about how it's my fault Sarah's up there. How she's going to kill all these people if

I don't get to her.

This time I notice when my feet leave the ground. It sends my heart racing and a little zap of electricity runs up my spine. I open my eyes.

Kat bites her lip.

Riley watches me hovering there, looking at me like he's having serious second thoughts, like maybe I can't do this and we should all be running while we can.

"Shut up, Perkins," I mutter.

"I didn't say anything."

"But you were thinking it."

I'm not going to let them down. I think about rising through the air. It works, and then I'm actually *moving*. I'm clutching the personality enhancer for dear life and have to make myself ease up, so I don't break it again, but at least I'm making progress. I keep my eyes focused on the building, because then I can't see how high up I am. Or how far away the ground is.

This building might be several stories tall, but it's not anywhere near as high as the Banking and Finances building. It really doesn't take that long before I'm almost to the roof, where Sarah has her back to me. She's staring at her phone, and there's something in the middle of the floor, something big, only it's hidden under a sheet, so I can't see what it is.

My pulse races from being so high up, and my palms sweat, but I try not to think about it. Instead, I keep my attention on the roof, noticing there's also a big metal cage, like the one I saw in the drawing at Sarah's house. It's big enough for a person. And maybe it's because I'm distracted, looking at the cage and getting this horrible sinking feeling in my stomach, or maybe it's because I misjudged how close I was to the ledge in my effort to not look down, but when I try to step onto the roof, I *miss*, and my foot finds empty air.

A wave of sharp panic lights up my nerves, and my power cuts out, and I'm actually *falling*.

For a split second, I'm weightless, with nothing below me but a sickening drop. I recognize the feeling of plummeting through the air. I'm going to die. And then adrenaline courses through my veins, and my flying power kicks back in, and I hurtle myself over the edge onto the building as fast as I can.

This time, I definitely don't land gracefully. I don't even land on my feet. Instead, I slide face first onto the roof. The crash knocks the wind out of me, and I accidentally let go of the personality enhancer. It goes skittering across the floor. I hurry to reach for it just as Sarah hears me and turns around.

"Seven fifty-nine," she says, slipping her phone into her pocket and pointing a raygun at me. "You're cutting it close."

The personality enhancer is several feet away. And well out of my reach. What I wouldn't give for Amelia's power right now. Not that I'd *ever* admit that to her, even if I don't die tonight.

I wonder if I could make a run for it and shoot Sarah before she shoots me.

But then Sarah fires her raygun at the ground between me and the device, blasting a chunk out of the floor of the roof. "Don't move," she says through clenched teeth. "You were *supposed* to call me, so I could let you in. Instead you used your hero power! As if you're not one hundred percent *villain*." She spits the word, making a disgusted face.

"Sarah. You don't mean that. You know I'm—"

"I know what you *think* you are!" She aims the raygun at me with both hands. She's right in front of me, and there's no way she'd miss if she fired.

My heart pounds. She's going to kill me.

At least I'm not wearing just swimming trunks this time. At least when I die, I'll be well dressed.

"Get up," Sarah says.

I get up. Lightning flickers in my palms. "You don't have to kill me. You don't have to kill *anyone*!"

"Get in the cage."

"What? No, I'm not—"

"Get in the cage, or everyone dies. And don't even think about zapping me. Because if anything happens to me, the bombs go off automatically, and you can say good-bye to Vilmore and everyone in it."

She's bluffing. Maybe. Okay, knowing Sarah, probably not. And I really don't want to die. And I don't want Kat to die. Or Riley. Or anyone at the dance, really. Well, except for Tristan, but I'd like to be the one to kill him.

I think about blasting Sarah with my lightning and making a grab for the personality enhancer. But I don't know if I can do it without killing her. And maybe it's come down to that, but ... I don't know that she's bluffing about blowing everything up.

I make the lightning go away.

"Good boy," Sarah says, as if she was talking to her dog. "Now *get in the cage.*"

I do what I'm told.

She closes the door and locks me in, then steps back, a smug grin on her face. "You should have embraced villainy, Damien. Because you thinking you have a heroic side? I meant it when I said it's your worst trait. It's the one that's going to get you killed. If you could have just admitted you're all villain, you could have walked away." She mimes walking away with her fingers.

"Sarah ... what are you talking about?"

She shrugs. "There aren't really any bombs. I wasn't going to hurt anybody—not without *your* help, anyway."

"*What?*" My stomach drops and my blood runs cold. I summon up lightning in my hands, because ... because maybe I don't know what I'm going to do, but I know I have to do *something.*

But then Sarah walks over to a control panel and presses a large red button.

As soon as she does, there's a whirring noise, like a machine turning on, and then the lightning in my hands gets sucked away, disappearing into the metal bars of the cage. It feels weird, like it's not just taking away what's already there, but actually *draining* me.

I stop using my power. And I don't know what's going on, but I pray that Kat and Riley didn't believe me about not dying up here. I hope they find a way in, and fast.

"It took me all week to build this," Sarah says, beaming proudly. "Well, not the cage so much as *this.*" She walks over to the thing in the middle of the roof and pulls off the sheet.

The thing underneath looks like a giant metal drill. It's as tall as Sarah, and twice as long, and it's pointed down, toward the event hall. There are also big wires running from it over to the cage I'm standing in.

Sarah gives the machine a loving pat. "This took a while. I had to miss school."

"And you think *I'm* dangerous?"

She grins. "You don't even know what it does yet. It's going to shoot a giant beam of lightning at everyone and obliterate them. I got the idea for it last weekend, when I saw you blow up part of Heroesworth. When I found out you have a villain power. You see, Damien, normally someone with your ability wouldn't be able to use that much energy all at once. You only could because you were so freaked out. Like those stories you hear about moms lifting a car off of their kid, because of the adrenaline rush. But just because they can do that in moments of panic doesn't mean it doesn't hurt them. Your body has limits, and if you use too much energy, if you push yourself too far, you could kill yourself. But that doesn't mean you don't *have* that much energy. Enough to power something like this." She pats the machine again.

"You can't *make* me power that thing."

"Can't I?" She laughs, like I'm an idiot. And Mom's right, Sarah probably would do well at Vilmore, or at least this version of her. Maybe a little too well. "Last weekend, you nearly killed a bunch of people with your villain power. This weekend, you're really going to. Only they're going to be villains, just like you, like they should have been all along."

"But you said if I turned myself in, you wouldn't hurt anyone else!"

"Oh, *did I*?" She trails a finger from her eye down across her cheek, pretending to shed a single tear. "I lied. But you should thank me, because you're going to die doing a good deed. You're going to destroy a generation of villains and make the world a *much* safer place."

"No, Sarah, I'm not going to do that! You can't make me hurt people! And I *know* you, and I know you don't really want to do this!"

She sighs. "I'd hoped you'd cooperate, but I guess I'm going to have to do this the hard way." She walks over to the control panel again.

"Sarah, what are you—"

She presses a black button this time, and a jolt of electricity hits me. It comes from the bars of the cage, from all directions. Liquid fire burns through my whole body. Everything hurts, and I feel like I'm going to burst apart. Like my bones and my veins and my muscles are about to explode. My heart races, and my vision blurs. I feel like I'm screaming, but I don't hear anything. I can't move.

Then it stops. It felt like it never would.

I take deep, gasping breaths. I'm shaking all over. My heart's still beating too fast and my muscles twitch uncontrollably. My whole body hurts, like I just got run over or something. "What ... what the hell was that?"

"You see?" Sarah says. "I can make you do whatever I

want. The wrong voltage could stop your heart. And too much exposure to electric shock will kill you. But I did a little research. You're immune to electricity, but only while you're using your power. So if you don't want to feel that again"—she hovers her finger over the button, and already panic races through my chest—"you'll turn on your lightning power."

"And then what? You're going to kill me either way, right?! So why should I—"

She presses the button.

It hurts worse this time. So. Much. Worse. More liquid fire ripples under my skin. My nerves scream out in sharp agony, and I've never felt anything so horrible. My muscles spasm so hard, it feels like my bones are going to crack. Everything aches. My heart races faster. Like it could beat right out of my chest.

Sarah says something to me, but I can't make it out. I can't pay attention to anything but the pain ripping me to pieces.

I don't want to kill people or help her power her crazy machine, but I don't want to die. And I don't think about it too hard—I can't think about much of anything—I just do what she wants. I turn on my power. It's the one thing that doesn't take any movement. Just one barely coherent thought, and it's there.

And suddenly I can breathe again. I can move and I can think. Tremors still run through my muscles, but they're slowing down, getting less violent.

"That's more like it," Sarah says.

"Sure it is." I can feel her machine draining me. It's a

weird tingling feeling all over as it steals the electricity from my body. And I think maybe this isn't so bad. I can feel it taking energy from me, and I'm already kind of tired from being shocked so badly, but I can handle this. At least for a while. At least long enough for Kat and Riley to find a way into the building and come stop her.

I'm not going to die.

The realization sends relief flooding through me. She's not going to kill anybody. Nobody has to die, not even me, and no one else is going to get hurt.

And then Sarah reaches for a knob on the control panel. She twists it really far to one side.

I scream as the cage's power cranks up, ripping electricity out of me. It feels like it's pulling it all the way from my bones. "Sarah, stop! You're going to—"

"Kill you? That's kind of the point."

"I'm not a villain." Sweat beads on my forehead and drips down my face. "You know me. You're my *sidekick*! You're just messed up right now, but deep down, you know I don't want to hurt people!"

"You think I'm messed up, just because I'm finally seeing the truth? You might not *want* to hurt people, but that doesn't stop you from doing it."

"I'm half hero, Sarah. I'm—" I grit my teeth against the pain, unable to go on for a second. "Maybe I'll never be all hero, but I'm not all villain, either!"

She shakes her head. "And that's what makes you so dangerous. It's tempting to think you're not all bad, but you are. You're worse, because you have hero genes and you're *still* a villain. You hurt *everyone*—not just the people

389

you know, but the whole city. And you being half hero means you had access to Heroesworth, where you brought an actual supervillain to the dance!"

"Kat didn't do anything! She wouldn't, and you know that!"

"You're right. She didn't. *You're* the one who blew up part of the school with your villain power! You could have hurt people!"

"It was an accident. I didn't mean to—"

"That just makes it worse! If you could control yourself, you could choose not to do it. But you can't. You don't belong at Heroesworth, even if you're half hero. You couldn't even answer a simple question, like what heroism means to you. Because it doesn't mean *anything*, does it?"

"That's not true!"

"You're the most dangerous one of all, Damien, because not only do you have that horrible villain power, but you *live* with heroes. You're a wolf among the sheep, just waiting to betray them even more than you already have. Well, you *were*. After tonight ..." She waves her hand, indicating that I won't be around anymore.

It's getting harder to breathe. My lungs feel so heavy. My whole body does. She's taken so much energy from me, and I wonder how close she is to powering her machine. I can't let her kill all those people, and if I'm going to die either way, I should just turn my power off now and be done with it.

But I can't give in yet. I just can't. And this is *Sarah*. Even if the personality enhancer screwed her up, she's still there, somewhere, isn't she?

"Sarah, you ..." My tongue feels like it's made of lead and my mouth doesn't want to form the words, making it hard to talk. "You say I'm a villain, but what about *you*? You're not a hero, either."

She scoffs, like she can't believe I would even question that. "I'm helping people. I'm making the world a safer place. I don't have to have an *H* on my thumb to do that."

"What about the ..." I falter, the pain getting worse. My head spins and my skin burns all over from so much electricity leaving my body so fast. Being torn out of it. "What about the League Treaty?"

"What about it?"

"You believe in it, right? In the rules?"

She takes a step closer to the cage, folding her arms and peering at me, like she thinks I might have gone crazy. "What does a *villain* know about the League Treaty?"

"I know the third rule says heroes don't cause unnecessary bodily harm. Not even to their enemies. That includes villains, Sarah."

She scoffs, like she can't believe I just quoted one of the League rules at her. It's the only one I know, thanks to Riley and our stupid school assignment, but I'm not going to tell her that part. "These villains are *going* to hurt people," she says. "I'm just getting to them first."

"You don't know that! And even if you did, it doesn't give you the right to kill them! You might not have signed anything, but you want to be a hero. You believe in the rules, but you're the one that broke them. Not me. I never hurt anybody, but you shot Kat and Riley! And you're hurting me now, and I—" I sink to my knees, gasping in pain. I can't keep this up. "You tell me *I'm* the villain, but I never broke the rules! That was all *you*. You're the one killing your best friend right now, so what does that say?!"

Her mouth falls open and her face sort of crumples. She blinks at me as what I said sinks in. "I broke the rules," she says, sounding numb, like she can't believe it. She drops the raygun and puts her hands to her mouth.

Right as the door to the roof bursts open and Kat appears. "Oh, my God, Damien!" she shrieks when she sees me in the cage.

I wonder where Riley is, and then I realize he must be invisible. I hear his footsteps as he darts across the roof, toward the personality enhancer.

Sarah grabs the raygun.

"Kat!" I scream. "Watch out!"

Kat runs straight at Sarah, which is not at all what I meant for her to do.

Sarah points the gun at her, her finger on the trigger. But then her face crumples a little, like it did a minute ago when I told her she'd broke the rules, and she hesitates.

And that's when Kat punches her in the face and knocks her to the floor.

Whoa.

On the other side of the roof, the personality enhancer moves and disappears. I know it must be Riley, that it didn't really move and go invisible on its own, and then a beam of light shoots out of it and hits Sarah while she's still lying on the floor.

Sarah sucks in a deep breath, like she's never breathed

before. Riley goes uninvisible and runs over to her. She sits up and puts her hands to her temples, looking really confused. Then realization hits her, and she looks over at me. In the cage. Dying. "*Oh, no,*" she says.

Kat hits some buttons on the control panel and turns the dial the other way. The cage stops draining me. I'm too afraid to stop using my power, though. What if it electrocutes me? What if that part's still on?

"Hit the black button!" Sarah shouts.

Kat hits the button, just as my body decides I can't keep my power going anymore. It's not a choice, it just happens. I collapse on the floor of the cage, exhausted and covered in sweat.

And really surprised to still be alive.

CHAPTER 30

Kat grabs the key from Sarah and unlocks the cage. She flings the door open.

I'm more tired than I've ever been in my entire life, and I still feel like I'm about to die, but I don't waste any time getting out of there. I scramble out of the cage on my hands and knees before getting to my feet.

Kat nearly knocks me over as she throws her arms around me and buries her face in my neck, squeezing me really tight.

I squeeze her back and say, unable to hide the awe in my voice, "You punched Sarah." Not that I wanted Sarah to get hurt or anything, but ... wow.

"She had it coming."

Over her shoulder, I see Riley kissing Sarah like he hasn't seen her in weeks, which I guess he sort of hasn't.

"But," I say to Kat, "you, like, knocked her down. With your *fist*. I didn't know you were so bad-ass."

"I didn't, either." She steps back and contemplates her knuckles, shaking her hand out a little. Then she glares at me and pokes me in the chest. "And I *told you* you shouldn't have come up here alone!"

I shake my head. "If I hadn't, she would have killed you." She would have fired at Kat as soon as we got to the roof. There wouldn't have been any hesitation.

"She almost killed *you*," Kat says, shooting Sarah a dirty look.

"It wasn't really her. I told you, the real Sarah would never—"

She cuts me off, like she doesn't want to hear it. "Are you okay?"

My whole body hurts, like I got hit by a truck. And like maybe it backed up over me a few times. My arms and legs are so heavy. I feel like I haven't eaten in a week, and like I could sleep for at least that long. My muscles are still sort of twitchy, and I'm overly aware of my nerves. But I'll live, and Kat's okay, and Sarah's back to normal. And a whole bunch of people didn't just get blown to smithereens. "I'm going to have to take a rain check on going to your room with you. Even though you being such a bad-ass is *super* hot."

She grins. "Wow, for you to pass that up, you must be pretty much—" She stops herself, the grin suddenly fading, not finishing that sentence, not saying, "you must be pretty much dead."

I'm about to tell her maybe we should have joined the circus after all—even working with lions and clowns and stuff has to be safer than this—when Sarah comes running up to me.

"I'm *so sorry*, Damien," she says. There's a giant bruise forming on her cheek where Kat hit her. "I don't know how to apologize for what I did, but ..." She stops and just sort of stares at me, her jaw trembling.

"It's okay, Sarah. All this ... it was my fault."

She shakes her head. "I almost killed you! I almost blew up all those people!" She takes a deep breath and then looks at Kat. "I'm sorry I shot you. And that I broke into your dad's company. I don't hate supervillains. Not as a general rule."

Kat's lip curls. "Gee, *thanks*."

"I mean it. I know we don't really know each other, and you probably think I'm psychotic after what I've done, but I would never do any of those things normally."

"Oh, you mean you *wouldn't* try to kill my boyfriend?!"

Sarah's eyes water. "Of course not! He's my—"

"What? Your superhero partner or whatever?"

"He's my best friend," Sarah finishes.

Kat's nostrils flare. Her hands curl into fists. "No, he's *my* best friend. *Not* yours."

And this would be why I never wanted them in the same room together. I put my hand on Kat's arm, because she looks like she might try and deck Sarah again. "You know, actually, I think I *do* want to go to your room." To, like, lie down and never get up. "Maybe we should go."

"Don't worry, Damien," Kat says. "I'm not going to kill her. That's what she—"

"Um, Sarah?!" Riley interrupts, sounding really panicked. "Is your machine *supposed* to be doing that?"

We all turn to look at the giant drill-looking thing in the middle of the roof. It's glowing, casting a bluish-white light all over, and there are bursts of sparks coming off of it.

"Oh, no." Sarah puts a hand to her forehead, her eyes going wide. "It must have crossed the energy threshold. I put in a failsafe, so it would still go off, if ..." She glances over at me, her face pale. "If something happened to you, or if someone tried to stop me. I made sure that as long as it had enough power, it would still go off, even if it wasn't as much as I'd wanted."

"So," Riley says, backing away from the machine, "what you're saying is, this thing is still going to shoot lightning at everyone?!"

Sarah nods. "We have to do something!"

"My dad's down there!" Kat cries.

"Can't you stop it?" I ask Sarah. "Isn't there a button you can press, and it will just self-destruct?!"

"I didn't put in anything like that! There isn't even an off switch. And, even if there was a self-destruct button, it would still explode and cause too much damage! There's way too much energy!"

"So, there's no way to stop it?!"

"We have to warn everyone—we have to get them out of there!" Sarah takes off for the door to the roof.

The rest of us take off after her, though my legs don't want to move, and it feels like I'm trying to run through water.

"How much time do we have?" Riley asks Sarah as we go inside the building and pile into the elevator.

"I don't know." She squeezes her eyes shut, trying to calculate. "I don't ... It doesn't matter. I *can't* let anyone else get hurt!"

Kat gets out her cell phone and dials her dad's number. He doesn't pick up. "Damn it," she mutters. She dials again, only to get the same result.

None of us says anything the rest of the way down. My heart pounds in the tense silence, expecting to hear an explosion any second. Then the elevator dings, and the doors open, and we're running for the event hall.

The dance is still really crowded. Maybe more so than when we left. People look at us kind of funny, possibly recognizing us from the videos. Or possibly just noticing that we're kind of bedraggled, and that some of us are underdressed, though at least it's not me this time.

"We have to get everyone out of here!" Kat shouts.

"How?" I ask her.

Sarah grabs some guy's arm and says, "You have to leave! The school's going to blow up!"

He looks at her like she's a freak and pulls away, backing up into the crowd and not running for the exit.

"Pull the fire alarm!" Riley says.

Which is a surprisingly good idea, especially coming from him. But before we can find an alarm to pull—before we can even *move*—a deafeningly loud blast hits the ceiling. It explodes, raining debris on everyone. Chaos erupts as people fall down and start screaming. Someone says the school's being attacked. Nobody has any idea what's really happening.

"You all have to run!" Sarah cries. "That was just the

opening shot!"

Riley grabs her arm. "Sarah, we can't stay here!"

"No! I have to stop this!" There are tears streaming down her face, because we all know there's nothing she can do.

But there *is* something *I* can do.

I take off for the middle of the room, right under the giant hole in the roof. I hear Kat call out my name, but I don't turn around. I have to push people out of the way, and it takes a lot of effort, and my muscles still don't want to work.

There's a flash of light and a loud crackle as a giant beam of lightning pours in through the ceiling. I throw myself forward and make my power work. I'm so drained, and I've lost so much energy already—energy that's now going to zap everyone and kill them if I can't do something —that my body resists using electricity. Like Sarah said, there's a limit. It's only through sheer force of will that I make it work, though it doesn't hurt that I can't help thinking about how horrible it would feel to get shocked again, sending a spike of adrenaline through my veins.

Sparks race along my arms, and then—

Then the giant beam of lightning hits me full on. It feels like a ton of bricks just dropped on top of me, and it almost knocks me to the floor. It's way too much, especially all at once. And even though I'm supposed to be immune to it, I can't absorb it all. I can't overpower it. My muscles freeze up, and I can't move. And at the same time, they spasm and twist in on themselves, threatening to break me. My vision goes blurry, and my bones ache, and

I feel like my insides are about to explode. My heart beats way too fast.

The beam doesn't stop. It's a steady stream of pain pouring into me, showing no signs of letting up. My skin burns, inside and out. My nerves are screaming.

I'm aware of people shouting. Of running. Of nobody getting too close. I think I hear Kat, but I can't tell. All I know is I don't want her to see this.

My bones are going to split apart. My muscles feel like they're on fire. My heart can't possibly be beating this fast. Racing so hard, like there's a finish line to get to.

The beam gets stronger, or maybe it just seems that way, because my body is breaking down. I'm not going to survive this. It's not a thought or a question, just something I suddenly *know*. But I wonder how much longer I can last, and if it will be enough to save everyone.

There's more commotion around me. Somewhere. I can't really tell anymore. A man's voice shouts something. It might be Kat's dad.

I think he says, "Hold on!"

Which is easy for him to say, since he's not the one getting electrocuted. He's not the one who can't breathe, whose heart is about to burst. He's not the one who—

The beam suddenly eases up. It doesn't stop, but it slows down a lot. Enough so that my electricity power counteracts it. I still hurt all over, but I'm no longer being shocked. I'm not frozen. My bones aren't trying to break. I take a deep, shuddering breath. The world slowly comes back into focus.

Kat's dad looks really freaked out. Though relief flickers

in his eyes when I turn my head to look at him. "I can't stop it," he says. "All I can do is slow it down."

It takes me a second to realize what he's talking about. That he must be using his power to communicate with Sarah's machine. That he's the only reason I'm not dead right now.

"Damien? Can you hear me?" he asks, sounding kind of panicked when I don't answer him. Like he thinks I'm not all here.

Which I might not be. I nod.

"You're going to be okay." He says that like he means it, but the worried look on his face tells me he's not so sure.

"How's this for a publicity opportunity?" I say, because I feel like I need to prove I can still speak, and those are the words that come out.

He shakes his head. "You're banned for life from all company events."

"Like that's going to stop me."

"I'm kind of saving your life right now. You want to at least humor me for a minute?"

"Yeah, sorry—I didn't mean to say that out loud."

He looks at me like that doesn't make it any better.

We don't say anything else, and I don't know how much time passes before the beam stops completely. It couldn't be that long, maybe only a minute, but it feels like much longer, especially since I'm *so* ready for this to be over. When the beam finally stops, I turn my lightning power off and feel like I'm going to collapse and never get back up again.

Did I say I could sleep for a week? I think I meant more like a month.

Kat's dad puts a hand on my shoulder and looks me in the eyes. "Are you okay? And," he adds, when I immediately start to tell him I'm fine, "do *not* lie to me."

My right arm hurts really bad. So does everything else, really, but I test my arm out a little, just to be sure. Not broken. My muscles still burn, and they're all jumpy and twitchy, and I feel really sore all over. My heart is beating like normal, though. "I think I'm okay," I tell him.

He nods and lets go of me. "You say something if you're not."

"You could have let me die."

"No, I couldn't."

"Does this mean I can marry Kat?"

He sighs and puts a hand to his face, like he can't believe I said that. "You're lucky you're alive. Don't push it."

Kat rushes past him and studies my face. "Are you—"

"I'm okay." I start to take a step toward her, but my legs are kind of wobbly. So instead I pull her to me. "Put *this* on the evening news," I say, and then I kiss her.

It's a deep, intimate kiss that lasts a long time. The kind I wouldn't normally want her dad to see, because then he might get ideas about all the *other* intimate things we do together. But I don't think that's exactly a secret at this point, plus I really don't care. And even though it's the kind of kiss that should make other people uncomfortable, I'm pretty sure they take pictures.

So all in all, not a bad evening.

CHAPTER 31

The rest of the night is one big blur. I vaguely remember getting into Riley's car to go home, but I must have passed out or fallen asleep after that, because I don't remember anything else. All I know for sure is that I wake up in my bed the next day, still in my clothes, minus the jacket and tie.

I blink at the red letters on my alarm clock, which say that it's one thirteen. Not at night, but in the afternoon, because there's sunlight bleeding through the curtains on the window. I slept for ... I don't know how long, but it must have been well over twelve hours.

I'm starving. And *so* thirsty. But I can't imagine going down the stairs, or even getting out of bed anytime soon. My whole body aches, especially my arms and legs, which still feel really heavy, and all I want to do is sleep some more.

"Damien?" Gordon's voice startles me. I had no idea

anyone else was in the room.

I turn over—which is no easy feat and makes me aware of just how sore all my muscles are—and see him sitting in a dining chair next to my bed. "Don't tell me you've been watching me sleep," I mutter, "because that's really creepy."

His face is pale and his eyes are red, like he hasn't slept in a long time. "I was worried. I thought ..." He takes a deep breath and rubs his eyes with his palms. "Half a dozen times last night, I thought you'd stopped breathing."

"You were here all night?" Has he really been sitting in here for that long? In that uncomfortable wooden chair?

He nods. "And I don't know what I would have done if ..." He runs his hands through his hair. "Do you know how dangerous that was? What you did last night?!"

I sit up, being careful not to bonk my head on the slanting wall, and stare at my knees. "I know you probably don't care, because they were all supervillains, but I couldn't let anybody get killed. I had the power to stop it, so I did."

"You almost *died*."

"But I didn't. And, look, I know you're pissed at me for going to Vilmore. Helen said it was okay, but it's not like I didn't know you'd still be mad. And you probably didn't need all those pictures of me fighting with Tristan blasted across the internet. Or of me almost getting electrocuted while stopping that beam to save a school full of supervillains. I blew up Heroesworth, but I saved Vilmore, and that *can't* look good. And I know you were already ashamed of me, because I ruined your career and your life and stuff. I know sorry isn't good enough, but I am. I mean, I'd still do it. I'd still go to Vilmore all over again, even if you told me not to, because I *had* to see Kat." And stop Sarah, though I hadn't known that part was going to happen. "But I didn't want to cause trouble for you or anything. It's not like I *want* you to—" I press my lips together and don't finish that. I can't say out loud that he hates me. "I know all I do is cause problems for you, and that you don't know what to do with me, and that this was probably the last straw, but ..." I squeeze my eyes shut. "Don't send me away, okay?"

"*What?* What are you talking about?"

"I can't promise to be better or different or anything, because we'd both know that would be a lie. I won't stop seeing Kat, and maybe I don't have a good reason for you to let me stay, but ..." My throat goes tight and my voice sort of sounds too high. "I don't want to go."

"Damien, that's ... Why would you think I would do that?"

"Mom did. What I did to her wasn't nearly so bad as what I did to you. I lived with her for sixteen years, not six months, and I thought she cared about me. I mean, she did, but then she still kicked me out, just like that." And didn't waste any time replacing me. Not that Gordon needs a replacement—he's already got three other kids.

He gets up from the chair and sits on the edge of my bed instead. "I don't care what your mother did—we don't kick people out in this family."

I shake my head. "I didn't think we did in mine—in hers—either."

"Damien, look at me."

I risk a glance at him, even though I really don't want to.

He grips my shoulders and peers into my eyes, concern creasing his forehead. "You're *not* going anywhere. Do you understand?"

"But—"

"I mean it. This is your home."

"I ruined your life."

He sighs. "Well, you certainly made it more complicated."

"What I did last weekend at Heroesworth was bad enough, and now ..." I shrug. "I made things that much worse for you."

"I can't fault you for saving people. I can't say I always like *how* you do it, and I wish you'd think about the consequences a bit more before you act. But a lot of people would be dead right now if it wasn't for you."

"I didn't go to Vilmore to save people. I went there to see Kat."

"I know why you went. Helen explained it to me."

"Yeah, so, if I hadn't almost died last night, you'd be yelling at me right now."

"I ..." He falters and shakes his head. "Look, I was mad at first, but I understand why it was important for you to go. Though maybe you could have done it *without* picking a fight?"

"He was a douche. So, no, I couldn't. But I'm pretty sure I would have won, if that helps."

"That's not ... My point is that I have a son who was

406

willing to risk his life to save a lot of people. And who would do anything for someone he cares about. Not everyone can say that, and I'm proud of you. Of who you are."

"The whole city hates you."

He flinches and puts a hand to his temple. "Damien, just ... Let me worry about it, all right?"

"I'm not going to let them cancel your show."

He gives me an exasperated look as he gets to his feet and says, "You need to rest now."

Which I think is code for "you need to stop talking."

There's a commotion in the living room, followed by running footsteps on the stairs. Obviously some crazy person who wants to die in a tragic stair-collapsing incident. Then my door flings open, and Kat comes in. She looks kind of surprised to see Gordon here. Her eyes flick over to him, like she thinks he's going to kick her out. Then she ignores him and rushes over, climbing onto the bed with me.

"Kat, you're here. In the *house*." I can't help smiling, even though I still hurt all over and feel like crap.

"I had to see you." She glances over her shoulder at the sound of more footsteps on the stairs, which must be Helen. Coming to tell her to get out. "I had to make sure you were okay."

"Aw, I told you I was fine."

She nods, her eyes watering a little. "I know you kept *saying* that, but you really didn't seem like it. And I watched you almost *die*. I thought you were really going to, and if I hadn't found my dad in time ... I couldn't sleep last night. I kept expecting to get a call, saying you weren't all right, that something horrible had happened and you'd had to go to the hospital, or that your heart had stopped. But then I realized there was no one who would call me and tell me that. Just you, and your phone was fried, and even if it wasn't, if you were unconscious or in the emergency room, or ... or dying ... then you couldn't have said anything." A couple of tears slide down her cheeks, and she sucks in a deep breath. "I had to stay at Vilmore with my dad, and you seemed so messed up when you left, and I kept thinking, what if that turned out to be the last time I ever saw you? What if you really weren't okay?"

I put my arms around her and pull her close to me, trying not to wince at how sore I am. "Kat, I promise I'm all right. You're always going to see me again." Then to Gordon, who's still standing there, watching us, I say, "Weren't you on your way *out*?"

He scowls at me, but before he can either confirm or deny that, Helen comes in the room.

She does *not* look pleased to see Kat on my bed, as if she just caught us about to have sex again, even though Gordon's *right there*. And even though I still feel like I got hit by a truck and am not exactly up for that right now, though I suppose she doesn't know that part. "You ran past me," she tells Kat. "You didn't give me a chance to say anything."

"I just had to see if he was okay. And now I have, so ..." Kat says that like she's going to leave, but she doesn't move.

Helen sighs. "I was *going* to tell you to come in. And

where Damien's new room was, but I see you already knew that."

"So, does that mean she can stay?" I ask. "You're not kicking her out?"

"That's right."

"Because I'm recovering from almost dying, or because she's allowed in the house?"

"Both. But there are going to be rules, and I don't want the two of you—"

"Having sex? Yeah, I *know*." I glare at her.

Kat brings up her knees and hides her face, looking like she's going to die of embarrassment.

"You're still only sixteen, and there are certain things that—"

Gordon puts a hand on her arm. "Helen, the kids are fine."

Her eyebrows shoot up in surprise.

"I know you worry about him, but I trust him. To be responsible about it." He clears his throat, looking uncomfortable. "So, let's just let it go for now."

Wow. I can't believe Gordon just stuck up for me. Especially about *that*.

Then again, he did just argue in favor of me sleeping with a supervillain. So maybe I shouldn't be too surprised.

Helen looks like she wants to ask him if he's really sure about that, but she doesn't. Instead, she sighs in defeat and goes to leave, but not without propping my door open on her way out. It's like living at Kat's house. Except without the really good chocolate chip cookies her mom makes.

"Do you need anything?" Gordon asks.

I am *so* tempted to say "condoms." But I restrain myself. "Actually … I could go for some tomato soup." And everything else in the kitchen.

He smiles and says he thinks we're out, but that he'll go to the store and get some.

I wait until he's gone, then say to Kat, "Close the door. I need your help with something."

She raises an eyebrow at me. "I'm glad you're feeling better, but there's *no way* I'm having sex with you while your parents are home."

I grin. "It's cool that your mind went there, what with you not being able to stop thinking about ripping my clothes off and all, but that's actually not what I meant."

"Uh-huh."

"I'm serious. Though I *am* going to get undressed, and we *are* going to make a video."

"Is this an audition tape for the circus? Because I was joking about your act actually being x-rated."

"*Our* act, Kat. And I don't think they take audition tapes. Plus, this has nothing to do with that. It's important, and … it's just something I have to do."

"Something that involves the door being closed and you not wearing anything?"

"I didn't say I wasn't going to wear anything. So, while you're up, could you grab my swimming trunks from the dresser?"

A curious expression tugs on her mouth, but she doesn't ask questions. She gets up to do what I asked and says, "I hope you know what you're doing."

I smile and say, "Don't I always?"

Even though I have no idea if this is going to work.

$$X \cdot X \cdot X$$

Riley comes over later that evening, after Kat's gone home. I half expected—or maybe just hoped—that Sarah would be with him, but she's not.

He sits in the dining chair next to my bed with his hands on his knees, looking really serious. Then he takes a deep breath and says, "Dude. I can't believe you like Superstar." He glances over at the poster on the wall.

"That's what you have to say to me? I nearly died, and you come in here and *insult* me?" I shake my head and cluck my tongue at him, even though really I'm trying not to laugh.

"What do you want me to say? That I thought you were going to die in my car last night?"

"I was just asleep."

"*Oh, no.* You weren't. You said some really weird stuff."

"I'm pretty sure that I didn't." I hesitate. "Like what?"

"You told me you loved me."

"*What?*" No wonder he thought I was about to die.

"Just kidding. What you actually said was that you were going to murder me if I ever told anyone you were afraid of heights. You sounded like you meant it, too. Like you *really* meant it. And you kept holding up your hand and threatening to zap me. Even though I was driving."

"I was delirious. I'm *reluctant* about heights. Not *afraid* of them. That's ridiculous."

He squints suspiciously at me, obviously not fooled.

"Kat said you could hardly get up the stairs."

"She was exaggerating. She didn't want me to go face Sarah alone."

"It's okay. I wasn't going to tell anybody, even before the death threats."

"There's nothing to tell."

"Oh, *right*." He presses his fingers together, shaking his head. "It's not like you're the only one who's afraid of stuff, you know."

"Yeah? What are *you* afraid of? Not getting straight *As*? Missing an episode of *Train Models*?" I say that a lot meaner than I meant to, then feel kind of bad about it.

"Losing people." He picks at a string hanging off the edge of his shirt. "My dad died a few years ago. Because he sacrificed himself to save that bus full of people, and ... I know it was the right thing. At least, that's what everyone always tell me. But ..." He presses his palms to his forehead, gripping his hair. "I really hate him for it, you know? Maybe it was the right thing for the people on that bus, but it wasn't the right thing for *me*. Or for Zach. Or my mom. And then *you*—" He swallows. "Look, X, I know we're not even that close or anything. It's stupid, but when I saw you throw yourself at that beam of lightning, and it was obvious that, even with your electricity power, you were going to die—that you were going to *sacrifice yourself* to save everyone, like an idiot—you just ... you scared the hell out of me!"

The sudden anger in his voice startles me. I blink at him. "You're seriously pissed at me for saving people?"

"*Yes*. No. I mean, I'm mad at you for throwing your life

away like that! And for what? A bunch of people you don't even know?! I *know* that's supposed to be heroic and all, but what was I supposed to tell Zach? And Sarah never would have gotten over it, if you'd done that, because of her."

"She wouldn't have gotten over killing all those people, either."

"I know. But ... It's just ... *How* could you do that? How could you do that to Kat and to Sarah?! And to your family?!"

"Whoa. Calm down, Perkins. It's okay."

"No, it's *not* okay! It was really stupid of you! I know everyone on the news and on those dumb websites is saying you're a hero—"

"They are?"

"Yeah, well, you did stop a whole bunch of people from getting killed."

"But they were supervillains."

"So?" He looks at me like I'm crazy. "Anyway, it wasn't heroic, it was really selfish of you. I mean, I was pretty freaked out."

"Because I almost died?"

"And because you were just going to give yourself up like that, and there was nothing I could do to stop it. I felt helpless, like I did when my dad died, and I wasn't even there for that." He meets my eyes real quick, then looks away again. "Don't tell anyone."

"I won't."

"I mean it."

"I *said* I won't."

413

"Okay, but I should ... I should probably get going, though."

"Come on, Perkins. You don't have to do that. I didn't die, okay? I'm sorry I freaked you out. And ..." I take a deep breath. "I *am* afraid of heights. Kat wasn't exaggerating. It's really bad, and if anything, she was downplaying it. So, now you know something about me I would never tell anyone." Not if I could help it. "You don't have to leave."

He nods, looking grateful for that. "I should still go soon, though. I have this project I'm working on, for Intro to Heroism. We finally started doing field work."

"You did?"

"We haven't actually been out on any missions yet, but we're supposed to in the next couple weeks."

"Let me guess. You're doing something stupid, like rescuing cats stuck in trees or helping old ladies cross the street."

He snorts. "This isn't the Boy Scouts. Or that stupid poster you made. How is any of that stuff going to help us stop bad guys and not get killed? How is that even a career?"

"It's not. It's useless. But I thought that's what Heroesworth was all about."

"Seriously?" He shakes his head. "We're supposed to be retrieving stolen goods. My group got assigned this painting that was taken from the Golden City Art Museum. The guy who stole it is this supervillain called the Cat Burglar. His superpower is not making any noise. We know it was him because he left his calling card at the

414

museum. It even said, *Come and get me, if you dare.* And there was an address."

"Wow." I know who he's talking about. It's not somebody I know personally or anything, but I've at least heard of him. "So, you're going to go after him?" That actually sounds kind of cool.

"*I* said we should, but everybody else in my group shot me down. They said it was easy enough for me to say we should go, since I can turn invisible, but they can't. They also said it's obviously a trap and way too dangerous for them."

"So, in other words, they *don't* dare."

"Exactly. And we're not allowed to go alone. Not that I'm crazy about going by myself or anything, because it *does* sound dangerous, but it's not even an option."

"How are you going to get the painting back, then?"

"Oh, there's some art auction coming up. We *think* he's going to try and sell it there. Well, actually, *we* don't, but Brian does, and he convinced Brittany and David that crashing the auction is our best chance at getting it back."

"What do you think?"

"I think it's going to be gone by then. And that even if it's not, there are going to be too many people at the auction. Probably a lot of supervillains. It's unpredictable. I get that they want to do it because it sounds safer, at least on the surface. But that doesn't mean it's a good idea." He sighs. "We're *so* going to fail this assignment."

"So, you finally get past all the boring crap and get to do something exciting, and they just want to sit there and fail? *Lame.*"

He grins. "See, I wish you were in my group. You can't turn invisible, but you'd still go with me to scope out the Cat Burglar's place."

"Yeah, I would." I'd go even if it wasn't an assignment. Which I guess it isn't, at least not for me.

"So, why did you have to go and get yourself expelled?"

I glare at him. "You're the one who told me I should quit."

He looks away guiltily and shrugs. "I was wrong. It's too bad you screwed up so royally."

"Gee, thanks."

"I just mean it's too bad you can't come back."

"Yeah, maybe it kind of is. But I'm a supervillain. I mean, half supervillain."

"You're half hero, too. And I don't really care *what* you are. You're braver than anybody else I know. Kind of stupid sometimes, but if you were in our group, we wouldn't be failing this. And even if the others were on board with chasing down the Cat Burglar, I'd *still* rather have you go with me than all of them."

Wow. "It's too bad I screwed up so much then."

"Yeah," he says. "It really is."

CHAPTER 32

I find Sarah in the park on Sunday afternoon after trying her house first. I expect her to be walking Heraldo, but instead she's picking up trash along the jogging trail. She looks up when I approach, her face going pale. She's still got a big bruise on her cheek from where Kat punched her.

"Hey, Sarah."

"What are you doing here?" she says.

I could ask her the same thing. "I had to make sure you were okay. You didn't come see me."

She bends down to pick up an empty water bottle and stuffs it into a big plastic bag she's got. "I didn't think it was a good idea. Not after what I did."

"Sarah, it wasn't you. It was the personality enhancer."

"That *I* made."

"Yeah, and that *I* broke. Everything that happened was my fault."

She bites her lip. "Damien, I was going to use it on you. I was going to try to *change* you."

Heraldo comes bounding up to her with a stick he must have been fetching. He gets really excited when he sees me and jams his nose in my crotch without letting go of the stick first, jabbing me in the leg, which is still sore.

"*Ow.*"

"Heraldo, *no*," Sarah scolds.

He backs off.

"Thanks, Sarah, that—" A couple of giant dog paws hit me in the chest as Heraldo jumps on me, unable to contain his excitement after all. He knocks me over, and I land on my back in the grass with an *oof*.

Sarah makes him get off of me and go lie down. Then she looms over me and offers me her hand to help me up. "See?" she says. "Being around me is dangerous."

I raise an eyebrow at her while I dust bits of grass and dirty paw prints off of myself. "You think you're the dangerous one? Because I'm pretty sure that's me."

"I saw the news, by the way," she says. "Congratulations."

"Yeah, well … thanks, I guess." Vilmore made a big public announcement today, offering me admission. And a full-ride scholarship. I saw it on the TV this morning at the same time as Gordon, who turned around and looked at me, like … Well, not like he was angry so much as just *hurt*. Like as soon as he heard them say the words, he knew that he'd lost me and was never going to see me again. "They just did it for the publicity."

"It's what you always wanted, though, right? So it

doesn't matter why they gave it to you."

I stick my hands in my pockets. "I'm not taking it."

She gets in my face and peers at me through her glasses. "Have you been to the doctor? Because I think all that electricity might have done more damage than you thought."

"I'm not crazy, Sarah."

"But you *have* to take it. No other schools want you, and it's a big opportunity." She shakes her head at me and bends down to pick up more garbage.

"Yeah, it is. But it doesn't feel right." She's also one of the last people I thought would be congratulating me about it. "And I thought you didn't want me to be a supervillain. You said you couldn't be my sidekick if I got a *V*."

"I've been rethinking my views on that. I was awfully villainous, and I didn't have *any* letter. So, you were right —as long as I agree with what you're doing, the technicalities shouldn't matter. But I think I'm going to be too busy for the foreseeable future to be your sidekick anyway."

She drops a candy bar wrapper as she's stuffing garbage into her bag, and I reach down to grab it for her.

Her mouth drops open in horror. "What are you *doing*?"

"Helping you."

"Don't!" She snatches the wrapper out of my hand. "This is *my* punishment, Damien."

"Punishment? For what?"

"See, you *do* have brain damage."

"I *don't*. Geez. I told you I'm all right."

419

"No, you said you weren't crazy, which is just what you *would* say if you were. And if you don't have brain damage, then you know exactly why I need to be punished. After everything I did, I can't just go back to normal and pretend nothing happened. Even if my personality enhancer changed me, I still committed crimes. I thought about turning myself in for what I did at Vilmore, since I didn't get caught. But then I decided to sentence myself to community service for a while instead. Besides picking up litter, I'm going to volunteer at a retirement home and at an animal shelter. I'll give it a few months, and if I'm not seeing results by then, I'll reconsider."

"Reconsider *what*? And what results?"

"If I don't feel like I'm making up for what I did, I'll reconsider turning myself in. I feel so guilty for everything, and if doing community service doesn't make it go away, then I'll know I need to be locked up."

"Wow. Are you sure *you're* not the crazy one?"

"I hurt you, Damien. A lot. I don't even know why you're talking to me right now. Maybe you broke the personality enhancer, but I shouldn't have built it in the first place. And I know why you threw yourself at that lightning beam. It wasn't just because you're heroic, but because you were trying to protect me. You didn't want me to be responsible for hurting those people. Killing them, I mean."

I poke at the grass with the toe of my shoe and scratch the back of my head. "Don't tell me you're mad at me for doing that, too."

She shakes her head. "I'm just glad everybody's okay."

"Right. Well, they *are*. We both messed up, but everybody's fine now. So, let's forget about it."

"Maybe everyone else is, but you're not. You got expelled from Heroesworth, because of what I did. If it wasn't for me hurting Kat, you wouldn't have lost control of your lightning."

"It was bound to happen eventually." Well, probably. I mean, we don't know *for sure* that I couldn't have kept my power in check and hidden it from everyone forever. Though I guess I can admit now that it does sound somewhat unlikely.

"But not like *that*. Even if someone found out about your power, it wouldn't have been because you blew up the gym. It wouldn't have been all over the news. And I can't make up for what I did to you, but if you take the offer from Vilmore, then at least *something* good will have come out of this."

"Sarah, you don't need to make it up to me. I should be making it up to *you*. And what about the Crimson Flash? How's it going to look for him if I go there?" I know how it would look for me, at least—like he was getting rid of me. Like he didn't want me around anymore.

"He wants you to be happy, doesn't he? Now you can still go to school. And you can be with Kat. You can't base your whole life on how it will look for him."

"I know, but ..." My stomach feels heavy, like there's a rock in it. I shift my weight from one foot to the other. "Maybe I don't want to go there anymore."

"I don't understand why you wouldn't. You spent

practically every waking moment with Kat this summer. And now you can essentially go live with her."

"Yeah, and it's not that I don't want that. And I'm not saying it's not hard, not getting to see her all the time. But I *do* still see her, and if I go to Vilmore, I'll be leaving all my other friends behind. I'll never see my family again, either."

"You can come home on weekends."

"I don't see that happening." Maybe Gordon won't disown me, like Mom did, but I've only lived with them for a little over half a year. If I moved out now, especially to go to Vilmore, of all places, then Gordon's house wouldn't feel like my home anymore. It would feel like I was giving up on being his son. "And I don't think never seeing you again is a good thing. I mean, is that what you want? To never see me again?"

"Of course not! But maybe it's for the best."

"Why? Because you think you're evil? Look, Sarah, remember when you were trying to get criminals to turn themselves in with those mind-control messages?"

"Don't remind me."

"Well, it was good people who did that. And I'm not saying that the people who didn't turn themselves in were sociopaths or whatever. But the people who did felt guilty, even about little everyday stuff they did wrong. And you feel *really bad* for what you did. You're trying to make up for it. You wouldn't be doing that if you were evil. You're a good person, Sarah."

She thinks about that for a second, her mouth falling open a little. Some of the worry disappears from her face.

"I might not be evil, but I don't see how you can forgive me. Even if you ignore all the stuff I did under the influence of the personality enhancer, I was still going to use it to change you."

"Yeah, and that sucks, and I wish you hadn't." I take a deep breath and let it out slowly. "I was being a jerk, though. Not that that makes it okay to use your gadgets on me, but I get why you wanted me and Riley to get along." Kat and Sarah are my closest friends, and it would be cool if I didn't have to worry about them murdering each other if they're ever in the same room. "And you were right. About us being friends once we got to know each other."

"I was?" She grins. Just for a second. Then she looks guilty again. "I shouldn't have tried to force you to be friends, though. It was wrong, and it wouldn't have worked, anyway. I see that now. And I shouldn't have tried to change you, either, Renegade. I like you how you are."

"That's right you do, Cosine." I smile at her.

"But if you and Riley are friends, then that means something good *did* come out of all this. So you don't have to go to Vilmore."

"Great. Thanks. Glad I have your permission."

"But if you don't take the offer, then what are you going to do?"

"Well, Gordon told me he's never kicking me out. So who needs school? And Kat's allowed in the house now. I'll just stay in the attic the rest of my life. Part of your community service can be visiting me and telling me about the outside world and stuff."

423

"I'm not going to be doing community service for *that* long."

"That's okay. I'm pretty sure I would die of boredom after only a couple weeks of being cooped up like that, anyway."

She calls over Heraldo, who's lying in the grass like she told him, watching us intently. I pick up his stick and throw it for him. He actually goes chasing after it right away this time, without looking to Sarah first. Hell must have frozen over while I wasn't looking.

"I don't really want you to go to Vilmore," Sarah admits.

"It's all right, Sarah. I know where I want to go."

"Where?"

"Back to Heroesworth."

She shakes her head. "That's not an option."

"Then I'll make it an option."

She pushes her glasses farther up on her nose and tilts her head, looking at me like I really am crazy. "Damien, you got *expelled*. For blowing up part of the school. With your *lightning* power. Millions of people saw it on YouTube. You got arrested for it. And your dad—the *Crimson Flash*—went on TV and said you were dangerous. One heroic act, especially one where you saved a bunch of supervillains, doesn't make up for that. So, even if you want to go to Heroesworth again, you can't. There's nothing you can do."

"Come on, Cosine. Do you really have so little faith in me?"

"My faith in you doesn't factor into this. It's impossible,

that's all."

"Well," I tell her, "we'll see about that."

X·X·X

Nobody stops me when I march into Heroesworth on Monday. It helps that it's the middle of third period, so the halls are empty. I go right to the dean's office. His secretary practically has a heart attack when I walk in, obviously recognizing me. Her eyes dart back and forth and she puts a hand to her chest, like she's afraid I'm here to blow up another chunk of the school.

"You can't go in there," she says when I walk right by her, not bothering to ask if the dean is in or if I can see him. Her hand hovers over the phone, as if she thinks she might need to call the police and wants to be ready.

I ignore her and go in anyway.

Dean Harold Scott—a middle-aged man with graying reddish-brown hair and about five used coffee mugs on his desk—looks up when I come in. So does Mr. Fitz, my former history teacher, who's apparently in a meeting with him. Or just chatting, but I can't imagine why anyone would ever willingly talk to him.

They both go silent as soon as they see me. Dean Scott gets to his feet and says, "You can't be here."

I'm not sure if he means in his office or in the school in general, but I'm guessing both.

Mr. Fitz's mustache twitches on overtime. "Mr. Locke," he says, looking kind of pissed, but also kind of amused, like he thinks he's going to get to watch me get arrested this time, "I believe you were expelled from this school over a week ago."

"Didn't you see the news?" I tell him. "I'm a hero now."

He glares at me. "I think we should skip calling the police and go right to the League. There's a dangerous supervillain at Heroesworth. One we apparently need a restraining order against."

God, I hate this guy. And if it wouldn't completely ruin my plans here today, I'd totally zap him. Not enough to kill him. Just enough to make him think twice about being such an ass. But since I can't, I ignore him and put my hands on the desk, looking right at the dean. "You want me back in this school."

To his credit, he doesn't laugh in my face. Though he does look annoyed. "I find that *extremely* hard to believe."

Mr. Fitz chuckles to himself, shaking his head. "Did you forget *why* you were expelled?"

"You know what happened Friday night," I tell Dean Scott. "There's no way you haven't heard about it."

"You stopped a rival school from getting destroyed, after blowing up part of this one. I'm not hearing a case."

"That's because that's not *why* you want me back."

"The boy's a little slow," Mr. Fitz says. "He doesn't understand that we don't want him back at all."

I clench my jaw and restrain myself from telling him to shut up. Which only goes to show just how heroic I am, since it's not exactly easy. I mean, look at me not killing this guy. That should get me reinstated right there.

"You look like you're pretty smart," I tell Dean Scott. Smarter than Mr. Fitz, anyway. "You look like you know a good deal when you hear one. And like you just said, Vilmore's a rival school. One that offered me admission and a full ride."

"Good for you," he mutters.

"No, good for *you*. I'm the guy who millions of people watched blow up part of Heroesworth. And now Vilmore's made a big deal over giving me this offer. They think I can't say no, and they're expecting me to take it. They need me to. Because if I do, it's like saying they're better than you. That you couldn't handle the half-villain son of the Crimson Flash, but they can."

Understanding flickers in his eyes. "And if you don't?"

"If I don't take it, then that kind of sucks for them." I shrug. "But if I don't take it *and* I go back to Heroesworth? *That* would be throwing it in their face. And after they made such a public spectacle out of it, it would make them look like idiots, because everyone would know I turned them down in favor of their rival. I got expelled from Heroesworth, but if I still choose it over Vilmore, when they're offering me a free education, it would really be sticking it to them." Not that I care about sticking it to Vilmore or anything, but it's my best bargaining chip. My only one, really. "And I'd never be able to go there after that. It's a permanent win for Heroesworth." Which makes me a little nervous, actually, but I've made up my mind. I meant what I told Sarah—Vilmore doesn't feel like the right place for me anymore, and I don't want to leave everyone behind.

Mr. Fitz rolls his eyes. "Oh, please. You expect us to listen to this?"

"Why don't you have a seat?" Dean Scott says.

I can't help shooting Mr. Fitz a smug grin as I take the other chair in front of the desk.

Dean Scott sits down, too. He presses the knuckle of his thumb to his mouth, thinking over what I said. "*If* you came back to Heroesworth, that would certainly look bad for Vilmore. Especially since, as you said, they made such a big deal out of this. But you haven't told me why it would look good for *us*."

"It wouldn't," Mr. Fitz snaps.

"You'd be stealing me away from them. The whole world thinks I'm this delinquent half villain—"

"Which you *are*."

"—but you'd be showing them that that doesn't matter. That you can take the least likely candidate and still make them a hero."

Mr. Fitz makes a *hmph* noise. "Just because he saved some supervillains doesn't mean he's not dangerous."

"I'm *not* dangerous. I mean," I add, when they both look at me like I just said I live on the moon, "I can be, when people threaten to hurt me and my friends. But what happened at Homecoming was a one-time event. So, unless you plan on trying to kill me, I don't see the problem."

Dean Scott nods, though his mouth is a thin, skeptical line. "Your father went on live TV and told the world that he endangered the lives of our students by enrolling you here. If I let you come back, then that would look like we didn't care about them, like we were knowingly putting our students and faculty in harm's way."

428

Or it would look like they made it up in the first place and that Gordon never did anything wrong. But I keep that thought to myself and instead say, "*Or* you could admit that I'm not a danger to them. I never hurt anybody. And don't pretend there aren't any hero powers that are dangerous. You've got to have kids here with light beams and freeze rays and super strength. But you don't worry about *them* walking the halls."

"They haven't given us a reason to."

"I panicked at Homecoming. What I did was an accident. One that won't happen again. But what I did at Vilmore, when I got in the way of that lightning beam, that was on purpose. And I would have done it whether I was saving villains or heroes or just regular people. It didn't matter who they were, only that I couldn't let them get hurt. So, by my count, I've prevented a lot of people from getting killed, and I never actually hurt anybody. Maybe those other kids haven't given you a reason not to trust them, but they haven't given you a reason why you *should*, either. I have."

Mr. Fitz shakes his head. I think a piece of crud falls from one of his giant eyebrows. "Dangerous or not, you don't belong here. You were purposely failing my class. It was only a matter of time before you flunked out of school completely."

"Yeah, I was *purposely* failing it. That means I didn't have to. And don't pretend like you weren't going out of your way to make that class hard for me. You wanted me to fail, because I'm half supervillain, and because you can't admit I might know some stuff that you don't."

"Are you hearing this, Harold?" Mr. Fitz asks the dean.

"Yes," he says, giving him a cold, thoughtful look, "I *am*."

Mr. Fitz swallows. "My class wasn't the only one you were failing," he adds nervously. "It wasn't just me."

"That doesn't mean I can't do better. It doesn't mean I *won't*. I'm ready to come back."

He scoffs, not buying it.

"Henry," Dean Scott says, addressing him, "can you give us a minute?"

It takes him a second to realize he's being dismissed. Then he glares at me really hard, as if I was the one who just told him to leave.

I smile angelically at him as he storms out of the room, which only makes him glare even harder, until it looks like his mustache is going to climb up his nose and suffocate him.

Dean Scott sighs once he's gone and takes a sip from one of his coffee mugs. Several of them are half filled and look a couple days old, but I'm going to assume this one is fresh. "You make a good argument. And I believe you about not being a danger to the other students. Or at least I believe you enough to give you a chance."

"You do?" I try not to sound too surprised when I say that—or too hopeful—but I think it comes through anyway.

"*But*," he adds, peering down his nose at me, "that doesn't mean I'm going to. As much as I would love to 'stick it' to Vilmore, as you put it, if you fail here, then Heroesworth is the one that ends up losing face. An awful lot of it. If we steal you from Vilmore and it becomes obvious that this *isn't* the right school for you, that there's no hope for you as a hero, then we look like fools."

"If I fail here, I won't have anywhere else to go. I'm not going to let that happen."

"You've proven you're heroic in the field—I'll give you that. That stunt at Vilmore should have killed you. But that's not enough to succeed at Heroesworth. You can promise not to fail all you want, but I don't have a reason to believe it. I think it's obvious you didn't try very hard while you were here."

"So, the only way for me to go is up. I can't possibly do worse than I did."

He shakes his head. "Your poster on heroism was blank."

"It was just a poster."

"It's one example. And, like your other 'work' here, it leaves me with nothing to go on. You say you're going to try harder, but that alone won't ensure your success. And until you give me a reason to believe you can take your assignments seriously, and that your best effort might actually *mean* something, I'm afraid my hands are tied."

"And what if I did? Prove it, I mean?"

"Then I'd think about it. But you'd really have to impress me."

I grip the edges of my chair and squeeze my eyes shut, not liking what I'm about to say. But he was probably going to see it anyway. The whole world is. "The new episode of my dad's show is on this afternoon. At four thirty. You should watch it."

He raises his eyebrows at me. "I'm a little old for it, don't you think?"

"You're never too old for safety," I tell him. "But, seriously. Just watch it. I think"—I *hope*—"that it will change your mind."

CHAPTER 33

I pace in the kitchen, not sure if I'm hungry or if I'm going to throw up. The numbers on the microwave say it's four thirty-five. Gordon's show has already started. And assuming Steve, the tech guy I talked to down at the studio, really did what I asked him to—which he said he would, after I made a convincing argument about this being a chance for the show to, like, *not* get canceled and for everyone there to *not* lose their jobs—then a whole lot of people are about to watch that video I made. Probably any minute now.

And I don't care how many people see me blowing up part of Heroesworth, but the idea of *anyone* watching this video, let alone the whole city, makes me want to die. And that's not including the fact that I'm sure it will end up online, too. And then absolutely everyone will see it, and I will probably have to move to Siberia after all.

But, on the bright side, no one here is going to be

watching it, at least not right now. Gordon doesn't watch his own show, and Amelia's over at Zach's house. So, even though Gordon's going to find out about it eventually—or, like, really soon—*I* don't have to see it.

Which is good, because then I think I really would throw up.

I hear Alex's footsteps in the living room, and then he turns on the TV. I run in there and see him changing it to Channel 12, the channel *The Crimson Flash and the Safety Kids* is on. Thankfully, there's a commercial playing.

He looks over at me when I come in, his eyes going wide.

"Hey, do you want to play trucks vs. dinosaurs?" I ask him. Anything to keep him from watching the show.

He shakes his head.

"You want to watch a movie with me? Or we could go *to* the movies." We'd probably miss dinner, but at least it would give me something else to think about. "I'm buying. We can see anything you want."

He hesitates this time, like he's tempted. But then he says, "I don't feel like it."

"Like watching a movie, or like watching it with *me*?"

"I just don't want to," he mumbles, looking away.

I get between him and the TV, which isn't as easy as it sounds, since he always sits so close to it, and press the power button.

"Hey!"

"We need to talk." And we really need to not watch Gordon's show today. I kneel down on the floor with him. "I know you've been avoiding me."

"No, I haven't," he says, though he doesn't sound at all convincing. More like he feels guilty because it's the truth and he's afraid to own up to it.

"Is it because of this?" I hold up my hands and make electricity arc between them.

Alex's face goes pale and he scoots back, ready to bolt, in case I lose control and shock him.

I make my hands go normal again and show them to him. "I'm still your brother, you know. You don't have to be afraid of me."

"Does it hurt?"

"No. Not me, anyway. It could hurt other people. But, Alex, you *know* me. You know I wouldn't do that. I'm still the same person who drew that excellent Velociraptor on your cast a month ago."

He glances down at the drawing on his arm—which still looks pretty good, even if the rest of his cast has gotten kind of dingy—then back up at me. "But you blew up your school. I saw it online. Everyone at my school saw it, too, and they said only supervillains can have lightning power."

"Well, yeah. But only superheroes can fly, and I can do that, too."

"You *don't*, though. And everyone's mad at you, for what you did at Heroesworth."

"I didn't do that because I'm a villain. I did that because I got scared. I thought Sarah was going to hurt Kat." Well, more than she already had, anyway. "But it was a misunderstanding. She's not going to hurt anyone. It's over now, and everyone's okay."

"Oh."

"Except, you know, for *me*, since my favorite brother doesn't want to hang out with me anymore."

He laughs. "I'm your *only* brother."

Ha. I wish. "Oh, great. So now if you don't want to have anything to do with me, then I'll have *no* brothers."

"I didn't say that. I still want to be your brother."

"Well, good, because I still want to be yours. And it's going to be Christmas in a few months, and that would have been one present down for each of us. I think we just dodged a bullet."

He grins.

I smile and hold out my fist.

He hesitates, still a little afraid to touch me, but then he risks it and bumps his fist against mine. He looks really relieved when he doesn't get electrocuted.

"So," I say, "now that we're cool again, how about we go—"

Amelia's door flings open upstairs.

Crap. I thought she wasn't home.

She comes racing down to the living room, shrieking, "Dad! *Dad!*"

Which I think is my cue to get the hell out of here. "Rain check," I tell Alex, jumping up from the floor.

Zach comes down the stairs, too. I guess they decided to come over here instead of going to his house. Though that doesn't explain why they were in her room, alone. With the door closed.

Amelia turns on the TV, and I should be making my escape, but instead I narrow my eyes at Zach. "What were you guys doing?"

He swallows. "Watching the show."

"Uh-huh. And what else?"

His face goes red. "*Nothing.*"

"It *better* have been nothing. Because I like you, Zach. I'd really hate to have to kill you."

Gordon comes running in from the backyard, looking pretty freaked out, like he expects to find a dead body in here. Which is understandable, given the way Amelia was screaming just now.

But before he can ask what's going on, he sees me on the screen. I'm sitting on my bed, wearing just my swimming trunks, the same as in the video of me from Homecoming.

"Damien," Gordon growls. "What the hell is this?"

And *that* really is my cue to go. I make a run for the door, but Gordon blocks me and grabs my shoulder, not letting me leave.

Then Helen comes in, carrying Jess, and now they're *all* here. Which is just great. Why not invite all the neighbors over, too? The whole block can be here to watch me die of embarrassment.

We missed the part where I introduce myself as the Crimson Flash's half-villain son. I thought I'd better make sure everyone was up to speed, just in case anyone watching has been living in a cave for the past week. On the screen, I grin at the camera, even though I look like hell. There are dark circles under my eyes, and my hair is kind of greasy, and my face looks pale. It's like I almost died the night before or something. "So"—it's weird, hearing my voice on the TV, and I cringe a little—"there was this assignment I was supposed to do at Heroesworth, about what heroism means to me. You probably heard about it. You probably heard *a lot* of things, but this one was true. I never really finished it. Well, actually, I did. I turned it in twice. The first time, I just said what I thought people wanted to hear. The second time is the one you probably heard about, when it was blank. And I know what you're all thinking. You're thinking, 'Yeah, that figures, what with him being a villain and all,' and that heroism doesn't actually mean anything to me." I take a deep breath. "That's what I *wanted* everyone to think. But it's a lie."

In real life, everyone turns to look at me. Gordon's grip on my shoulder tightens, and not in a friendly "I love my son" sort of way.

I will myself to pass out. Or to drop dead. Either one.

On the screen, I keep talking. "So, I'm finishing the assignment. For reals this time. I don't have a poster, just this video, but that's okay, because I think we all know by now that posters aren't really my strong point." I splay out my hands. "You guys thought you knew the Crimson Flash. You thought he was this great guy who was nice to kids and taught them safety tips and stuff, and that he was the type of person who would never hurt anyone. A superhero you could trust above all others. One who would *never* sleep with a supervillain, let alone in a—" I clear my throat, cutting myself off, since the details of him and my mom sleeping together aren't exactly public knowledge. "Believe me, I *live* with the guy, and I'd never expect that from him."

Gordon lets go of my shoulder. The blood drains from his face. He looks like he feels almost as sick as I do. "I asked you not to do anything," he says, sounding numb and completely devastated. Like this really was the last straw and I broke him.

"And now," the me on the screen goes on, "it turns out Golden City's most beloved superhero isn't who you thought he was. Because he has a half-villain son he didn't tell you about, who caused some trouble." I pause. "A lot of trouble. And you know what? You're right, Golden City. He's *not* who you thought he was. He's a whole hell of a lot *better* than that. Because he didn't even know I existed for sixteen years, but that didn't matter to him. When my mom kicked me out, he took me in, no questions asked. Seriously. *None.* And I know I'm not his ideal son or anything. Not even close. All I do is cause trouble for him. Well, for everyone. And I'm a reminder of the one stupid mistake he's ever made, and I never let him forget it. Though I can't say I'm not glad he made that particular mistake, what with enjoying being alive and all. But still. It's not easy for him, having me around. His life was pretty much perfect before I showed up. He didn't need me—he *doesn't*—but he still made me part of his family. And now I accidentally blew up part of Heroesworth, because I'm half villain. I *ruined* him. And it wasn't even his fault I was there—it was mine. He has absolutely no reason to keep me around, and every reason to get rid of me. But *that's not who he is.*"

I swallow, both in real life and on the screen.

"He's done everything he can to make me feel like I have a home. Like I can feel safe, no matter what. That no matter how badly I screw up, he's not going to give up on me. That I'm still his *son*." I tap my hand to my chest, emphasizing the word. I hadn't realized I'd done that. "It's easy to be a hero when everybody loves you. When they think you're perfect. But he's a hero even when everybody *hates* him. I know because the whole city turned on him, and he still stood by me. I'm his stupid screw-up son that he's only known for half a year, but he still sacrificed everything for me." I clench my hands, grasping at the air. "He didn't have to. He could have gotten rid of me. He could have *walked away*. I bet a lot of people expected him to. I know I did, and I wouldn't have blamed him for it. That's how badly I screwed up, and it's probably what I deserve. But he didn't. And he never will. And *that's* what heroism means to me."

On the screen, I press my hands to my knees, staring down at the bed for a second. Then I look up and say, "You can turn it off now."

The video cuts back to the episode of *The Crimson Flash and the Safety Kids*, as if nothing out of the ordinary just happened.

The whole house is deathly silent. No one says a word. I don't think anyone even breathes—I know I sure don't. I hold my breath until my lungs ache. I keep waiting for Gordon to speak. To tell me I was wrong in the video and that he can't stand to have me around for even one more second.

When I can't take it anymore, I look over at him.

He's staring at me. His eyes are wet. "Did you mean all that?"

No, I stripped down to my underwear and aired all my messy feelings on TV for *fun*. "Of course I—"

He doesn't let me finish. He pulls me into a hug, squeezing me so tight, I can't even breathe.

For a second, I'm too stunned to move. And then I hug him back. Even though everyone's gawking at us, as if seeing the most embarrassing moment of my life wasn't enough for them and they have to stick around for this, too.

"You were wrong about one thing, though," Gordon says, finally letting go of me.

"Yeah? What's that?"

"I *do* need you."

"Are you sure? Because I think I have a real shot at joining the circus."

He laughs and says, "Yes, Damien. I'm sure."

CHAPTER 34

"Zach, what are you doing? Get over here." I point to my side of the living room, where I'm having a Halloween party. It's been three weeks since everything that happened at Vilmore, and while it's not actually Halloween quite yet, it *is* Amelia's birthday.

She's also having a party. It's also in the living room.

Her party has significantly more guests than mine, since she's got about fifteen girls over—mostly her friends from our old school and a few new ones from Heroesworth —plus Zach, and I've only got Kat and Riley so far, since Sarah's running late.

Zach's holding a cupcake with pink icing. He was about to eat it, but now his mouth falls open as he looks back and forth between me and Amelia, who's too busy talking to her friend Tiffany under a giant sweet-sixteen banner to notice me trying to lure him over to the dark side.

"Come on." I tap my foot. "*I* invited you. You said you

were coming to my party. So get over here."

He swallows and looks really nervous, like he thinks he's actually hurting my feelings or something. "But Amelia invited me to her party, too."

I gape at him, pretending to be shocked. "And you thought you could go to both? Is that why you're not wearing a costume?"

He looks me up and down, taking in the 1920s-style pinstripe suit and fedora I'm wearing, as if he hadn't realized I don't always dress this awesome. Which is flattering, but it doesn't mean I'm going to stop messing with him. "Well, I—"

"I thought you were my friend. And I'm pretty sure I invited you first."

"But she told me about her party weeks ago! And she has cupcakes."

"Yeah, but did she put it in writing? I gave you an *invitation.*" It was one of those cheesy ones they make for little-kid parties. There was a picture of a smiling jack-o-lantern on it and a very non-threatening vampire bat. "So you'd better give me that"—I snatch the cupcake out of his hands—"and come over here."

He opens his mouth to protest some more, but then can't seem to think of a good argument. He sighs, his shoulders slumping, and crosses over to my side of the room.

Riley folds his arms, looking amused, and says, "He's just messing with you, Zach. You can be at both parties."

"I ... I knew that," Zach says, though not very convincingly. He holds out his hand for me to give the cupcake back, but I pretend not to notice and take a bite out of it.

Amelia spots him, letting out a horrified gasp, and shouts, "Zach! What are you doing? You're my boyfriend! You're supposed to be at *my* party! Not *his*."

"Don't listen to her," I tell him. "She can't love you like I can."

He wiggles his eyebrows at me and says, "I'll sneak back over later," before hurrying off.

Amelia glares at me. She holds out her hand and uses her power to make my cupcake appear in her palm. "These are for my *guests*," she says, setting it down before marching up to me. "You're not even supposed to be here."

"I live here."

"Mom said you could have a few friends over. She didn't say you could try to take over my party. And she *is* home, you know." She says that like I should be worried that Helen's going to find out I'm doing exactly what she said I could.

"I'm not taking over—I'm staying on my side. It's not my fault your guests find me so fascinating and keep defecting." And staring at me. And taking pictures. And trying to talk to me, but then giggling and running away instead. It's like I'm famous or something.

Amelia grits her teeth. "It's *my* birthday. My sixteenth. It's supposed to be *special*."

She means because her thumbprint's going to rearrange itself to form an *H* at midnight. Which is a once-in-a-lifetime event and is something she's been counting down the days for since I met her. "It can't be *that* special if you didn't even invite your own brother."

She scoffs.

I catch snippets of a conversation from across the room, hearing the words *shorts, video,* and *pretty much naked,* and look over to see a couple of Amelia's friends ogling me. I make eye contact with them, and they turn bright red and pretend like they weren't just picturing me without any clothes on.

They're lucky Kat's in the bathroom.

One side of Amelia's face twitches. "Everyone's supposed to be here for *me,* not you. Couldn't you have had your party *next* weekend?"

"Kat could only make it home *this* weekend. So, no. But if it makes you feel any better, I got you a present."

"You did?" Her face lights up, like she's willing to forget she doesn't want me here, at least for the moment, if it means getting another gift with her name on it.

"Yeah, but it's too big to wrap."

"What is it?"

"A stripper."

"*What?*" She grabs my arm in a death grip. "You'd better be joking."

"Don't worry—it's a male stripper. I know what you like."

Her nostrils flare in and out, and she makes an angry noise in the back of her throat that sounds kind of like a tea kettle about to go off. "Can't you guys go to your room or something?!"

"And miss the entertainment?"

One of her friends from Heroesworth *ever-so-casually* walks up to us, as if she can't tell Amelia's busy chewing me out—or trying to, anyway—and pretends like she doesn't notice me at first. Then she blinks, acting surprised, and says, "Oh, hey, Amelia, is this your brother? I didn't know he was going to be here."

"He's *leaving*, Kim," Amelia seethes, her fists clenched.

Kim holds up her phone. "Can I get a picture first? I thought you could—"

"Take it for you?" Amelia snaps. "Even though it's *my* birthday?!"

"*No*. God. I thought you could stand next to him, but I guess not." She puts her phone away and backs off.

Amelia glares at me, as if her losing her temper just now was somehow my fault. She points her finger at me and says, "You'd better not be here at midnight." Then she leaves to go find Zach.

"You didn't tell her we're going to the movies?" Riley asks.

We're going to go see *Pirate Zombies from Hell* once Sarah gets here. Kat might have gone to see it with all her friends, but I missed out, and now we're going to go see it with mine. "Nah, I don't want to ruin the surprise. But, speaking of ruining things, you're as bad as your brother. I told you this was a costume party." I shake my head at him, sighing in disappointment at the jeans and hooded sweatshirt he's got on.

"I'm *wearing* a costume."

"Going as yourself doesn't count."

"I'm not *me*. I'm a supervillain." He unzips his

sweatshirt to reveal a purple and gray Vilmore T-shirt. It says, VILMORE: VILLAINY AT ITS FINEST SINCE 1903, in swirly, vintage-looking letters. He holds up his thumb, where he drew a *V* on it in black marker.

"That's the best you could do?"

"My other idea was dressing up as a clown."

I point to the door. "*Get out.*"

He grins, like he thinks he's really hilarious.

I wonder what's taking Kat so long, then glance over and see her attempting to cross through enemy territory on her way back from the bathroom. She's wearing a dark-green flapper dress and one of those circles around her head with a feather sticking out of it. A couple of girls from Amelia's party have clustered around her and are now talking excitedly at her and holding up their phones.

"I dare you to wear that shirt to school on Monday," I tell Riley.

"How bad do you think Brian would flip out?"

Brian's one of the kids in our group in Intro to Heroism —the one Riley was complaining about before. He's got a lot of bad ideas and thinks people will listen to him if he just says everything forcefully enough and shoots down anyone who argues with him. A method that was working pretty well for him, actually, at least until I showed up. "I think he'd have an aneurism."

"Then I'll do it."

Kat makes her escape from the girls and their camera phones and hurries over to us. She drapes her arms around my neck and leans into me. "Save me, Damien. I only got away because I told them I'd be right back."

"Pretend to faint and I'll take you to my room."

She smiles. "Last night wasn't enough for you?"

The whole family—well, everyone except me—went over to Gordon's parents' house last night, so they could give Amelia her birthday presents. And even though I'm technically just as related to them as any of their other grandkids, I wasn't invited. Which is fine with me. I mean, I don't think they *hate* me anymore—not after that video I made, which has gone a long way toward putting the Crimson Flash back in everyone's good graces—but they're not exactly eager to get to know me or anything, and the feeling is mutual. Besides, one benefit of being the black sheep of the family is not having to visit stupid relatives with everyone. I can't say I minded having the house to myself. Or having my girlfriend over.

In my bed.

Several times.

"Come on, Kat," I say, tilting my fedora to one side. "You know I can never get enough of you."

She sighs. "Have I mentioned how hot you look in that outfit?"

"Likewise. Though it doesn't hurt that I can totally see down your dress right now."

She punches me in the arm.

"Dude," Riley says. "Either go to your room or don't, but *stop talking about it.*"

"And leave you alone to get poached by Amelia? I don't think so. We'll wait until we're in your car."

His eyebrows come together and he folds his arms over his chest, like he thinks I'm serious. "*Absolutely not.*"

There's a knock on the door. I go answer it and find Sarah in a Crimson Flash costume. Complete with a bright red cape.

"Whoa."

She adjusts her glasses and says, "I would have been here sooner, but my cape got stuck in a sticker bush."

She tries to move past me, but I hold up a hand. "Oh, no. You can't come in here dressed like that."

"You said to wear a costume."

"I didn't say to dress like my *dad*. That's weird."

"It's part of my plan to keep myself on track. I'm dressing as a positive role model."

"Oh. If *that's* all you need, then you can ditch the cape and borrow some of my clothes for tonight."

She rolls her eyes at me. "You're not a positive role model."

"Sure I am. I go to hero school. Why, just last night I captured a supervillain. More than once."

Her lip twitches in disgust. "Damien, I *don't* need to know about your love life."

"Fine. But you can't wear that. This is my party, plus you owe me."

"For what?"

"Oh, I don't know, maybe because your favorite show in the world just got renewed for another season because of me?" They just announced it yesterday, capitalizing on the positive publicity that's been building since my video aired. A *lot* of people have seen it, first on TV, then online. A fact I try really hard not to think about.

"You're the one who almost got it canceled in the first

place. And I didn't spend ten minutes picking this cape out of that stupid bush just to go change." She shoves me out of the way and steps inside.

Riley smiles when he sees her and gives her a thumbs-up. "*Nice.* It turned out great."

"What?" I narrow my eyes at him. "You knew about this? And you didn't stop her?"

"Why would I? It's awesome."

"The cape isn't very functional," Sarah says, "but otherwise, I like it."

Kat stands off to the side with her arms crossed and scowls. Like she was hoping Sarah wasn't going to show up tonight. "We'd better not miss the movie because of her," she mutters.

"Have I mentioned how awesome you are?" I ask her. Kat agreed to be civil to Sarah tonight—and, you know, not punch her—so I could have all my friends together in one place, even though Sarah's not exactly her favorite person in the world or anything. More like the opposite. And I'd say she and Sarah just need to get to know each other, but I'm not 100 percent certain that that wouldn't make things worse.

"Have *I* mentioned that we're learning how to hide dead bodies in one of my classes right now?"

"Wow, seriously?" I can't help the excitement in my voice, even though technically she was implying she was going to kill Sarah.

She smacks me in the chest. "*No.* You know that's one of the advanced classes. Would you regret your decision if we were, though?"

She means me turning down Vilmore in favor of Heroesworth. "That depends. Are you guys going to learn how to seduce supervillains to get information out of them?"

"You're *so* not learning that."

"Oh, aren't we?" I grin and raise a suggestive eyebrow.

Kat rolls her eyes at me just as Sarah comes up to us.

"I wanted to say I'm sorry," she says.

"You said that already." Kat's voice is icy, leaving off an implied "and it didn't work the first time."

"But I don't think you knew how much I meant it."

"So, I'm just supposed to forgive you for almost killing my boyfriend? Plus all that other stuff you did, just because you didn't *mean* it?" She shakes her head.

"Not all at once, but I thought it could happen in small increments. Over time."

"You mean you think I'm going to get over it."

"Well, once you realize I would never have done any of those things normally, your anger will start to fade, and then we might be able to be friends."

Kat makes this half-laughing, half-scoffing noise. "Yeah, right."

"I would never hurt Damien. Not on purpose. And I wouldn't hurt you, either. And since I went crazy and committed all those crimes, I've been more open-minded. About supervillains. You wouldn't have hurt anyone, but I did, and I didn't even have a *V* on my thumb. I wasn't myself, but I'm still the one who built all those machines. And I wouldn't have tried to hurt supervillains like that if I didn't already have some biases. What happened was my

451

fault, and I'm trying to take responsibility for it."

"Whatever," Kat says. "Just don't talk to me."

"But how are we going to get past this if we don't interact?"

"We're *not*."

Sarah gets this confused look on her face, like she just can't accept that answer. "But—"

"Will you look at the time?" I say, not actually looking at it. "We really have to get going."

"Yeah," Riley says, actually checking his phone. "There's always a line Saturday night, and I don't want to miss the previews."

Sarah looks like she still wants to protest, like she thinks she can *make* Kat like her if she just apologizes enough, but then she gives in and lets it go. At least for now.

Kat grabs her coat, and the four of us head outside. It's cold out, and I can see my breath in the air. Gordon's just pulled up, after going to the store to grab more party supplies for Amelia, and he gets out of the car, carrying a couple of grocery bags.

He notices Sarah's costume and chuckles to himself, like he thinks it's actually funny. "You guys leaving?" he asks me as the others climb into Riley's car.

"We're going to go see *Pirate Zombies from Hell*."

"I heard that one was really— Wait, isn't that rated R?"

It is. But Kat can shapeshift to look way old enough that no one would ever card her. Plus, Sarah has a fake ID, which she claims she got just in case she needs it for chasing down bad guys who try to hide in bars or night clubs. She said it would be stupid to only be able to catch criminals who are under twenty-one. "Don't worry," I tell Gordon. "I'll probably be too busy making out with Kat the whole time to be scarred for life by all the raunchy sex scenes."

"There are sex scenes? I thought it was about zombies."

"Hence the raunchiness."

He laughs. "But you're not seventeen. How are you—" He stops himself. "You know what? I don't want to know."

"A wise choice."

"Have fun."

He goes into the house, and I get into the backseat of Riley's car with Kat.

"What did your dad want?" she asks.

"Nothing. He just told me to enjoy the sex scenes extra for him." I lean toward the front and say to Sarah, "What do you think of your positive role model now?"

"He didn't say that. He told you to have fun. I was watching."

"Yeah, what do you think he meant by 'have fun'?"

"Not *that*."

"Are we ready to go?" Riley asks. "We're going to be late."

"Hold on." Sarah opens her door and pulls in part of her cape, then closes it again. "Okay. Now."

I sit back and put on my seat belt. Kat slips her hand into mine and leans her head against my shoulder. Riley starts driving, and Sarah changes the radio station. They start talking about who would win in a fight between a lion, a tiger, and a bear.

A commercial comes on, saying the circus is coming to town. Besides the usual stuff, like the trapeze and elephants and things, it gives a quick rundown of its top performers and their acts, as if they were rock stars or something and we should already know who they all are.

"Listen to that," Kat says. "That could have been *us*. We could have been *famous*."

"Yeah, but you know me, Kat. I don't really like to make a spectacle of myself."

She laughs. "It's a good thing you live such a low-key life, then. All that attention would kill you."

"Yep. So I'm definitely not planning to moan really loudly while making out with you at the theater until people throw popcorn at us. And I'm *definitely* not going to accidentally say Riley's name instead of yours."

"You're going to do *what*?" Riley says, glancing at me in the rearview mirror.

"Relax, Perkins. I just said I *wasn't* going to." I roll my eyes at him. "Well, not *again* anyway."

ACKNOWLEDGMENTS

This book almost didn't exist. Like, really. I know I could say that for the first book, too, but it's even more true for this one. I always wanted to continue the story (and I still do!), but the original publisher said no dice. They had the money and the resources and the Final Say, and they said no, not going to happen.

So that was it. It was a one-time shot, no sequel. No more of Damien's adventures. No more Golden City.

Except that it wasn't. Because the publisher might have said no, but the fans kept saying *yes*. "Please write more," they said, as if it was at all up to me. "Please, for the love of God, tell me there's going to be a sequel and when it's coming out!!!" they said, as if adding extra exclamation points was going to make any difference in things that were so clearly out of my control.

Well, it turns out it really *was* up to me and that things really *were* in my control. I wrote the sequel anyway. And the fans backed me up. And I still can't believe that this book, which is the most amazing thing I've ever written, really almost never came about. Or that you're holding it in your hands right now.

And so a huge thanks goes out to everyone who wrote to me over the years, whether it was through a heartfelt email or an encouraging comment on my blog, telling me how much you loved Renegade X. Your words have stuck with me, and I think about them a lot, especially on the days when the writing seems hard, the risks seem crazy big, and giving in to self-doubt seems easier than not. Without you, this book would not have been written.

There are also three people in particular I'd like to thank, who were all early readers and helped shape the outcome of this book: Chloë Tisdale, who discussed the story and characters endlessly with me, and who laughed in all the right places; Karen Kincy, beta reader and author-friend extraordinaire, who's always up for a good scheming session; and Raul Allen, who makes the most amazing covers a girl could ask for.

You guys all rock.

SPECIAL THANKS TO THE FOLLOWING CITIZENS OF GOLDEN CITY

Name and Alignment	Power
Ruby Gale, V	Summoning storms
The Spark, V	Zap lightning from fingertips
El Whinestro, V	Hunger-induced superwhine
Mirage, V	Invisibility
Pam Pyro Palmer, H	Is on fire … literally
The Mysterious Lady N, H	Makes people randomly exclaim, "Wow, you have long hair!"
Dodici, H	Can flip time forward or backward by precisely twelve hours
Electric Blue, H	Messing with electricity
Witchy Woman, V	Controls lightning
Robodendron, V	Spawns a robotic plant army
Nature Woman, H	Animal communication and control
FadeDestiny, H	Power mimicry
Lioness, H	Invulnerability
The Long-Sufferer, H	Able to withstand 2 + hour phone conversation with mother—and other verbose family and "friends"—without getting a word in edgewise

Thunderin, V	Controls electricity and lightning
Lustra, H	Light in the darkness
Zannalov, V	Can conjure and command ferrets (but easily distracted by shiny things)
Snowtronic, V	Teleportation
Shadow Killer, V	Turns into a shadow
Bookdragon, H	Able to hoard and protect books with a vengeance
The Crazy Algorithms Lady, H	Creates unexpectedly weird solutions to intractable problems
PocketGoddess, H	The power of mobile technology to save the day!
Wintersmith, V	"I am Winter"
The Alley Cat, V	Exudes a variety of strong odors on command
Coordination Man, H	Supreme organizational facilities
Dr. JS Dichotomy, H/V	Multiple personalities. Hero side can neutralize a villain's powers. Also has great healing ability. If the villain is out, then by simply looking upon him (at all—even one of his fingers), a person will be struck dead instantly
The Blue Avenger, V	Incredibly handsome criminal genius and master of all villainy

Space Wizard, H	Astrophysics
CleveRun, H	Superspeed
Plain White Andrew, H	Awesomeness
Mrs. Pilkington, H	Craftivism
Cindy the Super Librarian, H	Always finds the right book
Raymond Tracer, H	4D vision
Dark Thea, H	Morphing into any animal at will
Live Wire, H	Electromagnetism
Blizzard, H	Making and manipulating ice
Book Girl, H	Psychokinesis
Palindromeda, V	Ability to cause a state of complete confusion
The Mechanist, V	Control over machines
Dragonstar, H	Force-field manipulation
Kesal Exuo, V	Technopathy
The Spoiler, V	Instantly knows the ending of every book, movie, and TV show he touches, sees, or hears
Bibliotheca, H	Literary teleportation
Alexander, H	Worlds traveller
Suzie Smiley, H	Making people happy

Abtacha, V	Camouflage
Harold Scott, H	Superhuman reflexes
Fuego, V	Pyrokinesis
Oraclenoid, V	Manipulating time using a prehensile tail
Helisca, H	Pyromancy
Possibly, V	Manipulates chance, increasing the probability of a particular event's outcome. Results can range unpredictably from lucky guessing safe combinations to evading police due to a collision with an overturned fruit cart and a flock of unexpected emus
Josh "Styles" Creager, H	Positive attitude!!!
Quarrel, H	Never misses the target with her crossbow
The Candlemaker, V	Melting things
Norske Storm, H	Lights up the darkness
Cartoon, V	Blatant disregard of the laws of gravity
Silent Behemoth, V	Can walk into a room full of people and walk out with the fridge and nobody will notice
Lonedeath, H	Semi-speedster and spikes

Ice Girl, V	Freeze ray
Brendan Blaze, V	Flame thrower
Lynxia, H	Flame-wielding feline
Accelerator Ray, H	Kinetic manipulation
, V	Make the formatting look a little off
Uamada, H	Patience
Arctic Frost, V	Cryokinesis and communication with wolves
Thomas Zilling, H	Telekinetic power
Stephenie "Mogsy" Sheung, V	Rabid devourer of books
Quickwit, H	Super speed of body and mind
Corundum, V	Shapeshifting
James Pratt, H	Can fix anything
Autumn Pratt, H	Has a green thumb
Mega Meltdown Mike, H	Melts down and puts luck in everyone's pockets
Sue Pallas, H	Can withstand electric current

ABOUT THE AUTHOR

CHELSEA M. CAMPBELL grew up in the Pacific Northwest, where it rains a lot. And then rains some more. She finished her first novel when she was twelve, sent it out, and promptly got rejected. Since then, she's earned a degree in Latin and Ancient Greek, become an obsessive knitter and fiber artist, and started a collection of glass grapes.

Besides writing, studying ancient languages, and collecting useless objects, Chelsea is a pop-culture fangirl at heart and can often be found rewatching episodes of *Buffy the Vampire Slayer, Parks and Recreation,* or spending way too much time on Facebook. You can visit her online at www.chelseamcampbell.com.

CPSIA information can be obtained at www.ICGtesting.com
Printed in the USA
LVOW11s0719191215

467208LV00002B/410/P

9 780989 880718